His gaze turned sharp then his eyes narrowed. The temperature of the room dropped as shadows descended upon his face.

"Perhaps I'm not making myself clear," he said, his voice hard. "Or," his gaze traveled over her, studying her from head to toe, "you want me this way, on the verge of losing control."

She swallowed hard. His heated, predatory gaze fixed on her as his voice deepened. Dangerous sexual intent burned in his eyes as he downed his liquor, savoring it as if imagining it was her blood. His eyes roamed her body. A pure masculine smile softened his features, as his fangs grew longer.

Eva gasped. God, she wanted this vampire. She had to use every ounce of her rapidly depleting self-control *not* to throw herself at him.

"Danger," he grated past his fangs, "it excites you."

Books by Amanda J. Greene

Rulers of Darkness Series

Caressed by Moonlight

Caressed by Night

Caressed by a Crimson Moon

Caressed by a Crimson Moon

Amanda J. Greene

Publisher Amanda J. Greene

Copyright © 2013 by Amanda J. Greene

All rights reserved.

Cover art by Kim Killion

Author website: **www.amandajgreene.blogspotcom**

ISBN 978-0615803678

This book is dedicated to my loving and supportive family. Without their encouragement, none of this would be possible.

To my husband, who understands my crazy ways and knows that creativity does not work on a schedule.

I also need to say a special thank you to my Nana. She was the reader in our family and she shared the wonderful world of books with me. I will cherish every romance novel she ever gave me.

Acknowledgments

As always, thank you Rebecca Grimmius! You are such a huge help. You really do keep me on track and make sure my Rulers of Darkness facts are straight.

With immense gratitude Rosemarie Lopez, you got me through to the end. You are a wonderful Beta Reader.

And I would like to give a shout out to Perk It Up Editing. You ladies are amazing.

Glossary of Terms

Binding Ceremony: Takes place between a vampire and their mate through the exchange of blood. Their blood will mix and they both must consume the combined blood at the same time. They will bare the mark of their binding, a scar.

Black Knights: The protectors of the vampire royalty and nobility and the enforcers of vampiric law.

Bleeder: A human slave kept by a vampire for the use of feeding. This practice is outlawed, though it remains in use within the Outcast Society.

Death Curse: A spell cast by the Shaman upon any vampire that becomes ruler of a Clan. This curse was created to limit the power and reign of the monarchs. It begins by attacking what remains of the vampire's conscience (often times the king reports seeing the faces of those he has slain, thereby attacking their mind), hallucinations set in and the vampire begins to descend into madness. Next, the curse singles out the vampire's emotions (they become over come by grief, shame, loneliness, despair, etc.). While the curse twists their minds and emotions, an illness consumes the body. Death is always welcome in the end. The average reigning term of a monarch is 200 years. This has helped cut the numbers of the older, stronger, vampires.

Fathers: Cassius, Uro, and Imbrasus. These three of the four purebloods shared their blood with humans, thereby creating fledglings. They also formed the vampire clans. Fathers can also be addressed as Sire. (Dimitri is a leader of a clan, though he has never created fledglings and is addressed as Sire.) Began to change humans to vampires when civilizations became strong.

Fledglings: Humans that have been changed into vampires.
A vampire's strength is determined by four (4) factors.

> How hard the victim fought to hold on to their mortal life. The stronger the will to live the stronger the demon will be within them upon transformation.

> How strong the vampire is that is attempting to turn the human. The Purebloods have the most strength, while their direct fledglings are the second strongest and so on and so forth. As the blood continues to be shared

with humans, the vampire curse becomes more and more diluted. Example: the vampires that are made by the 16th generation will not be nearly as strong as those made by the 2nd, no matter what.

The more blood a vampire shares with their victim, the more poison (the curse) the human consumes. With more poison in the system, the transition is easier, though there is still no guarantee that the human will survive the transition.

The passage of time. As years turn into decades and decades into centuries, the demon within (the vampire) grows stronger and some develop extra senses: mind reading, mind control, teleportation, and visions of the future.

Mate: A vampire monarch's lover. The Shaman, with his ability to see far into the future, knew that one day a ruler would come into power (one for each vampire clan) that would want to bring peace into the world of darkness. In order to save these rulers from the Death Curse, the Shaman created their mates. If the vampire finds their mate, they will never fall victim to the Death Curse. Though there is no guarantee that the vampire will find their mate and if they do not, they will parish.

Mylonas Clan: The very first vampire Clan to be formed. Created by Cassius, their territory consists of Southern Europe, every country that lines the coast of the Mediterranean. *Reigning monarch: Dorian Vlakhos*

Outcast Society: Made up of vampires who have been banished from their Clans or were changed into vampires illegally (without the blessing or the approval of the King). Generally they are the weaker of the vampire race, with few exceptions. Their territory consists of the Untied States, with some small factions scattered about Canada and South America. To protect themselves from the Red Order, they form groups, banding together. *The two largest groups within the Outcast Society are lead by Gabriel Erhard and Boras Werner (competitive factions).* Also known as bastards, blood-bastards, or filthy-blood.

Pureblood: The original vampires cursed by the Shaw: Cassius, Uro, Imbrasus and Dimitri. The proper way to address a Pureblood is Sire.

Rightful Ruler: The intended monarch chosen by Fate to rule a vampire clan. They will bring about peace and be granted a mate through the spell created by the Shaman.

Second: Also known as heirs. They are chosen by the current reigning vampire ruler to be their successor.

Shaman: Leader of the Shaw. He is all-knowing and his magical abilities are limitless. He is continuously reincarnated; this helps his powers grow and insures that his knowledge of the past continues on. The Shaman can choose to retire, meaning he selects a fellow member of the tribe, generally from his direct bloodline, to pass on his strength and knowledge. Once he relinquishes his power and memories, he is free of the reincarnation cycle and will live out his life to finally pass on to the next realm.

Shape-shifters: A species that appear human but can take the form of an animal. Also known as Weres. They separate themselves by animal type and live in packs/tribes. Africa, Asia South America, and some parts of North America are split up amongst the different factions. Generally live in small groups and amongst people. They share much of their territory with the Outcast Society. War is popular within their communities and peace is always short lived. One cannot be changed into a Shape-shifter. They can breed with humans, producing Half-Breeds.

Shaw Priestess: Gifted witches who show great promise for strength. They are trained by the Shaman and are highly respected within their otherworldly community. They are Seers, able to look into the future. They are assistants to the Shaman and are members of his bloodline. Priestesses are pure of blood, meaning their blood, if given to a human, can grant immortality.

Shaw Witches: A peaceful tribe of witches possessing great magical power.

Soul Shattering: When a human is on the verge of death and receives vampire blood, the transition from human to vampire begins. The blood is poisonous to a human; it eats away at the soul and conscience until the next full moon. Once the full moon rises, the transition begins; excruciating pain claims the victim as their body begins to morph into that of a vampire. At this point, the soul is weak and splinters under the pressure. In most cases, the soul dies and the human does not survive the transition. If the soul does not die, it is forever shattered – in pieces. The human will awake a vampire possessing little humanity. They retain their memories and some of their emotions, though their conscience is almost nonexistent. However, there is a way around Soul Shattering. When the human is being given the vampire's blood, the vampire can press their hand over the human's heart, there by creating a shield around the soul, protecting it from the poison. A vampire is stronger if they possess their whole soul.

The Red Order: Witches who have very little magical power but possess great physical strength, they are the hunters of vampires. Also known as the Red Order Hunters.

Transition: The process by which a human is transformed into a vampire. The human must be near death from blood loss and receive a vampire's blood. Upon the next full moon, the change from human to vampire takes place. It is an agonizing event and most do not survive. Males dominate the vampire race because, for one reason or another, female's bodies do not absorb the vampire's poisonous blood well and often die when the blood first enters their system.

Validus Clan: Created by Imbrasus. They claim Eastern Europe, beginning with the Czech Republic and advancing East, with the exception of Russia. *Reigning monarch: Hadrian Lucretius.*

Voidukas Clan: The smallest of the vampire clans, created by Uro. Their territory consists of: Estonia, Latvia, Lithuania, Poland, Germany, Denmark, and Switzerland. *Reigning monarch: Sonya Rebane.*

Volkov Clan: Formed by the pureblood Dimitri. Territory belonging to this clan is Northern Europe and Russia. He created this Clan to give refuge to vampires over the years trying to escape persecution, slavery, and tyrannical rulers of their own Clans. *Reigning monarch: Dimitri Arsov.*

Prologue

London, England

"They must be destroyed. *Every last leech.*"

"Samuel is right."

The voices echoed in the dimly lit tunnels.

"Death is not always the answer. We could have peace."

Outraged rumbled the cavern. Fists pounded on the table as men continued to debate.

"Peace with those bloodsuckers? Never!" Samuel declared.

"Murderers. They are all murderers," Oliver added.

A slender young man came to his feet. "Look around you. We have been forced to live like rats beneath the city streets, scurrying from tunnel to tunnel and cave to cave. Our numbers are small. Our children suffer while our women are treated like broodmares. This has gone too far and has lasted too long. It is ruining us."

"Sit down, Carter."

"No, Lewis, I will not. This council needs to open their eyes and realize what this war is doing to our people."

"The vampires began this war. The king of the Mylonas Clan—"

"You seem to forget your history lessons, Samuel," Carter snapped. "Mark Wright, your ancestor, and the vampire, Kal Gracchus, devised this war. Kal desired to overthrow King Dorian Vlakhos and enlisted Wright's help. The council of 1814 never approved of this war, nor did they give any military or financial backing."

"The council could have stopped Wright. They could have taken his army and stripped him of his title. They chose to let this fake war progress." Richard said.

"Because vampires were dying," Samuel growled.

"Wright slaughtered indiscriminately, killing humans, torching entire villages. He turned his back on our vows, knowing full well that we are never to take human life," Carter argued. "And it was Vlakhos who drew his military back when he learned that this war was not sanctioned. Vlakhos had been willing to end the feud."

Richard nodded. "But instead, the Red Order launched a full scale attack."

Lewis shook his head. "Mark Wright was a general. We had to avenge his death. Vlakhos killed him. And it was your great, great, great grandfather that helped the king, Carter."

Carter knew his ancestor, Jacque, had helped Vlakhos. He was proud of his relative for doing what was right, even if it meant helping the enemy.

"Wright was a traitor to our Covenant," Carter said. "Peace with the Mylonas could have been ours by now, if we choose to make it so."

Samuel scowled. "Peace? Boy, you are young and naïve. Peace will only come when the last vampire meets the sun."

"We can't continue to live like this," Carter protested. "The Red Order will cease to exist. We have been losing this war."

Richard spoke up, "The Shaw live peacefully with the vampires. Queen Sonya—"

"The Shaw are a disgrace," Oliver snapped.

Samuel came to his feet so quick his chair toppled over, slamming a fist on the table, silencing the bickering that ensued. "This meeting is over. Until someone can devise a plan that will bring the vampires to their knees, the council will remain closed."

Wooden chair legs scraped against the unrelenting stone floor as grumbles and curses filled the cavern.

Carter stood alone in the council chambers. His shoulders slumped as he fervently prayed for strength.

Destitute. His people, the magnificent Red Order Hunters, the group that struck fear into the dead hearts of the vampires, now teetered on the brink of oblivion.

Two centuries. The war with the Mylonas had raged on for nearly two centuries. The vampires had only grown stronger while the Red Order had weakened and crumbled. It was only a matter of time before Dorian Vlakhos found their dilapidated, underground haven.

Carter shuddered as he thought of the children. With their population loss, boys were forced to become soldiers at thirteen. They were barely able to shoot straight and were quickly killed if they ever came face to face with a vampire. Sadly, their life expectancy was twenty-two. He, at twenty-nine, was considered an elder, hence his being elected to the council.

The fighting had to end. This fake war, built upon the greed of two men, would be the demise of the Reds. How could Samuel and Oliver not see the wisdom in his words? Lewis was on the fence, while Richard supported him.

"You are too progressive, councilman."

Carter spun around. A short, slim figure stood before him. She was draped in a crimson cloak, the hood casting shadows upon her face, distorting her delicate features.

"Peace is the answer," she said.

"Priestess, I—"

"Silence. I haven't much time." She held a small dark purple envelope. "As you know, there are those within the Shaw that are gifted with the ability of foresight. The Order's future is grave. Literally. Death will fall to all."

"Even the young? Please, spare them."

"I'm not the collector of souls. Save your bartering for *him*. I speak only of what I have seen."

"Then it is hopeless."

"Nothing is ever hopeless." She extended her arm, offering him the envelope.

"This is an official summons from the Shaman of the Shaw Tribe. The Red Order Council must attend. The five of you will travel to Tallinn, Estonia. The date and specific information is provided. You will come unarmed."

Carter shook his head. "They will never agree."

"Yes, they will." Her voice grew deeper as the air in the chamber turned frigid. "To deny the Shaw is to invite death."

Chapter One

Amazon, Brazil

The sweet tang of blood filled his mouth. Falcon's frustration tripled as he swallowed. That had been the fourth time he had to literally bite back a disrespectful comment. Arsenio, the alpha of the Silveria shape-shifting pack, let insults carelessly slip from his lips and Falcon was growing tired of Hadrian being referred to as the 'mad king'.

His fingers twitched as he thought about wrapping them around the grip of his gun. They had not unarmed him when he arrived. His long coat concealed his double holster, which cradled a pair of modified Springfield 1911's. He also had a vicious hunting knife strapped between his shoulder blades and two small daggers tucked into his boots. He came prepared. As a Black Knight, protector of the vampire nobility, packing heat was mandatory and he always made sure he had plenty of back up.

"Am I to understand that your king has returned from a self-imposed exile and would like to solidify our pact by having me give him one of my daughters as a ward?" Arsenio asked.

Falcon gave a tight nod, refusing to speak until his frustration dwindled.

Arsenio dropped his glowing yellow eyes to the documents in his lap. Falcon had brought along a copy of the treaty that had been signed by Arsenio's grandfather, who had been alpha at the time the alliance was formed.

"My grandfather was to give one of my aunts to the crazed vampire," the alpha said, his eyes still focused on the document.

Falcon's fingers curled into tight fists at his sides. "Yes, but he never did."

"Because your king was unfit."

Falcon inclined his head, he could not argue with that statement. "The contract was never fulfilled and my king wishes to rectify this oversight."

"As you can tell, the alpha of this pack has changed."

"If you continue to read the treaty, my lord, you will find that the change of alpha makes no difference. To maintain the peace and the alliance with my Clan, the current alpha must send one of his daughters to my king as a sign of good faith and loyalty."

Arsenio cursed as he found the stipulation within the contract.

"By not complying you will be breaking the agreement," Falcon added.

He honestly could not care less if the Silveria Pack complied. There were plenty of shifter packs his Clan could align with. Though he knew the Silveria Pack could not risk losing the vampires' support. War was a constant factor in the shape-shifting realm. Peace was fragile and the only reason the Silveria Pack maintained their territory was because they had vampires with superior strength and speed backing them.

"You think I will not honor this pact?" Arsenio demanded, his yellow eyes alight with anger.

"I meant no disrespect, but your reluctance is plain to see."

"Did you expect me to gladly give one of my daughters to your insane king?" he snapped.

Falcon sighed. He knew females were precious within shifter society. They were rare and needed to replenish their numbers lost during war. It was because of that fact Hadrian had agreed to the treaty hundreds of years ago. He knew that if he were given a female as a ward, the shifters would never do anything to endanger her life.

"My lord," a woman said, hesitantly taking a step forward. Her head was bowed, her eyes downcast. She had been the only female permitted within the meeting. She was the alpha's first wife, the most honored female within the pack. "Permission to speak?"

The alpha roughly grunted.

Her gaze remained on the floor as she came to a stop beside the throne. "May I make a suggestion?" Arsenio waved his hand, encouraging her to continue. "You have been wondering what to do with Eva, perhaps you can send her."

Falcon did not possess the ability to read minds, but he could feel the tension in the room ease. He watched as disgust twisted the alpha's lips at the mention of the female's name, then thoughtfulness sternly set his features before his decision brought a spark of light into his eyes.

Falcon mentally recited the names of the alpha's daughters. Eva was not one of them. *Unless, she is a bastard*, he thought.

"Thank you, Luisa."

The woman nodded and retreated back to where she had stood.

"I believe we can work something out, knight," Arsenio said, turning his attention back to Falcon. "That is, if you think your king is willing to compromise for a time."

"What is your proposal?"

"I have many bastard daughters, one of which is a half-breed."

Falcon's eyes narrowed. Half-breeds were shunned within shifter society, the lowest of the low, often times killed when born, if they managed to survive the birth. Hadrian had told him to expect this tactic. Though Falcon viewed this as an insult to his clan and his king, Hadrian had insisted that he accept a half-breed.

"The contract is specific."

Arsenio insisted, "I fully intend to honor the treaty, but you can hardly expect me to hand over one of my most prized possessions to a crazed vampire, king or not."

Falcon swallowed blood again as he waited for the alpha to explain.

"Upon your arrival you said your clan will be celebrating your majesty's return in three months. My proposal is this; I place my half-breed daughter into your care until the celebration. If no harm comes to the girl, I will arrange for one of my purebred, legitimate daughters to be sent to your clan. Think of the half-breed as a placeholder."

"What will happen to the girl when the other is sent?"

The alpha gave a lazy shrug.

Fury burned in his eyes as he gave a tight, accepting nod. He was no fool. He knew exactly what the shifter was implying. The alpha fully expected Hadrian to harm the girl. Was he merely testing Hadrian's sanity? Did he hope his king would kill her?

Falcon took in sharp, rapid breaths, desperately trying to maintain his control. Not only was this an insult to his king and his clan, but also downright disturbing. Falcon's gut twisted as he realized how little the alpha cared for his half-breed daughter. In Arsenio's eyes, he was offering this girl as a potential sacrifice.

"You little bitch!"

Eva did not flinch, she did not blink, nor did her head snap to the side when she was delivered a solid backhanded slap. After living within her father's pack for ten years, she had grown accustom to being hit.

"You did this," Teresa screeched.

"Like I said, I did not touch your clothes," Eva repeated, trying to remain calm. Her eyes flickered to the guards that stood outside the open door. Being the treasured first daughter of the alpha meant Teresa was never left unguarded. If Eva so much as got close enough to breathe on her, she would be dragged from the room to the courtyard and beaten before all.

"Liar! You ruined my clothes."

Eva rolled her eyes. Teresa had numerous younger siblings who enjoyed playing pranks and, unfortunately for Eva, she was usually blamed and punished for what those little brats did. This time, they had taken immense pleasure in shredding a few of Teresa's shirts.

"Don't you dare roll your eyes at me." Teresa slapped her again.

Eva took in a deep breath, a scathing retort ready on her lips. But her words were suddenly lodged in her throat as she was yanked back by her long braid.

"What is this all about?" Luisa asked.

"The abomination ruined my clothes," Teresa answered, her yellow eyes narrowed.

Luisa wrapped Eva's hair around her fist and pulled hard, bringing her to her knees. Eva refused to satisfy her half sister and stepmother with her pain. She gritted her teeth and ignored the tears that stung her eyes. "You are nothing but a jealous, filthy half-breed," Luisa said. "And this is where you belong, on your knees, and at my feet."

Eva's temper was rising to dangerous heights. She glanced over her shoulder at the guards. Their numbers had doubled with Luisa's presence. Eva swallowed a curse. Just once she would like to return their abuse. Teresa's lips curled into a wicked smile as she took in her mother's expression.

"I have come with news for you girls," Luisa announced returning an equally wicked, conspiratorial grin.

"Happy news?" Teresa asked.

Luisa nodded and said, "We will no longer have to suffer her presence."

Teresa happily clapped as excitement flushed her cheeks. Luisa released her hold on Eva's hair, only to deliver a forceful shove to her shoulder, knocking her flat on the floor. Eva quickly came to her feet, straightened her spine and squared her shoulders.

"So, it worked? Our plan?"

"Yes, my daughter."

Eva frowned, confusion and anger fought for control of her mind as she watched the women exchange knowing glances.

Luisa took in a breath and turned to her. "Have you heard about our recent visitor?"

Eva did not answer, though she had heard whispers of a vampire who had arrived that morning. The pack had been shocked to learn he could walk in sunlight, but they had been more frightened as to his reason for coming at all. The Black Knights were guardians of the vampire nobility, their clans located across the ocean in Europe. Everyone wanted to know why one had come to their small village deep within the Amazon.

"He came to claim one of the alpha's daughters."

The air in Eva's lungs turned to ice, though she kept all emotion from her eyes. She would not let them see her worry or fear.

What had her father done?

"You are obviously ignorant of pack politics and the alliance we have with the Validus Clan of vampires. Allow me to explain. Alpha Juan, our current alpha's grandfather, made a pact with these vampires and, to show trust, they agreed the alpha would place one of his daughters within the vampire's home to live as a ward. However, the vampire king, Hadrian Lucretius, went insane and exiled himself. Alpha Juan never fulfilled his obligation of providing one of his female offspring. Now, the vampire king has returned."

"And he wants his ward," Teresa added, her voice ringing with satisfaction.

Eva's fingers curled into shaking fists. Luisa did not need to finish. She knew she was going to be the "ward," the gift given to placate the vampire king or, judging by the evil glint in these women's eyes, the sacrifice.

"Naturally, our alpha would not give one of his treasured, purebred legitimate daughters to a crazed vampire. So, you will go." Luisa smiled. "I was a young girl when Hadrian first came to our village. He was only a noble in the Validus Clan then. He was a fierce warrior and helped Alpha Juan defeat his enemies." Her smile grew wider. "The vampire was a true beast, laying waste to villages, ripping the throats out of his victims in battle, feeding freely. His hunger for blood was matched only by his hunger for sex, taking more than one female to bed every night."

Teresa studied Eva from head to toe. "No doubt he will use your body. You will be all that is low in this world: a half-breed bastard, bleeder, and vampire's whore. He'll mount you good and I bet you'll pray for death before he is done with you."

"She will not survive past the month," Luisa added with a shrug. "Now, go pack your meager belongings. You leave with the vampire tonight."

Eva was unable to breathe, her heart frantically slammed against her ribcage. She swayed and stumbled back, hitting the wall. Her vision blurred as her mind rebelled against this horrific news.

She was to be given to a bloodthirsty, sex-crazed, mad vampire. Her father may as well have slit her throat himself. She had heard of Hadrian and shivered. Countless awful, bloody, gruesome tales were attached firmly to his name. Her father was truly offering her as a sacrifice.

As a half-breed she was barren and unable to take animal form. She possessed no supernatural abilities, although, her senses were slightly better than a human's and she could heal quicker. But she had the features of a shifter: dark hair, petite but lithe frame and amber eyes. In the end, she meant nothing to the pack for she could not produce any offspring. She had been shunned and reduced to the life of a slave amongst her father's pack, looked upon only with disgust and hatred. God, how she missed living within human society, but those years seemed like a millennia ago. Now, she would be sent to her death.

"Did you hear me?" Luisa demanded.

Eva blinked, clearing her vision. "Y–yes," Eva said, her voice cracking. Shock still rattled her system. She did not know if she should be more frightened or angry at this turn of events. But how she felt did not matter. She had no choice. She would go with the vampire willingly or not.

Tilting her chin up in defiance, she decided she would not fight. She would gladly leave for this all meant one thing. She would finally be free of her father's rule, free to live her life. And if the vampire was as rumors claimed, she would escape. She was small of frame, but she was not defenseless. Her uncle from her mother's side had taught her the skills necessary for Brazilian Jiu-Jitsu and she had learned the art of Capoeira from watching the young males of the pack train and practice. She was also confident that if she did manage to get away from the vampires, she could make a life for herself. Her mother's family had been from northern Europe and she could speak four different languages. Yes, she could escape and finally reclaim control of her life.

—
6

"Well, get on with it." Teresa grabbed Eva's arm, pulled her forward and shoved her towards the door.

Eva spun on her heel, her anger rising again. "Don't touch me!" she snapped.

Luisa's lip curled over her teeth, bearing her slightly elongated fangs. "How dare you," she growled before delivering a strong backhand. "You have not been handed over to the leeches yet, you still belong to this pack."

Eva stumbled back, her hand covering her cheek. Her eyes watered, her lip was already beginning to swell.

"Guards," Luisa barked. The four men filed into the room. "Hold her."

Eva dodged the first man's hands, barely escaped the second's, but was caught by the third. The guard snatched her wrists, twisting her arms, pulling her hands behind her back. She struggled, but it was no use, the guard held her firm.

"I would think after nearly ten years you would have learned your place," Luisa said as she came forward. "Though I do not believe you will survive a month with the vampire, I do not want you to embarrass us. You will not bring shame to your pack with your disrespect and blatant disdain for your superiors."

"My pack?" Eva repeated, her voice laced with dark laughter. "I don't belong to any pack. I am not an animal like you and your stuck-up bitch daughter—"

Another, even more violent blow landed and Eva bit back a scream. Tears slipped from her eyes, her cheek burned. Luisa's ring had cut her, blood tickled down Eva's face to drip off her cheek. She stiffened, bracing herself for another blow when Luisa raised her hand again.

In a flurry of movement, Eva was wrenched away from the guard, spun about and shoved against the wall, pinned there behind a tall man dressed all in black.

"What is going on here?" the stranger demanded.

Though her vision was blurred from tears and pain, Eva watched Luisa drop her hand and straighten her shoulders. She gave a slight bow of her head as Teresa curtseyed.

"Sir Kenwrec, my apologies. You should not have had to witness—"

"Is this the girl?" he asked, his voice cold.

"Yes, she is not cooperating. I was going to have her escorted to her room so that she may pack and be ready for your departure."

"Would that be before or after you beat her senseless?"

7

Eva's swollen lips twitched with a smile. She had never met a vampire before and all the stories she had heard painted them as evil, disgusting, loathsome creatures. But this Black Knight seemed to be a decent fellow. He had just saved her from another strike and, if history taught her anything, Luisa had been about to demand the guards take her in hand and "teach the half-breed a lesson".

"Sir, I—"

"Enough. I have grown tired of this jungle and would very much like to be on my way." Turning, he faced Eva. She tilted her head back to meet his hard, gray eyes. "I'm Sir Falcon Kenwrec." He gave a swift bow and straightened. "I've no doubt you have been informed of my business here and know that you are to accompany me to my Clan's lands and reside within our care as a ward to King Hadrian." Eva slowly nodded, struck momentarily speechless by the knight's ruggedly regal good looks. "I will escort you to your room so that you may collect your belongings. We will leave as soon as you are ready."

Eva opened her mouth to speak and winced. Her lip was bleeding and the coppery taste of blood made her stomach roll. She hated the sight and scent of blood, unlike her purebred relatives. She wiped at her face and mouth with the back of her hand, desperately trying to clean herself.

"Here."

She took the handkerchief he offered, startled by his kindness. "Th–thank you." Eva gently dabbed at her lip and cheek. "I know what you mean, about wanting to get out of here." Luisa shifted behind the knight and Eva gave her a sharp glare, shooting daggers with her eyes. "I only have one other shirt and a night gown," Eva shrugged, "nothing really worth taking with me."

He nodded. "Dense civilization is a few days boat ride from here, but I can arrange some time for us to shop in Rio de Janeiro while we wait for the jet to be readied."

"Shop?"

"Yes, my king insisted that you be outfitted with a new wardrobe. He remembers shifter society well and knew you would have little." In fact, Hadrian had warned him while on the phone a few moments ago that he may need to arrange medical care for the girl, not knowing in what condition she may be in. Falcon reigned in his anger and disgust. There was no telling how much abuse the girl had suffered under their care.

"It is settled." Turning back to the others, he said, "We leave now."

Chapter Two

Carpathian Mountains, Ukraine

Danger.

A sudden chill rattled Eva's bones as they entered the narrow pass, taking them deeper into the forbidden mountains. High, impossible to scale cliffs lined the road on either side. They seemed to rise endlessly into the gray frost of the angry clouds. The wind whipped flakes of ice and snow across the windshield of the Land Rover as it roared over the packed snow and hard rock.

Danger.

Eva shifted uncomfortably in her seat. A dark shadow had settled within her the moment they entered the mountains, an impression of menace. The feeling was growing steadily stronger as the vehicle charged through the unrelenting storm to its destination. Palatio Nocte, Palace of the Night, the lair of the mad king of the Validus Clan, the home of the beast amongst vampires, Hadrian Lucretius.

The tiny hairs on the back of her neck stood. They were being watched. No, they were being stalked. Her gaze frantically searched the road, but she could see nothing. The flurry of snow and shrieking wind limited her non-supernatural vision. Wolves howled in the distance and Eva shuddered.

Glancing over to the Black Knight, he seemed to be at ease as he steadily drove them onward. They had finally broken free of the pass. Tall trees surrounded them now, with the occasional white-knuckle turn that hugged the edge of sheer cliffs.

Sensing her unease, Falcon said, "We are almost there."

She nodded in response. They had been driving for what seemed like an eternity. Once off the plane, he had ushered her to the car and they set off. Though she was not in any way looking forward to reaching their destination, she was anxious to be free of the confines of the vehicle.

Peeking at the knight again, she gave an exasperated sigh as she once again thought of all the outrageous and purely evil stories she had been told of vampires. Thus far, Falcon, who insisted she use his given name, had proven all the rumors wrong. She did not doubt there were some bloodthirsty demons walking the earth with sharp fangs, but Falcon had been the embodiment of civility. His manners were impeccable, his speech was flawless and he was always polite. Then again, most would seem perfect compared to the animals of her father's pack.

"I hope you will find your new home to your liking," he said. "The construction and restoration projects have just been completed."

"So, there will be running water?"

He laughed, "Yes, all kinds of modern amenities."

"I was worried I wouldn't be able to take a shower and would have to bathe in some icy stream."

"We are not that rustic."

Eva shrugged. "I didn't know what to expect. My standards of living are very low these days. For the last ten years, I've lived in a poorly designed and horribly built hut. Living in a rainforest with a leaking roof—"

Her words caught in her throat as the castle came into view. Even from a distance it was impressively large and stood proudly atop another mountain. The road twisted and coiled, the incline was steep, but the Land Rover had no trouble.

"Oh, my god," Eva whispered as the knight pulled the vehicle to a stop. There was…nothing. The road had ended.

"I think if we back up and I stomp on the gas, we'll make it."

Eva turned wide eyes to Falcon. He smiled as her face paled.

"It's not that big of a gap. Maybe, twenty yards give or take a few." He laughed as Eva continued to stare at him. "The bridge we had was tattered. Like I said, we have just finished the construction improvements and restorations." He reached up and pushed a button on the sun visor. "This is one of the improvements," he pointed to the thick metal plates that slid out from the beneath the earth to connect the sides, "retractable bridge is much better and will help with security."

"Is this the only way to cross?"

"One way in and one way out."

Eva grabbed hold of the seat, her fingers dug into the leather as they rolled over the bridge. Once they had safely reached the other side, Falcon pressed the button again and the bridge promptly retreated back to its hiding place. They charged the rest of the way up the mountain. There were no tower walls, no ramparts or portcullis, unlike most castles Eva had seen in history books and on television. She pressed her face to the chilled glass as they pulled into a large circular driveway. Falcon parked the Land Rover at the foot of the steps that led to a set of daunting, ten foot tall, wood doors.

"You better zip up your jacket. I'll grab your bags and we'll make a mad dash up the stairs," Falcon directed before pulling the keys from the ignition. He took in a breath and threw the car door open, the wind slammed it shut behind him.

Eva released her seat belt with trembling fingers, never taking her gaze off the intimidating fortress. The keep's walls were dark, mostly shades of gray, with hardly any windows except for one long wall made entirely of glass. While she studied the imposing fortress the back of her nape began to tingle and she could not shake the feeling of being watched. Her eyes flickered to the wall of windows. Was there someone up there?

"Are you coming?" Falcon asked as he opened the back and drew out her new suitcases, packed full of new clothes.

His voice snapped her from her trance and she quickly zipped up her jacket. She had lived in a warm humid climate all her life and had never experienced the harshness of winter. Taking in a deep breath, she threw the door open and stepped out.

The icy wind lashed at her face. Her neatly braided hair was whipped about. Dark, silken strands were pried free by the angry storm. Her teeth chattered as she mumbled curse after curse. She shoved her hands in the pockets of her jacket and ran to catch up with the vampire, who was already halfway up the snow-covered steps. She slipped as she hurried towards the doors. Her entire body shivered uncontrollably as the wind drew tears from her eyes. Through the blur she saw the knight shove open the heavy doors, pushing them aside as if they weighed no more than dust.

Eva skid to a halt on the top step and watched the vampire disappear into the darkness of the fortress. Shards of ice blew against her cheeks as she regarded the entrance. She could feel the warmth that radiated from within and, yet, it did nothing to chase away the chill from her bones. The very atmosphere seemed to shimmer around her, time slowed and an oddly disorientating sensation and a sense of knowing took hold of her. The cold bite of the storm was quickly forgotten and replaced by a ruthless feeling of dread. She knew in that moment, if she entered Palatio Nocte she would never be able to turn back. Her life would never be the same.

"Have you lost your mind?" Falcon called as he came stomping from the shadows. He reached for her arm, but Eva retreated.

She said nothing, unable to form words as fear choked her. During the entire trip she had not been frightened, despite the fact she knew she was to live with a crazed vampire. She had tried to block out the stories she had heard of Hadrian, but now, they came at her all at once, robbing her of all logic and confidence. Hadrian had been a merciless Roman general, changed approximately two thousand years ago by Imbrasus, the pureblood vampire and Father of the Validus Clan. He had been selected to become a beast because of his skills in the art of war and his exceptional intelligence. It was said that Imbrasus had bestowed upon Hadrian his own dark needs of blood and death.

Rumors began to play like a broken record in her head; the voices ran together until they became a steady stream of fear: *He kills for sport and bathes in the blood of the slain. No one has ever met his rage and lived...He'll suck the life right out you, down to the marrow in your bones. He's a devil, that one, a beast straight from the fires of hell... You best behave and be cautious, vampires will eat you alive, little girl.*

Eva covered her ears, trying to block out the terrible voices. Her heart pounded in her chest as she gasped for air. A scream built in her chest, but she lacked the breath to free it.

"Eva, come inside."

"I–I can't," she answered, her teeth chattering viciously. She wrapped her arms tightly around herself as she hesitantly took a step back.

Sacrifice. She was a sacrifice to the vampire king.

Falcon's liquid silver gaze began to harden to gray. Fear. He could scent her fear.

"You will freeze out there. Please, come inside."

"N–No."

She stumbled down a few steps, briefly losing her footing on the ice.

"Eva," Falcon called out as he darted for her. He caught her arm and pulled her against him before she could tumble down the steps. She struggled against his hold, but he pinned her to his chest, his arms locked around her like steel bands as he carried her into the castle.

The doors slammed behind them and Eva let out the feral scream that had been building, shoving relentlessly against him. Falcon set her on her feet, placing himself between her and the door. Eva backed away from him, her eyes darting about the room as she tried to remain away from the shadows that seemed to surround them.

Danger.

It was a thick stench that clouded the air and Eva struggled for breath.

"What has brought this on?" he asked. "What frightened you?"

Eva shook her head. She had no answer. She did not know what had triggered her panic attack and she could feel her cheeks growing bright with a blush. Never had she acted this way. Her mother had taught her never to give in to fear, never to allow such a weak emotion to rule her and yet, it had just claimed her. She had never been so terrified in her life. When her mother had passed, leaving her alone in the world, she had not been scared. When her father and his men arrived to drag her off to their secluded village in the jungle just days after her mother's funeral, she had not betrayed her teaching. Never once while she lived amongst the shifters did she give in to any emotion, save anger. She could not begin to explain this.

She took in deep breaths, desperately trying to regain her composure, ruthlessly shoving aside her terror. She needed to be calm, focused. If there was danger, she needed to be aware and not be overcome by panic. She smoothed her wind swept hair back from her face and unzipped her jacket, suddenly feeling extremely warm and completely embarrassed.

"Eva, are you—"

"I'm fine."

Falcon's eyes narrowed as he studied her and Eva shifted beneath his scrutiny.

"Nothing is going to happen to you here," Falcon said, trying to soothe her. "You are a ward to my clan."

Eva wanted to believe his words, desperately needed to believe them, but alas doubt remained as a dark shadow in her mind.

"You are safe here," Falcon said, in what she knew was meant to be a reassuring voice.

The comment drew a sharp laugh from her and Falcon's brow wrinkled with a frown. He stepped toward her and Eva resisted the urge to retreat.

"I've no doubt you've heard…terrible stories of my king. I will not deny that his mind has been touched by darkness, but he is a good man."

Eva waited for him to continue, but he said no more. She wanted him to say Hadrian was nothing like the rumors claimed, that he would not harm her in any way. Instead, he offered her nothing. She swallowed hard and prayed that Falcon would be staying here with her. After spending the last few days with him, she felt she could trust him and that he would not let anyone hurt her. She hoped that included his king.

"There are so many rumors...I don't know what to believe."

"Understandable," he conceded. "I know all too well what people say. His reputation is legendary."

"Lethal," she added on a whisper.

Falcon did not protest and silence stretched between them. A piercing ring from the other room was a welcome interruption.

"That should be the main house," Falcon said as the phone's ring echoed through the keep. "I was to report in when we arrived. I will not be long. Stay here."

Eva nodded and Falcon entered the shadows. She removed her jacket and hung it on a tall iron coat rack. Heaving a heavy sigh, she stepped from the safety of the foyer. It was a small room, clearly used for the removal of snow-lined coats and other travel wear. It was a transition room, or, as Eva noted the holes within the ceiling with tiny spikes protruding from them, a last line of defense.

She crossed her arms over her chest and leaned against the wall. While she waited for Falcon to return, Eva silently chastised herself for acting like a fool and tried to analyze what had caused her fear.

Something had been here, in the shadows, she thought. *Something...evil.* And she had an odd feeling that it wanted her.

She could not allow herself to be scared and she refused to be intimidated. If she could endure and survive the pack's treatment of her, then she could survive this. Thus far, Falcon had not been rough or violent with her. He had given her no reason to distrust him or to be frightened. Then again, she had yet to meet the king. She would have to find a way to endure this too, no matter what lay ahead.

Eva closed her eyes as she recalled her last night with the pack. She had stood outside her father's office, waiting for Falcon. Teresa and a few of her other half-siblings circled about the hall, their eyes filled with twisted satisfaction.

An elderly servant, who had been a servant for the alpha's grandfather had rushed to her, eyes filled with horror.

"Oh, you sweet child," she said. She had reached out to take Eva's hands then quickly drew back. The woman may have felt sorrow for her, but she was not about to touch a half-breed. "I've only just heard you have been given to the vampires." Fear filled her eyes. "Take care."

She shuddered and opened her eyes. Was the king as brutal as rumors claimed?

"Or could he be worse?" she whispered.

Dear lord, what had her father done?

He sacrificed me. She snorted. *He couldn't send one of his precious purebred daughters off to what was surely her death.*

Eva pushed away from the wall and began to pace. Falcon had been gone for nearly fifteen minutes and her nerves were making her restless. Glancing about, she decided to take a little tour. She would not go far and, with luck, she may find the knight. Besides, if she remained immobile, consumed by her thoughts, she would soon have herself worked up into another fit of hysteria.

Deciding to head in the direction Falcon had, she did not enter the main hall though the large arched entrance directly in front of her. Instead, she turned left and headed down a long, dimly lit corridor. She paused outside each door she passed, she knocked and tried their knobs, but no one called from the other side and every door was locked.

After the fifth door, she gave up her search and allowed her curiosity to take over. The hall was lined with wood paneling decorated by sharply detailed paintings. Each featured a portrait of a man and was accompanied by a gold placard with his name. These were the kings of the Validus Clan.

The name of the last painting read Hadrian Lucretius, but the image had been savagely shredded. Stepping closer, Eva reached up, trying to place the pieces back together, wanting to get a look at the vampire.

A cool hand clamped over her mouth, stifling her scream as she was hauled back. Eva fought for freedom, twisting around, she jabbed her elbow in her attacker's side then kicked back, connecting with his shin. He growled in response and spun her about, trapping her with his body. His hands slammed into the wall, cracking the wood, on either side of her head.

"Little girls should not wander alone in the dark."

She closed her eyes and swallowed hard. His voice, it was dark, threatening—pure sex. He leaned his head down, his lips brushed her ear and, God help her, she shivered. Whether it was from fear or something entirely sexual, she did not know. Confusion, terror, and desire fought for control of her brain, as she remained pinned between the large, solid male and the wall.

"Bad things prowl in the dark," he whispered against her ear and Eva's knees went weak. His words were heavily accented, his voice deep. It echoed with evil and was laced with lust. "Bad things, like me."

15

Eva tried to speak, knowing she should demand he release her, or scream, but nothing came.

One of his hands dropped from the wall to encircle her wrist, the pad of his thumb gently brushed over her erratically beating pulse.

"Your scent," he said, his voice rough, the sound sending waves of need crashing over her.

His fingers lightly traced up her arm to cup her nape, tickling her sensitive flesh.

Eva's breathing grew shallow as her body began to burn.

Desire?

Yes. Oh, god, *yes.*

The menacing male drew closer, his second hand dropping to her shoulder, pressing her firmly against the wall. Danger, it radiated from him, yet desire flickered in his cold, black eyes. Instinct took hold of her. Eva wrapped her arms around his waist. Her hands pressed flat against his lower back, urging him closer. She arched her back trying in vain to close the space between them.

"Sweet...warm vanilla." His cool breath caressed the tender flesh of her throat, sending chills all the way down to her toes.

Was he going to bite her?

God, what was she doing? She had no idea who this man was let alone what he was doing to her. She should shove him away. She should bring her knee up and hit him where it counts. But she could not move. Her heart beat frantically, her blood rushed like lava through her veins as her body responded to this aggressive male.

"My king!"

Eva's sigh was a mix of relief and disappointment when she heard Falcon's voice.

"Release her."

The vampire's mystifying obsidian gaze held her captive as he asked, "Do you want to be rescued?"

No, but her self-preservation cried yes.

The vampire gently brushed her bottom lip with his thumb and Eva shuttered.

"My king," Falcon bellowed.

The stranger lifted his head and glared at Falcon for a long breathless moment. She could sense the tension that coiled in his body. Pure lethal power flowed from him like tidal waves.

Finally, he turned his attention back to her. Framing her jaw with his large hands, he bent his head down. Was he going to kiss her? Another rush of heat coursed through her and pooled at her core. She wished she could see his face. The shadows hid his features. All she

16

could see were his dark as midnight eyes, which burned in the darkness, full of violence and lust.

He leaned into her, his solid chest brushing her breasts, causing them to ache as he sank his lower body against her. Surrounded. Hot, aggressive male surrounded her and—wild, she was wild with need.

His cool lips brushed against hers as he whispered, "Until we meet again, little one." He disappeared.

Eva sagged against the wall, her body feeling bereft without him. Shock pulsed through her body and she struggled to make sense of what had just happened. Her initial reaction had been fear, but it had been quickly replaced by desire. She focused on her breathing, trying to calm herself as she gathered her scattered, confused thoughts.

He didn't kiss her. Why did he not—

"Did I not ask you to remain in the foyer, because I distinctly remember doing so?" Falcon asked.

"What?" she sputtered.

When she looked up at him, his expression was not what she had expected. His tone implied annoyance but his gaze was quizzical as he studied her, his brow furrowed in thought.

"Nothing," he said with a shake of his head.

Falcon cursed a string of obscenities, some in English but most in an old form of…French?

"Come on, I'll show you to your room so you can get settled."

He turned and continued back down the hall.

Eva shoved away from the wall and jogged to catch up to him. Her legs were still weak and she feared they might give out. She caught his arm and Falcon stopped.

"Was that…I mean, he was—"

"Hadrian Lucretius, King of the Validus Clan of vampires," he answered.

"I thought so," she said, her voice a faint whisper.

He sighed heavily and rubbed his brow. "Eva, he is not completely…stable," he paused as if searching for the right words, "He has his moments, like you just witnessed. It would be best if you tried to stay clear of him for a while, just until he gets used to having you around. He has lived alone for so long and it will take him some time to acclimate."

She nodded. "I understand."

Falcon said nothing more as they walked back to the foyer. He gathered her bags and mumbled for her to follow him. They entered the great hall, which was brightly lit by numerous, iron chandeliers. Eva was awed by the splendor of the room. It was wide open with lines of intricately carved columns that rose to high, vaulted ceilings. Tapers burned everywhere, dispelling the darkness, as a fire crackled and hissed in the wide-mouthed hearth. Thick, crimson drapes covered the windows, concealing the metal shades that blocked out the light from the setting sun. The room was nearly vacant of furniture, save a long table with rows of bench seats on either side, a throne like chair positioned at the head, and two smaller chairs flanking its sides.

The keep was a feast for the senses, the artwork and structure was beautiful, straight out of a fairytale, complete with a beast lurking in the shadows.

They mounted a wide, grand staircase that was newly carpeted in deep red. The banisters were polished and shined, reflecting the light. Falcon and Eva came to the third floor and turned right, to continue down a dark hall lined with doors.

"These are the guest quarters. The remaining levels and rooms belong to the clan members. At one time, this castle housed all of the Validus." He paused before a door on the left, shuffled the bags around, freeing his hand so that he could turn the knob. With a light kick, the door flew open. "This is your room. I hope you find it adequate."

Eva followed and blinked twice in surprise. The room was spacious. A long row of stain-glass windows covered the wall to the right. Their colored panes shimmered from the light of the red and gold flames that jumped within the fireplace to the left. The door faced a four-poster bed, piled high with thick quilts. The beautifully carved furniture glimmered in the firelight. She had never seen such a grand room and she could not believe it was for her.

Falcon gazed at the fire for a moment before shaking his head and setting her bags down beside the bed. "The bathroom and closet are through there," he said, waving toward a door in the left corner. "Are you hungry?"

"No," she answered absently as she wandered through the room.

"I will bring something up for you later. The kitchen should be well stocked."

"I can find it later and—"

"I think it would best if you remained in your room this evening."

She turned, her eyes narrowed. "Why?"

"Well, for one, this castle is very large and you can easily get lost. Two, I would like to give you an official tour and three, I would rather not have a repeat of what happened downstairs. I would like to speak with the king before you go wandering about on your own, again."

She winced. His tone had hardened upon his last word. Yes, she was fully aware she had made a mistake.

Her hand came up to her neck, her flesh still tingled from where his breath had teased her and she had to stop herself from wondering what would have happened if Falcon had not interrupted.

Interrupted? More like saved my ass, she thought. *The king had been about to snack on me.* Clinging to her rational thoughts, she ignored the strange primal excitement that he had ignited within her.

"I know shifters hate being confined, but you should be able to manage one night."

Eva nodded. Even though she was a half-breed, her spirit was still more animalistic than human and the thought of being caged in was loathsome. Their wild nature craved and demanded freedom, but she could tolerate one night. In truth, she had suffered many days and nights being locked away in her hut as punishment or, during the full moon, for her protection.

"Now, be prepared, I am a horrible cook. I apologize in advance if anything is undercooked, burnt, or flat out tastes horrid."

She could not stop the smile that curled her lips. "Noted."

"Unfortunately, I did not have the time to arrange for a cook," he explained. In truth, Hadrian's decision to collect a ward from the Silveria pack had been last minute. The construction and renovations had been completed only the week before and Falcon was glad the cleaning crew had finished before they arrived.

"Some fruit, bread with a little butter and water will work for me."

He frowned and looked her over from head to toe. "Is that what you usually eat?"

She nodded. "Just about."

"No wonder you are so thin."

Eva rolled her eyes. People always criticized her for her weight. She was short, not much over five feet, and a little on the skinny side, but she didn't look like she was starving.

"I'll give you some time to unpack," Falcon said in parting and closed the door behind him.

Her entire body tensed as she waited for the sound of a lock to slide into place as it always had when she was locked in her hut. But it never came.

Chapter Three

A familiar chill settled over Hadrian. The vicious wind lashed out, attacking him as he stepped out onto the balcony. Sharp shards of ice whipped at his face and arms, the sting a welcome distraction.

He closed his eyes as he took in a deep breath, filling his lungs with the crisp winter air. His fingers slowly curled into fists as he exhaled. The palms of his hands burned. Soft. The female's skin had been incredibly soft. Her delicious scent had been overwhelming and her response...

Gods, he had acted like a beast. If Falcon had not arrived Hadrian knew he would have taken her there, right then against the wall.

And she would have let you.

He cringed at the dark thought. He had behaved like the monster that he was. Poor girl, she had been frightened and the demon within him had loved it. He had fed off her response as if it were some kind of drug. Terror and lust, the heady scent still clouded his mind.

What had come over him? The instant he had seen the female, something within his mind had snapped. All he could think about was her, claiming her, drinking her.

He had not fed in nearly a week, perhaps that was why he had stalked her through the hall, but that would not explain away his intense sexual reaction to her. True, he enjoyed women and had enjoyed hundreds, if not thousands, of lovers over the course of his immortal life. Sex and blood was a wonderful combination, one he had been without for nearly three hundred and fifty years.

Hadrian shook his head. No matter the reason, he had lost control and he could not afford to do so again. There was no telling what would happen if he allowed the vampire within to take over, he could very well kill the girl. She was only a half-breed, not much stronger than a human, and humans were so frail. Like most other vampires, he preferred his lovers to be of his own kind, mortals were easily broken. Not to mention, he was sworn to protect the girl. She was his charge. He was responsible for her and he would never forgive himself if he harmed her.

Hadrian sighed and forced his troubled thoughts aside. He had experienced a moment of weakness, nothing more. Once he fed and perhaps took a woman or two to bed, all would be well. He knew he should apologize to the half-breed for his appalling behavior, but that could wait until he saw to his needs.

The soft sound of footsteps thudding up the stairs vibrated in his ears. He searched the hall outside the room with his senses. Turning from the balcony, he entered the room, closing the elegantly crafted stain-glass doors behind him, banishing the loving cold.

The door to the room opened and Falcon stepped inside.

"Your Highness, must you keep the guard on your power in place? I was unable to sense you. I've searched this entire castle for you. I was about to head out to the woods."

Hadrian ignored the irritation that roughed Falcon's voice and replied, "Habit."

Falcon snorted and closed the door. "My king, may I speak plainly?"

Hadrian cursed. Nothing good ever came of conversations that Falcon begun this way. "You know you need not ask permission to share your thoughts. At least not when we are alone. Speak your mind, if you must."

"What the hell happened in the hall?" Falcon demanded.

Hadrian turned his back on the knight and gazed out the colorful glass.

"Are you going to answer me?"

"It was a momentary loss of control."

Falcon shook his head. Doubt clouded his eyes and before he could voice his concerns, Hadrian added, "You needn't worry. It will not happen again. The girl must think I'm a monster." *And she would be right.*

"What was it about her…I mean, what do you think triggered"

"I was at the pass," he said, as he began to pace, his boots falling soundlessly on the stone floor.

"Yes, I sensed you. What were you doing out there in the storm?"

"Occasionally I like to go for a run. It is soothing." *And it helps focus my mind when the madness creeps in.* "I heard your vehicle and decided to head in your direction.

I followed you to the keep. Perhaps the chase triggered the vampire. Hunting, stalking prey." It was a plausible explanation for his hunger. He had gone months without feeding before, though one week should not drive him to such extremes as to attack the female in the hall. But the demon within him craved the hunt and she would be delicious prey.

Falcon rubbed the nape of his neck. Hadrian could be right, but for some reason, he did not believe that was the cause. With a shrug he said, "It is a possibility, but she did respond to you."

Hadrian scoffed, "Fear."

"More than that," he insisted.

When Falcon had come upon Eva in the hall he had seen the flush that colored her cheeks and the desire that filled her eyes. He had thought it such a strange response. Hadrian had a captivating way with the ladies, but Falcon highly doubted Eva was able to see his face in the darkness. No, she responded to something else entirely. Then, a thought had crossed his mind.

He shook his head as he had before. His mind was playing tricks on him. Just because Dorian, the king of the Mylonas Clan, and Dimitri, the king of the Volkov Clan had found their mates did not mean...But, he had never seen Hadrian in such a state. He enjoyed women, that was no secret, but the way he had behaved and the look on his face. Falcon would never forget Hadrian's eyes; they glowed blood red and were filled with malice for the one who had interrupted them. The glare had struck Falcon speechless, cementing him where he stood. Possessiveness jumped like flames in the crimson depths as he stared him down. Challenging him as a wolf might when it came to his mate. Then there was the fire burning in Eva's room. Hadrian must have lit it, which was a nice gesture for a recluse king.

"The animal spirit within her responded to the aggressive sexual threat I presented, nothing more."

Falcon sighed and rubbed his forehead, trying to release some of the tension that gripped his body. He did not know what to think and he had plenty of other things to worry about. Besides, if what he suspected was true, it would all work out and if he were wrong then nothing would change and Hadrian would be another victim of the Death Curse that had claimed all the kings of their race. The curse created by the Shaw witches to control the vampire population.

Hadrian relaxed a fraction when Falcon accepted his words. "Now, explain to me why we were given a half-breed. You were not very descriptive over the phone. As I recall, anger clipped your words."

Falcon shrugged off his worry for his king and his curiosity of what had happened in the hall. Business. It was clear Hadrian would rather discuss business and, at the moment, so did he.

"The alpha did just as you expected," Falcon said, "He was extremely reluctant to give us one of his legitimate, purebred daughters."

Hadrian clasped his hands behind his back, his pacing slowed.

"A test," his words were not a question, though he waited for Falcon to respond. The knight gave a tight nod and Hadrian came to a stop before the glass doors.

"It's shameful."

"Hm?"

"This test," Falcon clarified.

"He doesn't trust me and I cannot blame him."

"Not that. If he truly felt you can't be trusted and that you would be a threat to his daughter, he should have sent no one."

"And disgrace the memory of his grandfather by not upholding the treaty?" Hadrian countered.

"In his mind, he sent his half-breed daughter off as a potential sacrifice. It's sickening how little he cares for the girl. If you were to kill her, I don't think he would even bat an eye."

"Most likely not."

"This doesn't bother you?" Falcon demanded.

Hadrian turned, leaning his shoulders against the door. He crossed his arms over his chest. "Which part?"

Falcon's entire body tensed as anger sparked in his eyes. "All of it."

"I know well how shifter society works. He has no intention of insulting me by sending his half-breed bastard and every intention of protecting his most prized possessions, his purebred daughters. He has every right to be concerned for his daughter's safety. I did exile myself and have lived alone with only my madness to keep me company for over three hundred years."

"I think he is hoping the girl dies," Falcon spat.

Hadrian shrugged in reply. Falcon's thoughts were most likely true.

"What do you know of this girl?" Hadrian asked.

Falcon buried his anger and began to list what he knew of their ward.

"Her name, Eva Maldonado. Born to Isabelle Maldonado, who is said to have left Brazil the moment she realized she was with child. From birth to age fifteen she lived in Miami, Florida. That summer, they moved back to Rio de Janeiro where they lived with Isabella's brother. Unfortunately, right after Eva turned seventeen her mother died of cancer and her father claimed her immediately after the funeral. She has been with the Silveria pack for the past nine years."

Hadrian's brows drew together as he mulled over the very interesting information. He had spent years living amongst the shifters in South America and what Falcon had just described was highly unusual. Though, half-breeds were exceedingly rare.

"Eva," Hadrian whispered as if testing her name. "Truly a lovely name."

Falcon's eyes narrowed at his king's musings.

Shaking his head, Hadrian asked, "Anything else?"

"No, the alpha did not spend very much quality time with the girl."

Hadrian ignored Falcon's sharp tone. "What I'm concerned about is that the contract specifically states we are to be provided with a purebred. If this is not fulfilled, the treaty becomes null and void. Do we need to start contacting other shifter packs to maintain our Clan's influence in South America?"

"Not yet. Alpha Arsenio will be coming to your coronation ceremony. If Eva is unharmed and in good health, he will present you with one of his other daughters."

Hadrian nodded. One month. Eva would only be with them for one month. He felt torn and did not know if he should be relieved or saddened, which was a peculiar reaction. One month was nothing but a mere moment in time when one lived for eternity.

"I trust everything is in order for the ball."

"There are a few more details that must be sorted out, but everything is on track."

Hadrian would reintroduce himself to his entire Clan at the ball. It was his official coming out party. He would reclaim his throne by pledging his loyalty and life to his Clan and the Death Curse, that had taken the lives of all the rulers before him, would surely set upon him. How long he had before true death claimed him, he did not know, but he would do all he could to solidify his power and to make sure Falcon's succession to the throne would be smooth.

"The nobles of the Clan, do I have their support?" Falcon's silence was enough of an answer. "Do you think any will challenge me for the throne? By law, they have the right. I knew what I was doing when I renounced the throne. Naturally, I'm permitted to reclaim the crown; however, any noble within the Clan can challenge my claim."

"There may be one. Jefferson."

A slow smile curved Hadrian's lips. Jefferson had been a noble within the Validus Clan for centuries, repeatedly looked over as second. He was old, strong, and had never trusted Hadrian, not even when he was a general within the Validus army. Yes, Jefferson was a threat.

"You need to rebuild your strength. I've stocked the kitchen with plenty of bagged blood. You have no reason not to feed every day. If Jefferson decides to challenge you, it will not be an easy fight. Once Eva is settled, I will return to the Clan to check on preparations for the ball and the coronation ceremony. Rest assured, I will uncover any plots of rebellion, if they exist."

"Thank you, Falcon," Hadrian said, turning to face the stain glass doors.

Falcon stepped to the exit, his hand hovering over the doorknob. He could sense that Hadrian wanted to be alone, though he worried every time he left his king alone with his thoughts. His madness lurked just under the surface.

Falcon had come to this decaying castle and found his king—a shell of the vampire he once was. Insanity had claimed his mind while despair, regret, and self-loathing ravaged his soul. His body had been reduced to pale, white flesh covering dense bones, every hollow visible. Malnourished for centuries, Hadrian had miraculously survived on animal blood. Now, Hadrian had put on some weight, regaining muscle though his physique remained lean. But if he were to face a challenger…

Falcon glanced to the mini-fridge that was disguised as a cabinet in the built-in bookshelf that rose from floor to ceiling.

Dropping his hand, he went to the fridge and pulled out one of the many bags of blood inside. Then he crossed the room to Hadrian's desk. He set the crimson filled pouch beside Hadrian's crystal decanter and matching glasses.

The king stood perfectly still with his hands clasped behind his back, his gaze staring unfocused out the colorful glass doors. Without a word, Falcon headed back toward the exit. And with one last glance back at Hadrian, Falcon opened the door and left Hadrian alone with his thoughts, his madness and his blood.

Hadrian heard the door close. The sound was faint and light as if it was coming from a far off distance. He opened the balcony doors with his mind, the cool air rushed in causing the candle's flames to quiver.

He turned and his eyes narrowed as they fell upon the bagged blood. With slow, deliberate strides he approached his desk. For a long moment he stood, his eyes riveted on the bag, his body frozen.

Feed, he commanded himself.

His fangs lengthened in his mouth and yet, he could not bring himself to pick up the bag.

He circled the desk twice before lowering his frame onto the throne-like chair.

The beast within him was hungry. For a week, he had refused the demon's call to feed. He needed to rebuild his strength, but he loathed the vampire within him with such a passion that he would rather starve than give into its demands.

The bag glowed a seductive crimson in the candlelight, taunting him.

He brought his elbows up, resting them on the polished edge of the desk.

Remember the taste, his demon whispered. *Remember the warmth.*

Memories.

They always came with blood, united as one; memories of sin, torture, screams of fear, screams of unimaginable pain, and death. Always death.

Did he dare drink? Should he risk falling into a maddened rage?

He needed to feed. He needed to keep his strength up and build his power. Hadrian could feel his madness build in the back of his mind. Like a shadow, it lurked ever closer. A bloodcurdling shriek rang in his ears as his entire body began to shake.

No.

He gripped his head, his fingers dug into his skull. The stinging scent of smoke clouded around him as he struggled against the memories. A deep, satanic laughter filled his head. Imbrasus stood over his victims, who cowered in the corner of their crude hut, flames licked ever closer. A mother wrapped her arms about her children as her husband tried to combat the fire around them with his tattered cloak.

No. No!

His chest heaved as he desperately drew in the cool crisp air that surrounded him in reality. The memories…he was not there. He was in his castle. He was not there.

The flames grew higher as they advanced on the humans. Imbrasus's eyes danced with murderous laughter as he watched. He stood in the doorway, blocking the only exit. He held a woman by her hair as she wept, blood and bruises colored her face.

"You didn't listen, girl," Imbrasus snarled. "Perhaps I should feed the flames with your useless carcass as well."

Hadrian lashed out, sweeping his arm back. His chair spun across the room and splintered against the stone floor.

Burning flesh, the aroma was so strong he could taste it. Bile rose in his throat. He covered his nose as he staggered to the balcony, taking in gulp after gulp of clean winter air.

Anger filled his heart as the scene continued to play within his mind. If only he could have been there. He would have taken great pleasure in watching his maker, the Father of his clan, burn to ash.

Another scream sounded as the girl cried out for her family. Imbrasus continued to laugh as the shrieks of his victims vibrated the night, then he shoved the girl to the ground. She kicked and scratched as she fought the depraved vampire. Her fear was a sweet, alluring perfume, urging the beast on.

Rage began to pump like gasoline through Hadrian's veins as the scene continued. He found himself praying that he could save the girl, but he knew well how this memory ended, just like all the others.

He violently shook his head as his hips collided with the balcony wall.

When had he stepped outside? It didn't matter. He needed action to stop the memories.

Run.

With a glance to the snow covered lawn below, he jumped. His feet hit the ground without a sound, his boots leaving only the slightest impression. Shutting down his senses, blocking everything out, he ruthlessly shoved his maker's evil memories aside and ran. As fast as he could, he ran, tearing through the labyrinth, across the frozen lake, deep into the darkness, seeking refuge amongst the trees.

His rage fueled him on as he crashed through the dense forest.

Run. Keep running. Escape the memories. Escape the death.

Chapter Four

Eva groaned when the clock on the mantle elegantly chimed three. She slid from the bed and began to pace the room again. She couldn't stop thinking about her encounter with the king. He was a powerful, mysterious, and all together lethal vampire and he had made her desire him. She had struggled to find a logical explanation to her reaction, but came up with nothing. With a sigh, she acknowledged that her confinement was not helping her bewildering thoughts and restlessness.

She circled the room. Though the space was large and stylish, she felt trapped. At her father's village, she had been treated like a prisoner, always locked away, always caged. She craved movement and she wanted out. Now. But Falcon was right, she could easily get lost and she did not want to be caught by the king again.

Or did she?

No, of course not.

She paced by the door for the hundredth time, casting a longing glance at the knob. It wasn't locked. Maybe, if she just stepped out into the hall for a moment she would feel better. She shook her head. No, she would wander away. She would be unable to resist the urge to roam. In frustration, she threw her hands in the air. Hoping a shower might help calm her, she went to the dark polished dresser and pulled out a set of pajamas before stomping to the bathroom.

Having inspected the bathroom earlier, she had been pleased to find it stocked with all the necessities. After placing her neatly folded pajama pant and tank top set on the counter, she grabbed a bottle of body wash, then studied the collection of expensive shampoos and conditioners and randomly selected a French pair. She turned on the shower and quickly ditched her t-shirt and sweats.

The warm water that rained down from the numerous showerheads was soothing. She took her time bathing and washing her hair, savoring the heated water and privacy. For the past ten years she had bathed in a communal shower with chilled water. Well, no one had actually bathed with her, no one dared to be that close to the half-breed.

"Another positive check for the vampires," she said as she sat on the bench, basking in the heat and steam that gathered in the roomy glass shower stall.

God, she had missed true civilization. The shifters she had lived among envisioned themselves superior to the human race, deciding that living in the jungle with few modern amenities and technology was the way to go. She rubbed the back of her neck and snorted. The pack was nothing but backward, from their views of the world, of women, of war, everything. Why could they not be like most other shifter packs and live with humans? Have normal homes, eat at restaurants, and enjoy dance clubs and movie theaters.

Enjoy everything I once had.

She had lived within human society the majority of her life. She and her mother had lived happily together, just the two of them before cancer stole her mother's life and her father claimed hers. She had attended public schools, making friends with humans and even a few shifters. Never had they treated her like a leper or made her feel inferior.

With a sigh, she turned the water off, quickly dried and dressed. Out of habit, she brushed out her thick hair with her fingers, instead of using one of ivory combs, and fastened it in one long braid that extended to her hips. Next, she stoked the fire. Its flames came back to life with a vengeance and she happily greeted the warmth. Eva fell into a chair and brought her legs up. She hugged them to her chest and rested her chin on her knees. For a while she sat, gazing into the fire. The shower had helped, but she still fought the urge to glance at the door.

Never had she felt so restless, not even during a full moon when she was locked in her hut while the pack shifted into animal form. Their snarls, growls, and fights would echo in the night and, being a half-breed, she remained in human form. Her body grew tense as she tried to keep her focus on the elegant dancing flames.

When the clock's beautiful melody chimed four, Eva cursed and jumped to her feet.

"That's it."

She stormed back into the bathroom and threw open the door to the walk in closet. She wiggled free from her pajama pants and quickly pulled on a set of dark jeans, slid her feet into thick socks and tied on her snow boots. All the while, she silently thanked Falcon for purchasing these items for her. After she snatched a powder blue down jacket, matching beanie and gloves, she reentered her room. Eva paused before the door, her hand hovering just above the knob. She knew she should stay. She knew Falcon was right and the last thing she wanted was to get lost in this inexplicably large castle. Or to be found by the king...

An unseen force beckoned to her, calling to the dormant wildness within her. She wanted nothing more than to throw open the door and *run.*

Eva rubbed her temples and dropped her head.

"What is wrong with me?"

She had never craved movement so much in her life. She needed to be out of this castle. She longed to feel the cool wind whip at her cheeks, to feel the moon kiss her skin and...She frowned as her heart began to slam in her chest. There was something else. Something in the back of her mind demanded that she go into the night. She knew there was something out there. Something she...needed.

Eva opened the door and stuck her head out into the hall. She looked both ways before silently tiptoeing from the room, closing the door. She retraced her steps, descending to the main level and out the front door.

Relief filled her as the wind rushed over her. She quickly tucked her ears beneath the beanie and shoved her hands into her gloves. Taking in a deep breath, she filled her lungs with the clean scent of trees and freshly fallen snow.

"Okay, I'm outside. Where to now?"

An odd sensation compelled her to turn right. She walked along the wall of the castle and continued around until she came to a terrace. The furniture was covered with tarps weighted down by snow. Coming to the edge, she was shocked by what she could see. Below was a large labyrinth made of hedges, with a building made of glass at its center and a lake, frosted over by ice, towards the back. A village of cottages and small empty shops huddled together against a line of trees. The forest lay beyond and stretched to the horizon.

She quickly descended the steps from the terrace and paused when she came to the entrance of the labyrinth. Should she enter? Did she dare? Again, an odd feeling swept over her. Not one of fear, but of excitement. Confusion clouded her mind while instinct compelled her forward.

Eva slowly wound through the maze, using her photographic memory to find its center. She was almost certain the glass building was a green house and she was anxious to see what kind of tropical plants would be living such fragile lives in these unforgiving mountains.

Her steps faltered as she came to a bend. The hair on the back of her neck stood on end.

She was not alone.

Eva froze and strained her senses. Her hearing and eyesight were slightly better than a human's but nothing compared to a full shifter or—she swallowed hard—a vampire. Unable to detect anything, she slowly crept forward and peeked around the corner.

A man sat on a white marble bench, his elbows resting on his knees, his head hung low. She could only see his perfectly hard profile and her heart skipped a beat as her breath caught. High, bold cheekbones and a straight, stern jaw descended to thin, yet enticing lips. His hair was black and buzzed in an extremely short military fashion. To her disappointment, his eyes were closed, but she knew they would be intense. He was dressed in all black, a stark contrast to the white that surrounded him.

Raw power radiated from him. He was pure unadulterated male. Lethal. She knew instinctively that this vampire was the crazed king, Hadrian Lucretius; the man—no, the beast that had ensnared her in the hall.

His eyes remained closed as his lips pulled back from his long, white fangs tinted with red.

Blood.

She knew she ought to be horrified but as before…all she felt was lust. Her body was hot and heavy, her breath came in soft gasps, and heat spiraled through her core as she recalled the feel of his powerful body looming over her.

"I know you're there." His voice was deep and heavily accented though his style of speech was modern. He spoke again, but she did not comprehend his words. She closed her eyes and savored his voice. Dark. Seductive. She shivered, not from cold, but from pleasure.

Nothing made sense. She knew her reaction was insane. She knew she should be terrified and run as fast as she could back to the castle and the relative safety of her room. But, she couldn't bring herself to leave, nor did she want to run. Her heart stuttered at the thought of him chasing her and something wild roared to life deep within her.

In a rush of movement, she was pulled forward and spun around. Her back slammed against the hedge, a cool, strong hand wrapped around her throat. Her cry of shock quickly faded to a gasp of delight. He stood before her, pinning her to the hedge. Her senses flared, taking in his fresh scent. He smelled of pine, wilderness, and male. His eyes gazed deeply into hers as if searching for her very soul.

They were fathomless, obsidian pools that swirled with malice, grief and...desire.

   Her heart thundered in her ears as her lips parted, drawing in rapid breaths, filling her lungs with his irresistible scent. Again, she wondered at her response, but lust clouded her mind, blocking out all rational thought.

She dropped her gaze to his broad shoulders and chest, which were covered only by a short-sleeved black shirt. Her fingers twitched at the thought of running her hands over the wide expanse of hard muscle. He was lean, solidly built, and tall, clearly over six feet.

He crowded her. Trapping her.

She loved it.

Hadrian's gaze focused on her pulse. Eva's heart beat wildly, teasing him. His fangs felt heavy in his mouth and they ached to pierce her slender throat.

The run had helped him immensely, driving away those hateful memories. He thanked the Gods he had recovered before his Ward had stumbled upon him in the labyrinth. The memories always left his mind tainted.

He had wanted blood. No. Needed blood. Death. Yes, he had craved to taste death, to savor it. He had hunted in the forest and fed from a rabbit. Its tangy blood and tiny life had brought him precious little relief, but it was enough. It would keep him from tearing her throat open.

She would be spicy, exotic, and oh, so hot.

He ran his tongue over his fangs and Eva sighed. The scent of her desire grew stronger. He took in a deep breath and shuddered. Intoxicating. His erection strained against his pants as heat consumed him. He wanted to teleport her to his bed, feel her soft body beneath him, her hips rocking with his as he claimed her, filled her. Her lust sang to him like a siren's song and fired his icy blood.

"We meet again, little one." He brushed the elegant column of her throat with his thumb, pausing over her pulse with every stroke. "I did not expect it would be so soon."

Hadrian kept his hand on her neck as he stepped back to appraise his prey. He had known she was small, but his mind had been completely consumed with lust and hunger earlier to focus on the details. She was barely over five feet and slight of frame. Fragile. He could snap the poor girl; easily break her like a doll. He eased the pressure on her neck at the thought.

Her face was delicate with almond shaped eyes that were downcast, concealing their color. She also had well defined cheekbones and a stubborn chin. Her luscious, pouting lips were peach in color. Hadrian shivered as he imagined their taste. He could not remember the last time he had felt another's lips pressed against his. Never had he kissed the women he took to his bed…not since he had been a mortal man, not since his wife. But damn, her mouth was tempting.

He dropped his gaze to her body. She was tightly bundled in a thick jacket, the blue a perfect complement to her smooth sun-kissed skin. Her dark brown hair was pulled back and fastened in a braid that came to her hips. He resisted the urge of freeing her locks, having an absurd desire to run his fingers through her hair.

He released her throat to press his hands to the hedge on either side of her head. Her gaze met his and Hadrian bit back a curse. Amber. Pure amber stared back at him. Not yellow, as he thought before when he had found her in the hall.

Stunning.

For an instant, his gaze grew sharp. Eva tried to look away, but his hand caught her chin and forced her to face him.

"Look at me, little one."

She raised her hands, intending to shove him away, like she knew she should. This was wrong. He was a vampire. No, he was the crazed vampire king and she was, well, a lowly half-breed, who was also his Ward. Nothing could happen between them.

As if I would want something to happen between us, she told herself.

His thumb brushed over her bottom lip, the caress was simple and yet completely erotic. He sank his body into hers and Eva lost her breath.

Hadrian's hand slipped to her nape. His fingers began to play with the stray strands of hair that had escaped her braid while his ravenous gaze roamed her body. Despite the bulkiness of her jacket, he could feel her generous curves. The blue material covering her chest strained ever so slightly against her breasts as her hips cradled his, her stomach was flat and soft against his painful erection.

"Shall we continue what we started in the hall?"

Eva swallowed hard as she thought, *Oh, god, yes!*

His finger danced down to the zipper of her jacket. She watched as he slowly drew it down, heat coiled in her core. She couldn't move. The warmth of his strong hands burned through the thin material of her pajama tank top as he spanned her waist. She didn't notice the cold but shivered in anticipation. His fingers slowly slid up her sides and paused at her ribs, just below her aching breasts. She arched her back and he hissed.

"Terror," Hadrian whispered. "You should be feeling terror."

Eva squeaked in response, unable to speak.

He leaned his head down, his breath brushed along the sensitive flesh of her throat.

"You should run," he said. *Would I let her escape?* Yes, he would. He would use what remained of his will to restrain himself as she raced through the labyrinth. He knew, in this moment, he should set her from him and demand that she go.

Eva nodded, she knew he was right. She should be screaming. She should be praying that Falcon would come to her rescue. This dark vampire had her trapped. Hadrian, the mad king, had her at his mercy. She tried to remember the evil rumors, hoping they might be able to draw her back to reality. Nothing came. All she could think about was how much she wanted to feel his hands on her body, his lips against her skin and his—

"Touch me," Eva gasped. Desire controlled her mind, her actions.

His black gaze jumped with dangerous delight. He spun her around, forcing her back against his chest, his hands gripping her hips as he pressed her front towards the hedge.

Heaven help her, a bolt of treacherous excitement ran down her spine to curl her toes. She pressed her hips back and groaned at the feel of his hard cock against her ass.

"Do you know who I am?" he asked, his lips brushing her ear.

"Yes."

"Who?" His demand was rough and, god, she loved the anger that laced his voiced. On some level, she knew she must be losing her mind to desire this vampire. She did not care. She wanted him. Now. Primal, sexual need coursed through her in sweet agonizing pulsating waves.

"H–Hadrian Lu–Lucretius," she answered.

Eva cried out in surprised pleasure as he slowly scraped his fangs and drew his tongue over her rapidly beating pulse. She tilted her head to the side, giving him better access to her neck.

This was crazy; she should be begging him not to bite her, not panting for his touch. All her life she had been told a vampire's bite was ruthless and excruciatingly painful, something to be avoided at all costs. But she wanted this.

She frowned as she tried to analyze her reaction. She should be fighting him with every ounce of her strength. Instead she was aching with lust.

His tongue caressed her neck and her thoughts scattered. Her head lolled back against his chest.

Eva began to wriggle beneath his hold. She wanted to see him, to kiss his lips. It felt like an eternity since the last time she had been kissed. Would his fangs cut her? Something dark and wild in her roared at the thought. She tried to turn, but he kept her pinned.

"You crave." His fingers dug into her hips as he rubbed her against his shaft. He dipped his face down into the crook of her neck and took in a deep breath. She shuddered. He inhaled her scent, like an animal, like the beast that he was and it thrilled her. "I can sense your need."

She boldly covered his hands with her own and slid them brought them up to her breasts. She moaned when he gave a gentle squeeze. Her breasts were bare beneath her tank top and she hated the thin material for being in the way. She wanted to feel his palms against her hard nipples.

"Wild," Hadrian breathed.

She sighed and began to undulate her hips against him. He bit back a curse as fire spread through his veins.

Take her.

His fangs grew even longer, his nails lengthened to claws as his cock swelled. His eyes flicked from her to her pulse. The vampire within him howled as he thought of pushing her jeans down, revealing her sex. She would be so hot, so wet. He could tell by her scent she was ready. He could drive into her as he pierced her flesh and drank deeply.

Take her.

Eva reached back to circle her arms around his neck—

She stumbled face first into the hedge. Whirling around, she saw…nothing. Hadrian was gone. The absence of his body left her vulnerable to the cold and she quickly zipped up her jacket. She shook her head, trying to dislodge the sensual haze that clouded her thoughts.

Her neck tingled and Eva hesitantly raised her hand, her fingers met smooth skin. He had not bitten her. Her cheeks flooded with heat. She had wanted him to sink his fangs deep within her. Her blush grew even darker as clarity began to set in. She had freely offered herself to him, mind, body, and…blood. She had been his for the taking.

So why hadn't he claimed what she had clearly offered?

Eva walked over to the marble bench and sat. She rubbed her hands anxiously over her knees as she fought the urge to search him out, to find him and demand they continue. He had wakened something deeply feral within her and she frowned, one hundred percent confused.

Why had she acted this way? Why did she want him so badly? She bounced her legs, barely resisting the need to *hunt* him.

She knew vampires could control a human's mind. The ability made hunting and feeding much easier. Had he done that to her? Possibly. But, if he had reached into her mind, why had he let her go? Why had he not taken what he wanted?

"Because you're a half-breed," she spat.

No man in his right mind would want a half-breed.

But he isn't in his right mind, she thought, then mentally shook herself. *Stupid girl,* she chided. *Even if he hadn't used his power on me and I do truly desire him, it doesn't make a difference. He is a king and I'm a half-breed bastard that he's been saddled with as a ward.*

She sighed and leaned back, titling her head up to the clear sky. The night was still. Silent. Her breathing had begun to slow, her heart returning to a normal pace while her body still throbbed with need.

Out of all the rumors she had heard of Hadrian, none had warned her about how devastatingly handsome he is. Darkness clung to him and he wore power and malice like a second skin. Yet his touch had been gentle and—she shivered—deliciously firm. He could have ripped her throat out with his fangs or he could have slaked his lust on her. Instead, he deserted her.

A growl rumbled the night and Eva's brow furrowed. It sounded like a jaguar. She glanced about, straining her hearing, trying to discern where it had come from. To her knowledge, there were no shape-shifters here besides—She slapped a hand over her mouth—Her. *She* had made the noise. Never before had she been able to growl, to channel the feral animal that lurked within every shape-shifter.

She shook her head in disbelief. Something strange was happening to her. First, she had craved freedom from her room, and then followed her curiosity out of the castle. She had been compelled to enter the maze and this sexual madness with Hadrian. Everything pointed to what the pack called Drive, a behavior motivated by pure instinct. She was a half-breed and as such, she would never experience Drive. Or, *should* never.

Eva gave a heavy sigh, her shoulders slumping as she brought her hands up to massage her temples. Maybe she just needed some sleep. Jet lag could do strange things to people.

*   *   *   *

Dark.

Silent.

36

Hadrian materialized in the safety of the Clan's mausoleum. The scent of dust, fresh roses and decay was welcoming and oddly soothing to his ravaged mind.

He had almost taken Eva, there in the snow, like some animal. His fangs had been at her throat, his hands roaming her supple body. His cock was stiff and he groaned as he recalled the incredible sensations that swept through him as he pressed his hard length against her ass.

She had been ready for him, he could scent her arousal, feel the heat that radiated from her soft flesh. Gods, she had been a sweet fire in his arms.

The demon in him had roared in outrage when he pulled away, teleporting to the crypt.

His hands shook as he ran them over his head. He needed to regain control.

The visions he experienced had made him weak, leaving his true nature unrestricted and the vampire within him was starved for freedom. Until three hundred years ago, he had kept his other half under constant mental lock and key, then his madness set in. Tonight, his demon was at the fore and it wanted Eva, her body and her blood.

Terror struck him like a blow to the chest, sending him stumbling into the stone sarcophagus beside him.

Thank the Gods he had left her before…he couldn't bring himself to think of the things he could—No, *would* have done to her. Closing his eyes, he sucked in breath after breath. Leaning against the tomb, he desperately searched for some sense of calm.

He had lost control again and he would not be surprised if the girl demanded to be secured in another of his Clan's homes to escape him. How could he expect her to want to stay in a castle with a wild beast such as him? He had mucked things up and it was only her first night here. At the rate he was going, he would harm his Ward and give the alpha of the Silveria Pack every reason not to trust him with one of his purebred daughters.

The shifters needed this treaty. Without the Validus Clan's support they would be destroyed by their enemies, he thought, even though none of that excused his treatment of the girl. He had nearly claimed her innocence in the snow and they had yet to even be formally introduced.

She knew him. She had spoken his name, her words broken, her voice rasped with desire. Her head had lolled back, giving him complete access to her throat. She had taken his hands and drawn them up her body to cup her breasts.

He shuddered as a hiss passed his fangs. His body still burned for her as his cock strained against the roughness of his jeans.

"Fuck," he sighed, scrubbing his face with his hands as he slid to the floor, his back pressed against the chilled stone of the sarcophagus.

He had to get a handle on himself.

His predatory instincts had consumed him when he attacked Eva in the hall. Now, the vampire had nearly had its way with her in the labyrinth. He was vulnerable to the whims of the demon that resided in his soul. Under normal circumstances he would never attempt to take advantage of a woman.

The thought drew a dark laugh from him, the sound echoed through the centuries old mausoleum. He hadn't been "normal" for over three hundred years. He no longer understood the definition of the word.

Chapter Five

"This first level is considered the social floor. Here, you will find everything," Falcon had stated at the beginning of the tour and he was right.

He had kicked off the excursion with breakfast, showing Eva the massive kitchen, large enough to cook for an army, and the smaller dining room, which could easily seat fifty. While Falcon explained how he had done everything possible to maintain the historical integrity of the castle through the extensive restoration, Eva had savored a bowl of Frosted Flakes, a staple she had sorely missed while living deep within the Amazon.

When she had finished, it was on to the billiards room, complete with seven tables, a full bar that extended across one wall, along with a collection of old video arcade games. What interested her most were the various polished suits of armor and medieval weaponry that decorated the room.

Next, the monstrous movie theater with rows upon rows of oversized recliner seats, a popcorn machine, a slushy bar, and vending machines filled with a three-year supply of candy.

"I thought vampires couldn't eat food," she said as she paused to snag a Snickers bar, another delicacy she had been deprived of for far too long.

"It's not that we can't, but we generally abstain from food. Occasionally, I do like to enjoy a hot fudge sundae," he answered with a shrug. "Now, we have an obscenely large movie database which begins with silent films and ends with the latest box office releases. This theater is also connected to the Internet and you can instantly stream videos on the screen."

Eva's eyes grew wide with shock. She now knew what she would be doing for the next few days, catching up on all the films she had missed over the years.

As she tried to plan her movie marathon, debating whether she should begin with chick-flicks or horror, Falcon showed her the solarium, its wall-to-wall windows, were covered by heavy, retractable metal shades and housed only night blooming flowers.

Eva's jaw dropped when Falcon took her across the hall to the five-story library. Books extended from floor to ceiling and lined every wall. Tight, spiral staircases stood in each corner, every level accessible by wrought iron landings and walkways. It was a windowless space, except for a small reading nook tucked in the far left corner.

"My king's book collection is so extensive that we've changed many of the smaller rooms in the keep into storage. Feel free to read whatever you like, we have every genre you can think of, published in every language. Even a few from antiquity and various other periods."

Has the king read all of these books? Eva wondered.

Still dazed, Eva let Falcon guide her through the castle to the gym. She had never seen so many pieces of workout equipment. Dark blue mats covered the floor up to the full sized basketball court and stadium stands.

"I've saved the best for last," Falcon said ushering her from the gym. They entered the hall and ascended a wide staircase to the second level. He pushed open a set of double doors and Eva was swept away.

The pool was long and narrow with glistening, tropical blue water. Lounge chairs lined the sides while a fully stocked bar was situated along the back wall, which was lined with covered windows. White, smooth marble columns reached to the ceiling, which was also lined with steel window covers. At night, the shades would retract allowing the brilliant moon to light the pool. The stars would twinkle as snow fell all around. The room would look like something out of a travel magazine, a pool area that belonged to an extravagant hotel.

Eva was speechless as she wandered about the expansive room. This castle had everything. Never in her life had she imagined she would be staying in a place this beautiful.

Stepping to the edge, she knelt down, and dipped her fingers in the water. It was warm.

"Out there is a small balcony," Falcon pointed to a door, "When the weather grows warmer, it should be rather nice. Naturally, you will be left alone. We vampires can't sunbathe."

"But you can walk in the sun," she pointed out.

Falcon's hand went up to his chest, his fingers capturing something that dangled from a necklace, but was hidden by his shirt collar. "I'm fortunate," he muttered.

Not wanting to pry, Eva changed the subject, "Well, Falcon, I'm at a loss. This place is gorgeous. A huge step up from my little hovel in the jungle." *From one extreme to the other,* she thought. "I don't know where I should begin. Should I lounge here and enjoy the hot tub, or numb my brain with some flicks, or start hoarding books?"

Falcon chuckled as he glanced at his watch. "Well, I've arranged a few interviews today, hoping to find a chef. They should be arriving shortly."

"You, Mr. Occasional Hot Fudge Sundae, are going to interview cooks?" she teased with a smile.

"If you don't mind joining me, you can sample their food since each will be providing a demonstration."

"I can't wait," she beamed.

Falcon pulled a paper from the inside pocket of his blazer. "I almost forgot. I've drawn this up for you. It is a map of the castle and the grounds."

"Thank you," she said taking the paper. She quickly unfolded it and scanned the drawing. He had even provided a layout for the labyrinth and circled the greenhouse at the center.

Eva frowned as she noticed the entire west wing of the castle, with the exception of the first and second level were missing. Also, the hall made of windows she had seen earlier was not on the map.

How odd. Falcon must have done it for a reason...the king, maybe?

The west wing must belong to King Hadrian. She gave a little pout of disappointment. She had been looking forward to seeing the hall of windows, which was incredibly high up. The view would have been spectacular.

But I don't need another run in with that particular vampire, she reminded herself as she folded the map and placed it in the back pocket of her jeans.

"Well, I'll leave you to decide what you would like to do first and I'll see you in the kitchen."

He bowed his head slightly then turned on his heel and disappeared out the doors.

Eva sighed and sat on a lounge chair. What did she want to do first? She felt like a child at Disney World, too many options, and too many exciting things. After some thought, she decided to hit the library first to pick out a book or two. Then, she would sit in on the chef interviews and taste test with Falcon before rounding out her evening with a movie and a nice soak in the hot tub. While relaxing she would come up with an educational plan. She needed to catch up with human society if she were to blend in.

Standing, she exited the pool area and retraced her steps, not wanting to get lost.

Once she reached the first floor she cast a glance at the gym. Even though it looked nothing like her uncle's combined jiu-jitsu and yoga studio, it had reminded her of happier times. Every day after school, she and her mother would go to the studio. Two days a week they did yoga together, while the remaining three days were devoted to training. Her uncle taught her well. She had even participated in a few jiu-jitsu matches and had won them all.

Stepping over to one of the black punching bags, Eva tested it with a shove. She watched it swing a few times before steadying it. Then she took up her stance, dancing on the balls of her feet. Envisioning Teresa's face, she began to hit the bag, hesitantly at first, but her attack soon became wild. She delivered blow after blow with amazing speed, releasing pent-up aggression. She landed a few kicks, keeping her breathing controlled and even, like her uncle had taught her.

Pinpricks of awareness tickled her nape as she swung around for another hit, her arm raised, her fist tight. The loud smack of flesh-to-flesh impact rattled her eardrums in the silence of the gym.

"Hello, little one."

Eva's mind went numb. Hadrian stood before her, his lean muscled chest bare, lose workout shorts hugging his hips. A smile curled his sensual lips as she continued to stare. Her heart began to race as she lost control of her breathing. Lust exploded from her as her eyes focused on his chiseled abs.

"We keep running into each other," he said.

His voice caused her to shiver and drew her gaze to his.

Realizing she was standing, gaping at him with her mouth open, she snapped her jaw closed, shook her head and frowned. Why did her knuckles sting. Glancing down her eyes grew wide. He had caught her fist.

"Your skill is impressive. Who taught you how to fight?"

Did he just ask me a question? Oh, come on, Eva, you've seen plenty of bare-chested men. The males in the pack hardly ever wore shirts. She exhaled a breath she had not realized she had been holding. *But damn, none of them ever looked this drop dead sexy. Oh my god, focus!*

"I'm sorry. What?"

His perfect smile widened and she groaned from embarrassment.

"I had asked who taught you how to fight."

"My uncle." At his frown she hurried to explain, "My uncle on my mother's side. He was an instructor and owned his own Jiu-Jitsu studio in Rio."

Hadrian gave a nod and released her hand. "He taught you well."

"Thank you, Your Highness," she said. Dropping her gaze she felt her cheeks heat with a blush. "I was, ah, just heading out. Excuse me." Eva moved to step around the vampire king, but he blocked her retreat. She looked up and swallowed a surprised gasp. His eyes were narrowed, his expression hard. Had she done something wrong? Had she insulted him in some way? Did she not address him properly?

Crap, I only said 'Your Highness' once.

"Your eyes," he grated, his voice had turned cold, fitting his demeanor. He took a step forward, forcing her to tilt her head back to maintain eye contact. "What are you?"

Her eyes shimmered. Hadrian wondered what caused the beautiful, abnormal color? They were a beautiful shade of amber.

"I'm sorry, Your Majesty, I don't know what you—"

"What are you?" he demanded, cutting her off.

Squaring her shoulders, Eva stated firmly, "I'm half human and half jaguar shifter." She was not ashamed of her mixed blood, she was proud to be her mother's daughter.

Hadrian took another step, closing the space between them. Eva jumped as his chest brushed against her breasts, the contact sent heat straight to her core. She took in a deep breath, willing herself to remain calm, but his heady male scent attacked her senses. Her knees went weak and she leaned her shoulders against the punching bag for support, praying it would not swing and let her fall.

"No," Hadrian said, his eyes focused on hers as if searching for an answer to some mystery. "No, you are not." He snatched her wrist and raised it to his nose. While still holding her gaze, he inhaled her scent, his breath caressing over her pulse. "You are something more." He pressed a kiss to the inside of her wrist, drawing a longing sigh from her lips. "Shall I have a taste?"

She ran her tongue over her now dry lips.

"One drop," his fangs extended, his eyes grew even darker, "could tell me everything about you." He gently drew the pointed tips of his fangs across her skin and Eva's eyes closed against the pleasure. "May I have a taste, little one?"

43

Oh–god–yes, she wanted to scream. His voice was deep with need. His black eyes glittered with threatening passion and dangerous hunger. On some level she knew she should pull her arm back, but she couldn't move. Her entire body hummed with desire, her breasts swelled against the pressure of his hard chest.

Hadrian kissed her wrist again and drew his warm tongue over her erratically beating pulse, gently suckling before murmuring, "Please, sweet, allow me a taste."

Her moan was all the answer he needed. Hadrian inhaled her seductive vanilla scent once more as he pressed her wrist to his mouth. His body had responded the instant he came upon her in the gym, his shaft swelling as he watched her. Then, when she saw him, lust had exploded from her body; the delicious scent of her arousal hit him like an upper cut.

Just a taste, he told himself. *Control. Do not harm the girl.*

She felt his lips open over her pulse, her heart skipped as she sucked in a deep breath, holding it, waiting for him. He smiled against her wrist.

He would take a drop, no more.

Hadrian's predatory instincts flared. Someone was coming. He probed the hall outside the gym with his senses. A growl rumbled from his throat. The vampire within him howled in protest as he dropped her hand. He took a step back, then another, ignoring the foreign compulsion that demanded he return to her. His demon roared in outage at the loss of her warmth.

Eva blinked once, twice, then a third time. He hadn't bitten her.

Damn confusing vampire. Gets me all hot and bothered then stops. What the hell? Well, at least he didn't pull a 'now you see me, now you don't' like last time.

"Why did you not—"

"Hey, Eva, the chefs are arriving," Falcon called as he pushed open the door. "Do you want–Holy, mother of—Your Majesty, I was not expecting to find you here."

"I intended to go a few rounds," he said, his gaze still locked on Eva, whose cheeks were bright pink, his words hiding a naughty double meaning.

"I didn't sense your—"

"Yes, I apologize. I really must work on letting my guard down and revealing my energy."

Eva stepped to the side so that she could see Falcon. Hadrian had stopped because he knew the knight was coming and now he spoke with him as if nothing had just happened.

44

Nothing had happened, she chided herself.

"I don't believe the two of you have been formally introduced," Falcon said, coming to stand beside Hadrian.

"No, we have not *formally* met," Hadrian said with a charming smile that made Eva's blush darken.

"Your Highness, may I present our Ward, Miss Eva Maldonado of the Silveria Shifter Pack. Miss Maldonado," Falcon gave a bow, "His Royal Highness, Hadrian Lucretius, King of the Validus Clan."

Hadrian took Eva's hand and placed a soft kiss to her knuckles. "Charmed."

Eva gave a nervous curtsy.

"My king, I have arranged to interview a few chefs and Miss Maldonado has graciously offered her services as taste tester," Falcon said with smile.

Hadrian gave a light chuckle. The sound was warm and caught Eva completely by surprise. She already loved his voice, she thought she could come just from listening to him speak, but his laugh, lord, have mercy on her peace of mind.

"A more than suitable occupation for our young Ward," Hadrian replied. "Please, don't let me keep you from your work."

Eva took a step toward Falcon and Hadrian's entire body tensed. He barely resisted the urge to snatch her to him.

Falcon's scrutinizing gaze locked on Hadrian as he said, "The first few chefs have arrived and are waiting in the kitchen. Miss Maldonado, would you mind going alone? I would like a word with His Majesty."

"Sure." She headed toward the exit, but paused and gave another fumbling curtsy. "It was a *pleasure* to formally meet you, Your Highness."

Hadrian bit back a smile as she left.

"What happened?" Falcon demanded the instant the door closed.

"What do you mean?" Hadrian innocently asked.

"Do you think it has escaped my notice that the air is thick with lust?"

Hadrian couldn't stop himself from taking in a deep breath. The scent of warm vanilla sugar inflamed his desire once more.

"I know how much you love women, Hadrian, but this one is our Ward and an innocent."

His good humor gone, Hadrian replied, "I will not dishonor the girl."

"She is a good looking female, but—"

"That is enough, knight," he growled.

Falcon's teeth ground together as he mumbled, "Fine." He gave a low sweeping bow. "My apologies," he added, then turned toward the door.

"It's her eyes," Hadrian called after him.

Falcon paused in the threshold, slowly turning back to his king. "What?"

"Have you noticed their color?"

"They're yellow," Falcon answered.

"No," Hadrian said, contemplation deepening his voice, "they are not."

Falcon frowned. "I don't understand."

"She doesn't have shifter eyes."

"Of course she does," Falcon scoffed.

"The color is wrong."

"Impossible."

It was common knowledge that shifter genes were dominant when paired with that of a human's. In rare cases, if a half-breed survived birth, they would not possess a single physical attribute from their mortal parent. In fact, the only difference between a purebred and half-breed shifter was the dilution of magic within the blood, preventing half-breeds from shifting and locking away their animal instincts.

"Yes," Hadrian conceded. *It should be impossible.*

Chapter Six

It had been two days since Hadrian had found his pretty ward in the gym. Two days since he had nearly sank his fangs into her elegant, slender wrist. Even now, as he paced before the picturesque wall of windows in the solarium, his nerves were raw and his hunger ravenous. The demon within him wanted the half-breed. Her blood. Her body. It craved her very soul.

"Just one taste," he snorted.

He was disgusted by how easily he had lied to himself and to her. He had been a fool to believe he would be able to pull away once the sweetness of her blood caressed his lips.

Shaking his head, his steps quickened.

He would have drained her; greedily hastening her death so that he may savor the moment her soul departed her body. There was no doubt the beast within him would howl with delight as he watched the brilliant spark of life fade from her amber eyes.

Hadrian's wide shoulders shuddered at the thought.

How could he even think about taking the life of one so young, so innocent, so vibrant and beautiful? The female was gorgeous, from her mesmerizing eyes, to her lush lips, her curves and, most of all, her spirit. She was a fighter. Many in her position would have perished long ago under the harsh treatment of the pack.

Hadrian knew shifter society well, having lived amongst various packs for numerous years in South America. She was undoubtedly beaten on a regular basis, mocked, scorned, and looked upon with disgust. Judging by her slight frame, she most likely was malnourished, given scraps or had to fend for herself.

Worst of all, she had been given to a mad vampire king whose fangs ached to pierce her flesh, whose body burned with the desire to claim her.

Had the alpha been right in sending his lowly half-breed daughter? Would he kill the girl?

No, she was his ward. Honor dictated that he keep her safe from all, including himself. He would order Falcon to chain him in the dungeon before he harmed the girl.

Hadrian's lips twitched with a smile. Perhaps that was not such a horrible idea. His incarceration would certainly appease his mind. But locking himself away would do nothing to prepare him for returning to his clan. Eva was a temptation, and he would face countless temptations once he rejoined vampire society. The girl was not only a test given to him, but also a test for himself and he would not fail. He would prove everyone, himself included, that he could be civil, that he was no longer controlled by his madness.

Still, there was no denying that he wanted the half-breed. She plagued his every thought and when she was near, a high-level, intense buzz rocked his body, vibrating his very bones, firing his blood and provoking his hunger. Her delicate scent set him on edge and made his cock ache to be inside her. His need to take her was near impossible to ignore and his need to taste her blood was consuming when she was near.

Hadrian's eyes darkened as he continued to pace, his thoughts growing deeper as he analyzed his odd response to her.

He had not been with a woman for more centuries than he would like to even think about. Before his exile he had countless lovers, all faceless, nameless women, each as interchangeable as the last. None had been worth remembering. Over the past three hundred and fifty years he had been alone, lost in his mind, wading through chaotic memories. Was his body shaking free of his madness? Was he only interested in Eva because she was a readily available female? Could his response be due to his unsatisfied sexual appetite?

Hadrian paused and rubbed his brow. It was the most plausible explanation. His drive for sex had always been accompanied by his need for blood. Sex and blood, it was all he had ever needed or wanted from women. He made certain they all found their pleasure, while he remained guarded. Never sharing himself with anyone, never wanting any kind of intimacy.

He could think of no other explanation for his fierce reaction to the woman. One night filled with intense passion would surely cure his sexual desire for her, while carefully controlled bites would satisfy his hunger for her.

She is my Ward, he thought, appalled with himself.

He could never take her to his bed. He would never feel her soft body move against his while entangled in the sheets; never hear her sighs of pleasure. And never would he taste her sweet blood. He would not dishonor or disrespect Eva and her pack in such a way. She had been placed in his care to guard, not to use for his own amusements.

He should find another to see to his needs. If memory served, any female would do. He could easily teleport to Maggie's. Her brothel was still in business.

Perhaps his response to Eva was a positive sign. Was his mind truly healing? Could he return to the man he once was?

He scoffed.

I'm crazy. Not delusional.

Hadrian knew he would never be the same. Not after Titus's death and the destruction of his psyche. He was no longer able to control the demon and its evil memories would forever haunt him as they did now.

As if on cue, a montage of fire and death flickered in his mind as memories of the victim's pain sliced through him. Terrified screams echoed in his ears as he tried to remain calm, focusing on his breathing. Searing heat ignited in his chest and spread over his body until he could feel the flames whip at his flesh. Thick smoke seemed to fill his lungs as he was swept into the memory. Pale, cold corpses lay around the village, each with their throats ripped out. Fire wildly snapped as it consumed their huts and eagerly began to feed on the bodies. Imbrasus stood, hands on hips, his face smeared with blood, his clothing drenched to the point his tunic appeared to be black. Beside him stood a man, his fangs and claws still dripping with blood, his face the mirror image of Hadrian's.

Titus.

Imbrasus turned lightning white eyes to Hadrian's twin, his lips twisted with a murderous smile as he asked, "Shall we find your brother?"

The words ricocheted in Hadrian's mind. He knew Imbrasus had used Titus to get to him.

I am a vampire because of him...and Titus is dead because of me.

Hadrian opened his eyes. His hands shook uncontrollably as his anger heightened into rage. Claws extended. He needed to get out of the keep. He needed to run, to force out the vile tension that wracked his body.

Another scene blurred his vision as the high-pitched horrified screeches of children carved through the silence of the room. Imbrasus had enjoyed playing with his young victims.

Stay calm, he ordered himself. *Breathe. Breathe. Breathe!*

The nauseating scenes of torture would not stop. The raw stench of agony mixed with the heady scent of fear beckoned to the darkness within him. He could feel the madness coming. It crawled up his spine. Its claws ripped into his shoulders and entered his mind. The demon's sinful memories ensnared him, twisting reality.

The abyss. The blackness. The mouth of hell was open. Waiting for him to fall, waiting to consume his soul. He was on the edge, knowing if he slipped, he would never return. His mind would be lost forever.

Hadrian's heart stopped, his lungs froze, his body stilled as time slowed. His vision began to fade as all that surrounded him slowly turned gray as the darkness closed in on him. He felt himself sway; he knew he would hit the marble floor any moment.

The sound of a steady, strong heartbeat began to sing in his ears, faint at first until it became a roar. Vanilla filled his senses, the rush of the fresh scent washed over him, cleansing his body and freeing his mind. His heart slammed back into action as his lungs expanded with breath, taking in the warm aroma.

Clarity.

The darkness vanished; the abyss that wanted nothing more than to swallow him was gone. The memories fled, swiftly retreating to the recesses of his mind.

Hadrian stood dazed, gazing out the picturesque wall of windows, the scene more vivid than he could ever remember. Shock rattled his system and for the first time in his unnaturally long life he was thunderstruck.

What had just happened?

"Good god," a startled female gasped from behind him.

Snapping out of his stupor, Hadrian turned toward the entrance. The relief he felt a moment ago vanished as lust took hold of him.

Eva was at the door. She wore a simple, floor length causal yellow dress with thin straps and a low neckline. His gaze skipped over her face, lingering for a moment on her full peach colored lips, then her pulse before moving down to her breasts and lower. The dress complimented her figure and teased his desire.

Hadrian whispered a curse as he dragged his gaze from her. Damn the half-breed for being so alluring. Her scent was soothing, bringing calm to his mind, and yet, erotically intoxicating. His jeans grew tight. His fangs tingled as he tried to focus his gaze on anything other than the woman before him.

A disturbing thought glimmered in the back of his mind. Had it been the demon's sexual need and hunger that had drawn him back from oblivion? Or had it been Eva herself?

"Your Majesty," she said, regaining her composure, "I didn't know you were here."

Hadrian straightened his shoulders, deciding to reflect upon his bewildering experience and her role in it later. Now, he needed to practice control. He needed to prove to himself that he was capable of civility and decorum.

"Good evening, Miss Maldonado," he greeted, with a smooth voice.

"I apologize for disturbing you. I can go—"

"Nonsense. Won't you come in?"

Eva hesitantly entered the solarium and slowly came to stand at Hadrian's side. She shifted uneasily beneath his gaze.

"What brings you to the solarium this evening?" he asked.

"Um," she said, trying to collect her thoughts. Being this close to him was wreaking havoc on her senses and his rough, sexy voice was not helping her concentrate. Her eyes watched his lips move as he asked her another question. Damn, his mouth looked—*Snap out of it!*

"I thought a change of scenery would be nice. I've been in a movie coma for the past two days. There is so much that I've missed: *It's Complicated, The Hangover, The Avengers,* and all the *Saws.*"

Eva blushed when Hadrian smiled. She knew she sounded like a child with her enthusiasm.

"You have been terribly deprived," he said with a light laugh.

"You have no idea. Only this morning did I create a *Facebook* page."

"It seems you and I are in...I believe the term is 'the same boat'."

Eva laughed, causing an odd warmth to spread through Hadrian's chest.

"I suppose we are, Your Majesty," she sighed. "To be honest, I was hoping to go for a walk. I was on my way to change when I noticed the storm," she pointed out the windows, "I thought the solarium would be the next best thing."

"Yes, it is quite ugly out there."

Snow fell in a mad flurry as wind tore across the landscape.

"I wouldn't say that. Beauty can be found in chaos. I've experienced my fair share of storms. Hurricanes were always a worry where I grew up in Florida. My mom used to say, 'there is always hope after a storm'."

Sparing her a glance, he took notice of the grief that dulled her brilliant amber eyes. Sorrow rolled off her in cold waves. Hadrian raised his hand before deciding it was best if he did not touch her. He knew nothing of comforting others. As a mortal, he had been stern, a military man who had no need of kind words and as a vampire, well he had been no better.

"I'm sorry for your loss," he said hoping there was enough sympathy in his voice.

Eva mumbled her thanks before shrugging off her momentary depression. She was not an emotional person. Besides, her mother had taught her to never dwell on the past. 'Always live in the now, Eva'. And she would. Right now, she was staying in a castle that reminded her of her favorite childhood movie, *Beauty and Beast*. The man standing beside her was straight out of a dream, fangs and all. She was free of her father's rule. Free of the pack and the harassment she was forced to endure day after day.

'Today is what counts, forget about yesterday.' Yes, mama, you're right.

"Do you come to the solarium often?" Eva asked.

Hadrian shrugged and Eva watched his wide shoulders roll wanting nothing more than to feel them move beneath her fingers as he—*Stop right there. It is one thing to seize the day. It is quite another to throw yourself at a vampire king. Especially when you are the equivalent of a political captive.*

"Like you, I had hoped to roam the night, but alas, the storm has ruined my plans."

"I thought vampires weren't susceptible to the cold."

"You are correct in your assumption. However, I do not relish the thought of having snow and ice slap me repeatedly in the face."

Eva could not hold back her laugh. "Your old accent and choice of words make the strangest combination sometimes."

"I do my best to sound modern."

"I meant no offense, Your Majesty," Eva quickly said.

"No offense was taken," he assured her. "Tell me, what are your plans when you finish with the films?"

"I have made up a system. I will spend two days watching films, two days in the library reading, two days of music combined with web surfing, then repeat until I feel satisfied that I wouldn't make a fool of myself in the civilized world. So tomorrow I will be spending the entire day, and most of the night, in your very impressive library." She gave him a once over with her eyes before asking, "Have you really read all of those books?"

Hadrian sighed. He had never done so much reading in his life. Society had changed a great deal since he had begun his exile. For the past two months he had done nothing but read every book he could get his hands on: astronomy, political literature, history, philosophy, medical textbooks, and everything in between. He had watched film after film, every genre from comedy to documentary, beginning with silent movies and ending with the latest box office releases. For once, having no biological need for sleep worked to his advantage as he spent hours upon hours listening to music and marveling at the change and the varieties.

He had always been a firm believer in the cliché of knowledge is power, and he knew he would have to assimilate as best he could if he were to reclaim his throne.

"Yes, and then some," he answered. "There are more books, which have been spread about the various rooms of the castle, not to mention all of the e-books stored on numerous devices. Unlike you, I had hundreds of years to catch up on."

Eva's eyes grew wide from astonishment. "You must be a genius."

He shrugged again. "Some professors and various experts I have met recently, due to my studies, have compared my brain to a computer. The rate in which I absorb, process, and store new information astounds them."

Unfortunately, his intelligence had been one of the reasons Imbrasus had cursed him with immortality.

"That is truly amazing."

Eva did not know what to say. In two months Hadrian had advanced over three hundred years and had no culture shock? Then again, he was an ancient vampire, changing with the times was a skill he must have mastered long ago. She knew from stories told of him that Hadrian was near 2,000 years old, though he didn't look a day over thirty-two.

"Well, I haven't been apart from the world as long as you, but I'm surprised by how much things have changed in the last ten years."

"How old were you when you joined your father's pack?"

Eva scoffed, a very unladylike sound. "I was abducted when I was seventeen," she said.

Hadrian nodded. He knew it would not be long before he received a full report on Eva, in the mean time he could try to learn as much about her as he could. That is, if he could manage to keep his instincts in check. He struggled not to reach out and snatch her to him. She stood so close. Her lovely feminine scent set his blood on fire as the heat of her body chased away the cold that had long ago settled over him.

The woman was a puzzle. Her very existence was a mystery. Her upbringing was outside the norm for shifter society, even for a half-breed.

"If you don't mind me asking, what would you have done with your life had the pack not taken you?"

"For starters, I would have gone to my graduation. Then I think I would have moved back to the States and lived with a close friend of my mom's while I went into debt paying for college."

"What would you have studied?"

"I wanted to be a pediatrician."

Her answer intrigued him. "And you no longer do?"

"I'm still interested, but… at this point in my life that goal isn't realistic." She shrugged and continued, "Eventually, I would've gotten married and…well, you can guess the rest. Living in the human world, no one would have ever known I was a half-breed. I would probably have run into a few shifters here and there, but those in the States are much more progressive than those like my father's pack, who shun human society. I would've had a normal life."

Hadrian winced, "Normal."

"Yes. Average," she added with a smile.

He shook his head. "You are not average."

Eva's smile faded as she turned away from him. No, she was an unnatural being in a world of darkness.

"I could have led a perfectly normal, average, boring life if—"

Eva's breath caught as he spun her to face him, his large hands gently resting on her delicate shoulders. His black gaze held her captive, their depths mesmerizing.

"There is nothing normal, average, or boring about you," he said. "You are too special to lead an ordinary life."

Hadrian was shocked by his own words. *Where the hell had that speech come from,* he wondered.

She swallowed, her throat suddenly dry. "Special is a nice way of saying that I'm a freak. I know what I am, Your Majesty."

Hadrian's eyes narrowed. She was not a 'freak'. She was exotic.

"No, I don't believe that you really do know what you are."

"I'm a half-breed. An abomination. A creature that should not exist, that was never *meant* to exist."

Hadrian was taken aback as an odd unidentifiable emotion gripped his heart. She had spoken the words with such ease it disgusted him. Did she honestly believe she was so worthless?

Without thinking, Hadrian pulled her into his arms.

Eva gasped as an excited thrill sprinted down her spine. He bent his head, his lips hovered over hers and she held her breath waiting for his kiss. It had been so long since she had been kissed. Way too long.

Hadrian's hand cupped her nape while the other flattened against her lower back, arching her into him. His cock pulsed against her belly and Eva moaned as her body blossomed, growing ready for him. Silky wetness pooled between her thighs as tension coiled in her belly. God, she needed him to kiss her and he needed to do it now.

Wetting her lips, she whispered, "Y–Your Highness?"

His hold on her grew firm. With a simple thought he could teleport them to his room, where they could spend the remaining hours of the night in pleasure. Why would he deny his needs? She was a willing female and surely he could control his bloodlust, taking just enough from her to satisfy his hunger.

She gazed up at him expectantly and Hadrian stood, enthralled, immobile. Her eyes sparkled with desire and burned with need, but there was something else that shimmered in their amber depths.

Innocence.

She was an innocent.

For a few precious moments he could forget that she was his Ward and that he was plagued by madness. But never could he overlook the fact that she was a virgin and that he was not the sort of man that would be gentle.

Protect her, even from yourself.

Chapter Seven

Hadrian opened his eyes. He stood on the balcony of his room. Snow and wind lashed at him, punishing him for his weakness.

At the last moment, as his body began to fade, he released her, leaving Eva in the solarium while he materialized outside in the storm.

What had come over him? Good lord, he had been about to *kiss* her. He kissed no one. A kiss was personal and intimate, a connection he knew very little about. So much could be shared and revealed in a simple kiss: passion, doubt, fears, his very soul.

Hadrian scowled. His soul. His battered, poisoned soul was one thing he would never reveal.

But sweet heaven, Eva had felt incredible in his arms. Her soft, delicate form pressed tightly against his had made him wish there was no clothing separating them. Her heartbeat sang to him as their lust filled the air. Her eyes, brilliant swirling pools of amber, her lips had been parted — perhaps an invitation? He thought she had wanted him to kiss her, but he knew it would not end there. He would never be able to release her once he sampled her passion.

Hadrian took a deep breath, hoping the frigid air would bring him peace. He cursed. Vanilla. The teasingly sweet scent clung to him, filling his lungs once more, feeding his ragging lust.

He needed to gain control. He needed sex. And blood.

Turning, he threw open the double doors with his mind and stalked into his room.

He had spent little time in his newly furnished, freshly draped bedchamber. Falcon had done a wonderful job with the repairs. Up until a month ago, the keep had been the definition of chaos. Books had been stacked like columns shoulder height, old papers had covered the floors like carpet while the wood paneling on the walls bore deep claw marks, every window was shattered leaving the remaining glass shards to shimmer in the light of the moon. This room had been no different, covered with scares from his unleashed fury, but one would never know now. Everything was organized, assigned its own place, the books had been put away and were even alphabetized and grouped by genre, the room appeared untouched by madness.

Hadrian slammed the balcony doors closed with a thought as he rounded the raised dais his expansive bed stood upon and headed for the adjoining room, which had once been a sitting area but had been remodeled into a closet. Shoving the door open, he tore off his shirt, casting aside the offending vanilla scent and donning a fresh black button up.

His cock still throbbed with need and he muttered curse after curse as he forced it into a new set of jeans. His clean clothes felt confining as he pulled on a black leather jacket.

The demon in him roared for release. It cried out for Eva and Hadrian fought the images of her parted lips and her glowing eyes. He could have easily brought an end to his misery by teleporting her to his room. He could have laid her on his bed and slaked his wicked lust and drank deep of the luscious red wine that was her blood.

"She is my Ward. She is mortal. She is abhorrently virginal," he growled as he stomped back into his room.

Besides, any woman could grant him release. He just needed one or two or three. His craving for sex had to be due to his lack thereof. Nothing more. It was not Eva. It was not her feminine scent or the combination of her luscious curves and small frame. It was not her bewitching eyes or her mysterious background. Her mere presence set him on edge because of his own forgotten, untended desires. Also, he only craved her blood because he had not fed.

The night was still young and he desperately needed to gain control over his traitorous body.

Blood and sex, the combination was the key to his peace of mind. Once he had fed and taken as many women as necessary, his mind would clear, as it had so many times in the past. He would be free to focus on the mystery that surrounded the half-breed and, most importantly, his Clan. He'd no longer feel the urge to bury himself in Eva's depths over and over again or crave the intoxicating elixir that was her blood.

Without pause, he walked to the bookcase, yanked open the mini fridge, pulled out a bag of blood and viciously sank his fangs in as he prepared for the onslaught of Imbrasus's memories; instead, his mind whirled with erotic scenes of Eva. He silently cursed as he tore deeper into the bag, sucking down the stale blood gulp after gulp. Finished, he let the deflated bag drop to the floor and grabbed another. The demon within him roared to life as the blood nourished his deprived cells. He could feel his muscles grow and strengthen with every swallow.

Wiping his mouth with the back of his hand he closed his eyes, taking in one measured breath after another. For so long he had starved and he had forgotten how empowering feeding could be. His body hummed with life, yearned for action. And he would have it. Calling on his senses, he focused his energy on teleporting.

Gasps kissed his ears as he appeared in the brothel. The putrid scent of alcohol, smoke, sweat, and sex assaulted him as he opened his eyes. Not much had changed. The full bar extended across the back wall, with a row of televisions playing sports or pornography. The women lounged on large, overstuffed sofas, scantily clad. Some, who were entertaining customers with dances, paused for a brief moment but quickly recovered and resumed their work.

"Your Majesty," a woman dressed in a black corset, curve hugging latex black pants and blood-red blazer walked up to him.

"Hello, Maggie," he greeted the madam.

"We've been expecting you," she said, her ruby colored lips turning up with a sensual smile. "When I heard you had returned I had your bedchamber prepared."

He gave a nod as he scanned the room.

"It has been a long time, Your Majesty."

"Too long," Hadrian mumbled under his breath.

"I have recently acquired some new girls, ones that I'm sure will be to your liking." She clapped her hands and the women came to their feet, stopped their dancing, and even ran from the various halls that led to the bedrooms. They formed a line, shortest to tallest, each in different stages of undress.

"Most of the girls I had when you last visited have quit, having saved enough money to be independent," Maggie explained, "but I have replaced them well."

Hadrian regarded the women with a bored expression. He knew any man would be frothing at the mouth if presented with so many beautiful women and yet he stood completely unmoved by their bared breasts and come-hither gestures.

He shook his head. Every vampire knew madness touched him and yet here these females were, winking and blowing kisses at him. No doubt Maggie had told them he was a master of pleasure who would pay them generously for their services.

"Well, Your Majesty?" Maggie asked from beside him.

The moment he entered the brothel, his lust had vanished, his erection quickly fading. Hadrian silently cursed as he waited for his desire to return.

He gave a shrug and in a disinterested tone said, "Numbers four, seven, and twelve."

"Very good," Maggie said with a nod. "They will bathe and be sent to your room. In the mean time," she waved to a human girl who stood beside the bar, "may I interest you in a drink?"

Chapter Eight

Failure.

Hadrian materialized in his room.

A complete waste of time, he thought as he whispered a string of curses, his lips peeling away from his fangs as he growled viciously.

It was just after dawn. He had spent hours at the brothel and— nothing. He had selected the most beautiful females from Maggie's extensive collection and not one had truly sparked his interest. He had watched as they pleasured themselves and each other, but his lust had not stirred. What man on Earth would not be wild with lust after watching three very sexy women perform such an erotic show?

A crazed man.

Oh, the females had valiantly tried to entice him, but their touch had left him cold and more damn confused and frustrated than he had ever been.

Anger boiled his blood as he stalked to the washroom. Tearing at his clothes with his razor like claws, he started the shower with his mind. He needed to scrub free the rancid stench of lewd sex and absolute failure.

Not waiting for the water to heat, he stepped under the icy shower. Lathering a washcloth, he scrubbed his skin until it felt raw and burned red. Once satisfied he was clean, Hadrian pressed his palms flat against the porcelain tile. Arms locked and straight, his muscles tense. The water rained over his body in cool, soothing waves. Tiny droplets dripped from his chin and nose.

"That damn half-breed," he said with an exasperated sigh.

His pretty little Ward had gotten under his skin.

Even as he lay in bed with the women, their naked limbs brushing over him as they massaged his muscles, their lips skipping across his flesh, their fangs gently teasing his skin while their breasts caressed him, Eva had consumed his thoughts and his chest had ached in a bizarre way.

Had it been guilt? She was his ward, not his betrothed, not his wife. She was nothing but a pawn in a political battle of wills, and yet, as the women had kissed, licked, and suckled him, a nauseating sense of betrayal knotted his gut.

Had he actually felt shame?

Yes. As he lay beneath the women, he had found himself wishing he were with Eva. Wishing that she were the one kissing his chest while her elegant fingers pumped his cock.

A moan escaped his lips as he became hard. His eyes drifted closed, his imagination going wild. Her long, dark hair would fall around her waist in waves as she leaned over him. Her generous breasts would brush over his chest, her hard nipples teasing him as she slid down his body to his aching erection. She would trace the crown of his penis with her tongue before sucking him between her soft, pouting lips.

Hadrian's hand slipped from the wall to grip his shaft. His fist worked the hard length, his body growing taut as he envisioned Eva. Her smooth, golden skin would glow in the candlelight. He could almost feel her hips cradle his, her legs encircling his waist as he drove into her.

He shuddered as he came, his legs nearly giving out. Stumbling, he pressed his back to the cool wall. His chest rose and fell with rapid breaths as the intense pleasure of his orgasm receded. The relief and calm that accompanied his release quickly faded as his anger rose to the front.

Shutting off the water, he shoved open the glass door. It snapped back, the force causing it to shatter, sending shards of glass skittering across the floor. He stepped out, snatched a towel, and roughly dried himself. Feeling no pain as he padded over the sharp edges that covered the floor, he stormed from the bathroom.

After slipping on a pair of jeans, Hadrian collapsed in the chair behind his desk.

His hunger for blood was nothing he could not handle, having lived on the verge of starvation for so long. He was accustomed to the ache that came with the deprivation of his body. He understood his need for sex; he had often taken multiple women to his bed each night. He was not surprised his desire had come back to him in a rush.

What was not normal and what he could not understand was his absurd need for Eva. Never had he craved one woman in particular, never had he obsessed over a single female's blood or body. Rarely had he slept with the same woman twice.

He had hoped his mind was improving, but perhaps the opposite was taking place.

The scowl that creased his brow darkened.

Eva was not his type. She was too short, too slim, and mortal. He could easily snap her arm with just a pinch of his thumb and forefinger. He had always enjoyed robust women who could take and enjoy a rough tumble. But he could not deny the fact that despite her size, Eva was nicely proportioned with lush breasts and flaring hips. If only he were a human male with natural desires—

He lashed out, swiping his arm across his desk, sending the books and papers crashing to the floor.

He was a vampire. He was a king. And he was cursed with loathsome memories that would drag him to hell one way or another.

She was innocent. She was kind. He had no right to want her. No right to even fantasize about touching her. He had the beast in his bones, evil coursed through his veins, poisoning his heart and killing his soul. He was a murderous, bloodthirsty demon, nothing and no one could change that fact. He was a creature destined to bring death.

Just like his maker.

Much to his shame, he had been more like Imbrasus in the early years of his transformation than he cared to admit. He had slain and drank deep of innocent blood, but he never raped, he never tortured, and never once had he taken pleasure from another's pain.

Oh, how he had reveled in the sweet taste of blood and the addictive ecstasy of death. Feeling a mortal's pulse slow as the warmth of life faded from their flesh, the soft sound of their last gasps of air had tickled his ears, and then death. It had washed over him, heating his flesh until he felt as if the sun was burning him, the bliss numbing his mind.

Hadrian's fangs slipped from their sheaths as his lungs expanded with needless air. His senses grew sharp at the faint scent of vanilla. His eyes shot to the shirt that lay in a crumpled ball on the floor just inside his closet. Standing, he forced a fire to jump to life in the hearth across from his bed. Snatching up the offending fabric, he viciously threw it into the flames.

What had the half-breed done to him? Despite his earlier release in the shower, his body continued to ache for her. It was as if she had cast a spell on him.

The thought gave him pause but he brushed it aside.

With a heavy sigh, Hadrian went to his bed. His mind was weary and his limbs heavy. Praying for one day of peaceful, dreamless slumber, he laid back.

All his troubled thoughts and strange behavior could be contributed to his lack of rest. Counting back, he could not recall the last time he had slept. Perhaps a little sleep was all he needed. And blood. Yes, he would need more blood; the two bags he had drunk earlier had done little. Once he was well rested and fed, his attraction to Eva would surely become nonexistent.

Allowing his eyes to drift close, he braced himself for horrors that only *his* mind could possess. For when he slept he dreamed, and when he dreamed the hellish memories of his demon mixed with his own until he could no longer tell the two apart. He and the vampire became one and the same.

As sleep claimed him, Hadrian could only hope that his fragile sanity would survive the hell that he knew was to come.

Crimson flowed like rivers down his chest as he wiped it from his eyes. Imbrasus smirked as he stepped over one body, then another, and another, crossing the blood slick tavern floor.

The veil between Hadrian and the demon he carried evaporated, leaving him to feel every evil impulse that had belonged to his maker, Imbrasus.

Death surrounded him as bones cracked beneath his boots. His eyes darted about the tavern. One. There was one mortal that still lived. Her soft, frantic breaths drew him to her hiding place. His muscles flexed, his claws lengthened as he bared his fangs. Fear, it was delicious, the aroma made him hard.

Rounding the bar, he found a hatch in the floor.

Her scream pierced Hadrian's soul as she was wrenched up from the cellar. She hysterically pleaded for her life as his claws sliced the thin material of her sleeve, drawing blood.

Hadrian's stomach rolled in revolt but he could do nothing except relive the evil.

Snatching the woman to him, she trembled in his grasp and he felt his lips curl into a sadistic smile. With a swift swipe, he tore her bodice, revealing creamy breasts.

More pleas, her voice shook as she began to sob.

Anger.

It filled him, driving him to shove the female down. Blood splashed beneath her, coating her limbs as she struggled.

Laughter rumbled his chest.

Hadrian felt his lips move as he heard Imbrasus sneer, "Pathetic."

Hadrian fought against the nightmare, grappling to wake but the madness was too strong. It held him, trapped him within Imbrasus's body as the vampire pinned the woman beneath him and ripped at her clothing.

Hunger.

Blood.

In the recesses of his mind, he heard himself bellow as the victim screamed, while the tender flesh of her throat yielded to his sharp fangs.

The room began to spin as he choked on the terror-spiked blood.

Rain slipped down his face like tears and wind viciously whipped at him.

"No!" He heard himself yell as he was swept back to the night his life had changed forever.

Hadrian blinked, clearing his vision. His chest felt heavy, as if a steel cage imprisoned his lungs. Agony like he had never known tore at him with poisonous talons.

Closing his eyes, he refused to look down. He knew this scene all too well. He had relived this moment thousands of times, praying it had ended differently, that he had fallen to his death instead.

"Titus," the anguished roar ripped from his throat, the force brought him to his knees.

He could feel the barrier that divided him from Imbrasus's demon crack. With every passing second, his mind crumbled. His world was collapsing into chaos.

Again and again he shouted. Sorrow shattered his heart as guilt crippled his soul. The sound of his pain echoed through the night. The trees swayed from the impact while the mountains cringed. A demon had risen.

Hadrian opened his eyes. Blood dripped from his fingers. Was it his own or did it belong to Titus?

Struggling to maintain his control, he mentally clutched the shreds that remained of his sanity. He wiped his shaking hands on his white tunic, forever staining the pure fabric, branding him a murderer.

"No," he breathlessly gasped.

The mental wall he had spent years building and fortifying fell. The sulfuric scent of unadulterated evil burned his nose and scalded his lungs as Imbrasus's essences invaded his body. Visions of death and carnage filled his mind as his grief mixed with hate and anger.

Gripping his head, his nails drawing blood, he began to rock back and forth on his knees.

This was not *real. This could* not *be real. Titus could* not *be dead.*

Shoving himself to his feet, he stumbled toward the stone railing. Lightning flashed, cracking the night sky and with it the last of his sanity.

Titus laid stories below, impaled; the steel cross of the castle's rooftop protruding from his chest. The rain fell and washed away the blood that covered his body.

"Titus. Titus! Brother, no! Come back to me. Come back!" His throat grew tight; his voice became hoarse as he screamed until he could speak no more.

Please, he prayed, please come back. You cannot be dead. You cannot be—

Hadrian's mind snapped as he collapsed to his knees, his shoulders slumped. His head hung low as the world faded from his sight, leaving his eyes vacant obsidian pools.

Ice settled in his bones, never to be removed, his reality melted away.

Falling. He was falling into the abyss. He felt his lungs expand as he tried to scream, but only silence met his ears. Darkness reached for him as insanity welcomed him to Hell with open arms.

Hadrian came awake with a violent jolt. Blinking repeatedly, he frowned. Had he teleported to the lake just outside the labyrinth or had he been sleep walking? And why would he come here? Why not teleport to Titus's grave or the cursed Hall of Mirrors like all the times before? After reliving that fateful night, he usually awoke where his nightmare had taken place…where his brother had died.

Deciding there was no logical explanation for his illogical action, he turned his eyes to the dark sky—peaceful, loving night. The cold was a balm to his raw emotions and tortured mind. His lips turned up in a rueful smile, as he whispered, "No rest for the wicked. No cliché has ever been more true."

Chapter Nine

With a frustrated sigh, Eva snapped the book shut and tossed it on the bed beside her.

God, her head ached. Rubbing her temples, she leaned back against the pillows. She had gotten little sleep the night before and tonight was not shaping up to be any better.

No matter how hard she tried, she could not stop herself from obsessing over Hadrian and the almost kiss. She had lain awake until sunrise wondering what the hell had happened. One second they were talking, next she was in his arms with her body tightly pressed against his. The evidence of his arousal had rubbed against her belly, flaming her already raging desire. His dark eyes had burned with lust and consuming hunger.

Yet, he recoiled. Did she disgust him? Or had he been revolted by the fact that he had been about to kiss her? Surely, that was it. She was an 'abomination' after all. And, why would someone like him want someone like her. He was a king for god's sake while she was too low for anyone of worth to notice.

Upon reflection, Eva surmised that the incident was most likely caused by Hadrian's lack of feeding. She had over heard Falcon complaining to someone on the phone about how Hadrian refused to eat and even refused to sleep. His hunger could have driven him to—

Eva shook her head remembering the pained expression on his face and the sympathy in his cold black eyes when he had pulled her to him. He had seemed genuinely upset by her words. Could he possibly relate to her feelings?

No, he must have agreed with what I said, she thought, *why else would he refuse to kiss me?*

Besides, if it had been blood he wanted, Eva knew she would have freely given it. Yes, she knew that was a shameful confession, but when it came to the mad king, all her good sense vanished.

Then again, I don't know if I truly want him. He could be using his powers on me. He could be making me think I want him.

Eva rolled her eyes at her absurd thoughts. *Why would a vampire use their power of compulsion and not capitalize on it? That made absolutely no sense, unless he is some twisted bastard who enjoys playing mind games. He was beaten with the crazy stick after all. He could be on a power trip.*

Yet she doubted the thought. Hadrian was a sexy man, plain and simple. A woman would have to be a fool to not find him attractive, and she was no fool.

"What I am is sexually deprived," she huffed.

She had enjoyed the boyfriends she had when she was a free spirited teenager, but her life and fun ended way too soon.

Now, she was a woman who wanted to know all the life experiences that had been denied her. And she was trapped in a castle with a devastatingly sexy vampire who seemed to be physically attracted to her, if nothing else.

His eyes were hypnotic, his lips sensual and his face ruggedly handsome. He was tall and built, but by no means bulky. He was all solid, lean muscle. And his penis, from what she had felt from the times he had pressed her to him, was thick and long.

A moan escaped her lips as she imagined what it would feel like, his body dominating hers, pressing her down into the mattress as he drove into her.

Her thoughts were an endless vicious cycle. She had tossed and turned last night as her mind raced with questions. She restlessly wandered the castle all day as she desperately fought to come up with answers, and every time she ended up envisioning Hadrian's powerful body moving over her as he—

Eva gasped as the thundering sound of a jungle cat's purr met her ears. Her hands shot to her throat. Her body went cold; her breath froze in her lungs as she waited for the sound to happen again.

Silence.

Tension slowly eased from her body as confusion set in. As if she did not already have enough to contemplate she had to add this weird shifter like phenomenon to the list of questions that desperately needed answers.

She could not have made that sound. She *should* not have been able to make that sound. She was a half-breed and though she possessed every physical trait of her father's line, her blood was diluted. She did not possess enough magic to tap into her animal spirit and yet, she had growled and purred.

Impossible.

God, she wished she had someone to talk to, someone to help her find answers. That was what Eva missed most about her mother. She had always been there to listen, to guide, to help her smile in spite of her problems, and helped her find a way to solve them. She had never judged, never chastised or betrayed her. She always gave her support.

Eva blinked away her tears, refusing to let them fall. She had to be strong; her mother would have wanted her to be strong. And she would not live in the past.

Coming to her feet, Eva donned her snow boots and snatched her jacket.

She needed some fresh air and a walk would help her clear her mind and maybe grant her peace, if only for a little while.

The storm had broken early in the morning, leaving behind fresh snow and a clear sky. As she walked, the snow rhythmically crunched beneath her boots and Eva found the sound oddly soothing. For a moment her mind was calm, her mass of questions and troubling thoughts forgotten. She idly wandered through the maze, occasionally plucking a frosted leaf from the hedges. She took in deep, cleansing breaths of fresh night air and sighed in contentment.

Her mind finally cleared and her thoughts became serene for the first time that day. She rounded the last corner of the maze and—*he* was there. Hadrian stood on the ice-covered lake, his face turned up toward the moon, basking in the soft glow. Dark jeans that hung low on his hips were all he wore and Eva could not resist running her tongue over her lips as her eyes devoured him. He was all lean muscle, his pale skin smooth and perfect.

She caught and held her breath as he slowly turned to face her. His chest and abdomen were flawlessly formed, all hard and chiseled, like a Roman sculpture.

"Enjoying the view?" he asked.

Eva nodded, sweeping him with her gaze once more. Her breasts felt heavy as she drew in breaths. Her bra felt tight and she sighed, the thin material caressing her now hard nipples.

Get a grip, Eva, she chided herself.

Snapping her gaze from his body, she met his stare. She stumbled back as if she had been struck. His black eyes whirled with rage, loathing, torment and... primal hunger.

Hadrian's chest heaved, his hands curled into fists, his fangs glinted in the moonlight. He looked wild.

Eva knew she should be frightened. He appeared ready for battle, the hard lines of his face set. Threatening power radiated from him as he continued to stare at her. Would he rip her head off, or shred her clothing and—Self-preservation sparked in the back of her mind, she should leave, but instinct told her if she ran, he would give chase.

Her pulse leapt with excitement as she envisioned the vampire tearing through the labyrinth. He would catch her, ensnare her in his arms and pin her down with his body…

Hadrian's dark eyes narrowed with predatory delight. Eva felt a blush creep to her cheeks. She knew he could read her body. Her heart pounded with anxious anticipation, as her breaths grew shallow. She had no doubt he knew she wanted him.

Which is insane, she told herself.

She should not be standing here, gaping at him as if he were a wild animal on a nature reserve and she on a tour. She should apologize for interrupting whatever he was doing out in the snow half-dressed and go back to her room and that damn book.

"I asked you a question, little one."

Eva barely resisted a sigh when he spoke. His voice was like velvet and despite her good sense, her body heated for him. Wetting her lips she said, "W–what was the question, Your Majesty?"

Hadrian's lips curled into a perfect sensual smile; his fangs grew even longer, greedy and ready. "No matter," he said as he appraised her from head to toe. "What brings you to the lake this evening?"

"I thought a nice walk would help me relax and sort out my thoughts."

"And has it?" he asked, taking a step toward her.

"It was helping," she admitted.

Hadrian took another step in her direction and Eva suddenly felt skittish. He was moving like a cat, slowly closing in on its prey. Was he trying to distract her with conversation?

"*Was* helping?"

She swallowed hard as he drew closer. "Y–yes."

"Perhaps, if you share your troubles with me, I could help ease your mind."

Eva shuddered. *Oh, I know you could.*

"Tell me, little one," Hadrian coaxed, his voice smooth and pliant.

"My thoughts are of you," she answered with a squeak.

Hadrian stopped and disappointment spread through her chest. She wanted him to come to her, to take her in his arms like he had the night before. She had dreamed of what his lips would feel like against hers, how he would taste, and she needed to know, now.

"Of me?"

Her cheeks were on fire, from embarrassment or arousal, she could not say. "I think we should talk about what happened, or, well, what *almost* happened—" Eva's words lodged in her throat as his breath brushed her ear. She had not seen him move.

"Has our encounter of last eve plagued your thoughts?" he asked, from beside her.

All Eva could do was nod. Her voice had abandoned her.

"Do you really wish to talk about what *almost* happened?"

She shook her head. No. She did not want to talk about it, she wanted to continue and finish what they had started.

Hadrian's lips caressed her ear as he asked, "What is it you really want?"

Sensual heat fired her blood. Struggling to find her voice, she swallowed hard and whispered her confession, "You."

The scent of her arousal set alarms off in his head. Need slammed into Hadrian so hard it rocked his entire body, making him tremble with urgent desire.

"You shouldn't," he grated, forcing himself to move away from her. The sexual heat of her body was an inferno and he needed the bite of the cold to maintain his ever-slipping, ever-fragile control.

Eva's sigh was one of frustration as she rounded to face him. "Do you honestly think I don't know that?" she snapped.

The corners of Hadrian's lips twitched, but he did not smile.

"I apologize for my tone—"

"This is not a formal conversation, you may speak freely."

Eva shook her head. "This was a mistake," she said cursing herself for telling Hadrian she wanted him.

Nothing could happen between them. They were too different, he a king, she a bastard peasant half-breed who meant nothing. He was crazy and she, well, she wasn't sure that she didn't have a few screws loose herself after last night. Hell, they weren't even the same species!

Deciding it would be best if she returned to the castle before she suffered any more embarrassment and before her self-esteem took a hit, she had to get one thing off her chest.

"We can pretend this," she waved a hand at the space between them, "never happened, but I—"

"Why would we pretend this," he mimicked her, "never happened?"

Refusing to answer, Eva continued, "I need to know. Have you planted thoughts in my head making me believe I'm attracted to you?"

Hadrian balked as if she had gravely insulted him. "I have never invaded your mind. Your emotions and thoughts are your own."

Eva ground her teeth. If he was telling the truth then she was in more trouble than she wanted to admit. It would be easier to blame the vampire for the turmoil that raged within her. Shaking her head, she could not think about this right now. She just needed to get away from him and his intoxicatingly fresh male scent and hungry eyes.

She brushed past him and headed for the labyrinth.

"Wait."

It was not a command, but a request and Eva's body froze against her will.

"What happened in the solarium and…all the other times, I want you to know that…it will not happen again. I'm deeply sorry for causing you confusion."

"Forget it, nothing ever actually happened." *And nothing ever will.*

She turned back toward the maze, but he stood, blocking the entrance.

His large frame shook, his muscles strained as if he were forcing himself to remain still. His eyes focused on the snow that covered his bare feet.

When he spoke his words were strained, "I must make you understand."

Was he going to try to scare her into not wanting him?

He looked up, his gaze meeting hers. Eva swayed from the force of her shock.

His eyes were an impossible blood red, the white completely consumed by the deep crimson.

"As you can see, I am not like other vampires. I am the monster that demons fear. And," his eyes slowly roamed over her body, she gasped as if he had physically caressed her, "I want you. I want to drain you as I claim your body. I want to feel your heart slow beneath my lips as I come deep within you."

Eva closed her eyes as his words settled over her. How could she find what he was saying sexy? God, she had to be twisted. After all the time living amongst her father's pack her mind must have snapped. He was describing how he wanted to kill her and she was getting hot?

"My grip on reality is fragile, my control razor thin."

The harshness of his voice faltered ever so slightly and Eva snapped her eyes open.

Anguish. Despair. Loneliness. Hate. It was plain to see the emotions that flickered to life within his red eyes. He spoke of being a monster, but all she saw was a tortured man. She did not doubt what he said was true, yet, as she stood bewitched by his glowing red eyes, she knew evil was not his true nature.

Slowly, she raised a hand, cautiously reaching out to him. She expected him to growl at her, to slap her hand away or vanish. Instead, he stood firm as a marble statue. His hellish gaze fixed on her.

Comfort. Something within her cried out to comfort this vampire.

He admitted he wants to kill me.

Eva snapped her hand back preparing to scream as loud as she could. Taking in a large gulp of air, she prayed that Falcon would find her. Rescue her from—

"No," his whisper was barely audible. "Touch me." She had not seen him move, but now, he towered over her. "Please." His eyes narrowed as if willing her to reach out to him. "Please, Eva, I *need* you to touch me."

Chapter Ten

Hadrian needed to feel her hands on him. He ached for her to chase away the loneliness that tore at his soul, even if for a moment.

Eva hesitantly came closer as he battled the demon for control. He did not want to frighten her, though he should. He ought to strike terror in the girl, show her what sort of beast he truly was. He was a vampire, death incarnate, but with her—for her he could be more.

Her fingers hovered just above his heart. He shivered. Her warmth was inviting and torturous.

Leaning forward, he silently encouraged her.

Eva's tongue slid out, wetting her upper lip before she bit the lower. Hadrian groaned. Waves of need pulsated through his shaft, swelling it, making it even harder. He wanted to take her lips, to feel their fullness beneath his, to taste her tongue.

She tentatively placed her palm flat on his chest and he flinched. She scalded him, her heat banishing the chill that resided in his very bones and surrounded his heart.

"More," he bit out.

Eva brought up her other hand and traced the lines of his muscles with her fingertips, making him shudder. Her delicate hands moved over his chest, down his sides, and over his abdomen. She stopped before reaching his hips, drawing away.

He could not suppress his growl. Was it a warning or a demand that she continue?

Her hands came back to his flesh, this time beginning at his abs and, with agonizing slowness, worked their way up his solid pecs to his shoulders.

Eva's vanilla scent surrounded him. It invaded his lungs and attacked his mind, soothing his thoughts, chasing away his guilt, and sending Imbrasus's memories back into hiding.

Unable to resist a moment longer, Hadrian snatched her to him. Her breath escaped her lungs as her soft body slammed into his. One massive hand fisted her jacket as the other cupped her nape, his fingers entwined with her dark, luxurious satin hair.

Hadrian did nothing more than gaze into her eyes and Eva began to tremble from the force of his sexually charged stare. Pure, animalistic desire glittered the depths of his eyes.

God, what was she doing? Just a moment ago, he had detailed how he wanted to kill her. She had seen the bloodlust flicker like flames in his unholy red eyes, but she did not want to believe he was evil. She did not want to believe that he was a lost cause, that he was crazed like the rumors claimed. But, the truth had been standing before her. His demonic eyes had bore into her, searching for her soul, as his long, lethal razor sharp fangs stood proud and ready to tear at the tender flesh of her throat.

His hold tightened as if he sensed her inner turmoil. He pressed her even more tightly to him, molding her form to his.

Nervously, she asked, "Are you going to kiss me?"

Hadrian stared at her perfect lips for what seemed like an eternity before dragging his gaze back to hers. "No."

"Why not?" Eva knew disappointment rang in her voice and she dropped her head, hiding the confusion that surely clouded her eyes.

Eva's pulse stuttered and a gasp of surprised pleasure caught in her throat as his lips brushed her ear taking the sensitive lobe into his mouth.

"W–wait," Eva panted. This was not right. He had just said this would not—his lips moved to her neck. *No. Focus.* This should not be happening. "Your Highness," she squeaked, "We shouldn't be—"

"Hadrian," he grated, his voice deep and husky, "During moments like these, please, call me by my given name."

Eva could not help but nod in agreement as he tasted her flesh with his tongue, drawing circles over her throat, pausing at her pulse. A thrill of excited fear rushed down her spine curling her toes.

Trying one last time to hold on to her senses, she tried to pull back, but his arms were like unyielding steel bands. Deciding it might be best to use her fighting skills, she hooked her boot catching his ankle. Tripping him, he went crashing to the ground, but he took her with him. They rolled through the snow until he pinned beneath him and capture arms, restraining them above her head.

His expression was one of surprise while his eyes darkened. Eva knew in that moment that he would not let her get away. This was happening, whether it should or not and something deep within her roared with triumph.

Hadrian lay over her, his eyes studying her as if carefully calculating his options. Finally, with his voice rough with need, Hadrian vowed, "I will bring you pleasure."

If Eva had suffered as he had since their last encounter, then he would ease her. His heart began to beat in time with hers and he prayed he would be able to maintain control.

Hadrian shifted, his erection pressing between her thighs. Freeing one hand, he held her wrists in the other. He traced her jaw with his index finger before his hand slipped to her throat, brushing the pad of his thumb over her pulse. His hot gaze followed his fingers, searing her skin.

Running his tongue over his fangs, he frowned. Her bulky jacket was in the way, concealing her ample breasts. With a frustrated snarl, he bent his head, took the zipper between his teeth, and tugged.

Eva wore a black sweater with a deep V-neckline. It clung to her breasts, hugged her waist, and then flared at her hips.

His lethal yet delicate hand drifted over her newly exposed skin until his palm hovered above her breast. Eva's back arched, thrusting her breasts upward, but he did not touch her. His gaze lingered on the tops of her honey colored swells. His eyes traveled lower, his hand following down her side to her hip. He looked over his shoulder at her legs that were spread wide to accommodate his size.

Was he envisioning her naked?

Hadrian's obsidian gaze captured hers. Eva's heart pounded out of control, her breaths came in painful gasps as unadulterated lust laced her blood. His eyes promised lethal passion.

Finding her voice, Eva asked, "W-why are you looking at me like that?"

"Like what?"

"Like you want to devour me."

Hadrian's lips pulled back from his gruesomely sexy fangs as he snarled, "Because I do."

As if to prove his hunger for her, he ground his hips against her, his solid shaft stroked over her center.

"Oh...God," she sighed.

Eva's eyes slipped closed as he continued to move over her. Again and again he thrust his hips forward, rocking his hardness against her core. Instinctively, her knees came up, her snow covered boots hooked around his thighs. Her fingers curled, her nails biting half-moon imprints into her palms. She struggled against his hold on her wrists, craving to feel his muscles move beneath her hands. His grip tightened and he pressed her more firmly to the ground. Did he think she was trying to flee?

Hadrian's lips descended to her throat. His teeth grazed her soft skin, his fangs tickled and teased. Trailing kisses down her neck, he nipped at her collarbone as he slowly ran his free hand over her hip and up her side to cup her breast. His powerful fingers massaged her and occasionally gave a pinch to a hard peak.

Fire. She was on fire. Her clothes felt rough against her sensitive skin. She wanted to feel his hands on her body, his lips on her breasts, his fingers on her sex as he tongued her nipples.

As if knowing exactly what she desired, Hadrian tugged at her shirt, pulling the sleeve and bra strap down, revealing one shoulder and her breast.

She cried out as he took her aching nipple into his hot mouth, suckling her through the transparent material of her bra. He tongued and nipped at her while his hand continued to massage her other breast.

Each sigh that escaped her luscious lips drove him closer and closer to the edge of madness, but he couldn't stop, wouldn't stop. He had vowed to bring her pleasure and he would.

Eva arched beneath him, her arms straining for freedom. She wanted to clutch his head to her breast. She wanted to run her hands over his back as he worked his hips against hers.

He growled, refusing to release her. "I want to hear you scream my name," he whispered.

She knew she would.

Craving to taste her flesh, Hadrian roughly ripped her shirt open as his teeth tore at the thin black fabric of her bra. He traced his fangs along the curve of her exposed breasts, his tongue lightly teasing, sending delicious chills over her body. Then, he captured her nipple again with his lips and Eva's cry echoed in the night.

Eva trembled beneath him as he savagely assaulted her breast. Dear god, she had never known pleasure like this.

With a husky groan, Hadrian's thrusts grew wild as he aggressively pumped his swollen cock against her. Eva rocked her hips, matching his tempo. The world melted around her until there was nothing but Hadrian and the wonderfully torturous things he was doing to her.

Urgent, undeniable want consumed them as their movements became frenzied. The rougher Hadrian became, the more Eva cried out in bliss.

Take her, the beast within him whispered.

He took in a deep breath. God, she was ready for him. He could scent her arousal, she was drenched in sweet honey…He could easily undo her jeans, shove his down and slide into her.

His entire body quaked. He could almost feel her clenching around him, milking him as she came. To drive into her would be bliss, a heaven he did not deserve.

The vampire in him roared, demanding that he mark her.

His fangs began to tingle as he thought of sinking them into the tender flesh of her breast. Her pulse pounded the sweetest of rhythms in his ears, luring him like a sinful siren's song, as her body writhed with need. Hadrian grazed her nipple with his fangs and Eva gave a small cry of ecstasy. Again, she tried to wrench her hands free, but he tightened his grip. Hadrian knew he had precious little control. He was barely hanging on, barely able to keep the beast in its cage.

Releasing her wrists would be dangerous, the things she could do with her hands—He couldn't think about that now. This moment was not for him. He would give her the release she desperately craved and leave. Or, at least, he prayed he would leave.

"Please, Hadrian," Eva sighed, snapping him from his thoughts.

She was close, so very close. Reluctantly freeing her nipple, Hadrian drew himself up. Arching his back, he pounded against her.

Dear lord, she was lovely. Her eyes were closed and her brow was creased as she sought her orgasm. Her lips were parted, begging him for a forbidden kiss. The moonlight glittered over her dark hair and made her skin glow. A goddess lay writhing beneath him. Gorgeous.

Free of inhibitions, Eva matched his thrusts. She arched her back, causing her breasts to brush against his chest with every frantic thrust. Grinding up against him, she moaned, whispering his name again and again.

Every muscle in his body tensed, his control stretched razor thin. The beast was just beneath the surface, ready to drink her, ready to claim her. There was no stopping.

"*Yes…Hadrian…Yes.*"

"Come hard for me," he rasped.

Her thighs clenched his hips as she threw her head back. "I'm…Oh, Hadrian…you are making me—"

Eva cried out, her body fragmenting into a thousand pieces. Shock after shock ripped through her. Her legs wrapped tight around his hips as she rode out her pleasure, savoring her explosive orgasm.

Hadrian became deathly still. An odd pain tore through his chest as he slowly released her wrists. He pulled her tattered sweater back into place; every fiber of his being protested as he came to his feet, and stepped away from the heat of her body. Curling his fingers into fists, his claws cut into his palms; blood trickled from the cuts to the pristine snow, marring its purity.

His shaft twitched and pulsed painfully, straining against his pants. His sack was heavy with seed and the demon…it screamed for him to take her. Every instinct demanded for him to claim this woman.

Images of her in his bed, her hair spread across his crimson sheets, plagued his thoughts. Her thighs open, her lips curled with an inviting smile, her wrists shackled—

This moment was for her, only for her.

Control. Protect her. Keep her safe.

The words were a never-ending mantra playing in his head. Though he could not ignore nor shake free the strange feelings that coursed through his body, hunger like nothing he had ever experienced made his throat clench, desire beyond imagining raged within him and his soul, a part of him he had thought dead, yearned for her soft caress.

What was happening to him?

"Hadrian."

Her voice was elegant and musical; bringing precious relief to his battered soul and frayed nerves.

"You didn't…I mean you haven't come."

He shuddered as the last word fell from her flawless lips.

How could he have let this happen? Directly after telling her these types of encounters would not happen between them again, he had pressed her to the ground, thrusting against her until she came.

"Hadrian," she called, coming to her feet.

Hadrian's angered roar shook the night as he clutched his head. He could not have her. She was not his.

He had to get away from her. He had to get her scent off him. Without looking back and without a word, he dematerialized. Leaving her in the night, he took form in his washroom. Kicking free of his jeans, he stepped under the waterfall of ice cold water in his shower. He had to clear his mind. He had to wash away her essence.

As the chilled water cascaded over his head, he punched the tiled wall, cracking the porcelain. The water rinsed away the blood on his knuckles to reveal already healed flesh in stark contrast to the damaged tiles. He envisioned his soul looked just like the circular indent. Each fissure and fracture of the tile representing the damage his battered soul bore.

He was evil.

He was insane.

He was…empty.
He did not deserve her.

Chapter Eleven

Falcon watched as Hadrian dropped the thin file folder on the antique, mahogany table and began to pace the expanse of the council chamber. Falcon could not remember the last time this room had been used, but tonight, a meeting was in session. Subject for discussion: Eva Maldonado, half-breed daughter of the Silveria alpha, and ward of the Validus Clan.

"This is all the information our men were able to find?" Hadrian asked.

Falcon nodded. "It is very little."

"It is next to nothing," Hadrian corrected.

"I apologize, my king. We can have more—"

"No, it is not necessary."

There was no point in wasting more time on this task. From the report, it was clear that someone had not wanted this information to be found. Shadows surrounded Eva's background. Why?

It seemed as if Isabella, Eva's mother, had not existed before she moved to Brazil at the age of nineteen. They only knew she had come from Estonia because Eva had shared that fact with Falcon. Isabella had worked as a waitress and had lived with a few different female roommates in Rio de Janeiro. When interviewed, the women claimed Isabella was rarely home and they could not remember ever seeing her with any men.

They knew she had been twenty-four when she met Arsenio. Their relationship consisted of one night and about a month later Isabella packed up and moved to Miami, Florida. She gave birth to Eva approximately eight months later. Had she known she was with child when she left Brazil?

Mother and daughter lived with a 'family friend' named Jenna while Isabella worked nights and attended nursing school. When Eva was seven, her mother bought a small two-bedroom house where they lived alone until they returned to Brazil.

Why had Isabella decided to return to Rio? Perhaps she returned because of her brother, Joseph Maldonado. He had moved to Brazil from Estonia a year before the mother, daughter pair. Hadrian stifled a shudder. It was possible that Isabella knew she was ill. The relocation could have been for Eva's benefit. Surely, Isabella would have wanted to leave her daughter in the care of a family member. Approximately two years after moving back to Brazil, Isabella passed of leukemia.

"He has no right to her." Eva's words sounded in his mind as he continued to analyze the mystery. Her uncle must have been speaking of Arsenio. Had Isabella reached out to the alpha when she returned? If so, why? There had been no evidence of their communicating before she and Eva relocated to Rio and Arsenio was not interested in sharing any details.

The entire situation was...odd. And it was mystery that he needed to solve.

"Have you tried talking with Eva?" Falcon asked.

The knight's question made Hadrian's pacing pause for a brief moment. "We have spoken."

"She should be able to help. Surely, her mother told her something about her family."

Hadrian shook his head. No. Eva's mother had gone to great lengths to conceal her past and most likely would have revealed little to her daughter.

"What of Isabella's brother?"

"He moved to France about six months after Arsenio took her. After living there for two years, he dropped off the radar. We have been unable to track him down."

Yet another conundrum to add to the list, Hadrian thought.

"Are you certain our ward isn't exactly as she claims, half human-half shifter?"

"Positive."

"My king," Falcon sighed, "her eyes are yellow."

Hadrian's hurried pacing stopped, his gaze dropping to the file. "No, they are the purest shade of amber."

Falcon's eyes narrowed as he studied the ancient vampire before him. Hadrian's expression had softened, his tone had thickened, and his eyes had grown distant, even though he looked down upon the file folder.

"Has something happened between you and Miss Maldonado?"

The question seemed to snap Hadrian from his daydream.

"Nothing worth sharing," the king answered. He cleared his throat then fixed his cold eyes on Falcon. "You are leaving for the main house tomorrow, correct?"

Falcon responded, but not before he noted how quickly Hadrian had changed the subject.

"The final decisions for the coronation ceremony need to be made. While there I will do recon, just as you requested."

Hadrian sighed. He had mixed feelings about the Clan returning to his sanctuary. "I will face my challengers and, as customary, take my oath as king before the hearth in the main hall."

"Everything will be arranged properly. Besides, the Hall of Mirrors would not provide enough space for a proper challenge."

Chills swept over Falcon as a blast of grief and rage filled room.

"We don't have to host the celebration party in that particular ballroom. There are numerous others within the castle we could use," Falcon suggested. "The nobles will understand if you want to keep that room closed off."

Everyone knew Hadrian's brother, Titus, had fallen to his death from the balcony of that glittering, enchanting ballroom.

"No. It has to be there," Hadrian said, his voice hard and edged with ice.

Needing to distract his king, Falcon said, "I conducted a little recon mission the last time I was at the main house and, assuming not much has changed, I don't think you will have many challengers."

"Can you give me a number?"

Falcon blinked, surprised by Hadrian's smooth, detached tone. "Most of the Clan are eager for your return."

"You did not answer my question."

"There are a few wary nobles, but they do not possess the strength or necessary skills to go against you. Except for one, but we have already discussed him."

Hadrian nodded. Jefferson had been his rival when he first claimed the throne all those centuries ago. It was only fitting the vampire would want to confront him now.

"May I ask you something, Falcon?"

"Anything," the knight insisted.

"Why are *you* not challenging me?"

Falcon stood with a blank stare, speechless.

"As my Second, you should have ascended to the throne the moment I renounced my claim," Hadrian continued, "You have every right to the crown."

Falcon shook his head. "You are the rightful king."

"I did not become king the traditional way," Hadrian countered.

"You did what was right."

"Did I?" Hadrian mused. "I drove our Clan into civil war and killed the reigning king and his heir in battle."

"Have you forgotten the nobles voted for you? They elected you to be our king."

Images of the war flashed through his mind until they faded, leaving behind the scene of *that* night. The night his brother met everlasting death.

Titus's words began as mere whispers, steadily growing louder and louder. *I was to be king!*

Hadrian flinched as he tried to ignore the screams in his head. Rubbing his brow he confessed, "And every day I have questioned whether or not they made the right choice. Perhaps they should have selected Jefferson. I'm certain the nobles regret their decision."

"They voted for the better man," Falcons stated.

Hadrian's dark laughter echoed in the large, empty council room. *If only you knew what I have done.*

"You don't owe me your loyalty, nor am I worthy of it."

Falcon balked. "Everything I am, I owe to you. When you found me, centuries ago, I was on the verge of death. You gave me your blood while others told you I wouldn't survive the transition because I was half Shaw. You took me in, treated me like a brother, taught me how to control my hunger and harness the power of my inner demon. You are a good, honest, noble man, Hadrian."

"Somehow you never fail to see the good in people. I've always admired that about you."

Falcon shrugged. "Just a little something I learned from my Shaw mother."

Hadrian turned somber eyes to Falcon. "Thank you."

"For what?"

"Never giving up on me."

Chapter Twelve

Snow slowly fell outside and the flakes began to pile along the windowsill. Eva sat on the bench in the alcove of the library, leaning towers made of various discarded books were stacked high on the floor around her. She had been gazing, unseeing out across the white-blanketed landscape for what seemed like days but she knew only minutes had passed. The scene was tranquil and serene. This little space tucked away in the massive, windowless library was the only place where she could think.

Last night, she had gone for a walk hoping to clear her mind. Instead she had ended up with more questions and more confusing emotions.

She had not expected to find Hadrian, half-dressed and standing out on the frozen lake. Nor did she think she would ever admit her desire for him, but she had and he had shot her down, assuring her that their heated encounters would not happen again. He had revealed his inner vampire: bone-chilling red eyes, gruesome fangs, and lethal claws. She knew he intended to frighten her by describing how he craved to feel her pulse slow to a stop beneath his mouth. And yet, his words had enticed her while his eyes…

Eva sighed and leaned back against the wall. His eyes had revealed so much more than his words. She did not doubt the predator in him wanted the kill, natural instinct was hard to ignore, but his gaze had been filled with such longing. Heart breaking loneliness made his fathomless black eyes glitter as they swirled with despair, guilt and…self-loathing?

She understood misery all too well. She had been alone since her mother's passing. No one cared for a half-breed, she could drop dead tomorrow and no one would even remember her. It had been years since she had been held, since she had even been touched with a gentle hand. And she knew it had been much longer for Hadrian. He had lived for centuries alone, battling his madness and harboring his secrets. Had he been looking for comfort and reassurance in her touch?

He pulled away, she reminded herself.

He had vowed to bring her pleasure and he certainly had, but after she came, he grew dangerously distant and had vanished. Why had he not taken his own pleasure? And, again he had not kissed her.

She blushed. *Well, he kissed me just about everywhere else.*

Rubbing her temples she cursed. He was giving her a headache. *Damn confusing sexy vampire.*

Eva knew she could not place all the blame on the king, even though she wanted to. If he could be believed, and thus far he had given her no reason to distrust him, then all her thoughts, emotions, and reactions towards him were all her own. Which meant she was truly attracted to him. But was it Hadrian or was it that he was a good-looking available male?

Falcon is a handsome man, tall, muscled, with brown hair and unique silver eyes, but one look from him doesn't make me hot and his voice doesn't make me shiver.

Shaking her head, Eva knew the answer and she knew she had to speak with Hadrian.

He was attracted to her. Perhaps they could work something out. By no means was she looking for a relationship and even if she was, she had no chance with Hadrian on that level. She was his ward. He was a king. Hell, they weren't even the same species. Nothing emotional could happen between them, but that did not mean they could not enjoy each other's company. And, to be brutally honest, she was so over being a virgin.

In her father's village, she couldn't have given herself to anyone. She was just a filthy half-breed to them. But Hadrian had been more than ready to give her exactly what she wanted, what she craved. Sex.

A strange tingling sensation began at the base of her spine before branching throughout her nervous system. A whisper to her senses drew her eyes to the entrance of the library. Dark spice misted the air with a hint of menace. A shadowy figure advanced down the hall.

Hadrian?

Her heart quickened and instinct took over. Jumping to her feet, she followed. Eva slipped from the library and slinked down the hall to the lobby of the second floor. She saw the heel of Hadrian's shoe as he rounded the corner to the stairs. Eva silently made her way to the third level to spy Hadrian mounting another set of stairs that led to the off limits west wing.

"I don't recall this section of the castle being on the map," a familiar voice said from behind her.

Eva slowly turned to face Falcon.

"What are you doing?" he demanded.

"Exploring," she squeaked, her eyes downcast. She felt like a child who had just been caught being naughty.

"Please, stick to the areas on the map I gave you. I wouldn't want you getting lost." He glanced up the stairwell before settling his eyes back on her to continue, "Why are you up here?"

Eva shrugged. "Curiosity got the better of me."

Falcon's silver gaze turned sharp and Eva shifted uneasily. Did he know she had been following Hadrian?

"I must warn you against your mission."

Eva tried to stay calm. She knew Falcon would be able to sense her nervousness. "What do you mean?"

"You are looking for the king. I left the council room with His Highness and saw you follow him from the library."

Busted, Eva thought.

"If you would like an audience with the king, I can arrange one. Seeking him out in his private quarters is not wise."

She could not argue. He was most likely right. Eva studied Falcon, taking note of his stern set jaw. His silver eyes were now stone. Why was he warning her away from Hadrian? The king's intense sexuality threatened her peace of mind, his touch made her burn, and his lips did wonderful things to her, but he had never been violent. Though, she was certain he was more than capable of rending a man's head from his body.

"Tell me, Falcon," she said as she paced back towards the vampire. "Do you honestly think your king will harm me?"

Falcon's eyes narrowed. "Are you willing to test him?"

Eva wished she knew. She did not believe Hadrian would use his force against her, but how well did she know him?

Not well at all.

"Or, do you have a death wish?" Falcon asked, his tone hardened with challenge.

Eva blinked in surprise. "Do you think he would kill me?"

"He can."

"And so *can* you," she countered.

Falcon's sigh was filled with irritation. "Hadrian is not stable. He could snap at any moment. And he is…capable of horrific deeds."

"I hate to be the one to point this out to you, but everyone, especially vampires, is capable of horrific deeds. Everyone is capable of anything under the right circumstances."

It may have been a trick of the light, but Eva could have sworn Falcon's lips twitched with a smile for a second.

"You have courage, I'll give you that," he said, stepping closer to her, towering over her. "What do you want with him?" he demanded, his tone firm.

What did she want with the mad vampire king? She knew she wanted to continue whatever it was they were about to do last night.

She wanted to feel his hands on her body once more and his cool breath on her neck. It had been so long since she had been touched or kissed, too long since anyone had shown her desire or sparked her lust. Hadrian had ignited an inferno within her. His demon had triggered her inner animal spirit and she wanted him.

"It's a private matter," she answered.

Falcon raised a brow, when it was clear she would say nothing more, he warned, "The king is…better left alone. Whether you want to believe it or not, he is dangerous."

Eva nodded. Of that, she had no doubt and in a twisted way, that was part of Hadrian's appeal: the mysterious, dark, tortured, sinfully sexy, dangerous vampire.

"I know."

"Eva," Falcon sighed warily, "Use caution."

"Wait. You're not going to try to stop me from finding him?" Falcon had just advised her to stay away from Hadrian and now he was…giving up? Something was not right.

"I have a feeling I couldn't even if I tried. Well, short of locking you in the dungeon. However, you're an honored guest and that is not the way the Validus Clan treats their guests. But, when things go badly, which I'm sure they will, please, scream as loud as you possibly can so that I may find you."

Without another word, Falcon turned and walked away. Eva stared after him, more confused and conflicted than before. Was she being foolish?

Probably, she thought with a shrug as she mounted the stairs. She still wanted to speak with Hadrian. Only he could answer her questions and his answers would hopefully help her get her thoughts in order.

A flicker of movement caught her eye when she reached the landing. Instinct whispered to turn left and she did, cautiously making her way down the dark hall. There were no lights, no sconces or candles, leaving the corridor crowded by shadows. The hall ended at a set of ten-foot high double doors, each adorned with an intricately carved, roaring lion's head.

Eva's steps stuttered to a stop as a chill snaked up her spine, causing the hair on her nape to stand. This was insane. She was insane and she was quickly tipping over into stalker territory. Here she was, standing outside his room and hunting him through the halls like an animal.

That thought struck her like an upper cut. She was a half-breed. She didn't hunt people. She was more human than animal...wasn't she?

With a frustrated huff, Eva decided it would be best if she went back to the library.

Turning, she collided with a solid form that was concealed by the shadows.

"What are you doing here?"

Her gasp lodged in her throat as the cool, deep voice sent waves of startled pleasure through her body.

"Your Highness—"

"You were warned against coming here."

How long had Hadrian been behind her? Had he overheard her conversation with Falcon?

The sconces nearest to them blazed to life as Hadrian cupped her chin with his thumb and index finger, lowering his head to gaze directly into her eyes.

"I–I—"

"Wanted to speak with me again," he finished. "Would you like to step into my bedchamber and...discuss whatever it is you want in private?"

Eva could do nothing but squeak in response as Hadrian brushed her bottom lip with his thumb. His burning, black gaze lingered on her mouth before descending her body. Her heartbeat quickened as her breaths grew shallow, heat spread through her center while her breasts swelled. Lust. With a look or a simple word, this vampire could make her lust.

Focus, you came up here for a reason and it isn't to jump his bones, she chastised herself. She had a few choice things she wanted to say to this dark, menacing, drop-dead sexy, and absolutely arrogant vampire.

"You should leave."

Hadrian dropped his hand and Eva waited for him to disappear. Instead, he stepped around her and shoved the double doors open to enter his dimly lit, private chambers.

Eva exhaled a long breath she had not realized she had been holding. If he had not wanted her to follow, he would have teleported. So, she went after him.

A few candles burned, casting eerie shadows along the walls. She shivered from the lack of heat. A large bed dominated the room. The mahogany wood was thick and ornately decorated with scenes of ancient battles and the sheets were a deep crimson. To the right, a wide desk stood, the papers and books neatly organized atop the smooth polished surface.

A crystal decanter filled with a strange glowing silver liquid rested on a matching cut crystal tray, accompanied with glasses. Bookshelves covered the walls from floor to ceiling. Everything seemed a little too perfect, too organized, and much more normal than she had expected to find the vampire king's chambers.

The door slammed behind her, the force shaking the room.

Quicker than a blink, cool fingers wrapped around her throat as he dragged her toward him. Their bodies collided and a violent thrill of excitement frayed her nerves.

"I told you to leave," Hadrian roughly whispered in her ear.

"You also invited me into your room," she countered.

He spun her about and they went crashing to the bed. Hadrian moved over her, his hand leaving her neck to wrap her braid about his fist. He trapped her with his chest, pushing her into the mattress. Heat licked between her thighs as his hips settled over hers. Eva gasped for breath. God, this male was raw sexuality.

"A monster haunts these halls, little one," he hissed. "A bloodthirsty, half crazed demon that likes to make snacks out of little ladies like you."

Eva shivered as he ran his tongue over his fangs.

"If you're trying to scare me off, it isn't going to work."

He bent his head and inhaled a deep breath, his lips hovering over her pulse.

"You want my bite, don't you?"

Eva closed her eyes and swallowed hard. God help her, she did. From the moment they met, she wanted to feel his fangs sink into her flesh, to feel his tongue sweep over her pulse as he gently sucked.

Hadrian tugged on her hair, exposing her neck even more as his tongue lightly caressed the line of her throat. Eva moaned, slipping her arms around his shoulders. Damn, this man knew how to fire her blood. His lips teased their way up to her sensitive earlobe. Her fingers curled, her nails dug into his shoulders, drawing a hard growl from him.

In a flash of movement, he was across the room. His back turned to her.

"Run along," he grated.

Eva moved from the bed, her legs weak. "No," she said squaring her shoulders. "I really must speak with—"

"I'm not in a talkative mood, little one. I suggest you go."

Standing her ground, Eva lifted her chin in defiance. "Why haven't you kissed me?"

Hadrian turned, his eyes full of indecision. His gaze focused on her lips.

She had not seen him move, though he now stood behind her. "I have kissed you," his fingers skimmed over her neck to her shoulder, "here," his hands brushed the sides of her breasts, "and here."

A shiver raced up her spine as she held her breath hoping he would cup her breasts. Good lord—how could Hadrian make her so hot that her blood nearly boiled? How could he make her thoughts fade away until there was nothing but him?

"H–Hadrian," she said, her voice a soft whisper.

His lips tickled her ear as he spoke. "Yes, little one."

Her head lolled back against his shoulder as she struggled to regain her composure. She had been angry. She had wanted—Hadrian's lips caressed the tender flesh below her ear. Eva tried to focus, but her mind was consumed with a mess of erotic thoughts. Would he take her now? Would he lay her back onto the bed?

"Eva," he rasped against her ear, "you need to leave." His voice sounded torn, full of desire and yet still determined to push her away and end this.

No! This could not end. Not now. She wanted more, needed more. And she had come here with a mission. She had followed him because she had questions…right?

Hadrian felt his control slipping. His hands shook as he pulled away from her.

Eva slowly turned to face him and he had to look away. Her eyes glowed and reflected her need for him, her arousal and sweet vanilla scent was overwhelming. His fangs grew to lethal points, slicing his lower lip as his cock hardened and strained against the confines of his jeans.

How could he still crave her blood? He had fed.

Was Eva destined to be his next victim? Gods, he craved to kill her. His demon roared, delighting in the thought of draining her and slashing his own vein for her—

Make her mine.

Her heartbeat was a steady rhythm in his ears. It would be so easy. All he had to do was reach out…

Hadrian snatched her arm, his fingers encircling her wrist, the coolness of his flesh felt like steel wrapping around her. Eva did not resist when he pulled her to him.

He said nothing as he continued to stare at her as if he were contemplating tackling her to the ground and ripping her clothes from her body. The thought sent a jolt of pleasure skittering down her spine.

His black eyes shimmered with carnal need and undeniable desire. Then, with a simple blink, his gaze became void of all emotion, soulless and empty. His expression was unreadable. The sudden change told her that he was a master at hiding his true feelings, his true nature.

Hadrian silently struggled against his instincts to throw her back on the bed and claim her body, her blood, and her life. Releasing her, he forced himself to step back, retreating from the welcoming heat of her body.

"It is not safe for you here," he coldly stated, impressed that his words did not falter.

Eva watched him take another step back. Hadrian honestly believed he was a threat to her. Her stomach twisted as the rumors flooded her mind. *He'll suck the life right out you, down to the marrow in your bones. He's a devil, that one, a beast straight from the fires of hell.* Falcon, his closest friend, had warned her just moments ago about Hadrian being dangerous.

Knowing he was reaching his breaking point, Hadrian barked, "Have you no sense, woman? Get out."

His hard voice shattered her thoughts.

"I have questions."

"For the love of all the gods," he sighed. "It is not safe for you to be near me."

"Will you rip my throat out? Will you suck the marrow from my bones? Or will you play cat and mouse with me first, drawing out my death while you laugh?" No response. "I don't think you will."

"What makes you so sure?" he countered, his voice deepening.

"If killing me was your plan, you've had ample opportunities to do the deed."

Hadrian scrubbed his face with shaking hands as he turned and stalked to his desk. He needed a drink. With luck, the liquor would help to calm his roiling emotions. His fingers wrapped around the fragile neck of the crystal decanter as he poured the glowing silver liquid into a tumbler. The liquor burned in a delicious way as he gulped it down. Wiping his mouth with the back of his hand, he poured another glass.

Eva watched as he continued to drink the strange, glowing fluid. She had never seen anything like it and could only assume it was Silver Moon. She had heard about the liquor. It was rumored to be the only thing that could get a vampire drunk.

Great, Eva, you've driven him to drink.

Praying that the liquor would soothe his demon, she decided this would be the best time to start with her questions. Wetting her lips she asked, "Why did you leave me sitting in the snow?"

Hadrian carefully set the tumbler on his desk, idly tracing the rim with his index finger. "If I had not abandoned you, I would have torn your jeans from your limbs. And as I savagely thrust into you over and over again, I would have sunk my fangs into your lovely, elegant throat."

His voice was smooth as he poured himself another drink. His manner was relaxed and detached. Yet, Eva could sense the demon lurked just beneath the calm surface.

"Your blood would sweeten with your orgasm. The taste would have driven me to madness and as I came, I would have drawn on your vein until every last drop of your precious blood touched my tongue. Then, as I released your body, I would have ripped your throat out with my teeth and left you to be buried by the falling snow," he shrugged, "or to be eaten by wolves."

"You had me excited until that last part," Eva said.

"I was losing control. If I had not pulled away…" A twisted smile graced his perfect lips. "My demon wanted to kill, more than it has wanted anything in its entire unholy existence."

Was he trying to scare her again?

No matter what he said, fact was, he had done none of the things he described. He had recognized he was becoming dangerous and vanished.

"But you didn't hurt me. Well, except my pride. No woman wants to be left in the snow like that."

His gaze turned sharp then his eyes narrowed. The temperature of the room dropped as shadows descended upon his face.

"Perhaps I'm not making myself clear," he said, his voice hard. "Or," his gaze traveled over her, studying her from head to toe, "you want me this way, on the verge of losing control."

She swallowed hard. His heated, predatory gaze fixed on her as his voice deepened. Dangerous sexual intent burned in his eyes as he downed his liquor, savoring it as if imagining it was her blood. His eyes roamed her body. A pure masculine smile softened his features, as his fangs grew longer.

Eva gasped. God, she wanted this vampire. She had to use every ounce of her rapidly depleting self-control *not* to throw herself at him.

"Danger," he grated past his fangs, "it excites you."

Eva opened her mouth, ready to deny his words, but she knew whatever she said would be a lie. Was danger the reason she was so attracted to Hadrian? She always had a thing for bad boys and Hadrian was the worst kind. His reputation was deadly. His looks combined with his sexuality were lethal. He was a king amongst the vampires with nearly unmatched power, strength, and speed. He was the embodiment of all that had been denied her for the past nine years. He was sex, danger, and excitement. He was a true alpha male and she wanted him to claim her. Dominate her.

"Come here, Eva."

His voice sent waves of sensual vibrations throughout her body. Without a thought or a care, she came forward. In a whirl of movement, he spun her about, pinning her against the desk, trapping her with his body.

"I warned you," he whispered, "you should have left while you had the chance." His cool breath brushed her neck. "A feral beast haunts this castle and," his hands gripped her hips as his lips brushed her ear, "that beast is me."

His hands slowly moved up her sides, tracing the contours of her body. He removed her shirt and his fingers brushed over the exposed flesh of her breasts, outlined by her sheer lace bra.

Hadrian stroked his velvet tongue down the column of her throat. His hand dipped inside her bra. As he rolled her hardened nipples between his fingers, he pressed her forward with his chest, forcing her to lean over the desk. He nipped at her jugular and her knees went weak. He caught her to him, effortlessly supporting her with his body.

"I'll try to control myself for as long as I can. But you want me to behave like a savage, do you not?"

He gathered her floor length skirt in his fists, drawing it over her legs inch by painstaking inch. Eva bit her lower lip. She wanted to scream at him to rip the skirt away, but instead she worked to savor the sweet, torturous anxiety. Her breaths came in pants as fire skipped along her flesh. Heat collected between her thighs.

God, she wanted this male. She needed him. Now. Hard and fast. She needed him to claim her, to make her feel alive after so many years of pain and neglect. She had been waiting for this, dreaming of this moment for far too long. And now she had a stunning vampire as hot for her as she was for him, caution be damned.

Using his knee, he pushed her legs open, giving him better access to her. Eva moaned as he drew a finger over her damp panties. All he had to do was move the thin material of her thong aside...

"You're so hot," he said. His finger brushed her again and her entire body quaked. "So wet." Shifting, he held her skirt in one hand, bunching the material around her waist. He ran his fingers from her navel, between the valley of her breasts to cup her jaw. Turning her head, he ran his tongue over her sensitive earlobe before taking the tender flesh between his teeth. "Gods, you are ready," he whispered, as he rocked his hips against her. "You want the demon?"

Eva gasped as he moved against her again, brushing his hard length over her ass.

"You want me?"

All she could do was nod in response.

Hadrian took her hand in his and slowly drew their entwined fingers down her body, pausing to massage her breasts in turn, then her hip and then lower.

Eva's breath caught as he traced their fingers over her panties. A violent wave of pleasure washed over her as he drew her index finger along her silt.

Hadrian released her hand and pushed her forward, making her rise up on her toes. In this position, her skirt was pinned between her hips and the desk. With both of his hands free, he captured her wrists and placed her palms on the smooth polished surface, giving a silent command not to move.

He cupped her ass, then leisurely ran his strong hands up her arched back, over her shoulders, then down to her breasts. He kneaded her breasts and Eva silently prayed he would remove her bra.

Releasing her breasts, he moved his masterful fingers lower. One hand flattened against her belly, his fingers splayed, filling the area between her hips as the other continued down. He began to stroke her through her panties, the pad of his index finger casually rubbing along her clitoris.

Eva trembled. If desire had not robbed her of her voice, she would beg him to tear her panties away and demand he bury himself deep within her. She knew there would be pain at first, but she was on the verge of coming and craved to feel him filling her.

"Tell me what you want," he grated.

She could hear the change in his voice and sense the darkness rising within him. His fangs would soon extend, if they hadn't already.

Their stark white would shimmer in the candlelight, long and razor sharp. Would he bite her? Dear heaven, she wished he would.

He increased the pressure and speed as he worked his hand over her, drawing sigh after sigh from her lips.

"Say it, Eva," Hadrian rasped. "Tell me what you *crave*."

Her breath seized in her lungs as his fingers moved to the edge of her panties and...stopped. He gently teased the flesh along the hemline. Her rapidly beating heart skipped a beat as he toyed with her, tortured her. God, surely the anticipation would kill her.

"Come on, little one," he urged.

She swallowed, praying her voice would work, "Hadrian."

"Hm?"

"I–I want you." Eva's words ended with a gasp as the tips of his fingers curled beneath the seam of her panties.

When she wriggled her hips in anticipation and moaned with sexual frustration, he chuckled, "Sorry, sweet, but," he pressed his hard length firmly against her backside once more, "can you be a little more specific?"

"P–please, Hadrian."

"Tell this demon what you want," he encouraged as he flicked her clit with his thumb.

Eva moaned as her body arched in pleasure. Damn, she was close to coming.

"This is your last chance, Eva. Tell me what you want and I will show you every bit of the monster I am or leave."

Eva blinked in surprise. Hadrian was offering her an out. If she did not answer him, he would pull away and deny her—No. He would deny them both.

A shadow of doubt crept into her mind. Was he truly worried he would lose control, that he would harm her...or worse? She knew his style of lovemaking was rumored to be rough. Did he think she was too frail?

Eva shoved her doubts aside. They had come this far and there was no turning back. She gave a silent prayer in the hopes that she would not regret her decision and took in a deep breath. She had to focus on creating a cohesive sentence. Her mind was consumed with desire, her body burning with need, but she would give him exactly what he wanted. She may be a virgin, but shy was not an element in her personality.

"Vampire," she bit out as if it were a curse, "I want you to take me. I want you to drive your cock into me again and again. I want you to make me come so hard I scream."

His growl shook the room as he tore her panties from her. The destroyed silk drifted to the floor as he pulled her hips roughly against him. He dipped a long finger inside her and began to circle her clit with his thumb.

Eva's arms weakened and she slid further along the desk. He inserted a second finger, curling them upward. The delectable sensation sent her over the edge. Her back arched, her nails bit into the desk, marring its smooth façade as she wildly rocked her hips against his hand. He groaned as he followed her rhythm, thrusting his shaft against her backside.

"You're so tight," he hissed past his fangs.

Eva came with a scream, her inner muscles clenching his fingers. Her body shook as waves of ecstasy crashed over her. Hadrian didn't stop, forcing her to ride out her pleasure as he continued to work her with his hand. Glorious tension began to build within her again as he stoked her passion to dangerous heights.

She heard his zipper release. Licking her lips in anticipation, she reached out to steady herself, preparing for his invasion. Her hand brushed something cool and sharp; an annoying sting penetrated her lust-clouded mind.

Hadrian frozen and Eva groaned. She couldn't wait anymore.

"No. No, don't stop," she gasped between pants, vaguely aware of the sticky moisture pooling beneath her palm.

She pressed her hips back in invitation, but he released her. Unable to support herself on trembling legs, Eva sagged against the desk. Was he taking off his pants? Eva peeked over her shoulder. Hadrian was still as a grave, his face etched with harsh lines of hunger, his black eyes sharp and feral. His chest heaved, the sound of his ragged breathing was deafening as he fought to maintain control.

She tried to push herself up, but her hand slipped and she fell to her elbows.

"What the hell?" she whispered, glancing down. A gold letter opener rested just beneath her fingers.

Blood.

Rivulets of crimson snaked down her fingers and smeared over the desk. The sight was as effective as a bucket of ice water, extinguishing her lust.

Eva cautiously stood, careful to make no sudden movements. Her skirt fell down her legs. She didn't bother looking for her shirt as she turned to face the vampire.

Hadrian took a step back. His hands fisted at his side, his muscles strained from the effort to remain still.

His black as death eyes remained fixated on her hand. Eva tried to will herself to stop bleeding, but she wasn't a vampire and couldn't command her body to heal. And her mixed blood prevented her from healing as quickly as a purebred.

"Your blood," he said, his voice deep and harsh, no longer his own. "So...sweet. You smell so sweet. Like warm vanilla sugar." His tongue traced over one long fang then the other.

Hadrian struggled to look away as memories assailed him. The scent of her blood acted as a catalyst. Images of Imbrasus slaughtering whole shifter packs made his stomach roll. The taste of virginal shifter blood filled his mouth as Imbrasus greedily fed from a young woman's thigh. God, Eva's blood would be even better, the right blend of spices. She was the perfect combination of...

Attack. Pin her down. Take her body. Take her blood.

Hadrian trembled as he grappled with his demon. Using every bit of self-control he possessed to restrain his basic instincts, he rasped, "Scream."

Chapter Thirteen

Eva felt her cheeks pale and her eyes widen with alarm.

A demon stood before her, ready and eager for a kill. A terrified chill shook her as he licked his lips, then his fangs. The whites of his eyes were completely consumed by unholy black; their depths glowed red hot, like flames from the bowls of hell.

In that moment, she knew she was staring at death.

He wanted her to scream, but her throat was too tight. Swallowing hard, she tried to dislodge the lump of terror that choked her.

"Damn it, Eva, scream!" He rasped again.

Fighting to mask her fear, she calmly nodded. She took in one measured breath, then another. If she showed any signs of fear, his predatory instinct may take over and she would be a nice snack.

As she filled her lungs once more, she wondered if he had overheard her conversation with Falcon. The knight had instructed her to scream when things took a turn for the worse and...they just had.

It took every ounce of strength Hadrian possessed not to lunge at her. Tension coiled within him. His hands fisted, clenched and released only to repeat the pattern.

Take her. Drink her. Claim. The demon chanted as scenes of the past played like a silent film in his mind. Smoke, flames, the scent of burning flesh, the taste of blood, and the glorious sensation of feeling a mortal's life end.

He prayed for strength.

Eva took a hesitant step toward the door. His heart stopped, his lungs froze as if filled with cement as every muscle in his body clenched.

She thinks to flee.

The thought enraged him. He snarled and advanced. This delectable little half-breed would not escape him. She *belonged* to him. Her body, her blood, even her very soul was *his*.

"Hadrian," she whispered, finally finding her voice. His eyes shimmered with deadly intent. Filling her lungs to capacity, she screamed and his lips twitched with a delightfully, evil smile.

He reached out, his claws swiping at air as she was whirled away.

Falcon faced his king and shoved Eva behind him, blocking her with his body. Hadrian studied the knight with wild, intelligent eyes. Holding up his hands, Falcon stepped forward.

"I have no weapon," he said in an even tone.

Hadrian growled, his lip curling over his dagger like fangs.

"Breathe," Falcon calmly instructed, "Just breathe. Slow and steady. Focus."

"Her blood," Hadrian hissed.

Falcon did not take his eyes off his king as he picked up Eva's shirt. Tossing the balled fabric her way, he ordered her to cover her wound. She quickly wrapped her injured hand, concealing the wound as best she could. Though the intoxicating scent of her blood still filled the room and teased the king's senses.

Closing his eyes, Hadrian's chest rose and fell as he took in deep breaths. His claws vanished as his fangs slowly receded.

Her heart clenched when he opened his eyes and whispered, "I'm sorry." His simple words possessed an undertone of shame.

"Wait," she called as he faded into nothing.

Sorrow, regret, fear, hunger, need, and hate. Every emotion swirled like a storm within his eyes. His soul. In that one unguarded look, she had seen his *soul*. She had seen *him*.

Falcon turned on her. "What the hell just happened?"

Eva jumped at the force of his voice. Falcon stalked to her, snatched her wrist and unwrapped her hand, revealing her wound. Blood ran freely and dripped from her fingertips. With a curse, he shredded the shirt, using only the unsoiled strips to gently dab at the gash that extended from the base of her left palm diagonally to the tip of her index finger.

"We need to clean this," he said. Tugging on her wrist, he led her to the bathroom, which was skillfully camouflaged by the wood paneling, the door blending seamlessly into the wall. Releasing her, he handed her a towel to provide her more modesty and turned to rummage through the cabinets.

Eva set her destroyed shirt on the counter. Squeezing her eyes shut, she rinsed the blood from her hand. She had not noticed the pain or the coppery stench until Hadrian had vanished. Now, her stomach rolled as she imagined how her hand must look.

"Here, let me see," Falcon insisted.

Eva blindly turned toward his voice.

He chuckled as his fingers encircled her wrist once again. "Don't like blood?"

She shook her head. "Never have."

He teased, "You would make for a terrible vampire."

"I would die of starvation, if that is even possible. I can't stand the sight, smell, or taste of blood." *But when I saw Hadrian's blood, I wanted to lick it.*

"This is going to sting," Falcon warned before brushing a cotton ball over her palm.

Eva winced, but kept her eyes closed.

"What is that?"

"The closest thing to an antiseptic/antibiotic I can find."

She heard Falcon unscrew a cap and set it on the marble countertop. The pungent odor of the salve stung her nose.

"Smells like something I want rubbed into my gaping wound."

Her sarcasm was not lost on Falcon. "Believe me, this is the best. It is what we use to treat injuries caused by poison tipped weapons."

Eva nodded, she knew there was only one type of poison in existence that could kill a vampire…but she did not know what it was or how to get it. The vampires tried their best to keep their weaknesses secret.

"It is made by the Shaw and works wonders," he explained.

The Shaw. She had heard the name once or twice, but the pack had known very little of the powerful witch tribe.

"You can open your eyes now."

Eva heard Falcon turn the water on. He rinsed off his hands while she decided to brave a peek at her hand. Falling against the counter, Eva gazed at her hand, speechless.

"The Shaw know their stuff," he added, drying his hands.

Shaking free her shock, Eva said, "That is amazing."

"Just like magic," Falcon chuckled as he leaned against the counter, crossing his arms over his chest. "So, are you going to tell me what happened?"

Eva groaned. How was she going to explain this?

100

"Is this," he motioned to her ruined shirt, "why you followed me?"

"No." Falcon raised a brow and Eva amended, "Well, not the only reason."

"Eva, it doesn't matter to me if the two of you decide to enjoy each other's company," he stated. "It would not be the first time a king had relations with his ward." She opened her mouth to speak, but he held up a hand and said, "Just explain what caused the drama."

"I cut my hand on a letter opener," she answered. Falcon was not interested in details and she was not interested in sharing. "That is when his vampire side came out to play."

"The scent and sight of the blood," he said nodding his head in understanding.

"Do you think His Majesty will be okay?" she asked, nervously biting her lower lip.

Falcon rubbed the back of his neck and let out a heavy sigh, "He hasn't been tested like this and his mind…I really don't know. I think it would be wise if you were to stay at another of our Clan's properties, at least until things…settle. We have a manor house not far from here. I'll be heading there tomorrow. You should come with me. The nobles will be gracious hosts."

Sadness and guilt combined to choke her. This was her fault. If only she had listened to Falcon, Hadrian would not be dangling on the cliff of madness right now. And the knight was right. It would be for the best if she relocated. She had become obsessed with the king; he plagued her thoughts and appeared in her dreams. There was also that explosive sexual chemistry between them. Her body went liquid every time they were together and her self-preservation deserted her. Their passion was lethal. Yes, she should leave.

A sharp pain pierced her heart and spread through her chest leaving her feeling numb as something inside roared in revolt. Outrage fired her blood as resignation and depression formed a cloud in her mind.

Eva massaged her temples with trembling fingers as a tornado of conflicting emotions swept through her. Her rational side firmly agreed with Falcon, while something deep within her seethed. As the thought of packing her bags in the morning surfaced, her skin crawled and her stomach twisted, leaving her feeling sick.

Eva swallowed hard, hoping to suppress the growl she could feel ascending in her throat. This reaction was not normal. Well, not normal for her. The inner turmoil she was currently feeling could be compared to what a purebred female might experience when contemplating leaving her mate.

Don't be ridiculous, she chided. *I'm no purebred and even if I were, the likelihood of a vampire being my intended mate is slim to none.*

Nevertheless, this was confusing and only strengthened her rational side's argument. She would pack and she would leave with Falcon. She was no good for Hadrian in his current state and to stay would be selfish.

*　　　　*　　　　*　　　　*

A brutal, unholy roar ripped through the night, the force vibrating the ancient mausoleum, dust and rubble rained down upon Hadrian. He howled until his lungs felt as if they would burst. Gripping his head with shaking hands, he fell to his knees between the stone tombs.

Her blood.

He shuddered.

Sweetly exotic, his mouth had watered while the demon begged for a taste. His fangs ached and his throat burned. Hunger twisted his gut as bloodlust shoved him over the edge into the black, bottomless pit of madness.

Deranged.

He had been seconds from attacking Eva, seconds from sinking his fangs deep into the tender flesh of her elegant neck and feasting on her intoxicating essence.

Hunt her, the vampire chanted.

Lashing out, he turned his murderous desire towards the floor. His knuckles cracked, bled, healed, cracked, bled, and healed again and again as he wildly punched the stone, which quickly turned to powder beneath his blows.

Scrubbing his face with dust-covered hands, he leaned back on his heels. "Control," he rasped as he sucked in rapid breaths, drowning Eva's scent with the decaying odor of the crypt. Frantically trying to deaden his senses.

The evil, sickening, memories began to retreat to the fringes of his mind as the tension of his body slowly eased, leaving him feeling drained. Hadrian collapsed and landed with a resounding thud. He sprawled out, allowing the bone chilling cold of the floor to seep into his skin.

He should have teleported the instant she followed him into his room. All rational thought vanished when it came to Eva. His sense of honor, decency, and responsibility became non-existent when they were together.

If he had thought last night had gone too far, tonight had been worse. Why could he not control himself? Whenever they were alone he behaved like an untried lad. His body yearned to feel her soft and pliant beneath him and he found it impossible to keep his hands off her. And he wanted—no, needed her. Only her. Only Eva.

Hadrian cursed. Eva had been brought here to be his ward, not his mistress. She deserved better. She deserved not to be attacked or used and he knew he could offer her nothing more in his damaged state. He had meant what he told her by the lake, these encounters would have to end and yet, he had almost taken her virginity and her life twice since then.

Fuck, he was a twisted piece of work.

And her blood, he thought with a low growl. *It would taste like ambrosia, the food of the gods.*

Closing his eyes, Hadrian imagined biting into her plump lower lip. He would sweep his tongue over the ruby droplets before claiming her mouth with a soul satisfying kiss.

A vicious snarl rumbled his throat as his fists slammed against the floor, cracking the stone.

He could not allow himself to think of such things, especially when his control was this razor thin. He could very well snap, teleport to Eva's room and—

Hadrian refused to finish that thought.

Instead he shifted his thinking to what he had discovered. All drama aside, he had finally lifted the veil of mystery that surrounded Eva. Her blood had revealed everything.

Half witch, half jaguar shifter, a perfectly stunning and lethal combination.

As he lie, gazing at the high, arched ceiling, realization hit him like a blow to the chest.

On the next full moon, Eva might transition. She had raw, untainted power in her veins; magic so strong it had hit him like a physical force when she had cut her hand. It hadn't been the scent or sight of her tempting blood, but the strength of her magic that had struck him, as he had been about to thrust into her.

Why had he not noticed the signs?

You were distracted by her charms.

From the moment she had entered the castle, Eva had been exhibiting the classic symptoms of a pre-transitioned shifter. Restlessness, she could hardly remain still. As she watched a film, she constantly shifted in her seat. While reading, Eva would twirl her hair and bounce her leg. Insomnia, Eva wandered the keep and grounds for hours, spending many sleepless nights exploring. Then there was her appetite. Over the last few days Eva had begun to double her caloric intake. Her body needed the energy for her upcoming transformation. And her sex drive…

"I want you."

He groaned. He would never forget the sound of her voice when she said those simple words.

"She doesn't want you. She is confused," he told himself as he fought the memories of Eva bent over his desk, ready, willing…begging him to take her.

Hadrian's cold body instantly came to life. An excited thrill sprinted down his spine as he bit out a string of curses that would make a demon blink in shock.

A low, deep growl echoed in the mausoleum as his body went up in flames. His cock strained and his sac ached as he struggled to keep his fantasies under control. He would give what remained of his shattered soul to be the male to service Eva. Closing his eyes, he gave into the erotic images of her riding him, her amber eyes glowing with desire as she licked her luscious lips and rocked her hips against his, taking him deep.

It would never happen.

He refused to take advantage of her. She would be helpless, vulnerable, and delirious with need. And he would allow no other male to see to her needs. Jealously exploded within him at the thought. If he couldn't have her, then no one could. Of course, this news meant that she would not be under his protection forever.

Mine, the demon within him roared. Eva was his. She belonged with him. Rage boiled his blood as he thought of another touching her.

"Gods," he groaned, "what is wrong with me?"

Eva belonged to no one, least of all him.

Right now, he needed to wrap his mind around his discovery and somehow find a way to tell her. How was he to convince Eva she was part witch? Hell, she thought she was half-human. And, he needed to find out if she would transition.

Why had Eva's mother not told her of her heritage? Also, why had Isabella not made arrangements for Eva to be sent to live amongst her family, the Shaw witch tribe, after her death? Had Isabella known Arsenio would take Eva? And why would he abduct her, with Eva being half-witch, shifter law did not apply to her. She owed no loyalty to the pack.

Eva had hungered for freedom for nearly nine years, never knowing she could walk away at any time. What reason could the alpha have for locking Eva away from the world? Did he and Isabella have some type of understanding? And, knowing that Eva was not the typical half-breed, why would he have sent her to live amongst the vampires? Unless, he didn't know Isabella was a witch.

There were too many questions, too many conflicting possible answers crowding his mind. The confusion was a welcome distraction from his madness and hunger.

Hadrian pushed himself up and came to his feet. Dusting off his clothing, he calmly ran his hands over his short hair. He would solve the puzzle that was Eva, but he must prioritize and formulate a plan.

First, he needed to know if she would transition. Judging by the scent of her blood, her magic was ripe and if she changed it would take place on the next full moon.

"Tomorrow."

Chapter Fourteen

A prickling sense of awareness skittered across his nape.

Sun rise.

Closing his eyes he imagined what it looked like. Brilliant shades of glittering gold, burnt orange and light pink would dance together as the sun peaked over the white-capped mountains. Centuries had passed since he had seen the magnificent sun. Much to his dismay, Hadrian had yet to develop the ability to walk in daylight like Dorian Vlakhos, king of Mylonas Clan had. Then again, the vampire was two thousand years older than he and also possessed the ability to read other's thoughts, another trait Hadrian did not hold, thank the good lord above. He had enough troubles.

Exhaling a heavy sigh, Hadrian glanced to the bookshelf and saw the bright red spine of the journal that could possibly hold the answers he sought. Imbrasus had spent centuries studying the shifter tribes while taking detailed notes. He documented his findings, observations, and the results of the horrific experiments he performed on his subjects within that journal.

Another tingling sensation spread down his spine. His senses grew sharp as he stilled.

He was not alone.

"Reveal yourself, witch," he commanded.

"Now there is no reason to snarl."

The air sparked with electricity as a young woman took form. Her red, crushed velvet robe swirled around her legs as her black, shoulder length hair whipped back from a nonexistent wind.

"I only wish to help," she insisted, her broad smile touching her deep brown eyes. The darkness of her hair and eyes made a shocking contrast to her pale, porcelain face and ruby lips.

Hadrian recognized the witch immediately. She had been Queen Kerstyn's maid of honor.

"Forgive me, priestess," Hadrian said, giving a stiff bow. "I did not realize it was you."

She shrugged, "No worries, and please, call me Silvie. I really hate being formal. It's just so…odd. Then again, I'm still new with," she waved a hand at her robe, "all of this. May I have leave to address you by your given name?" He nodded. "Wonderful. You're looking well, insanity does suit you"

"Why have you come?"

"You need my help. Unless you don't want to know how to save your Ward."

"Save Eva from what?"

His question was a demand. Silvie's smile grew brighter. "She's got you sprung."

He frowned, obviously lost.

"You need to study more phrase books."

"Later. Tell me, what or who threatens Eva."

Silvie sat, her small frame swallowed by the high backed, oversized leather chair that stood just before Hadrian's desk. She smoothed her robe over her lap then tucked her hair behind her ears. Her eyes drifted toward the bookshelf and the crimson journal. "*His* accounts will not help you." Returning her gaze to Hadrian she continued, "Nor will his demon's memories."

Hadrian was not at all surprised the priestess knew of his dark secret, the reason for his insanity.

"Are you stalling, witch?" Hadrian snapped.

"Not at all," Silvie insisted with a shake of her head.

"Who threatens Eva?"

"Your Ward threatens herself."

Hadrian's frown darkened, casting shadows over his obsidian eyes. "Explain."

"According to my uncle, the Shaman, there have been a total of three cases where shifters and witches have produced offspring." Silvie leaned forward, her fingers gingerly wrapped around the hilt of the gold letter opener.

Hadrian cursed. Had he been holding his breath? Yes, his entire body tensed the instant Silvie's eyes fell on the small, glittering dagger.

Silvie slowly turned the letter opener over in her hand.

"You got a good whiff of her blood, did you not? Tell me, what do you predict will happen to Eva come the full moon tonight?"

Hadrian forced his gaze from the gleaming metal. Though Falcon had washed away her blood, Eva's scent lingered. His fingers twitched as he thought of snatching the letter opener from her.

He cleared his throat, "Her blood is thick with magic and I believe she will transform."

"It's possible, she may experience the change," she shrugged, "but that is up to you." Silvie set the letter opener back on the desk and Hadrian resisted the violent urge to grab for it. His demon snarled, how dare the witch touch what did not belong to her.

Silvie gave him a wink as if she'd heard his thoughts. "Oh, yeah, you've got it bad."

"If you are implying that I'm in love with my Ward, you are mistaken," he hissed.

Denial, Silvie thought, as she held up her hands in mock surrender. "I am implying nothing." *I'm stating a fact,* she mentally finished. She didn't need to rile the king. She had plenty of other things to do and she didn't need to add any more stress or drama to her life. Silvie had thought becoming a priestess of her tribe would simplify things. A life without complications: no men, no sex, no love and no children. Nothing messy. Boy, had she been wrong.

Silvie shook her head. Now was not the time for reflection. Selecting her words carefully, just as her uncle taught her, she continued, "Unlike a shifter-human hybrid, Eva's magic is not diluted. As a matter of fact, she is pure magic. Human half-breeds cannot change, or use the powers of their animal spirit because they are too weak. So, what is Eva's problem? She is too strong. Shifter. Witch. Both dominate, both fighting to subdue the other. The animal within her wants to transform and run through the trees, wild. But witches don't take the forms of animals."

A tick developed in Hadrian's jaw as he intensely listened, absorbing and processing the information.

Eva was a threat to herself. Her very own DNA was warring with itself. His gut twisted as if he had been stabbed with a jagged dagger. He knew what Silvie implied.

"Tonight, when the full moon rises, Eva will begin the change, but she will die."

Hadrian's fists slammed on the desk as he stood. His chair flew back, colliding with the wall. Black rage consumed his eyes. His demon howled.

The witch didn't cower, nor did she tremble or scream. Silvie gazed up at him, calm and perfectly serene.

"Death cannot have her," Hadrian roared.

His fists clenched and unclenched at his sides. His chest was deathly still as he took in no breath. His heart frozen in time, the blood in his veins paused as he grappled with his demon.

"Control, Your Majesty," Silvie cautioned. "Please, sit."

With a thought, Hadrian drew his chair back, but he did not reclaim his seat. His muscles were too stiff.

"First," she leaned back, thrumming her fingers on the arms of her chair, "what are your feelings towards your Ward?"

Blinking, Hadrian fell back in his seat. "What?"

Feelings? He had none besides rage and lust.

"Never mind. My question was nothing but a distraction," she said with a shaking of her head. "There is only one way to save Eva from the bony, icy grip of death." She paused and Hadrian wondered if the witch were doing it for dramatic effect, to collect her thoughts, or to torture him. He gripped the desk in an effort to maintain control, his claws cutting the wood.

Silvie smirked. Hadrian eagerly, desperately, leaned forward. His gaze was sharp and determined as he silently waited for her to continue.

Yep, poor vampire is in love, Silvie thought before her uncle's voice invaded her mind. *Everything is falling into place.*

"What are you willing to sacrifice?"

"Name the price," he demanded. Hadrian would gladly sell what remained of his shattered soul to save Eva.

"Very well," Silvie stood, "Death."

"Done." Hadrian came to his feet, tearing his shirt from his chest. "Do you require a weapon? I have many." He motioned to the array of glinting swords and knives, which hung amongst an assortment of ancient weapons that decorated the stone walls of the room.

Silvie fought to not look at Hadrian's sculpted abs and chiseled arms.

"You misunderstand."

"Please, take my life. I offer it willingly."

"If you are to save Eva, you must sacrifice death."

Hadrian could not move, could not form a simple thought as Silvie's words circled around and around in his mind until they became a part of him, piercing his heart and branding his soul.

Sacrifice death.

He wished for death to claim him daily. He longed to never hear the voices again, to never again feel the unquenchable, burning bloodlust. For centuries, his only solace was in knowing that death would eventually come for him. The reaper would escort him to hell and he would drag his demon along with him.

He prayed for one moment of peace. No battles within himself. No overpowering desire to kill, to maim, to feel a mortal's life fade beneath his lips, to claim Eva. Peace. Death was peace.

Eternity. His torment would last for eternity. Forever suffering. Forever haunted by the bloodcurdling screams of the innocents slain by the demon lurking within him. Forever enduring the smell of burning flesh and the pale, stricken faces of the corpses.

He had hoped by returning to his clan, he could help restore his people to glory and then the curse that befell all the rulers of darkness would claim him.

"What of the Death Curse?"

"You will be exempt, like King Dorian of the Mylonas Clan," Silvie answered.

His claws grew even longer, digging into the desk.

Why could he not just exchange his life for Eva's? Why could he not die?

You will never be rid of me, the demon whispered.

Despair welled within him as the demon laughed.

A roar ripped from his chest as his fists slammed down upon the desk.

"You know, most would gladly relinquish the possibility of death."

"Most don't know my torment," he snarled, dragging his claws across his chest, slicing his flesh.

Silvie barely resisted the urge to cringe as the vampire's skin tore and knitted back together. His eyes glowed with an evil light, his fangs lengthened to razor sharp points as his jaw snapped like a crocodile's.

Deep down Hadrian knew he didn't deserve the peace of death. The demon was more a part of him than his own soul. But in this he could not—would not be selfish. Eva's life was more important. She was young, her life only just beginning. Who was he to take her life from her? Beautiful, precious Eva deserved to live and if it meant he would have to suffer than so be it.

"Tell me what needs to be done," he said, his voice deep and unnaturally rough. The demon was perilously close to the surface.

"You will bind Eva to you. Her life force will forever be intertwined with yours. As long as you live, she lives. So you see, to save her from death, you can never die."

Hadrian knew nothing of the bonding act except that Dorian, the king of Mylonas Clan of vampires, had somehow tied his mate, Victoria's life to his own. She was not a vampire, but she was no longer human. Victoria didn't crave blood, though she could consume the sweet, coppery wine. She could walk in the sunlight and was as strong as any vampire. She would also never age and never fall ill.

"You will take her blood."

Hadrian's black eyes jumped with evil excitement as his lips curled with a cold smile. Silvie worked to suppress the instinct to recoil. "Drain her to the point of death, then share with her your own."

"As if making a fledgling?"

"No, don't give her that much, just enough to mix your blood. Then, you both must consume your combined blood. I hear a kiss is the easiest way. Simply nip her." Silvie ran her finger over her lower lip.

Hadrian's eyes closed as the scorching heat of lust licked at him like flames. His blood pounded in his temples as his shaft grew hard.

He would take her blood. It would warm his soul. Then, to feel her mouth at his pulse, drawing gently on his vein...to kiss Eva, to feel her silken lips beneath his, to take her breath into his lungs as their combined blood sweetened their tongues—Heaven.

Oh, fuck. He shuddered.

"Remember, Hadrian, control. You must keep your demon in check. Eva will be teetering on the edge of death, her body fighting itself. You will need to draw her back."

Hadrian gave a stiff nod and sent a silent plea to the heavens for help.

"Once I...bind Eva to me, what then? Will she be able to take animal form?"

Silvie's pupils dilated, constricted, dilated again then returned to normal. "I don't know. The future," she paused, shaking her head to clear the smoky haze of her premonition, "is unclear. Though I doubt she will *completely* transform. You know, become a large jungle cat. Her witch side is more dominant, after all. Her hearing, speed, and eyesight may improve. Or, she might be able to use the strengths of the jaguar at will, such as the cat's agility. Eva could get all the perks of being a shifter, without the side affects. No fur, no tail, and no hairballs. If they cough up hair balls," Silvie shrugged, "I don't really know."

Hadrian ran his hands over his head, his claws slowly retracting. Anything could happen. It was completely out of his control and beyond his knowledge and he hated that. Eva was one of nature's great experiments.

"This is a lot to wrap your mind around, but it will be even worse for your Ward. Have you thought of how you will break the news of her unusual parentage?"

Hadrian simply blinked at her. Damn, the witch was barely giving him time to think.

"Well, I think it would be best if you *show* her rather than tell her."

Chapter Fifteen

Instinct and the sound of clicking glass lured Eva toward the solarium. The metal shutters retracted as she entered, signaling the setting of the sun. The only source of light was a small desk lamp burning brightly on the second floor, casting shadows throughout the massive room.

Eva dropped her packed bags and mounted the winding iron staircase that led to the solarium's loft study. She was not surprised when she found Hadrian. Her instincts seemed to repeatedly draw her to him. He was busy riffling through a china cabinet filled with various dried flowers and foliage, which were kept in glass vials and beakers.

"Welcome," he said over his shoulder.

"Good evening, Your Majesty."

Without even glancing her way, he said, "You have packed."

The statement made Eva wince. "Falcon has made arrangements for me to stay at another of your properties."

"Yes, he has shared his plans with me."

Hadrian turned from the cabinet, holding a jar full of wolfsbane. Crossing to the cool steel table, he gently set the jar beside a sheathed dagger, a beaker of clear solution, and a less than full, tall glass of blood.

Had he been drinking it?

He is a vampire. Drinking blood is nothing out of the ordinary. She frowned as she realized she wanted to see him take a sip. She wanted to watch him put the rim to his perfect lips.

"Do you want to leave?"

Eva's attention snapped back to the king. "After what happened…Falcon thinks I should go—"

"You did not answer my question." Hadrian's hand shot out, his cool fingers wrapped around her wrist and pulled her forward, making her lean over the table towards him. "Do you *want* to leave, Eva?"

Wetting her suddenly dry lips, she answered with a quaking voice, "No."

Hadrian brushed her palm with the pad of his thumb in rhythmic circles. "Your wound has healed nicely."

"It was treated with a Shaw salve."

He absently nodded as he turned her palm upward. Slowly raising her hand to his lips, he whispered, "You have beautiful skin."

He kissed her palm and Eva sighed as her entire body began to tingle.

"I pray you can forgive me for my actions of last night." His breath skipped along her wrist causing her pulse to flutter.

"Y–Your Majesty, I should be the one to apologize. If I had not followed you—"

Hadrian pressed another kiss to her palm, making Eva's words end on a gasp.

"I should have exercised more restraint." His eyes darkened as they traveled down her body, desire flickered in their cold, black depths. "My behavior was not at all kingly."

Releasing his hold, Hadrian pulled away. Eva barely resisted the urge to reach out and draw him back.

"So, what is this project," she asked, trying to sound casual, if possible.

"This is a test conducted on all new fledglings to determine how strong they will become," he explained.

Eva stepped closer. Focusing on the flowers, she tried her best to ignore the blood.

"New fledglings? You mean, newly transformed vampires?"

He nodded and withdrew three shriveled flowers still attached to their stems from the jar.

"Have you changed someone?" she asked, glancing about the loft. They were alone.

"I have changed only one mortal. Falcon," he answered. "I have put this test together for you."

"Me? I have no magic in my blood."

"I suspect that you do."

114

His statement surprised her. What was it about her that made him think she was anything more than a weak half-breed?

"I'll participate, but don't get your hopes up. I'm only half-shifter."

"These dried flowers were once blooms of wolfsbane. If magic is present in your blood it will come back to life. The quicker it is revived and the brighter the colors glow—the stronger the magic. Do you know what determines a vampire's strength?"

"No."

"By sharing our cursed blood we can transform humans into demons. The magic that runs in our veins is very potent. The stronger the curse, the stronger the magic, the stronger the blood," he explained.

"The stronger the vampire," she added.

He nodded.

"Do you plan to test that blood?" She pointed to the glass.

"Yes, I want to show you the difference between mortal's blood and ours."

"I don't think anything is going to happen, but I'm game. I'm warning you though. I'm squeamish when it comes to blood. Can't even look at the stuff and the smell..." her words trailed off with a shiver.

Hadrian smiled and unsheathed the dagger. He dipped the tip into the cooled blood and then held it over the first flower. The crimson liquid dripped onto the shriveled petals.

"Nothing happen," Eva whispered.

"And nothing will. Human's possess no magic."

Hadrian licked the remainder of the blood from the blade before dunking it into the clear solution. When he raised the blade, the unmistakable scent of alcohol assailed her senses.

At least this is sanitary, she thought.

Hadrian pricked the tip of his index finger. Blood welled and he held his hand over the second sprig.

Eva didn't notice the gasp that escaped her lips as she stepped forward, hitting her hips on the edge of the table. Her gaze locked on the flower. Brilliant, vibrant hues of blue and purple blossomed to life as the stem began to sprout.

"Amazing," she breathlessly whispered. "I have never seen anything like that. Well, except on TV. Your blood must be really strong."

"I was sired by one of the original vampires," he stated coldly. He rounded the table to stand beside her. "Now, it is your turn."

"Damn," she sighed, nervousness bubbled in her stomach.

He rinsed the blade again. "Your blood taunted me last night," he said, his voice deepening, his breath sweeping along her ear. He drew a finger over her palm, mimicking her healed wound. "And it revealed your secrets."

"Secrets?" Hell, she could not think straight with this man so close.

Her blood. He had been talking about her blood.

"I know what you are, little one."

"What do you mean?"

"Allow me to show you."

Eva knew she should close her eyes. He was going to prick her finger. He was going to draw blood. The thought made her stomach twist and she prayed she would able to hold down her Fruit Loops, but she could not look away.

She felt no pain as the blade pricked her finger. A tiny bead of blood welled and Hadrian held her hand over the last dried flower. One. Two. Three drops fell.

Eva's heart hammered against her ribs as her breath seized. Shock cartwheeled down her spine. She felt her jaw drop and her legs went weak. Hadrian caught her to him, supporting her weight with his body. A bomb went off in her head and, for the first time in her life, she swore she would faint. Awe, confusion, astonishment, and fear whirled together like a hurricane in her mind.

This was…inconceivable. It had to be a mistake. It *was* a mistake. When Hadrian cut her finger, his blood must have mixed with hers. That was the only possible explanation for the wolfsbane blooming.

"It–That–I don't…" Eva shook her head. Closing her eyes, she began to take in one slow, deep breath after the other. Collecting her scattered thoughts, she began again, "I think your blood mixed with mine."

"It did not."

"This has to be some kind of trick," she argued.

"Never have I led you falsely."

"But this," she waved at her once shriveled sprig, its colors so intense it appeared to be glowing, "is impossible. I'm a half-breed. My blood is weak. Diluted."

"Magic is thick in your veins."

"No. It's not. It *really* is not," she protested. "I demand a retest."

"By all means," Hadrian insisted. Plucking another dried flower from the jar he laid it on the table before her.

"Do you have something else I can use to draw blood?"

Hadrian went to the china cabinet and retrieved a small pocketknife. He sanitized it with fresh alcohol, flipped it in his hand and offered her the hilt.

Eva reached out with trembling fingers. She hoped she would have the courage to cut herself.

Time froze as she struggled to calm her nerves and ignore the storm of mixed emotions that whirled through her.

Squeezing her eyes shut, she held her breath as the cool metal pierced her thumb. Peeking from beneath her lashes, Eva watched her blood drip onto the new flower.

She expected to hit the floor, but Hadrian caught her. Her body was numb, her muscles slack, her breathing was shallow while her heart beat out of control as the blossoming flower stared up at her.

Eva sputtered, her head reeling. It took some time before she could finally speak. "This isn't possible. I'm a half-breed."

"Yes, but you are not half-human."

"W–what am I?" Eva's voice quaked and angry tears stung her eyes as she silently prayed for strength. Chaos. Her thoughts were complete chaos as her world collapsed around her, falling like shards of glass from a perfectly polished, beautifully destroyed mirror. "What kind of freak am I?" she demanded, her hands forming shaking fists as the red of rage colored her vision.

"You are no 'freak,' little one, but a true treasure."

She snorted, "Spare me the 'you are special' speech. What the hell am I?"

"You are of shifter and Shaw descendent."

"Shaw? No." She shook her head. "This can't be. My mother was not a witch. She was mortal. She was human. She was…normal."

"You have magic in your blood; there is no escaping, no hiding from what you are."

"No." She shoved against his chest. "I don't have magic. This has to be a mistake."

"Science does not lie," he stated simply.

"No!" Eva began to thrash and Hadrian's arms tightened like steal bands, trapping her. "My mother was not a Shaw," she railed. Unleashing the storm of emotions that roiled within her, she pummeled his chest with her tiny fists. She kicked at his shins and scratched at his arms. Hadrian held her firm, absorbing every hit she delivered.

How could she not have known? Why had her mother said nothing? God, she had lived her entire life believing she was mortal and now…She had no idea what she was or what she would become.

117

"Let it out," Hadrian crooned as she continued to fight. "Let all your anger out."

After what seemed like a tortured eternity to Eva, her wild punches slowed until she sagged against his solid chest. She trembled as tears slipped down her cheeks like tiny rivulets, soaking his shirt. Hadrian gathered her closer, as if he were trying to shield her from the pain.

Fury simmered within her as confusion clouded her mind. She couldn't breathe. She couldn't focus. Everything she knew about herself, everything she knew about her parents had been a lie. Her vision wavered as the sharp, gnarled edge of betrayal pierced her heart. Why did her mother never tell her about her true heritage?

"All my life, I was lead to believe—Why would she do this?" Eva sniffled.

"I wish I knew."

"And my father, do you think he knows?"

Hadrian rested his chin atop her head. He began to stroke her hair, the long silken strands slipping through his fingers. Eva burrowed her face into his chest. His warmth chased away the chill of shock that had taken root in her bones.

Closing her eyes, she savored the comfort he offered and wrapped her arms around his waist, hugging him tightly. No one had held her or shown her compassion since childhood.

The sound of a slow, steady heartbeat lulled her as he began to massage her shoulders, her neck, and her back. The tension in her body slowly eased until she was completely relaxed and…purring?

Yes and she felt completely content and exhausted. Her head ached and her eyes burned with tears. She needed a nice, long soak in the tub, hot chocolate, and some Ibuprofen. But there was one question she had to ask before she could slink off to her room to self-medicate and hide away from the world.

"I've growled and I was just purring. I haven't been able to sleep because I crave movement. Every night I pace my room for hours or swim laps in the pool. With every passing day I find it more and more difficult to stay still long enough to watch a movie." Gathering her courage, she stepped back and she asked, "What is happening to me?"

Chapter Sixteen

Hadrian didn't answer. He did not have to confirm what she could sense. Instinct told her a full moon would rise tonight. When it reached its peak, she would change. Her body would contort. Her muscles would tear, her bones would snap as the animal within her awakened.

"Oh, god," she whispered on a shaking breath. Her pulse pounded like a drum in her ears, her anxiety deafening. "Will I become a jaguar?"

"I don't believe so. Your witch DNA should prevent a complete transformation."

"*Should?*" she asked. Her fingers trembled as she nervously played with her hair, twisting and braiding it.

"Last night, I did some research and found nothing of value. I spent nearly fifty years living amongst the various packs that inhabit Central and South America. I learned all that I could of shifter history, biology, physiology and anatomy. I studied their war prone and often war torn cultures. I observed behaviors, interactions, and ceremonies. Not once, in all the time I spent with the packs, did I hear of one such as you."

Eva's shoulders slumped. "Are you saying there has never been a half-breed like me?"

Should he share with Eva what the Shaw priestess had told him? All those like her had died, none surviving past the change, but she would be different. He would save her. He would share his blood with her, the vile essence of his soul, and bind her life force with his.

Hadrian felt his incisors sharpen. Running his tongue over them, he groaned. Eva's blood, he would finally know the taste of

Eva's blood. He had spent countless hours imagining how sweet, how hot she would be.

"So there is no telling what will happen to me?"

Eva's distressed, musical voice slapped him back to attention. "No," he answered.

Fear's icy grip claimed her. There was nothing worse than the unknown. Had there truly been no others like her? The Shaw lived in Europe while shifters were scattered about the Americas and Africa, with a few remaining in Asia. It was highly unlikely the two would have ever crossed paths.

Or, she thought with a horrified shutter, *none had survived to complete maturity.*

Lifting her chin, she used all the strength she had to combat her fear. Fate had dealt her another bad hand, but she would not fold.

She stepped back, breaking Hadrian's hold on her. "I just need to know one thing. Could I die?"

Hadrian's jaw clenched and she could hear his teeth grind together. His eyes flashed between turbulent red and deadly black as he grated, "I will not allow death to take you."

Eva exhaled the breath she had not realized she was holding. Swallowing hard, she fought the dread that threatened to choke her. Death was a possibility.

Silence pounded in her ears. She stood cemented to the floor. The stillness was deafening as realization seeped into her. Tonight, when the full moon rose, she could die, painfully and bloody.

Hadrian watched Eva. Would she faint? Would she run? Would she ever break free of the fear-induced trance that had settled over her? Her breathing was slow, shallow as she continued to stare, unseeing, unblinking. Gods, he wished he could hear her thoughts.

He hesitantly stepped closer. Instinct roared within him, demanding he take her back into his arms, that he try to reassure her with gentle words. But he knew nothing of comforting others and touching her—

"Hadrian." Her voice was low, barely a whisper.

He moved closer. He could feel the delicious heat of her body.

"When I transition…will you stay with me?"

Unable to resist, Hadrian gently brushed her hair from her face, the curls erotically slipping through his fingers.

"I vow, I will *not* leave you."

"Thank you."

Hadrian felt her shiver and steeled himself against the urge to pull her to him.

"I never thought I would die a virgin," she sighed.

"You will not die," he snapped.

The violent force of his voice shocked her.

"Did you hear me, Eva?" His fingers circled her wrist, bruising her. He pulled her to him, leaning over her, his lips a scant whisper from hers. "Death will not have you. Ever."

"Okay," she gasped, her fear, her anxiety of the coming night forgotten, replaced by undeniable need. God, she loved it when he was rough, something dark within her reveled in it. "You're right. No need to stress over something that may not happen."

"That *will not* happen," he corrected.

Eva nodded. If Hadrian said she was not going to be shaking hands with the Grim Reaper tonight, then she would believe him.

"Put death from your mind," he commanded. "All we must think on is whether you will turn jaguar or not. Until midnight, we will play the waiting game," he added.

Laughter bubbled within her, destroying the glass cage of uncertainty and anger that surrounded her heart. She loved when Hadrian used modern phrases. It clashed with his old accent and regal demeanor.

Enchanting was the only word Hadrian could find to describe Eva's laugh. He stood, spellbound. Damn, she was beautiful. Her eyes sparkled despite the fear that lurked in their amber depths. She was brave, willing and ready to face whatever came at her. Hadrian found himself wishing this strong and gorgeous woman could be his.

Eva wetted her perfect lips and Hadrian groaned. They were inviting—no, begging for a kiss and, sweet hell, he needed to sample her passion.

Unable to rein in his desire any longer, he leaned into her, melding their bodies together. Her breasts pressed hard against his chest, her hips cradled his erection perfectly.

Delicious tension coiled through her and gathered at her center. She could sense his resolve weakening and she eagerly rubbed against him, her fingers ran up from his wrists, over the roped muscles of his arms, and continued to his wide shoulders.

Her breath caught as his lips brushed hers. Not a kiss, but a tender caress. She trembled. Anticipation mounting, her pulse hammered in her ears, drowning out the world. All that existed was Hadrian. The betrayal of her mother was forgotten and the news of her impending transformation became a faint memory.

Hadrian's hands moved into her hair as his body enveloped her. His low, deep growl vibrated her chest and she would have swooned if he had not been holding her.

Digging her fingers into his shoulders, she rose to her tiptoes. Their lips brushed again. He groaned as she sighed. His grip tightened. A shot of lightening sprinted down her spine. She stroked his bottom lip with her tongue.

Hadrian whirled away and she stumbled back, hitting the table. His back was to her, his fists clenching at his sides. She could see the whites of his knuckles as his shoulders heaved.

Her hand shot to her mouth. Her lips tingled. Her body burned. She fought the tears triggered by the sharp pain of inadequacy, and the dull ache of disappointment. She wanted to scream. She wanted to hit him over the head with a very large, very heavy book—repeatedly!

"Why do you always pull away?" Eva demanded. "Is it because I'm a half-breed?"

"I care not of your parentage." *And I'm not good enough for you,* he finished, his jaw clenched.

"Don't lie!" Her words ended in a threatening growl. "What is wrong with me?"

"Nothing," Hadrian snapped.

Eva roughly ran her hands through her hair, barely able to contain her disappointment, anger and sexual frustration.

"I don't understand. There has to be a reason for you to continue to shut me down." She shook her head. Maybe his refusal was not personal. "Is it because I'm your ward?"

Hadrian cursed then said, "It isn't proper for us to have sexual relations."

Eva shrugged. She could care less about what was right. She existed alone on the fringes of otherworldly society, why should she care about what others thought? They would judge her and shun her for her birth regardless. Why should she also worry about what they thought of her actions?

"It's not as if the alpha would challenge you to a duel in order to defend my honor and I highly doubt he would demand for you to marry me." *My father may have sent me here hoping you would kill me. Or he sent me here knowing I would transition and possibly–No, don't you even dare finish that thought.*

"It is not honorable," he firmly stated. "You are my ward. As such, you have been placed in my charge. I will not use my position to take liberties—"

"Careful, your age is showing," she chided. "And you shouldn't feel as if you're taking advantage of your sweetly innocent ward. Have you forgotten what I confessed last night? I want you. Since we met I've been practically throwing myself at you."

Sweetly innocent, her words sliced his heart like a samurai sword. She was an innocent, a virgin and he was a depraved monster who would do more than ravage her. Eva deserved better than that, more than what he could offer. She needed a man who would be kind and gentle to her, who would go slow and—His fangs lengthened. A murderous rage built like a firestorm within him as he thought of another touching her, making her cry out in pleasure.

Hadrian scrubbed his face with his hands, the stubble on his cheeks scratching his palms.

"Why don't you want me?"

Hadrian's gaze snapped to her. His lips pulled back from his fangs as he hissed, "How can you doubt that I want you?" He advanced, his eyes narrowed. "You plague my every thought. I dream of touching you, of kissing you," his cool fingers wrapped around her upper arm, his grip hard, "of claiming you in one position after another. Every cell within my body craves to possess you."

Lust rolled off of him in violent waves. Eva was helpless against the tide. She was swept away by his seductively dark eyes and his velvet voice.

He tenderly brushed the back of his knuckles along her cheek. "So fragile. So mortal," he sighed. "You set me ablaze, little one. Your vanilla scent haunts me, ever taunting, ever inviting." He took in a deep breath and Eva's knees went weak. "You bring the demon out in me, forcing me to fight for control, for my very sanity." He released her, folding his arms over his chest, his shoulders slumping as if he were trying to shield himself. "Eva, you make me dangerous and I think–I know, making love to you would drive me insane." He took another step back. "And I couldn't bear it if I hurt you. Orworse."

The chilling sting of sadness pierced her heart. He was honestly afraid he would harm her, but she could prove to him he was not a beast.

"I want to be with you."

Fathomless, obsidian eyes stared at her. They glowed with a demonic light. "You do not know what you want. If you knew me…"

"I know you want me as much as I want you."

"Why?" His whisper was rough, his sharp, crudely intelligent, predatory stare challenging her. "Why do *you* want me?"

Chapter Seventeen

Words failed her as she gazed into his haunted obsidian eyes. She could see past Hadrian's ruthless exterior and the evil the vampire cloaked itself in. She saw his vulnerability, his uncertainty, and his pain. She could see his soul. Beaten and bruised, a perfect match to hers.

Mine, her instincts screamed. *He is mine.*

She did not know how she knew Hadrian was hers. She did not understand where the compelling sensation came from. But she could feel it in her heart, in her soul that this dark vampire belonged to her and she had to have him. She needed to claim him and she would. Tonight. To hell with her transition and death be damned.

"There is something about you. About us." She took a step toward him. Hadrian did not retreat, but his arms remained crossed, his expression stern, scrutinizing. "I can't explain it, but I'm drawn to you, consumed by my desire for you. I feel…I need you." She nervously wet her lips. "When you touch me, the world falls away. It's as if nothing exists except me and you." She closed the space between them. He continued to stare her down. "Being with you feels right. It's as if we are meant to be together."

Hadrian was not the only one staggered by her confession.

Exhaling, he whispered her name and lowered his arms. "The change could be affecting your emotions."

Eva expected his analytical mind would come up with a rational explanation for her feelings. So, she decided to show him exactly what she meant.

"There is something happening between us. You must sense it too. Why do you fight it?"

Without warning, she rose to her tiptoes, her ballet flats slipped off her heels. She cupped his face and kissed him.

Hadrian was stunned, swept away by a torrent of sensation. She was kissing him. Her silken lips firmly pressed against his as if daring him to pull away. He was too shocked to move, to respond.

It had been centuries since he had felt another's lips caress his. A kiss was an intimate act, a connection - a couple sharing their souls as their breaths intertwine. But he had nothing to share.

He did not wrap his arms around her. He wasn't even kissing her back. Hadrian stood like an ancient Roman statue, still and cold.

Eva stepped back, releasing him, ending the kiss. A red-hot blush burned her cheeks as she nervously tucked her hair behind her ears.

Epic fail.

She bit her lower lip, unable to look Hadrian in the eye. Anxiety fluttered like butterfly wings in her belly as her heart pounded. The word embarrassment did not even begin to describe how she felt. Eva risked a peek at him, glancing up at him from beneath her lashes. The hard look on Hadrian's face did nothing to help her self-esteem. She had finally gained the courage to kiss him and he glared at her as if she had just committed the worst kind of sin against him.

Hadrian could not believe Eva had just kissed him. His lips tingled and his body burned. He wanted to snatch her to him, to feel her body pressed tightly to his. Most of all, he wanted to claim her mouth and swallow her gasps as he buried himself within her. His hands fisted at his side, his jaw clenched, his muscles tensed. He fought the overwhelming need to pull her to him, to lay claim to her lips, her body, and her soul.

He could not have her. No matter how much he desired her, no matter how much she may want him, it was dangerous, and it was unwise. He had reasons, good reasons. So, why was his resolve weakening?

For the precious seconds her lips had caressed his, his feral, tattered soul had come to life. Unfamiliar emotions surged violently through him and wreaked havoc on his already chaotic mind. He was dazed, unable to process what was happening to him, unable to form a coherent thought past having Eva beneath him crying out in pleasure.

Eva took a step back, retreating, and his demon growled. Was she trying to get away from him? No. His heart slammed in his chest, his breaths came fast and hard. She would not escape him. She had unchained his lust and now she would pay.

"I'm sorry. I shouldn't have—"

Hadrian's hand shot out, his fingers circling her wrist, he pulled her to him. They collided and with a deep, animalistic growl,

Hadrian surrendered to his need, embracing his hunger. His resolve gone and his reasons forgotten, Hadrian captured her lips.

Eva gasped, overcome by his intensity, swept up in the torrent of his passion and need, which matched her own.

His teeth nipped at her bottom lip, demanding entrance. Eva complied and Hadrian swept his tongue inside, exploring, conquering. His fingers plowed through her hair. One hand cupped her nape as the other slid down her back to grip her hip.

Eva could not think as Hadrian continued to plunder her mouth, stealing her breath. He kissed her like a man about to meet the executioner.

Vanilla. She tasted so sweet. Her kiss was drugging, addicting and he knew he would never get enough. After this slight taste of heaven, he would never be able to deny her again. Divine. Eva was divine.

More, the demon chanted and Hadrian would oblige. He would claim her. Tonight, Eva would be his.

A growl rumbled his chest; his hands slipped down to cup her ass. He drew her up his body and Eva wrapped her legs around his waist. His erection strained against his jeans and Eva rocked her hips, grinding herself against his solid, thick length.

Drowning, she was drowning. Eva's fingers dug into his shoulders, desperately she clung to him. He would not pull away; he would not deny her this time. Hadrian, the dark king, would be hers.

Hadrian's grip tightened on her and Eva felt the air whirl around them. Gravity shifted for a moment as the world around them plummeted into darkness. Peeking, she saw candles eagerly spark to life, dispelling the shadows. A cool breeze swept in through the open balcony windows, carrying the clean scent of freshly fallen snow and forest, but she did not feel the cold.

Hadrian broke the kiss and drifted his lips over her jaw, down the hollow of her throat before drawing his tongue up to her ear.

A shiver of pleasure ran through her to him like an electric shock.

His muscles were tight, his need for her a painful ache. His hunger raged. He felt the beast within roar and he knew he was rapidly approaching the point of no return.

Hadrian reluctantly set her on her feet. His entire body trembled as he battled to maintain control of his dangerous passion. He did not want to frighten her with his intensity or strength. She was so small, so fragile. He needed to be gentle even though the last thing he wanted was to be gentle. He wanted to throw her on the bed, tear her jeans from her limbs with his claws and thrust in deep and hard.

Eva stumbled back a step, the backs of her legs hitting the mattress. Was he going to disappear? Was he going to spout off his reasons as to why they should not sleep together? Panic rose in her throat. She would not let him deny them again. Never again.

"Eva," he rasped. "Last chance." He towered over her, a dark warrior king. Her dark warrior king. "I intend to have you." He advanced, his movements smooth as if he were stalking prey, prepared to pounce if she tried to flee. But she wasn't going anywhere besides his bed.

She stared up at him, her amber eyes swirling with desire and undeniable hunger. She ran her hands down his chest, over his flat belly to the hem of his black shirt. He allowed her to remove the garment. His hands fisted as he stood, waiting for to her speak.

Hadrian groaned as her tiny tongue caressed her bottom lip and then growled as she tugged that same lip between her perfect white teeth. She lightly traced the lines of his muscled abdomen, following the lines lower until her nails skimmed over his hipbones.

He caught her wrists, holding them away from him. His chest heaved as he sucked in breath after breath. The heady scent of arousal clouded the air. He was on the verge of oblivion. One more touch, one more kiss, hell, one more heated glance from her would send him into a state of frenzy. He was barely hanging on to the shreds of his sanity. If she did not leave now, there would be no turning back. He would not be able to let her go.

"No–escape," he grated.

She slipped off her shoes and slid back onto the mattress, pulling him with her. Hadrian leaned over her, his large, powerful hands pressing into the blankets on either side of her.

"I will be gentle, I swear."

Hadrian prayed to every god he could name that his words were true. He did not want to frighten her, but more importantly, he did not want to hurt her. His strength was immense and his vampiric urges demanding.

His eyes flickered to her throat, her rapidly beating pulse beckoning him for a taste. The demon snarled and his fangs lengthened.

"Hadrian," she whispered, drawing his gaze to hers. His black as night eyes smoldered with need, insatiable hunger, and…possessiveness. A low growl slipped past her lips as waves of heat flooded through her. Eva gripped his biceps, her nails creating half-moon imprints on his pale skin. "I've waited too long and you've teased me too much. It ends now."

With a hard tug, she pulled him down on top of her.

Hadrian claimed her lips once more. Her tongue met his thrust for thrust, fueling the inferno of need within him. There was a whole other world within their kiss. Heaven and hell, blissful torture and he never wanted it to end. His little half-breed had unleashed a demon that would take immense pleasure in devouring her.

The sound of tearing fabric kissed her ears as Hadrian ripped her sweater, revealing her black, silk bra. His hands made quick work of the button and zipper of her skinny jeans. He peeled the dark denim from her legs.

Never did his lips leave hers. He kissed her frantically, deeply. Need roared within her, making her blood burn, and her core ache for him. He was drugging her with lust, her body responding of its own accord. Her legs locked around his waist, her hips rolled, her back arched as her sensitive flesh brushed against his shaft and soft pleas fell from her lips. She wanted, no craved to feel his cock press against her. She gasped as she imagined the crown slipping over her clitoris.

Eva could not wait anymore. She tugged at the waistline of his jeans, her fingers fumbled with the button. Her breath caught when she managed to liberate the metal. She found the zipper, pinching it between her thumb and index. Eva began to draw it down. After all their "encounters" she suspected he went commando. Breaking the kiss, she leaned up and angled herself so she could watch his shaft spring free.

Hadrian caught her wrists and pinned her arms over her head. Too fast, this was moving too fast, spiraling out of control.

"Not yet," he said when she turned her disappointed gaze up to him. "Now, be a good little girl and lace your fingers together." She complied. "You will keep them there until I say otherwise."

Closing her eyes, she bit her bottom lip and nodded.

This was completely out of character for him. True, he enjoyed being commanding in bed, but he also took and gave pleasure hard and fast. Making the act as impersonal as possible, but not with Eva. Never with Eva. He wanted to take his time with her. He wanted to savor every caress, every kiss, and every sigh that fell from her exquisite lips. For the first time in over a thousand years, he wanted to go slow, needed to go slow.

She had truly awakened him in more ways than one.

Hadrian rose up and stood bracing himself for his first view of her naked form. He had felt her body intimately pressed against his, he had cupped her breasts and stroked her sex, but he had never seen her completely bare.

The light of the candles caressed her body. Eva's eyes remained closed as he studied her angelic face, his eyes pausing on her enticing lips. Her dark hair fanned across the mattress, the locks tousled. His gaze slowly traveled lower to the elegant curve of her neck. As his eyes skipped over her pulse his fangs sharpened. A groan ripped from his chest as his gaze fell to her high, full, breasts that were tipped with hard, dark rosy nipples. They beckoned him. His eyes continued lower, to her narrow ribcage, over her flat, trim belly, flaring hips and smooth thighs.

With trembling hands, he removed her red thong.

The sweetest of curses fell silently from his lips. His mind went blank at the first sight of her female flesh. Glistening petals. He traced her folds with the tip of his finger…wet, hot, and unbelievably soft.

He took in a shuddering breath. *Control. Maintain control. Do not hurt her. Do not frighten her. Only pleasure.*

His voice was wicked and rough, his accent thick as he whispered, "I am going to make you come until you can't breathe."

Hadrian hooked his hands beneath her knees and drew her to the edge of the bed.

Control.

He knelt, settling his upper body between her thighs.

Control.

He circled one taunt nipple with his tongue and smiled when she arched, begging for more.

Control.

Hadrian skimmed his fingers up the insides of her thighs, over her stomach to cup her breasts. They filled his hands, her stiff nipples sensually teasing his palms. He brushed light kisses over her chest, nibbled at her collarbone.

"Hadrian, please. T–too slow." Her words ended on a gasp as his hot mouth clamped over a nipple.

He drew lazy circles with his tongue, flicking the hard nub. Her body writhed beneath him as he began to suck, hard. Harder.

She was gasping for breath when he finally released her nipple. Their eyes locked as he drew his tongue down the valley of her breasts. His fangs gently scraped her flesh and her body went liquid with heat. Her head fell back.

Hadrian seized her other nipple. Torture. Searing. Blissful agony coursed through her and gathered at her core. She restlessly moved against him, her hips undulated beneath his heavy torso, as her back arched, pressing her breast firmly to his mouth.

With every draw of his lips, with every tease of his tongue and nip of his teeth, Eva came closer and closer to the razor's edge. Her breath came in rapid gasps. Her body ached, pleading for release.

He cupped her breasts, kneading the sensitive flesh with his strong fingers, suckling each nipple in turn, and drawing out her torment until the world splintered. Eva cried out as the storm of ecstasy swept her away. Her hands fell, she gripped his head.

Hadrian swiftly snatched her wrists again, imprisoning them. Gripping her chin with his other hand, he forced her to meet his gaze. Her vision was blurry, pleasure still hummed through her body. His face was set in harsh lines. His eyes. A spark of fear raced up Eva's spine. His eyes were consumed by dark crimson.

"My control is...fragile," he said, his tone even, his voice rough yet soothing. His hold on her jaw loosened, his fingers slipping back to her nape to caress her tangled hair. "Please, my sweet Eva." He drew her hands above her head once more. He gave a rough squeeze to her wrists before releasing her. She heard him whisper, "Only pleasure," as he moved down her body.

His lips burned her as he kissed a path from her chin, down her throat, and across her breasts. She locked her fingers together, her nails digging into the backs of her hands as he stoked the fire of her desire. He pressed his lips to every rib as he slowly descended her body. His fangs teased her hipbones. Her body went up in flames. An uncontrollable inferno claimed her as delicious pleasure began to build within her again. It coiled tighter and tighter.

His mouth hovered just above her clitoris, his cool breath teasing, taunting.

"Oh, Hadrian," she moaned, her legs restlessly scissored against him. Her body writhed, inviting, her sighs a pleading whisper. She needed to feel his lips on her sex, his tongue...

Hadrian took in a deep breath, branding her scent into his memory. His fangs dripped in anticipation.

"Please."

"Please, what, my sweet?"

Eva's growl made him smile. Hadrian skimmed his fingers over her breasts, pinching her nipples before running his hands down her sides to grip her hips, pinning her to the bed.

"Control," he whispered, too softly for Eva to hear. Hadrian lowered his head. "Is this what you want?" He stroked her with his tongue and groaned.

Eva shuddered. Her breath seized as her muscles tightened and her heart pounded out of control. He circled her clitoris with his velvet tongue before capturing it with his lips, suckling her relentlessly. He heard her breath catch, felt her muscles tense, and tasted her orgasm. She screamed and Hadrian grew more forceful. He licked at her. His tongue thrust into her again and again, as her honey filled his mouth. Her hips rocked, riding his mouth as she would soon ride his cock.

He growled. He had never tasted anything as sweet as this woman. His woman. His Eva. She was all warm vanilla, delicious and dangerously addictive. Another of her orgasms drenched his tongue. Her body convulsed and his name echoed through the halls.

His instincts roared as the world around him fell into darkness. Eva whimpered, her head thrashing against the pillows, her muscles tensed, strained and then released with orgasm after orgasm. Hadrian groaned low in his throat, the sound rough, primal.

He was mindless. Insatiable flames of passion consumed him. He was dying to be inside her, but she needed to be ready for his invasion.

Hadrian skimmed his hand over her thigh, pushed past her folds, and buried a finger deep inside her. Eva bowed, her hands gripping and tearing the sheets. He continued to work her clitoris with his tongue. Inserting another finger, he began pumping in and out.

"Again, Eva," he growled.

He drove into her, a fast, hard rhythm, curling his fingers upward and spreading as he thrust. Her knees fell open wide as moans slipped from her lips. Eva fought for air. The firestorm of pleasure became unbearable.

"I'm—Yes, H–Hadrian. I'm going to…" Her words ended on a scream of ecstasy as her orgasm claimed her. Frenzied with pleasure, she gripped at his shoulders. Her inner muscles clenched around his fingers, gripping him so tightly he nearly came in his jeans.

Hadrian pushed to his feet. He could take the torture no longer. He had to be inside her. Now. He tore at his zipper and stepped free of the rough, confining fabric.

He came down, his slim hips settling between her thighs. He supported his weight with his arms, his hands pressing into the mattress on either side of her head. It took every ounce of his strength to resist thrusting into her, savagely claiming her innocence.

"Please," she whispered, her voice was rough from her cries of pleasure.

Their gaze met and held. She was trembling beneath him, sated yet desire still glittered in those amber orbs. Her passion and hunger mirrored his own, matching his need. He peered down at her in awe. She was ready, willing, and demanding more.

She arched her back. The head of his cock brushed over her folds, slipping over her swollen, sensitive clitoris. Hadrian suppressed a shudder as her moan kissed his ears.

"Eva," he whispered. He ached. He ached for her. His body, his fangs, his heart, even his tattered soul *ached* for her and only her.

Hadrian pressed a kiss to her temple as he rotated his hips, rocking his long shaft against her. "I'm going to be inside you."

Eva struggled for breath, anticipation pounding through her veins as flames of need devoured them.

He pressed forward, working the crown of his cock into her. Eva gave a short, stunned sigh as he slowly entered her, stretching her.

"Gods, Eva," Hadrian moaned. She was slick with need... hot, tight silk.

Mine. He inched in further. *Claim.* His fangs throbbed in his mouth, her rapid heartbeat a flawless melody. *Take.* He could feel the darkness rising within him. He wanted to mark her, to score her perfect as silk skin with his razor like fangs. He wanted to spill his seed deep within her as he savagely fed, tearing at her throat.

Hadrian stilled. Closing his eyes, he battled his violent urges. This was not about him or his demon. This was for Eva. Only Eva.

"Is something wrong?"

Her soft voice drew him back, smoothing away his worries, his doubts, calming his beast.

"No."

"Good." She wrapped her arms around his neck. "No escape," she said, her breath brushing over his lips.

He took her mouth, their kiss long and slow. He savored the feel, the taste, and the beautiful new, frightening sensations that spread through his chest, warming him, heating his cold heart and damaged soul.

There would be no escape for either of them. Clenching his jaw, he thrust forward, swift, hard, deep. Hadrian's harsh growl was drowned by Eva's cry of pained pleasure.

"Oh, Gods," he exhaled as he trembled.

Perfection. He knew she would feel this way. Exquisitely tight and hell fire hot—Heaven.

"I know what you mean," she whispered.

He slowly withdrew, inch by inch, then thrust in again, hitting the top of her sex.

Gentle. Control. He chanted as he gritted his teeth.

Eva's head fell back, her hands slipped from his neck to his biceps, her nails carving into his hard muscle as he found a torturous rhythm. She writhed beneath him, her hips rocking to meet his slow, measured thrusts. His body quaked as he battled against his instincts to feed, to mark her, to…dominate.

His fangs pulsed as his gaze dropped to her throat. He could hear her heart beating. The sound of her blood rushing through her veins was deafening. The scent of her sex, her arousal, and their combined lust filled the room and burned his lungs like thick, black smoke. Her blood would be rich and thick with her pleasure, sweetly erotic. One simple taste would be enough to drive him over the edge.

Focus. He needed to focus. Hadrian's heart slammed against his chest, matching the frantic rhythm of Eva's. Catching her jaw, he held her still. Look at me," he commanded. Her pure, ethereal, molten amber, eyes swirled with need.

Eva struggled to keep her eyes open, the pleasure was drugging, demanding. Hadrian's intense, dark eyes smoldered with untamed need and wild hunger. Yet he resisted his cravings. He fought for her, to be gentle, patient. She brushed the tips of her fingers along his jaw. He turned toward her hand, pressing his lips against her palm and Eva felt her heart melt.

Focusing on Eva, he watched as her pleasure mounted. Her eyes glazed over, losing focus. Her cheeks flushed, her lips parted, her sighs and moans a soothing symphony to his tattered soul.

He nearly shouted as her back arched, her breasts thrusting upward, her nipples abrading his chest. His name was a strangled whisper as she came, her body rippled around him, her heat gripping him tightly.

Glorious, he thought.

His trusts quickened.

Again. He needed to feel her climax again. He bent his head and captured a rosy nipple. He licked, suckled, and grazed the hard bud with the tip of his fangs. He drew his tongue down the valley of her breasts before kissing his way to her other nipple.

Eva gripped the back of his head, holding him to her. "Harder," she moaned.

A dangerous thrill danced down his spine as he complied. His hips began to pound against her, hard. His body raged for release, a terrible need only she could fill. He was soaring as her body clenched around him. Her head thrashed as another orgasm slammed into her. Her hot sheath tightened, demanding. He thrust, helpless against the onslaught of emotions and exquisite sensations that pounded through him. Wild. Uninhibited. Urgent. His body took hers, claimed hers, demanding full possession.

White-hot lightning arced and snapped between them. The friction building and building, the tension increasing until the world fragmented around them and faded into nothing, time was lost and reality was nonexistent as their passion exploded.

They soared, falling into the warmth of perfect ecstasy together. A shocked, blissful roar tore from his chest, hot seed jetted from him. Spasms wracked his body as his orgasm went on and on, filling her, spilling to her thighs.

At last, Hadrian's arms gave out and he collapsed, his heavy frame shaking the bed. He lay beside her, his chest heavy, his heart matching the frantic pace of hers.

As the last quake of pleasure left his body, bloodlust slammed into him. The need pumped through his veins like thick lava. His nails turned into talons, tearing the sheets, his vision went red. He tried to swallow, but his throat was like sandpaper, raw.

Hadrian's gaze swept over Eva's body. Virgin's blood smeared the apex of her thighs. The scent was maddening, mouthwatering...*irresistible*. It called to him, beckoning the demon that prowled the darkness of his mind. Heat engulfed him; suddenly his skin was too tight.

Eva tensed, sensing the change in Hadrian. She looked up at him from beneath her lashes. His face was pale, too pale. Red devoured his pupils, bleeding to consume his black irises, seeping into the white until they glowed like the fires of hell, jumping with greedy flames.

"Hadrian, what's wrong?"

She reached for him, her fingers brushing his shoulder.

He violently flinched as if her touch were a searing brand, charring his flesh. He slid from the bed with a predatory grace, his demonic gaze locked on her. His muscles strained and shook as he fought to hold himself back. She could see every vein, every line and hollow of his body. Shadows sliced across his face, his eyes burning like hot embers in the darkness.

His lips curled back revealing long, lethal fangs. The sound of Eva's blood rushing, ebbing and flowing, flourishing with life, taunted him.

"Eva." Her name a strangled whisper.

"Hadrian, what can I do?"

"Can't—" He wrapped his arms around his middle. He had not fed.

Attack. Feed. Claim her.

134

He stumbled back. The demon's screams were piercing, his skull pounded from the noise. His lips felt dry and cracked as the need to taste her blood continued to overwhelm him. The scent of sex and blood burned his nose and stabbed his lungs like a bunch of needles.

"Blood? Oh god, you need to feed," she gasped.

"I have...to go." His words broke on an agonized moan, his body convulsed.

Chapter Eighteen

Hadrian materialized in the kitchen, the small action draining the remaining energy from his exhausted body. He staggered, almost blind, his hands outstretched, his bare feet slapping the cold tile. He could scent the blood within the refrigerator. His stomach rolled with disgust even as thirst scorched his throat.

He lurched forward, his clawed fingers splayed across the surface of the hidden refrigerator its façade blending seamlessly with the line of pristine, white cabinets. Throwing open the door, he snatched a bag of blood. His fangs ripped into the plastic, freeing the crimson liquid. At once the rush hit him, seeping into his starved cells. Images of Eva assailed him, sweeping him away. Her cries of ecstasy still rang in his ears, the heat of her body still clung to him and the intoxicating scent of her arousal drowned his senses.

Hadrian tore into a second bag. Eva, he could still see her beneath him. Her face flushed with pleasure, her eyes sparkling with desire for him, only him. Her lips parted as she gasped for precious air, her climax claiming her. She had thrown her head back in sweet abandon as her body convulsed around him, drawing on him, milking him.

He groaned low in his throat as he reached for another bag allowing the second to join the first, empty on the floor.

The demon howled for Eva. Enraged. Craving. Her. Only her. Only Eva.

The chilled blood settled like a rock in his stomach as the tangy flavor of plastic filled his mouth.

One taste, the vampire pleaded, *just one taste of heaven, of Eva.*

Hadrian growled, forcing himself to swallow the repugnant blood.

The demon railed even as his hunger ebbed. Hadrian raised a shaking hand to grab another sack of blood. More, he needed more. He needed Eva. He needed her soft touch, the soothing sound of her voice, the warmth of her soul.

When he released the last drained bag, he stumbled back. His legs buckled, but he caught himself, clutching the edge of the marble countertop.

His teeth gnashed together as his chest pumped, frantically drawing in unnecessary breaths as he waited for the crazed hunger to wane. His muscles began to relax and his fangs slowly retreated. He could feel every cell in his body swell with life as the nourishing blood flowed through his system.

He cursed himself for being a selfish idiot. He should have known better. He had told himself he would feed regularly, a lie. He had intended to keep his bloodlust at bay while Eva resided within the fortress, but a part of him still refused to drink. He no longer enjoyed the act of feeding; he only took sustenance when it was vital he do so. He loathed the contact required to take directly from the source, from humans. It was too intimate. He found sinking his fangs into a bag of blood just as revolting. But deprivation only bred destruction.

Power coursed through him like lightning as he grew stronger. The demanding storm of hunger faded as a hurricane of overwhelming, unidentifiable emotions tore through him. His body pulsed, his heart thundered, and his soul...he could *feel* his soul. For the first time in centuries, he could feel the flutter of life within his chest, warming his heart. The broken pieces of his soul blazed, the heat so intense as they began to weld together.

Eva. She had somehow triggered this change within him.

What did it mean?

For hundreds of years he had existed void of all real emotion, knowing his soul was damaged. He had known no love, no true joy, only anger, sorrow and guilt, the demon's favorites. But Eva made him feel everything in a flood. Even hope, a sensation he believed he would never know again. And rightly so, he did not deserve love or happiness, especially not hope.

His heart ached and swelled as his soul burgeoned with life and a strange, euphoric sense of contentment settled over him.

Gods, what was happening?

The lights suddenly flipped on, sending him reeling back. He buried his claws in the smooth, polished surface of the counter. His vision blurred as bright colors burst all around him. Hissing, he raised a hand to shield his sensitive eyes.

"Hadrian?" Falcon called from the doorway.

Hadrian muttered a curse when the knight rushed forward. He knew he looked like hell: naked, his face smeared with blood.

"My Latin is rusty, but I'm not a snake born of a whoring bitch," Falcon said with a light laugh. "You look terrible."

Prying back one finger at a time, Hadrian removed his hand. He blinked trying to clear his vision.

"This is the last place I thought I would find you, especially in this condition."

Hadrian scowled.

"Here." Falcon unzipped the duffle bag he carried and tossed Hadrian a pair of loose workout shorts.

Hadrian caught the clothing on reflex alone, his vision still blurred. His claws retreated and he leaned his weight against the cabinets behind him, his legs still weak.

Falcon glanced about. "Is Eva with you?"

"No."

He ignored the knight's frown and stepped into the shorts.

"Where is she?" Falcon demanded, his tone harsh, all humor gone.

Against his will, Hadrian's senses sought Eva. He found her easily.

"I believe she is heading towards her room," he answered as nonchalantly as possible, even though he longed to flash to her. Was she going to shower? He longed to join her. Or was she going to change and search for him. He felt a twinge of heat rise in his cheeks. He had ruined her clothes.

"What happened?"

Hadrian growled, the demon not liking Falcon's accusatory tone.

"That does not concern you."

"You slept with her?"

Hadrian said nothing as his fingers skimmed over the counter, searching for a towel. When he found one, he wiped the blood from his mouth.

"For god's sake, Hadrian, she is mortal."

"The girl is unharmed, if that is what worries you." Folding the now ruined cloth, Hadrian straightened, his now sound and strong body. "I'm not a total beast." His words, spoken in defense, suddenly struck him as truth. He had managed to be gentle, to hold himself back, to deny his very nature for Eva, for her pleasure. He had not ravished her, though he could not deny he still wanted to devour the sweet half-breed.

Falcon rubbed his nape. "I didn't say that you were. It's just, well, I've known you for so long. You aren't exactly known for…I mean," he sighed, "shit."

Hadrian held up a hand, stopping his friend. He knew what Falcon was trying to say, he was not known for being a tender lover. "People can change."

Falcon's eyes narrowed. "Yes, *people* can change."

Hadrian shrugged off Falcon's implication and pushed the secret, blood stocked, refrigerator closed, the door seamlessly blending in with the cabinets.

He swooped down to collect the empty bags of blood. Popping open the lid of the trashcan, he tossed them inside, concealing the evidence of his frenzied feeding.

His senses strayed again, finding Eva still in her room.

"Eva's scent."

Hadrian frowned as Falcon's words cut into his thoughts. He shook himself. How long had the knight been speaking? What had he said? *Eva's scent, he had followed her scent to the kitchen,* he thought.

"The car is packed and the main house is awaiting our arrival," Falcon continued.

"Miss Maldonado will not be joining you," Hadrian said.

"Listen, Hadrian, I understand there is…something happening between you two, but you must think of her safety."

"I am," he stated as he walked down the length of the cabinets to the main fridge. His fingers wrapped around the stainless steel handle, with a simple tug, the bright light within flashed on, momentarily burning his eyes. Squinting, he scanned the contents. Various deli meats and cheeses rested in a drawer below a shelf full of plastic and glass containers. The chef they had hired only came to the castle once a week. She kept the kitchen stocked and prepared complete meals for Eva.

"I thought we agreed it would be best if she stayed at another property until the coronation ball."

"No agreement was reached. You expressed your concerns for our ward's safety and suggested that she leave."

"But—"

"The girl stays," Hadrian snapped, his fangs flashing.

Waves of violence pulsed through the air. Falcon held up his hands, palms out.

"Okay, fine. Topic dropped."

Hadrian nodded and pulled a bowl of green grapes from the fridge along with some cheese and thick slices of turkey, left over from the meal Eva had the night the before.

Falcon watched the king as he opened one cupboard after another, withdrawing a plate, a glass, and some crackers. He filled the glass with water, and then began to arrange grapes, cheese, saltines, and meat in a circle on the plate. Surely he was not planning on eating. In all the years he had known Hadrian, he had never seen the vampire eat.

"Will you tell me what's going on?" Falcon asked.

"When you administered aid to Eva's wound, did you notice anything unusual?"

Falcon frowned. What did Eva's injury have to do with anything that just took place between his king and their ward? It was clear Hadrian had not fed from her, if he had, there would have been no reason for him to suck four bags of blood dry.

"No," he answered. "I washed her hand with some soap then applied a Shaw salve." Falcon's words lodged in his throat as realization slapped him, dropping his jaw. "Her hand healed immediately. As a mortal it should have taken at least thirty minutes for her skin to repair itself."

Falcon wondered how he had not noticed. He should have recognized the sign. *Well, my thoughts were preoccupied with Hadrian and worrying if he had gone on a murderous rampage in town.*

"There is much more to our ward than even she knows."

Falcon sank onto one of the stools that lined the breakfast bar of the island.

"What do you mean?"

"Eva is of Shaw heritage."

"I don't...how...that is..." Falcon shook his head, trying to organize his thoughts. "I don't understand."

"It is simple, her mother was Shaw, her father a shifter," Hadrian explained with a shrug, his gaze still on the plate. Should he rearrange the cheese and crackers? Maybe put the grapes in a bowl?

"What does this mean? Do you think Eva will experience the change?" Falcon leaned forward, his elbows resting on the counter. "No, she shouldn't. Witch magic is stronger than shifter." He dropped his head in his hands. "I've never heard of such a match."

"Eva is truly unique," Hadrian agreed.

"We should reach out to the Shaw. Perhaps they have some record or knowledge about her kind. They may even want to claim her. As a witch, her father has no right to her."

"I already contacted the witches."

Falcon waited for Hadrian to continue, but instead, the king returned to the fridge and removed a glass container of sliced strawberries and mangos.

"And," Falcon prompted.

"I received a visit from the Shaw High Priestess herself."

Anxiety gripped Falcon's heart, the pain spreading through his chest, piercing his lungs. The High Priestess did not make house calls for the hell of it.

"There have been others like Eva."

"Did she say what happened to them?"

"Yes," Hadrian answered, his voice cold.

The king's tone sent warning signals off in Falcon's mind.

"All experienced the transition. None survived."

Falcon dropped his head to his hands. He felt the blood drain from his face. Eva was such a sweet girl, despite all the crap she had been through in her short life. It did not seem right that she should die, yet biology worked against her. Witches can't take another form while shifters must in order to survive.

"Eva's shifter side has laid dormant, waiting for her to reach full maturity. Tonight, when the full moon rises, her shifter cells will awaken and her body will war with itself."

"The witch in her will fight to suppress the shifter while the shifter will struggle for release," Falcon said, nodding in understanding. Eva's body will fight itself. "Is there something we can do to save her?"

"Yes," Hadrian's voice was rough, demonic.

Falcon's head snapped up, his muscles tensing as he sensed the darkness shift within Hadrian. The king's eyes flickered between bone chilling black and hell fire ruby. His fangs sharpened as bloodlust radiated from him.

"What?"

Hadrian ran his tongue over his canines. Every second drew her transformation closer. He knew her taste would be unforgettable, just like everything else about her.

You cannot keep her. She is not yours, he reminded himself. He knew making love to her had been a mistake. He should never have allowed her to kiss him. He should never have crushed her to him and he certainly never should have teleported her to his room. No, he would not regret what happened between them, but he could never let it happen again. She was of Shaw decent, she was not bound to the law of the pack nor could she be used for the treaty. She could leave whenever she liked and he would let her. Wouldn't he?

Hadrian's thoughts turned dark as he considered the possibilities. He would make sure she lived, he would unite their life forces and he would help her start anew, away from his Clan, her father's pack, and away from him.

"Hadrian, what did the priestess say?" Falcon pressed.

"She told me how to save Eva."

"Oh, god, don't tell me you plan to change her."

Chapter Nineteen

Hadrian's features twisted into a mask of disgust. "Never."

Falcon let out a heavy exhale, "Good. You would surely kill her if you tried."

"The witch gave me instructions," Hadrian stated, not wishing to delve into the details. He did not want Falcon knowing his plans. Especially since he had doubts. Silvie had told him how to bind Eva to him, but she had not told him everything. Hadrian sensed there was more to the bonding than what the witch had shared, but he did not have time to think about the possibilities now. "Eva will live."

"Would you like me to stay? I could delay my trip for a few days and help," Falcon offered.

"That is unnecessary. Besides, you would be more help to me at the main house. Now that we have discovered the secret of Eva's heritage, we can no longer hold her as a ward."

Falcon nodded. As a Shaw descendant, Eva did not fall under shifter law.

"I would like you to terminate our treaty with the Silveria pack."

"Should I find another shifter group?"

Hadrian shrugged. "If the noble counsel deems it necessary. Our Clan already has a large presence in South America."

"You do know that without our support the Silveria pack will be destroyed."

"Arsenio has many enemies," Hadrian conceded. "If he meets his end, then so be it."

"What are we going to do with Eva? We can't keep her here."

Hadrian pinched the bridge of his nose. No, he could not keep Eva here. And he did not want to keep her. She was not his.

"Once she has recovered from her transition, she will be free to leave. She will finally be able to live the life she has always wanted."

He would pay for her to relocate to the city of her choice, arrange for an apartment, a car, and schooling. Once she established herself, he would sever all ties. He could erase her from his thoughts, banish her from his dreams, and cherish her in his memories.

"I will set up an account for her," Falcon said. "Once she has selected a location I will arrange the necessary paper work: birth certificate, identification, passport, social security and the like. Then again, the Shaw may welcome her."

"If she so desires, she may join their fold. That is where she belongs." *She certainly does not belong with you,* he reminded himself.

"May I speak freely?"

Hadrian's chest compressed with a heavy sigh. "Yes."

"I don't know what is happening between you and Eva, but I can guess." Hadrian bit back a curse when Falcon waved a hand at him indicating his lack of clothing and he knew he reeked of sex. "Do you really want to let her go?"

"It matters not what I want," Hadrian flatly stated.

"But what if she wanted to stay?"

"She won't."

"Well, I think—"

"I'm insane, Falcon. My mind is broken, my soul nearly nonexistent, I have nothing. It was a miracle I was able to hold back when we…She deserves more."

"You are a better man than you know," Falcon said.

Hadrian scrubbed his face with his hands. Gods, he needed a drink. His thoughts were a mess and these new emotions were of no help, only inflicting more pain. His demon was unwilling to let Eva go while his soul wept for her.

A wave of vanilla rushed the air. His head snapped to the kitchen door. His lungs expanded as he breathed in that wonderful scent.

"Hadrian," Eva called as she came running into the kitchen. She slid to a stop, almost tumbling head over ballet flats when her gaze fell on Falcon. His eyes were sharp, studying, probing, as if he were seeing her for the first time. "Your Majesty, Sir Kenwrec, I apologize. I did not mean to interrupt."

"There is no need for titles," Hadrian said. "Come in."

Eva crossed the kitchen to sit beside him at the breakfast bar. Falcon's gaze moved to his king, who watched Eva with the glowing eyes of a loving predator.

"So, Hadrian told you about the secret lurking in my blood," Eva asked, shattering the heavy silence that had settled over them.

"Yes. I don't know if I should congratulate you or offer my condolences."

Eva playfully punched Falcon's shoulder. "You could wish me luck. I may die tonight."

"You will not," Hadrian snapped.

"I have to say, I really didn't think I would ever find you in here," Eva said, her eyes traveling over Hadrian's bare chest. "I thought you might be in the solarium or out by the lake again."

"Why did you look here?" Falcon asked.

Eva shrugged. "Instinct."

Falcon's eyes narrowed as a frown ceased his brow. Ever since Hadrian had begun shielding his power, he had found it nearly impossible to locate the vampire and they shared a blood bond. Hadrian was his maker. But Eva could easily find Hadrian and she had yet to go through her transition. Her shifter instincts were buried.

Falcon was barely able to hide his shock when realization went off in his mind like a bomb. Drive. Eva was experiencing Drive. That was the only explanation. A shifter was drawn to their mate, guided by instinct rather than scent or sight. Eva's animal spirit recognized Hadrian as her male.

A sudden heart wrenching thought slashed through his mind. Hadrian had not told him what solution the Shaw Priestess had suggested, but Falcon would bet his soul he knew the solution. No potion or spell could save her from such a fate. Eva would die if Hadrian did not bind her to his life force.

Dear, god. Hadrian had no idea what was about to happen.

"I was going to bring this to you," Hadrian said, pushing the plate and fruit salad towards Eva. "You should eat. You will need your strength."

Eva smiled and accepted the fork Hadrian offered. "Thank you."

"It was nothing."

Falcon blinked. Was Hadrian blushing?

Eva began to pick at the fruit. "I guess you know I'm not going with you now," she said, turning to Falcon.

Falcon swallowed the lump of shock that had formed in his throat. "Yeah."

"Are you feeling okay? You are paler than usual," Eva asked.

Hadrian's gaze fell on him and Falcon shoved his thoughts aside, locking them away. "I think I'm experiencing information overload."

"Oh, I hear you on that," she said rolling her eyes.

"Well, I should be going." Falcon stood. "The snow has let up and I need to take advantage of the break."

"Drive safely."

"I want a report every night."

"I will be careful," Falcon said giving Eva a smile. Turning to his king, he gave a respectful nod. "I will provide you with all the information that I can and I will only act in the Clan's best interest."

"You have my trust," Hadrian said.

Falcon bowed, turned on his heel and strode from the kitchen.

"How long will he be away?" Eva asked.

He shrugged. "Nearly a week."

"We are going to be completely alone."

"Yes. Now, please, eat."

"I was starving." Her vision blurred. "But now, I feel kind of weird."

Her fork slipped from her suddenly trembling fingers. Eva rubbed her nape as a dull pain gathered at the base of her skull. It quickly spread, branching throughout her body, sending sparks of pain to every nerve. Her pulse spiked, her eyes dilated, and her beautiful, smooth skin became splotchy with fever.

"Hadrian." She swayed. "I don't f–feel w—"

Chapter Twenty

Hadrian rounded the island and caught her before she hit the floor. Cradling Eva in his arms, he rushed from the kitchen. Her head bounced as he crossed to the stairs, her hair falling over his arm like dark silk. He took the steps two at a time and sped down the hall to her room.

"T–too early," she whispered, her teeth chattering.

"Save your energy," he ordered, shoving the door open.

He did not have to glance at the clock on the mantel to know it was just past ten. Shifters did not begin their transformation until midnight, but Eva was not the typical shifter. There were no set rules.

Hadrian pulled back the sheets before gingerly laying her down.

"Cold," she gasped, her entire body trembling.

"It is the fever," he said. When Hadrian turned from her she cried out. "Quiet, little one, I'm just going to get a damp towel."

She nodded, curling to her side, her arms wrapping around her middle. Her eyelids were heavy. Her lungs burned, her head throbbed, and her body ached. Nausea rolled over her, bile climbed in her throat as her stomach twisted.

Hadrian quickly returned and she hissed when he pressed the washcloth to her brow.

"I need to undress you," he said and Eva weakly nodded. If her body were to take another form, the confinement of her clothing would only make it more difficult.

Setting the towel on the nightstand, Hadrian removed her sweater, slipped her jeans free, then made quick work of her undergarments. Her small form that had been trembling in pleasure a mere hour before was now wrecked with pain.

Her lips moved as she tried to speak.

"I will not leave you," he vowed.

Her quaking smile vanished as her bone-shattering cries pierced his soul. Her back bowed. The sickening sound of bones cracking vibrated the air like the snap of a whip. Her eyes rolled back and Eva fell victim to the blackness of unconsciousness.

Hadrian felt a tainted sense of relief. She could no longer feel the pain of her bones breaking and her muscles tearing, but she could easily slip away, surrender to the peace that existed in the darkness.

Her body twisted, contorted, her legs kicked out, her hands twitched, the spasms involuntary. Sweat dripped from her body, soaking the sheets. Tiny whimpers fell from her lips, occasionally she mumbled incoherently. Hadrian wiped at her brow, desperately praying he could take her pain.

It seemed like centuries before the clock struck midnight. The enchanting musical notes fell on deaf ears as everything went silent. Eva became still. Deathly still. Leaning down, he listened intently for her heartbeat, it was slow, weak. Her breaths were alarmingly shallow. The fever broke, leaving her cool to the touch. Her luscious lips tinted blue as the color faded from her skin.

This was it. Hadrian was disgusted by how easily his fangs lengthened; the vampire was delighted and greedy for a taste.

"Just enough," he whispered.

Hadrian laced his fingers with hers. With his free hand he brushed away the dampened curls that clung to her neck. He shifted, his chest hovering above her, careful not to touch.

"Just enough," he said again, his breath brushing her throat.

Control. If he took too much, he would kill her. Eva was already on the brink of death, every breath grew shorter, every heartbeat weaker than the last.

He pressed his lips to her pulse. "Control."

His fangs sank into the column of her throat, slicing through her artery. Her blood filled his mouth, the sweetest ambrosia. It was like electricity on his tongue. He swallowed and groaned from the intense pleasure. Nothing had ever been more perfect and he doubted he could ever relinquish this heaven. Addictive, just like he knew she would be. Her blood was the right mixture of sugar and spice, the best of vanilla.

Fire spread throughout his body. His heart began to pound with newfound life; he could feel his soul mending. Closing his eyes, he surrendered to the sensations. His mouth fed, frantically drawing her in, welcoming her essence into his body. The darkness in him stirred as he felt her pulse begin to stutter. Her breathing became dangerously slow.

He needed to pull away. He needed to stop before he killed her. But, gods, she was wonderful, the definition of perfection.

The air chilled. He could sense the familiar presence of death. He opened his eyes and with a growl, he ripped away. His heart slammed wildly against his ribs, his entire body hummed with life. Beneath him, Eva struggled for breath, her body laboring from the effort.

Hadrian tightened his hold on her fingers as he raised his free hand to his mouth. He drew his wrist across his fangs, tearing open his flesh. Blood flowed in an obliging rush. He pressed the wound to her lips.

"Eva," he whispered. "Come on, little one, drink." No response. He squeezed his wrist, forcing the blood to run more freely. Her skin was growing colder with every passing second. "No, Eva. You cannot die." Releasing her hand, he squeezed her jaw, forcing her mouth open. "Drink. Please, no. Death cannot have you." He slammed a fist into the mattress; the bed quaked from the impact. "Eva, come back to me," his words a broken sob.

Her heart stopped.

Chapter Twenty-One

Eva was floating, completely weightless. Light enveloped her. Warm. Welcoming. A hazy figure dressed in white approached. She blinked, trying to clear her vision. It came closer, taking the shape of a woman. Dark hair floated about her waist in waves of curls, her smile was bright, and her eyes soft.

"Mom?"

Her voice echoed in the expanses of nothingness. The woman waved. Eva felt tears gather in her eyes. The figure spoke, but she heard nothing. Eva wanted to run to her, to throw her arms around her and never let go. She tried to step forward, but something tugged her back. A deep, husky male voice called to her, the words distant and garbled. She ignored the strange voice and struggled to move. Her limbs were weak, her body suddenly aching; her skin felt as if millions of tiny needles pricked her all at once. Eva brushed at her mouth with the back of her hand. Blood colored her lips. She braced herself for the taste of copper, but all she could taste and smell was warm cinnamon spice.

Her mother's figure began to dissolve into mist as the bright white light slowly dimmed.

"Live, my Eva." The male voice pleaded.

Eva slammed back into her body as if she had fallen ten stories, landing broken and twisted, everything hurt. She cried out, her scream muffled as another rush of that cinnamon spice taste flooded her mouth. She swallowed reflexively. It burned deliciously as it slipped down her throat. God, she had never tasted anything like this. It warmed her cold body, chased away the pain and brought beautiful, peaceful quiet to her mind.

More. She needed more.

Hadrian carefully adjusted their position, shifting Eva from his wrist to his neck. He now leaned back against the headboard, tilting his head to the side, allowing Eva better accesses. Her lips pulled at his flesh as her tongue swept along his pulse, her draws grew more demanding almost frantic as she fed from him. Closing his eyes, he willed himself to remain calm, relaxed. Her hair spilled about him, covering his chest. He stroked her arms, her shoulders as he whispered encouragements. He did not know if she could hear him or if she was even aware of what was happening, but that did not stop him from becoming hard. Gods, he had never experienced anything as erotic as Eva's mouth working at his pulse.

Her skin began to heat once more beneath his touch, with every swallow her heartbeat grew stronger.

"Thank the gods," he sighed, staring up at the ceiling.

For precious seconds he had lost her, tears still stained his cheeks, but he had brought her back. He had saved her. He had pulled her from the brink, just as she had done to him the first night they met. Madness was ripe in his mind, poisoning his thoughts, fueling his bloodlust, but she was a light that chased away the shadows.

He rolled his eyes, when had he become a romantic? He was being ridiculous. Lust was all that existed between them. Sure, he cared for the girl. Eva was nice, gentle, sweet, and good, everything he was not. And she deserved to live, even if he did not. He would suffer through eternity, baring his curse so that she may live a happy, fulfilled life.

Hadrian felt his heart begin to slow. He had allowed her to take too much.

"Eva," he whispered, "No more."

She nipped at him. Hadrian's body jerked as a spike of need hammered through him.

Eva was not free of danger yet. The effects of his blood would only work for so long. The pain would return and so would death. He had to complete the bonding.

Forcing his lust aside, he gripped her shoulders and pulled away. Eva growled in protest. She reached for him. He caught her hands with his, lacing their fingers together. Her body still weak, she collapsed back on the pillows. Hadrian followed her, leaning over her once more. Eva's eyes fluttered, but she was unable to keep them open. She swallowed hard, her lips moving, but she could not speak.

Hadrian pressed his lips to her brow. Her skin was warm, clammy, the fever had returned. She began to shiver, her skin covered in goose-bumps. He kissed a path down the line of her nose. Again, she tried to talk, but all that passed her lips were whimpers and sobs as the pain began to take hold.

A kiss. The priestess had suggested a kiss. They both needed to taste the combined blood at the same time. He could nip her lip and draw the tiniest bead of blood. Their blood, mixed together, it flowed through her veins, giving her life. Pride swelled within him. Hadrian frowned, banishing the odd feeling.

She managed to groan his name, her lips trembling. Tears slipped from the corners of her eyes and fell like tiny diamonds down her cheeks to soak the pillow.

Summoning all the will he possessed, Hadrian bent his head. He traced her bottom lip with his tongue. His fangs ached and his stomach clenched. His throat was suddenly dry and rough like sandpaper. Gods, he craved another taste. He bit her, his fang slicing through her plump, tender lip. Eva flinched. He whispered apologies as he watched the perfect bead of crimson well. Hypnotizing.

"Eva," his breath caressed her cheek.

She knew she was falling fast. Her body was cold as electric shockwaves of agony pulsed through her. Just one kiss, her last kiss. She could think of no better way to part from this world.

Hadrian's lips were hot, searing, as they pressed against hers. His tongue swept against hers, demanding as he delved into her mouth. Luscious vanilla and spicy cinnamon swirled together as he deepened the kiss. His fingers tightened on hers. Fire burned her wrists. The flames spread up her arm, weaving through her veins and arteries until striking her heart, her soul.

Hadrian threw his head back. The scent of burning flesh stung his nose, white-hot heat sliced through him, so intense it branded his soul.

Eva convulsed. Her teeth gnashed together, her breaths came in harsh pants, her lungs franticly expanding and compressing. Her head fell back as her back arched, her eyes opened, glowing a vibrant yellow. Her nails extended to claws as a long and pure animalistic roar tore from her throat.

Then all went silent. Still. Calm still.

Her muscles relaxed, her breathing and heart rate mellowed to an even, healthy pace. But he did not let her go. He remained by her side for hours, their fingers locked together.

Her claws retracted and the bright light faded until her eyes became soft amber once more. She had not taken jaguar form, but it was now clear that she possessed some of the features of the jungle cat.

Hadrian vaguely recalled the clock chiming four A.M. He carefully extracted his hands from her grasp. She mumbled, but remained asleep. He stood and drew the sheets up, tucking her in. He knew he looked like hell. Stress streaked his face, worry furrowed his brow, and he still wore nothing but the shorts Falcon had generously tossed at him. He should shower, dress, and prepare her another meal. He knew she would be starving when she awoke. Yet, he was reluctant to leave her.

He rubbed his hands over his short hair, the stubble a welcome prickling sensation. The slightest aroma of charred flesh wafted in the air. He dropped his hands to look at them, palms up.

Terror rose like bile, burning his throat as the chilled grip of realization crushed his windpipe. His eyes flamed red as rage ripped through him like a firestorm.

"No," he hissed past his fangs.

Chapter Twenty-Two

Hadrian stumbled to the bathroom. His hips collided with the counter as he fumbled with the faucet, his hands shaking from anger or…fear, he did not know. His heart thundered so loud, he could hear nothing else.

He cursed as the warm water ran over his wrist, despite the sting, he scrubbed at the raw flesh.

This could not be happening. It was impossible. He, the mad king everyone whispered about, could not be the Rightful King of legend. He could not possibly be the monarch chosen by Fate to bring about peace and reign over his clan forever. This was wrong. A mistake. A hallucination. Anything but true.

Hadrian snarled as he rubbed at the wound.

Once, long ago, his people believed he was their savior, that he would finally bring an end to the strife that plagued his clan. His land had been divided by civil war after civil war; his subjects, vampire and humans alike, endured the reigns of numerous tyrants, all driven by greed and bloodlust. They deserved peace, stability, and security. But how could he provide for them what he did not possess? His mind was still afflicted by madness, his soul fractured. He could snap, lose control at any moment.

Blood rinsed away with the water as he frantically tried to scrub his skin clean. But he was branded, a circle within a circle, the mark of a mated vampire.

Until Dorian's success, Hadrian had believed the stories of the Rightful Kings and their mates to be nothing but falsehoods, legends created by past vampire nobles and rulers who sought hope, who longed for peace and the freedom of death.

Hadrian's hands curled, his fists shaking as he battled to contain the inferno of rage that violently ripped through him. The demon snarled, demanding blood of the one who had betrayed him; the one who had tricked him.

The witch.

Silvie. The Shaw priestess, the seer of all, she had known. She had arranged this scenario nicely and played him perfectly.

Like a typical Shaw witch.

She could have warned him. She could have told him what Eva meant...His shoulders shook with a dark laugh. He knew. He had always known what Eva meant to him. He had been blinded by his stubbornness and self-loathing, but deep down he knew. His soul had recognized her for what she was. His mate.

Mate. The word sounded so foreign as if belonging to some ancient, forgotten language.

A dark laugh shook his shoulders as he met his gaze in the mirror. Dark crimson eyes stared back at him. His lips curled into an evil smile, peeling back from his fangs. Shadows twisted the contours of his face and slashed across his chest. The demon glared at him. Taunting him as it always did. It had not changed, not in three and half centuries since he last met its gaze.

Hadrian lashed out, releasing his imprisoned rage. His fist slammed into the glass, shattering the mirror. Splitters of glass cascaded down, covering his arms, coating the white marble countertop and clattering to the floor. He delivered blow after blow until he could see his reflection no longer. Bloody knuckles continued to pound against the bare stone wall, cracking the wall as a roar filled the room.

Hate was not a strong enough word for what he felt. He loathed the demon, despised the bastard with every fiber of his being and yet, it was a part of him, attached to his very core.

It did not deserve Eva. *It* did not deserve happiness and it could not be the bearer of peace and prosperity. All his demon ever brought was death and pain. *It* murdered. *It* raped. *It* tortured and laughed with twisted delight at his victims' screams. And because of the abomination he carried inside him, he could never have Eva. It did not matter that she was his mate. He would never allow the monster within him to have her. Never.

The slightest sound of footsteps drew his attention to the bathroom door. Eva gripped the door jam so tightly her knuckles were white. Her hair fell in a tangled mass about her, floating about her breasts and her hips. Her legs shook from the effort of standing.

"Hadrian," she called, blinking. He had not turned the light on in the bathroom. Could she see him? The moon shown through the window above the shower, it's rays glittering over the glass that covered the counter and floor.

"Wait there," he ordered, not wanting her to cut herself.

Eva nodded. Whether or not she could see him did not matter, she obviously had heard him.

He watched as she slowly slid to the floor, sitting just outside the bathroom, her knees drawn to her chest.

Hadrian closed his eyes and cursed. He had lost control. He had potentially put Eva's life in danger. He forced his muscles to relax, flexing his fingers. Then he focused on his lungs, which had stopped. It was not necessary for vampires to breathe, but he found it soothing. Inhale. Exhale. He concentrated on keeping his breathing even.

When he had calmed, he opened his eyes. Eva was resting her head on her knees, her arms wrapped around her legs. He listened to her steady heartbeat, normal pulse and her breathing until it matched his own.

"You shouldn't be out of bed."

"Shower," she whispered, her voice low and weak. "I need a shower."

Hadrian nodded and stepped to the counter. Brushing the glass into the sink, he pulled the hand towel free from its chrome ring on the wall, spreading it out, creating a place for Eva to sit.

The showerhead hissed to life as he crossed the small room and gently lifted her into his arms. He placed her on the counter then stalked into her room, quickly returning with a tank top and pajama pants in hand.

She tried to smile, but found even the muscles in her face hurt. Her gums ached, her throat was raw, and her eyes watered, suddenly too sensitive to the light. Blinking, she tried to track Hadrian as he moved about the room. He had set the clothes beside her then opened the glass door to the shower and checked the temperature with his hand.

He scooped her up and carried her to the shower. She welcomed the humidity and heat with a sigh. He slowly eased her under the rainfall. Eva let her head fall back, the water cascaded over her face and down her neck. Hadrian gently dropped her feet to the ground.

"Thank you," she whispered, leaning her weight against him.

Titling her head back, she soaked her hair. Hadrian grabbed a shampoo bottle and washed her hair, massaging her scalp until she moaned. She tried to speak, but her voice failed, so she pointed to the conditioner. He lathered her unruly locks until they rinsed smooth, combing through the length with his fingers. She rinsed her hair as he took up a bar of soap and began to caress her skin, every curve, every dip, leaving nothing untouched. Turning her gently under the spray, the water washed the suds away.

"Your shorts?" she asked, her voice cracking as she spoke.

He said nothing as he stared down at her. His gaze intense, his jaw set. Eva shrugged. She was in no mood to get frisky. She just wanted to see him naked, but this view would do. The soaked shorts molded to his body and she could see every line of his massive hard-on.

Hadrian shut the water off, stepped out and snatched a towel. He draped it over her shoulders, taking her up again he returned her to the counter. He was careful drying her. Eva helped as best she could. She hated feeling helpless, but her limbs were like jelly and very uncooperative.

He brought her a second towel that she wrapped around her hair after he slipped the shirt over her head. Hadrian kicked the glass aside with his bare feet, clearing a space for her. Eva slid from the counter and stepped into the blue, flannel pajama pants.

"Do you know where the linens are kept?" he asked carrying her into the bedroom.

Eva nodded toward a tall cabinet beside the closet.

Hadrian placed her in the comfort of the armchair before the hearth. She watched him from her perch as he worked. He stripped the bed, balling the sweat soaked sheets and tossing them over by the door. He quickly redressed the bed then came for her.

Eva pushed herself to her feet. Shaking out her hair, she dropped the towel beside the chair. Hadrian watched her with sharp eyes, studying her movements as she slowly crossed to the bed. She combed through her damp hair with her fingers, trying to appear casual, but her legs quaked and promptly gave out. He quickly caught her, scooped her up, and gently laid her down in the bed. Eva snuggled into the fresh satin with an appreciative sigh.

He frowned at her and she smiled. She knew this behavior was out character for him. She doubted he ever had to tend to someone, especially not a woman. He had been a warrior in his human life and aside from possibly dressing wounds, she doubted he had ever had to care for another.

She could not remember much of her transition. Her mind was clouded, her thoughts hazy. The pain, that she recalled with alarming clarity and—she swallowed hard—she had seen her mother. But Hadrian had brought her back. He had given her his blood. She buried her face in the pillow to hide her blush. She had liked it.

Why lie, she thought. *I loved it.*

She peeked up and found Hadrian kneeling, stoking a fire. Flames grew and danced, banishing the chill that hung in the room. His wet shorts hugged his hips and clung to his backside. He straightened as if he could feel her gaze upon him.

"How are you feeling?"

"Like hell," she croaked.

His lips twitched at the corners, but he did not smile. He came to stand beside the bed. "You need to rest." He drew the sheets up to her chin. "The pain will be gone when you wake, I promise."

"How?"

He shrugged. "Your unlocked magic will heal your body."

Eva sighed, thankful to know her arms and legs would be in working order soon. She hated feeling trapped and right now, her physical limitations were holding her captive.

"Thank you," she tried to clear her throat and winced, "for staying with me."

"I would never leave you," he said, stroking his knuckles over her cheek.

"And thank you for saving my life."

Eva kissed his fingers. He abruptly dropped his hand, but she was too tired to care why at the moment. Sleep tugged at her mind and she no longer had the strength to fight it off.

Chapter Twenty-Three

The thick stone wall trembled when Hadrian slammed his bedchamber door closed. He needed to feed again. His body was not used to sharing blood and he could feel the fatigue of hunger beginning to set in. He cringed as he thought of the bagged blood. He had hated it before, and after tasting Eva…would he ever be able to stomach the vile contents again?

He crossed to the closet, bypassing the bathroom. He knew he should bathe properly, but he had no patience for that. Answers. He needed answers. Now.

Hadrian discarded the dripping shorts and donned a pair of dark jeans and a black t-shirt. Deciding it would be best to hunt some game, he slipped on some socks before roughly tugging on his boots.

He stalked back into his room, throwing the balcony doors open with his mind.

Taking in a deep breath, he did his best to bury his frustration. He would not receive the answers he sought by tearing the meddling witch apart, though his fingers twitched with excitement at the thought.

"Witch!" he bellowed.

"No need to shout," Silvie chided as she appeared on the balcony beside him. Her scarlet robe whipped about her legs as her hood blew back, revealing her face. "Wow, this really is a beautiful view."

Snowflakes caught in her long, black lashes. The witch was enchanting with her dark hair, smooth pale skin and ruby lips, but she was nothing compared his exotic Eva.

She is not mine. I cannot have her, even if she is my mate.

"You tricked me," he snapped.

Silvie sighed and turned, reluctant to draw her gaze from the mesmerizing scene of pure snow, the crisp green forest, and the frosted lake. She was not surprised to find the king scowling. His glower was dark and menacing. She had seen worse.

"No tricks," she said, entering the vampire's lair. "I simply withheld a little information."

"You knew what she was to me and yet you said nothing."

Silvie did not even attempt to stop the sly smile that graced her lips. "Mate. She is your mate. Is the word so difficult to say? Or do you find it distasteful."

"Witch," he growled. A warning.

"Your Eva would have died if you had not bound her to yourself. I just failed to mention that the only way you can bind someone to one such as you, a vampire, is if they are your intended, your other half. *Your soul mate.* Only mates can share this bond." She held up her hand, preventing his next accusation. "I had to do it. The two of you were taking *forever* to get together." Silvie shook her head. She pitied Eva because the stupid vampire had played hard to get. "I felt I needed to step in."

Hadrian began to pace, needing some type of outlet for his frustration.

"This changes nothing." He would still send Eva away.

"Oh, really?" She laughed. "This changes everything, Your Majesty. Or do you still believe you can allow her to leave? That you can buy her a plane ticket and dump her at the airport without a second glance? Perhaps, you should speak with King Dorian first. He can share with you the mind numbing pain and heart wrenching loneliness that consumes you after being separated from your mate for long periods of time. He learned quickly after leaving Queen Victoria behind for a battle with the Red Order. You see, the Shaman crafted this spell, focusing on every detail." *Intending to avoid this exact situation,* she thought. Her uncle was a crafty SOB planning everyone's life, including hers.

Hadrian's hand fisted as his eyes began to jump with angry flames.

"What are you really upset about?"

Silvie walked a slow circle around him, looking him up and down, inspecting him? No, reading him. Could the witch hear his thoughts? He doubted it but reinforced his barriers anyway.

"The demon." She came to a stop just before him. "You don't want to share. I would think being a twin you would have impeccable sharing skills."

His jaw popped, his anger tipping over to rage.

"Oh, sorry. I forgot, touchy subject. I've got too many thoughts knocking around in my brain lately, hard to keep my ducks in row."

Hadrian released an irritated sigh, wondering if the witch may be as crazy as he.

"A few months ago you were incapable of a normal, civilized, coherent conversation. You have made tremendous progress with rebuilding the wall between you and Imbrasus's demon."

His eyes narrowed to slits.

She smiled. "Yes. I know many secrets. Such as, you are not like the other vampires. You killed your maker in a very special way. He changed you on the night of a full moon. When he gave you his blood you transitioned instantly. You sank your fangs in deep, anchoring yourself to his wrist. Your claws were buried in his arm making it impossible for him to shake you free. And you bled him dry, consuming every last drop until his body fell to the cold sand beside you."

Hadrian suppressed the curse that burned his tongue. Shivers raced along his spine, his demon howled, the sound echoed in his head. He had not thought of that night in centuries. Rage had taken root in his soul, fueling him to kill and dominate his prey—Imbrasus.

"Because you drained him and you were in mid-transition, instead of the curse creating a vampire to ravage your soul, you took Imbrasus's demon. Unlike other vampires who have a new demon born within them during their change, you house an original vampire, just like Sire Dimitri"

Hadrian stumbled back, horrified, as if the witch had swung an executioner's ax at him. How did she know? He had shared the facts of his change with no one. Not Dimitri or Dorian, not even Falcon. He intended to take this secret to hell with him.

"How do you know this?"

Silvie's expression turned sullen. "The Shaman of our tribe is all knowing and he shared some of his memories with me."

Hadrian slowly nodded as his brain kicked back into gear. Falcon always shared the latest gossip with him. Rumors circled that the Shaman was retiring, which meant he would no longer undergo reincarnation and would have to give his memories and powers to a successor. Instinct told him the chosen heir stood before him.

He cleared his throat, shoving his shock aside. He needed answers.

"Why did you not warn me of Eva?"

"I didn't tell you Eva is your mate because you may have decided not to save her."

Silvie's confession stung. Would he have let Eva die? If she had, he could have joined her in death. He could have known peace and serenity in the afterlife. He could have cast off his demon, leaving it to burn in the eternal fires of hell.

"And now would probably be a good time to confirm that she will go into heat."

A tortured groan escaped his lips.

"That was one of your questions, right? How does it work," she tapped her chin, "Oh, right. Three days after the transition, a female will go into heat and her breeding cycles will follow every six months."

He slowly nodded, fighting the erotic images that flooded his mind. Eva's golden skin would be flush with desire, her eyes bright with need. He would palm her breasts as she rode him. Her back would arch as he pounded into her from behind. Rolling her over, her nails would score his back as he thrust into her.

No! He would do none of those things. One night, that is all. They could not risk being together again. He had nearly lost control. He had nearly bitten her when they made love the first time. He shuddered. Her blood had been heaven and would be mind numbingly, blissful if sweetened by her orgasms. His fangs exploded in his mouth, his cock swelled. He hissed as it pressed against the zipper of his jeans.

Twenty-four hours of pleasure or, if he did not service her, she would experience twenty-four hours of hell. Females suffered excruciating pain if they did not have sex. Most compared the pain to that of their transition. He would have to restrain her. He could not have her escaping to town to prey on unsuspecting males. The drive to breed was overwhelming, all consuming, clouding the mind until the body reacted on pure instinct. But there was a drug that could dull the pain. How was he going to get it? Shifters were leery of vampires, thanks to Imbrasus.

"Let me guess, you are thinking about this," Silvie said holding up a sealed, sterile bottle and capped syringe. She smiled at his frown and shrugged, "Magic. I abuse it, sue me."

Hadrian's jaw clenched. The witch had come prepared. Suspicious. "You never cease to amaze."

"This stuff is hard to come by. Not many shifter packs have the resources to make it."

"Never once, in all the time I lived amongst the packs was I allowed to see it made or used. I learned from hearsay that unmated females found it useful and it loosens the tongue during interrogations. It must have been expensive."

"It was granted to me after magical compensation was provided," she answered.

"I know Shaw practices well," Hadrian stated. "Gifts of this magnitude are never free."

"If I recall my history lesson correctly, the Validus and the Shaw were not on friendly terms when you were last out and about." She shrugged. "News flash, times have changed. We now seek to obtain and maintain peace with all vampire kind. Unfortunately, in this particular situation I do require a concession from you."

"What is your price?"

"Simple. I want Sir Falcon Kenwrec."

Hadrian's scowl grew darker. "I do not understand."

"His fealty is to you."

"His fealty is to the Validus Clan."

"No." Silvie shook her head, sending her tight ringlets bouncing about her shoulders. "If his loyalty were to the clan, then he would have become king long ago."

"He is my second. I cannot release him from that pact."

"Unless he does something worthy of banishment," Silvie added. "I'm not asking for you to release him of his obligations. I merely require his services."

"You want him as your guard?" he asked.

"It is an ancient tradition. One not practiced much these days because of security systems, LoJack, and the aforementioned seeking and maintaining of peace. However, a girl could still use a bodyguard from time to time."

"You have no need for a personal guard. The Voidukas provide your tribe with plenty of knights and I've no doubt you are more than capable of protecting yourself."

"Look," Silvie sighed, pinching the bridge of her nose. "I know I'm supposed to talk in riddles and be cryptic, but I keep failing the test. So, I'm going to be as straight with you as I can. Something is going to happen in the coming weeks that will force the gallant, chivalrous Sir Kenwrec to make a decision that will cost him everything." She drew her index finger across her throat and clucked her tongue. "But you can save him by releasing him to me. Right now. All you have to do is say the words. Falcon can remain here, with you and your clan. I do not require his physical presence."

Stress pounded at his temples. Despite her argument, the witch was speaking in riddles. What could she possibly want with Falcon? And what would drive him to turn his back on his clan? Hadrian wracked his brain, desperately seeking the answer. He thought of every possible scenario and every outcome. None would lead to Falcon's banishment or death...except Sonya.

Silvie smiled as if she knew his thoughts. "This will be our secret," she said with a wink.

Chapter Twenty-Four

Eva stretched, reaching for the ceiling. Bending about the waits, she wrapped her hands around her ankles and pulled her chest flat to her thighs, her chin touching her knees.

Amazing. There was no other word for the way she felt. The pain of her transition was gone, nothing but a horrific memory. Hadrian had been right. She woke up feeling wonderful, her mind buzzing from her super sexy dreams of the sinfully sexy vampire king. The world was brighter, her vision sharper. She had quickly found out her hearing had improved as well. Eva had come down to the gym for a quick and simple yoga session, a brisk jog and a few rounds with the punching bag—her morning routine. Hopping on the treadmill, she popped her ear buds in, fired up her iPod, and cranked the volume, as usual. But this time she nearly died of a heart attack. Her ears were still ringing and she had run ten miles and even pummeled the punching bag.

She laughed when she checked her watch, normally she would be feeling tired by now, panting, craving water, breakfast and good shower. But she felt fine—no, better than fine. She was not even close to winded.

Improved stamina? Score one for my shifter side. Exercise will be a breeze.

She could definitely give Hadrian a workout in the sack. That is, if they ever ended up in bed together again. Eva prayed yesterday was not a one time thing. He had given her exactly what she craved and more. She'd had orgasms before, but nothing like what he had given her.

Eva had once wondered how people became sex addicts. Well, now she had her answer. All she could think about was Hadrian's lips on hers, his hands caressing her body, his hard chest pressing her down into the mattress, her thighs gripping his hips as he pumped into her.

Maybe she could use a shower after all, a cold one.

Sometime in the night, when she was surely snoring like a lion, Hadrian had come in and cleaned up the glass. She had briefly thought about asking what happened, but decided against it. The man was not the sharing type and she would not press him to tell her what had made him snap.

Eva gathered her things: a small white towel, her iPod, and a roll of Ace bandage that she used to wrap her knuckles, and jogged to her room. Her muscles relaxed and her body heated when she reached her room. Hadrian had just been here. His scent still lingered in the air.

"I guess my sense of smell also improved," she said to herself, as she closed the bedroom door.

She kicked off her running shoes, slipped out of her yoga pants and tossed her tank top to the floor as she crossed to the bathroom. She paused, her gaze falling on a large white box resting on the bed.

Excitement shot through her as she rushed forward. A present? Hadrian had brought her a gift.

Her fingers made quick work of the red bow. Impatiently, she threw the top of the box aside, her hands diving into the white tissue paper. Eva's breath caught. A floor length, silk, crimson gown was gently folded and snuggled in the box. She stumbled forward, her toes hitting something hard. She bent down and found a pair of black, strapped heels. Taking them up, she set the shoes beside the box on the bed.

"Wow," she sighed. It was so lovely, she was almost afraid to touch it. She lightly traced the deep v-neckline, her fingers barely skipping over the material.

She snatched the envelope that was propped against the pillows. She ripped it open, not caring where the paper landed.

She squealed with excitement. Hadrian was inviting her to dinner.

A date, she wondered, and prayed that it was, even though she had been telling herself all morning not to expect anything from the vampire. *Don't get your hopes up*, she thought. They had slept together, he stuck by her side during the transition, and cared for her when it was over, but that did not mean he wanted anything more.

She spun and headed into the bathroom. Flipping on the light she was pleased to discover a new mirror had been mounted. She stripped and studied her reflection. Leaning over the counter she inspected her teeth; her incisors looked a little longer. She ran her tongue over them and winced, they were sharper. Glancing down at her hands she tried to get her nails to grow. Earlier in the gym they had lengthened to claws as she attacked the punching bag. Now, they did nothing.

She shrugged. Maybe they were triggered by adrenaline. She turned her hands over. Frowning, she studied the odd-shaped scar on the inside of her right wrist. She had first noticed the mark when she was brushing her teeth. It didn't hurt, it wasn't even red, but white like it had been there for years.

"Could be a weird witch thing," she said, turning away from the mirror. She would ask Hadrian if he knew anything about it at dinner.

Deciding to pamper herself, Eva filled the Jacuzzi tub and sprinkled some aromatherapy bath salts into the water. She settled beneath the bubbles. Leaning her head back, she let out a long sigh and allowed her mind to wander. It did not take long for her thoughts to focus on the interesting subject of Hadrian and his body.

She ran her tongue over her lips as she thought about tasting him. She wanted to stroke his shaft with her hands and take him into her mouth...

What would they talk about tonight? She certainly had more questions about what she could expect. Would she go into heat? The transition only came when the body fully matured. Females generally went through their first cycle of heat three days after their change, which meant she had two days. Would Hadrian help her through the need? Her body tingled from head to toe as she thought of a sexual marathon with her dark vampire.

No, not mine, she chided herself. Eva would not delude herself. Sure, she had been a virgin and yes, that made her experience with Hadrian all the more special. But she was also a twenty-six year old and knew how the world worked, even if she had spent the last nine years in a jungle.

Besides, the rational and sensible part of her wondered if she should want a relationship with Hadrian. It wouldn't work. There were two simple facts that could not be overcome: he is a king, and she is a half-breed. He was just returning to society after being lost in a sea of insanity and he had a Clan to integrate into. Having her on his arm would only make things more complicated. Once everything about her transition was figured out, she would leave and most likely never see Hadrian again.

A low growl slipped past her lips as something within her rebelled. Eva shifted, suddenly physically uncomfortable, her muscles coiled with tension despite the hot water and her claws scraped along the porcelain bottom of the tub.

Mine.

Eva took in ten measured breaths to calm her sudden need to hunt Hadrian. Something primal roared within her to take the vampire and…mark him. Images of entwined limbs, twisted sheets, teeth and blood danced in her mind.

Mine. Bite. Mark. The words whispered over and over.

Eva shook head trying to cast aside the feral desire. Why was her shifter side obsessed with Hadrian?

Mate, her instincts screamed.

Chapter Twenty-Five

Hadrian paced like a caged lion before the open mouth of the hearth in the main hall. He was eager to see Eva. Too eager. All he could think about was tasting her lips again as he buried himself deep inside her body.

Gods, those sounds she made when she came...

He growled, his steps growing faster. He would never hear those sounds again. Never. He could not allow himself to grow accustomed to her presence and her warmth. She would be leaving soon and he would go back to his life and to focusing on his Clan.

He rubbed his chest. Why did he feel as if someone had just driven a dagger into his heart?

Hadrian sighed and turned towards the table. The new butler he had hired this morning had spared no expense, but wasn't that what he had told the man? New China, crystal, and linens had been purchased, along with numerous floral arrangements. The man had done an amazing job selecting a dress for Eva. Hadrian hoped it fit since he had guessed her size. He had also arranged for the chef to come tonight and from what he smelled, the food would be excellent.

His mind began to wander, as it had all day while he lay in his bed refusing the siren call of sleep.

Did Eva think this was a date? Had he intended it be? He didn't know, but a part of him hoped it was. He had read about dating, seen how it was portrayed in films, and even observed the custom during one of his rare visits to town. Mortals placed a high value on the social ritual. Besides, he wanted to give her something normal.

Hadrian winced. He was so far from normal it was laughable.

Rolling his shoulders he tried to loosen the tension that wound about his muscles. The black jacket he wore stretched, the seams protesting his movements.

The garments were confining and he was glad he had decided against the tie. Instead, he left the collar of his black button up open. He prayed he looked suitable; he had been unwilling to check his reflection, terrified of what he would find. He could not bear to yet again see Titus's image staring back at him or the vile demon.

He let loose a string of curses and took up his pacing once more. This was ridiculous. What had he been thinking? A date would not change anything. It would not soothe his heartache when she left. He had told himself repeatedly that he needed to protect her and the best way would her leaving. No attachments. Yet here he was.

Gods, was he trying to change himself for her? He had always hated wearing finery, he was a soldier to the core and he felt more at home in armor and leather. Well, now it would be jeans and a t-shirt, but this suit certainly was not him. Nor were the candles or the flowers that were arranged on the table. He glanced back at the place settings and cringed. Hell, he was considering eating for Eva, to make her feel more comfortable. It had been 1,967 years since he last ate. He remembered his last meal perfectly, a skin of wine and a loaf of rustic bread.

Hadrian's steps paused, his gaze falling to the fire. His stomach knotted. He had barely been able to swallow the food; he had been consumed by anger, pumping through his veins like boiling tar. Revenge. He had spent a fortnight hunting the demon that had taken his brother.

Taken, Hadrian scoffed, his hands curling into fists. A trap. It had been a perfectly planned trap organized by Imbrasus himself. The vampire had stalked him for months, learning all his strengths and seizing upon his only weakness, his twin.

Fury spotted his vision as he continued to stare into the flames.

Titus had not been taken. Titus had embraced the evil that wanted to claim their souls.

"I could not bear to be alone. I need you. I need my brother." He heard the words as if Titus were standing at his side.

The flames in the hearth flickered as the memories assailed him. The soldiers had whispered of a pale man with white as lightning eyes stalking the battlefields. Hadrian had thought it was a rumor spread by the locals to frighten his men and ruin moral. But the beast was real and it had captured Titus.

Hadrian's body shook as violent waves of rage coursed through him, burning his veins. His fangs elongated, his eyes sparked with hell fire. The impulse to kill, to maim, to destroy was consuming. He took in a breath, his lungs filling with heated air. His chest expanded as a roar built in his throat. The demon sneered as it pawed back and forth in his mind, ready, eager for release.

The delicate scent of vanilla crashed over him in a rush. The comforting aroma was like physical caress. As if on command, his body relaxed, his mental shield went up blocking the vampire. He exhaled an easy sigh.

The sweet perfume drew his gaze to the main staircase. His jaw slackened as his eyes fell on Eva. The red dress clung to her like a second skin and flowed with every step. Her hair was swept up in a mass of curls fastened by a red rose clip, exposing her long, elegant neck. Her pulse drew his attention before his eyes continued their decent. The plunging neckline complimented her full, high breasts. Her tanned skin shimmered like gold in the candlelight.

She was beautiful, radiant.

He took a deep breath in through his nose, his body hardening. And when she smiled, his heart stopped.

My mate. My Eva.

He shook himself mentally. He had bound them together, but no promises had been made. He could not afford to grow attached to Eva, even if she was his mate. She desired freedom and he would give it to her. Besides, he was not what women would call 'relationship material.'

"Good evening," he greeted, coming forward. He met her at the bottom of the stairs. She took his arm and allowed him to escort her to the table.

"This looks lovely," she said, taking her seat beside him at the head of the table. "And thank you for the dress. It is beautiful."

Hadrian leaned in, his lips brushing her ear as he whispered, "You look delicious."

She smiled. "So do you."

He pulled back, his gaze lingering on her lips. Chills of anticipation sprinted down her spine.

The sound of hurried footsteps shattered the moment.

Eva glanced about wondering who could be coming their way. The footfalls sounded nothing like Clare's, the chef. A short man dressed in all black, with the exception of his white gloves, appeared carrying a bottle of wine. He paused at the end of the table and bowed. Hadrian waved him forward.

"Eva, this is Mr. Banik. I hired him this morning. He is the new butler."

"My lady," the man said with another bow.

"Hi," Eva said, unsure how to greet the man. She had never been addressed as 'my lady' and it threw her.

"Wine, Your Majesty?"

Hadrian nodded then instructed Mr. Banik to leave the bottle at the table.

"Shall we have a toast?" Hadrian asked once Mr. Banik hurried off. He waited for Eva to take up her glass. "To life."

She smiled and took her very first sip of wine. The red liquor felt heavy and pleasantly warm. She returned the glass to the table with a smile.

"What is your secret?"

Eva laughed. "I've never had wine before. When I was younger, I did sneak a beer or two from my uncle's fridge, but that's all."

"Is it to your liking?"

She nodded and leaned back in her seat. Mr. Banik had returned, serving the soup course.

Eva took up her spoon and waited to see if Hadrian would do the same. He did not.

Hadrian eyed the spinach cream soup with apprehension. Would he have to force his digestive tract to function or would it work on its own? It had been so long since he used those organs. Would it be painful or just cause a mild discomfort?

"You don't have to eat," she said as if reading his troubled thoughts.

Hadrian hesitantly wrapped his fingers around his spoon. Fortifying his resolve, he took a sip. Nothing happened. His stomach did not revolt like he had suspected. It felt...normal; just as it had when he was mortal. He sighed in relief and pushed the bowl aside.

Mr. Banik brought the next course, sautéed shrimp over a bed of chopped cherry tomatoes and bell peppers.

After a few bites, she noticed he did not try this dish.

"So, are you like Falcon and only like hot fudge sundaes?"

Hadrian frowned. "I have never had a hot fudge sundae."

"Really? Wow, you don't know what you are missing."

"Perhaps you can show me."

Eva bit her lip as she envisioned Hadrian licking ice cream and chocolate syrup from her body.

"Truth be known, I have not eaten a single morsel since my transformation," he said.

She set her fork down. "Really? I can't imagine going without food for that long. I enjoy it way too much." *Probably because I've lived on the edge of starvation for so long,* she thought. "If you don't mind me asking, when were you changed?"

He was silent for a moment before answering, "I was born in 14 A.D." He paused. "I became a vampire when I was thirty-two."

Eva sipped her wine. The air thickened with tension. They needed a subject change. "On the topic of transitions, I don't remember much of last night, aside from the excruciating pain. But I vaguely remember you giving me your blood."

He straightened in his throne-like chair. "Yes, I apologize. I know you despise the sight, scent, and taste of blood."

"I liked it," she said a little too quickly. She blushed and dropped her gaze to her lap.

Mr. Banik was back. He cleared away the plates and presented an asparagus salad.

"Why did you give me your blood?"

Chapter Twenty-Six

"The priestess I spoke with suggested I share my blood with you."

"Well, it lessened the pain." Eva poked at the salad with her fork. "Was it to help me—did you do it to...Why is this so hard to say?"

She took up her wine again, suddenly needing the courage only liquor could provide. It was difficult to think of how close she had come to dying.

No, I did die, she told herself. She had seen the great white light and...her mother. A shiver rocked her.

Clearing her throat, she tried again, "Is that why I survived?"

Hadrian came forward, placing his elbows on the table. He laced his fingers together. How much should he tell her? It had been his blood that brought her back to the realm of the living. What did she think of the brand on her wrist? Would she ask about it or should he tell her? What would he say? All day he had been unable to think of how to deliver the information, words failed him. How was he to explain that her life was forever bound to his?

He sighed, and rubbed his brow. If he could he would tell her nothing of their bond, but for now, he would give simple answers. He would go into detail later, after she had some time to process this new information.

"Yes, my blood saved you from death," he said, his voice was rough like gravel.

Eva sullenly nodded. "Did the priestess happen to mention whether or not I will experience estrus?" she asked, deciding to use the technical term. Somehow it made the situation feel a little less personal, a little less...real.

"The witch is a seer," he stated, "according to her visions, you will."

Eva finished her wine and Hadrian refilled her glass.

She had heard the compulsion to breed was overwhelming. It drove women to attack men, their animal side completely exposed. It could easily get bloody and violent, if the female's needs were not met.

"I have acquired some Levo to ease your need. It will not put you under like other remedies, but it will relax you and keep you calm."

Eva blinked. "You think of everything."

How the hell had he gotten his hands on Levo? The drug was elusive, expensive, and was definitely not for sale to vampires.

The drug of choice for the females in most packs was morphine. It did not stop the need; it just made the women blissfully unaware of the pain. The females who were left un-medicated were untamed and uncontrollable, overcome with the violent need for sex. Levo would leave her lucid, but numbed out. The pain would be dulled and so too would the cravings.

Eva's body heated, desire rushed through her as her imagination went wild. She would give anything to make love with Hadrian for twenty-four hours. She would die of ecstasy. Problem was, she did not know if he would be game.

Gathering her courage, she asked, "What if I don't want to take it?"

His brow wrinkled. "It is my understanding that if not treated, females suffer painfully."

"Yeah, but what I'm asking…" Eva allowed her words to fade. How pathetic and embarrassing. Had she really been about to ask the vampire to tend to her needs? The man hadn't offered and she would not beg. "Forget it."

Hadrian shifted in his seat trying to relieve some of the pressure building within him. His body had hardened. He knew the line of her thoughts. Eva had been about to ask him to service her and he knew he would be unable to deny such a request. He craved to drive the hardest part of himself into her, to feel her come around him, on him. The thought had him itching to clear the table with a swift swipe of his arm, lay her down, raise her dress and thrust into her.

Needing to focus on anything other than his thoughts, he said, "I do have some good news; because of your mother, you have no obligations to the pack."

Eva's gaze shot back to meet his. "What does that mean?"

"You are free of them and of my Clan. You may leave Palatio Nocte when you are ready. However, I suggest you wait until your estrus has passed."

Relief and angry hostility flooded her. To be free, to be finished with the pack forever was her dream. She had tried to run away countless times, only to be caught, dragged back, and punished. Why her father cared so much about her escaping she would never know. But with her independence from the pack came her release from the Validus Clan.

A ward was required for the treaty to be upheld. Who would be sent to take her place? Would it be Teresa? The thought was laughable. Yes, the pack lived deep in the jungle, but Teresa and her mother spent much of their time in town with servants in tow. She could never survive here, secluded without anyone to pamper her and cater to her every whim. Jealousy took root within her as she thought of Teresa living in the castle alone with Hadrian. If the shifter ever gave Hadrian an interested glance, Eva would scratch her eyes out.

No, I won't be here when the new girl comes. I will be far, far away. Finally living my life, she reminded herself. *I will be far away from Hadrian.*

A sharp pain speared her chest. She nearly doubled over. Rubbing her hand over her heart she tried to breath, but her lungs were heavy. Why did she suddenly feel as if someone had ripped out her heart?

"So, who will be taking my place?" she asked, unable to silence her jealousy. She had to know.

"No one. As of today the treaty has been terminated."

Her jaw dropped. "What? Why?"

Hadrian gave a slow shrug, the jacket straining over his wide shoulders. "Arsenio cannot be trusted. The contract specifically states a purebred is to be given to the Validus Clan. He did not hold up his end, and now that we have discovered your true linage, I am extremely suspicious of his motives."

"Because of me you ended your alliance?"

"He had to have known your mother was a Shaw. Their magic is incredibly strong. A shifter of his abilities would be able to scent her a mile away. He allowed her to leave Brazil with you because he knew he had no right to claim you. Perhaps he hoped the two of you would never return."

"But we did."

"Yes, and he captured you." Hadrian's hands clenched, the whites of his knuckles flashing. "I wish I knew why."

176

"You and me both," she sighed, pushing her plate away. Her appetite had vanished, which was a shame, the lamb looked and smelled delicious. "But, it doesn't really matter. What is done is done. There is no going back." She took up her wine glass once more. "I will never see him again, just as I had planned when I left."

"You intended to escape?' Hadrian said, every muscle in his body tensed as if preparing for a chase.

She will never escape me.

He took a breath and forced himself to relax. She was not running from him, he was letting her leave.

"Somehow," she confirmed. "I underestimated how far from civilization the castle would be and I certainly did not expect that interesting draw bridge."

Eva would not tell him, but she had devised an escape plan. She would wait until the night of the ball, the night her father was to come collect her and haul her back to Brazil. She knew there would hundreds if not thousands of guests. She could easily blend in and sneak about unnoticed. She would steal a car, if she could remember what Jose, her boyfriend from junior year, had showed her. She assumed the bridge would be left extended because of the amount of traffic. Simple.

"Well, you needn't worry about that. When Falcon returns he will take you to Ivano-Frankivsk. It is the closest city with an international airport."

Eva almost dropped her glass. She finished the wine, then carefully returned the crystal to the table, her fingers trembling.

"And when will Falcon be back?"

"Wednesday."

"Wednesday," she repeated, her voice cracking. Her heart stopped, her blood crystallized in her veins, and her vision swayed. Three days. Hadrian was sending her away in three days.

He nodded. "I have arranged for our jet to take you back to Florida. That is where you had said you would like to live. I also had someone contact your mother's friend. Francis would be glad to have you stay with her. Or, if you decide you would rather have a place of your own, my people have found some apartments you may like. I have also spoken with the universities in the area. You could apply and start next semester, if you so desire. I will fund your education." He reached for her hands, but pulled back. "I want you to know that no matter where you go or what you decide to do, you will have the support and protection of the Validus."

She did not know if she should thank him or dump her plate in his lap. Here he was, offering her everything she had said she wanted, except him. He was making it possible for her to return to her old life in the States and attend school. She could become a pediatrician just like she had dreamed.

He was presenting her with a normal, average, boring life, but it no longer held its appeal. She didn't want normal. She wanted excitement. She didn't want average, she wanted everything that a life here with him had to offer and she could not go back to boring after living with Hadrian.

She tried to tell herself that it was good. This was what she wanted, but her head could not convince her heart. Even though she knew she shouldn't, she had hoped for more.

"Eva," he said with a frown. When she did not respond, he shook her shoulder.

She shrugged his hand off and turned to face him. Her eyes clouded, the amber depths swirled with emotions he could hardly name. He recognized sorrow and anger, but the others...he did not understand. He had thought Eva would be happy to know she would never have to return to the pack, that she could live her life the way she chose. She said she wanted normal and safe. He could give neither. He was a vampire, plagued with the demon of his maker, and he was dangerous.

"You have devised a very nice plan," she said, her words cold, her tone flat. "Would you allow me to stay here until I came up with my own plan?'"

"I will not force you to vacate."

She nodded slowly. Silence stretched between them. Mr. Banik came and went, offering a new bottle of wine. Hadrian declined and the butler swiftly disappeared.

"Eva," he sighed, leaning towards her. "This is a lot of information and a lot of changes all at once. I will not pressure you to make a decision." His fingers twitched to touch her. He wanted to cup her face and capture her lips with his. The memory of her taste, the soft gentle glide of her tongue against his, the feel of her breath against his skin, was maddening.

"I appreciate that," she replied, pushing her seat away from the table. "Excuse me."

Hadrian reached for her, impulse driving him. He caught her hand and pulled her back. "Wait. Eva, I need to know...Last night—"

"I have no regrets," she said, tilting her chin up, "You don't have to worry, Hadrian. I know that you never intended to sleep with me and that it just happened. I'm glad that it did. In hindsight, it may have been a mistake, but it was a mistake worth making."

"Eva, I wish things were different, that I was...different."

"I'm not expecting anything from you."

He winced. He wanted more, but it was impossible.

"Just so that we are clear, tell me, why can't I expect anything from you. Or, should I say, from us? And don't give me the same excuses. I may not heal instantaneously like you, but I will mend quickly enough. You will not have to worry about being too rough. I'm also no longer your ward."

Hadrian froze. The truth. He had to tell her the truth. He is a beast, a murderer. He had killed the only person he had ever truly loved in cold blood. The act unleashed the demon. It swept through him, taking hold of his very bones and poisoned his soul. Twisting him. Breaking him. Leaving him hollow. He had been lost for centuries, unable to discern the vampire's memories from his own. They bled together until reality no longer existed. Only now was he beginning to climb out of the madness. His mind was mending, the mental barrier between him and the demon grew stronger every day, but he still could not be trusted. If he hurt her, if he even inflicted the slightest scratch, he would never be able to forgive himself.

It was better for her to leave now. If she stayed, it would only be harder to let her go later.

His soul wept as he hardened his heart. *I must do what is best for her*. And he was not it.

"I could not bear to see you hurt," he began. "I am a monster, Eva."

"I don't believe that."

"If you knew what I have done, you would think differently."

"Then tell me."

Dark shadows fell over his face. "You need to forget about me, Eva. I am no good for you. All I can give you is pain."

Eva wanted to cry, her roiling emotions were becoming too much. Her frustration simmered as sorrow pumped through her veins. She wished Hadrian could see himself through her eyes. Just once. There was darkness within him, menacing and terrifying, but there was light within him too. He was fighting so hard to protect her. Deep down, Eva knew the truth. He was protecting himself. He wore his madness like a shield.

If he would just talk to her, open up and share the secrets that ate at his soul, he would heal. He would finally be able to let go of the self-loathing that dulled his brilliant obsidian eyes and shake free the guilt that looped around his neck like a noose.

"What happened last night cannot happen again. Please, understand that it isn't you—"

Something within her snapped. The anger that she held bottled inside exploded.

"Stop," she growled, yanking her hand from his grasp. "Don't you dare feed me that cliché."

"You are angry."

Eva tossed her napkin on the table. "You're damn right, I'm angry."

Mr. Banik had to enter at that exact moment. The man kept his head down, his eyes focused on the warmed dinner rolls he carried. After setting them on the table he fled back to the safety of the kitchen.

"I'm tired of people making plans for my life. For the past nine years I've had my life run by a dictator. I want you to know, I will leave when I decide to leave." Eva came to her feet. "And I know it isn't me. It is you. You're damaged, right? You lost your rocks when your brother died. I'm sure there is more to your story, something dark and twisted. Some secret that you keep buried in your soul, a secret so damning it is destroying you from the inside out. Maybe you have survivors' guilt or maybe he was the only thing you had that made life worth living. I don't know and I'm willing to bet no one knows because you share nothing. You even lock Falcon out of your heart. The knight loves you like a brother."

"Eva that is enough. You speak of things you do not understand."

"I could," she countered. She smoothed her dress and noticed her hands were shaking. Her emotions swept through her, a violent unstoppable maelstrom.

"You are not the only one who has ever suffered, Hadrian. I couldn't eat, I couldn't sleep, and I couldn't breathe when my mother passed. And just days after we laid her to rest I was taken. I was seventeen. My entire world, my life, was ripped from me and I was thrust into hell. People who hated me, who treated me as if I were an abomination, an affront to God, were now my caregivers. I know loneliness. I know what it is like to have nothing and no one. Nine years. I lost nine years of my life."

Eva straightened her back and refused the tears that burned her eyes. She would not cry. *Ever*.

"Do you think I'm this thin by choice? I know my hipbones stick out and you can count my ribs. Those savages I was forced to live among couldn't be bothered to feed the half-breed. They preferred to pretend I did not exist. I had to scavenge, forage, and hunt what I could in order to stay alive. Can you imagine how terrifying that would be for a seventeen year old girl who had known nothing but love and kindness until that point?"

She raised her hands to her hips. Her temper rising, hate laced every word. "But they didn't break me. They could never break me. It didn't matter how many insults or condemning looks they cast my way. It didn't matter that my 'step-mother' made up excuses so she could have me beaten. And now here I am." She threw her arms out wide. "My sperm donor must have sent me here hoping this castle would be my tomb and that his shameful secret would die with me. But I'm still kicking because you are not as crazed, ruthless, and soulless as everyone, including yourself, believes."

Eva took in a deep breath and slowly exhaled, her body shuddered. Adrenaline pounded through her veins and her heart drummed in her ears. Hadrian stared at her, his eyes flashing red, and a muscle ticked in his jaw as he ground his teeth together. He could be mad, hell, he could spin into a rage, but she did not care. He needed to hear this.

"Shit, Hadrian, after all of that has happened and almost happened between us, I still want you." She stepped around her chair and descended the dais. "But we can't be together. You won't let us happen. You have this idea of who and what you are that is so...wrong. You say you want to protect me from emotional and possible physical pain. Well, I've got news for you. I'm much stronger than I appear. I can hold my own." She pinned him with a hard glare. "And I see you, Hadrian. I see the *real* you. We are so similar. Our souls bear wounds, but what separates us, is that despite everything, I have not closed myself off from the world. I want to live." She rubbed her temples and released a heavy sigh. "When you stop reciting your reasons why we can't and shouldn't be together and you finally throw away your pity party hat, come knock on my door. I'll answer. Well, that is if I haven't already left."

With that, Eva turned and exited the hall, ascending the stairs with graceful, elegant strides.

Chapter Twenty-Seven

Wind pounded against the castle as lightning cut the sky and thunder roared. The storm had unleashed its fury when Eva slammed her bedroom door.

Hours had passed since she left Hadrian downstairs at the table to digest her words.

She punched her pillow.

God, she had lost it and she felt awful; her stomach was in knots, her heart ached and her emotions were a tangled mess. She did not regret what she had said, but the way she had said it. Venom had dripped from her words.

Rolling to her back, she let out a heavy sigh.

Should she hunt Hadrian down and apologize? Or should she pack her things and head out as soon as the storm passed?

Eva snorted. She would not take the coward's way out, no matter how appealing it sounded.

She knew she should get some sleep; it would help her clear her mind and organize her thoughts. Then she could find Hadrian. Besides, she was willing to bet he did not want to see her right now.

Eva closed her eyes and tried to will herself to sleep, but the image of Hadrian sitting at the table, his jaw tightly set, his black gaze filled with raw pain.

"Damn it," she hissed, tossing off the sheets.

Eva got out of bed. She kicked her feet into her slippers and grabbed her robe. She had to talk to Hadrian, she had to apologize, only then would she be able to sleep.

She paused in the hall outside her room. Surrendering to her senses, she sought him out, relieved to find that he was in the castle. She did not want to have to brave the storm and try to have a teeth chattering conversation by the lake.

Her footsteps were silent as she wound her way through the keep until she found the west wing and the hall of windows. Glancing out the windows as she walked, she watched the storm ravage the landscape. Ice slapped the glass as the angry wind thrashed. She slowly made her way through the long, glass-enclosed corridor. A set of floor to ceiling doors proudly stood at the end of the hall.

The hairs on the back of her neck rose as goose bumps pricked her skin. The king was inside.

Eva straightened her spine and squared her shoulders. She gathered her courage and tucked her emotions aside, clearing her mind. She forced herself to be calm and controlled. Ready for anything.

She shoved open the doors and stumbled in. She had expected them to be heavier, or was she stronger? She shrugged, deciding to test her strength later. Her eyes adjusted quickly. The walls and ceiling were lined with mirrors. Rays of moonlight peaked through the windows. The glass shimmered. The ballroom glittered with a luminescent glow, ethereal and otherworldly. The balcony doors were thrown wide, snow fluttered in to cover the gleaming, polished marble floor.

Instinct told her he was here. She glanced about the room, squinting as she peered into the shadows. She could not find him.

Frowning, Eva crossed the room and stepped out onto the balcony. The wind had increased, the clouds boiled against the dark sky and snow swirled, the flakes catching in her hair and frosting her lashes. Lightning sizzled and thunder shattered the serene silence.

Hadrian watched her from the shadows. The white silk of her robe clung to her, hugging the swell of her breasts and the curve of her hips. All around her nature erupted. She looked like an ancient Roman goddess. She was breathtaking.

Eva slowly turned, her eyes searching the ballroom. She could feel the heat and hunger in his gaze; it called to something primitive within her. Eva stepped back into the castle, the wind brushed past her, carrying her vanilla scent.

"Why are you here?" he demanded, his forceful tone echoed through the ballroom and made the crystal chandelier sway.

Ignoring the sharp warning in his voice, she said, "This room is gorgeous."

Chilled fingers wrapped around her throat as Hadrian appeared before her. His eyes flickered with red, his fangs bared. His elegant suit was torn, the jacket hanging from him in shreds, the shirt ripped open, framing his hard chest. He looked wild.

"I asked you a question."

Eva shoved at his shoulder and he released his hold.

"I came to apologize."

The room spun as she was twirled around and pushed against the wall of mirrors. The glass was cool on her face.

Hadrian laced an arm around her waist, gathering her robe and nightgown in his fist, pinning her. With his free hand he nudged her panties aside.

"I will take your apology from here."

Eva's thoughts would not keep up with his swift movements, but her body responded. Heat gathered, pooling at her core. She was ready for him. Her heart raced in anticipation.

His hands moved to grip her hips, pulling her roughly against him. She moaned as his hard length brushed against her.

A low growl rumbled through the room. He shoved away and Eva fell against the wall. She straightened her clothing and whirled around.

"Gods, Eva," Hadrian groaned, his hands trembled as he covered his face. "You make me crazed."

She heard him suck in one deep breath after another until his lungs and his heart stopped. She blinked, unsettled by the change.

He turned and stalked through the shadows. A throne stood against the back wall, the high back was cushioned by red velvet, the wood trimmed in gold. Roaring lion's heads formed the arms. He mounted the steps and fell onto the seat. His long legs stretched out before him as he reclined. He looked worn, his face sunken, his eyes rimmed with dark circles and his gaze unfocused.

"State your piece and go," he commanded with a regal air.

Eva approached the raised dais. "I want to say I'm sorry."

He scoffed, unsheathing a long dagger that dangled from a leather strap, which was hooked around one of the lion's teeth. The blade glinted in the darkness.

"Why?"

"Well, I, huh…" Words failed her as Hadrian playfully fingered the tip of the dagger. "I want to be clear. I'm not sorry for what I said, but I should have said it differently. I had no right talking about your brother like that." She shifted nervously, crossing her arms over her chest. He was turning the blade over in his hand. "I've never exploded like that before and it wasn't fair of me to dump everything on you like I did."

He slowly drew the blade across his palm, lying open his skin. "Apology not accepted."

"Whatever," she snapped. "Enjoy." Turning, she headed for the door.

"Wait," he called, as she was about to walk out.

Against her better judgment, Eva paused. She did not look back.

"You were right."

"What?" she whispered, turning to face him.

Hadrian beckoned her to come forward. She stopped at the foot of the steps that lead up to him.

"Titus," he grated, slicing his hand again. Eva winced. The wound heeled immediately, his flesh knitting back together as if nothing had happened. "My twin. He stood exactly where you are the night I killed him."

Chapter Twenty-Seven

Eva went numb. She did not know what to say, what to think or feel. She could not believe Hadrian could have murdered his own brother.

She sank to her knees, sitting back on her heels, her robe pooled about her. Eva folded her hands in her lap and waited patiently for him to continue. She would not push, she would not demand or question. She would listen, that was what he needed, someone to listen and to understand.

"There are many sins that tear at my soul, but this...I have never shared with anyone." He shook his head. The deepest of sorrow filled his eyes as regret thickened his voice. "I did not come to power the traditional way. Imbrasus, the Father of my Clan, built a great army. He searched the world for the most ruthless, bloodthirsty, unforgiving warriors."

Eva ignored the taunting glint of the dagger. The cinnamon scent of his blood spiced the air and then instantly vanished.

"Warlords make pathetic kings. For centuries, tyrants ruled my clan. Civil war was constant. Death stalked these mountains, claiming vampires and humans with no discrimination.

"In 1654, Avery Moreau ascended the throne," he paused and his gaze flickered to hers. "I had been in South America when that monster was crowned."

Hadrian growled. He sounded like a beast ready to attack. He turned away from her. "Moreau was an avid supporter of human slavery. He kept bleeders as pets, locking them in cages, using them for his own amusements. They never lived long. He believed that vampires were a superior race. Humans were nothing but animals to him and his supporters. He had even devised a breeding program."

Hadrian's lips twisted as disgust sharpened his eyes. His fangs lengthened and Eva winced as he cut himself again. The sound of the blade rending flesh made her stomach churn and she wished she knew why he was cutting himself.

"Can you imagine infants and children used as bleeders?" he snarled. "I could not allow such evil and I returned home. I organized and led a rebellion. The war lasted five years. I cut Moreau down on the battlefield, claiming his and his heir's head. Leaving no clear successor, the nobles of the clan gathered and voted for a new ruler. They elected me and I was crowned in 1659. Twelve years later, my world ended."

He shifted, craning his neck away as if suddenly frightened of his reflection. He fixed his eyes on the wall of windows and stared unseeing into the storm.

"Every year around Halloween, my clan hosts a masked ball. Nobles from all the families gathered for the gala. It was that night, the party had ended and dawn was near. Titus had requested I meet him here, in the Hall of Mirrors." The dagger clattered to the floor. His fingers gripped the lion's heads, his knuckles turning white, his claws extending. "He threw a sword at my feet," he swallowed hard. "He challenged me. At first, I thought it was amusing. Why would my own brother challenge me for the throne?" His body shook with a violent shiver. "He attacked, lunging and swinging his sword. I defended myself.

"As we fought I demanded to know the meaning behind his madness. I had no idea that for the last twelve years he had plotted against me, arranging one failed assassination after another. He was angered and declared I had betrayed him by naming Falcon my heir instead of him." Hadrian's voice dropped to a whisper. "I could not have chosen Titus to be my Second. He had not joined me during the rebellion, claiming it was his duty as a Black Knight to protect the monarchy, despite Moreau's behavior and actions. Falcon had stood by my side and charged into battle with me, never flinching, never doubting that what we were fighting for was right...Falcon is the most honorable man I have ever known. His loyalty knows no bounds."

He ran shaking hands down his face. Taking in a deep breath, he prayed to every god he could name for the strength to finish his confession.

"Our swords clashed. I tried to talk to him, to reason with him, but murder burned within his eyes. The fight led us out to the balcony. I pinned him against the railing, knocking his sword away." His voice cracked as the world began to close in on him. "I told him we were finished. I told him to forget his rage, to lay down his jealousy. I turned my back on him..."

187

Silence crowded the room and thickened the air until Eva found it difficult to breath.

"It was raining. Thunder and lightning splintered the heavens." His gaze dropped to the weapon that now lay abandoned on the floor at his feet. "I heard him unsheathe a dagger."

Eva's hands clenched in her lap, her claws extended. The delicate sound of ripping silk hit her ears like a shock wave of an exploding grenade.

Oh, god, no, she silently pleaded.

"He rushed me, the blade nicked by throat." Hadrian fell forward, his knees smacking the marble platform. His fingers gripped his head and dug into his skull as the memories attacked. He could feel the rain hit his face. He could hear the deafening stillness of death. The image of Titus's impaled, lifeless body flashed through his mind.

"In that moment, I did not see Titus as my brother. I saw him as a twisted, demented beast. I saw our sire, Imbrasus, glaring at me through his eyes." He doubled over, his arms wrapping around his middle. Eva forced herself to remain still. He needed to say these words. He needed to share his sins. He needed to release his guilt so he could heal. "For the first time, I saw Titus, the true Titus. He was no longer my brother. He was not the Titus I knew growing up." Hadrian began to rock back and forth on his knees, his head hung low, his eyes squeezed closed. "In that moment...I wanted to kill him."

Hadrian's voice caught, the words he so desperately needed to say were choking him as the memory of that night played like a silent film through his mind. He could feel the madness. It flowed like thick poison through his veins.

Say it, he demanded. *Say the words. Tell her what you have done. Prove to her that you are a monster, that you are unworthy of her kindness and affection.*

He knew he should tell her his actions. They would disgust her. They would make her flee. It would be easier for the both of them if she hated him. But damn the gods, he could not lose her. Eva had been the only good thing his insanity had brought him. She was a ray of light, a beacon of hope and his soul cried out for her.

Hadrian drew in rapid breaths, filling his lungs with her delicate scent. He imagined her hands stroking his back, her warmth seeping into him. The chaos in his mind slowly began to fade.

Gathering his strength, he shoved the madness aside, banishing it to the recesses of his mind. It would not stop him from confessing his sins, it would no longer keep him from asking for forgiveness and he desperately needed to be forgiven.

He sucked in a trembling breath and forced the words to pass his lips, "Titus swung his blade, aiming for my heart and I shoved him. He stumbled back. Titus tried to steady himself, but the balcony was slick from the rain and the railing was short...I watched my brother plummet to his death."

No longer able to hold back, Eva sprang to her feet and darted up the steps. Wrapping her arms around him, she pulled him to her. His wide shoulders shook as a pained cry wrenched from his chest. Her eyes stung with tears. She cried for him, for his loss. She understood his guilt. He believed he was a murderer, a monster, but it had been an accident, or according to some laws, a justifiable homicide. Titus had meant to kill him. His twin was the beast and Hadrian the victim. For hundreds of years he had carried this dark secret and it tore at his soul.

"You were defending yourself and it was an accident."

He shook his head, his cheek rubbing against her chest. "No, Eva. I murdered him. I should not have pushed him so hard. I should have wrested the dagger from him. I should have done something, anything other than killing him. No matter what he had become, no matter how evil he may have been...he was my brother. My twin."

She tightened her arms around him. "You did what you had to do."

He shoved her away. "It should have been me. I should have died that day, not Titus. Never Titus. He was weak and impressionable. I was to protect him. Always protect him." Red bled into the whites of his eyes. "I failed him."

"He was a grown man, not a child," Eva reasoned. "He made his own decisions."

"I never should have abandoned him to travel. I should never have allowed Moreau to come between us."

"You need to let go of the guilt. If Titus had not surrendered to his jealously and greed, none of this would have happened."

His fiery eyes glazed over as he stared past her. Eva glanced over her shoulder. There was nothing, no one. Was he reliving the fight?

After a long moment of silence he finally spoke, his words cold, his tone haunting. "I did die that night."

Eva frowned. She wished she knew what was going on in his mind. Had her mother possessed any special gifts that she could have passed on to her? She wished she could see into his past or read his thoughts. She wanted to help him. She felt as if it were her right and responsibility to take care of him, to soothe his wounds and mend his soul. Instinct demanded she do...something.

She cupped his face, her thumbs stroking over his cheeks. His turbulent emotions attacked her senses. She could feel his hate heat his skin, hear the regret that laced his voice, and taste his despair. Her heart wept for him.

"Oh, Eva, the worst has yet to be told."

He focused on his reflection and sneered. His face twisted in the mirror revealing the demon.

Tell her everything. She needs to know everything. Then she will understand why we cannot be together. She will see why I am dangerous. She will leave.

The vampire cried out, begging him to keep quiet. Odd, the fiend feared the truth. Until now, it had reveled in its deeds, proud of the pain it had inflicted.

He drew away from her. Eva's hands fell to her sides.

"I killed my maker, Imbrasus, the Father of the Validus. I sentenced that bastard to Hell. I drained him. I consumed every last drop of evil that resided in his soul. I took his demon."

"I don't understand."

A hard laugh escaped him. "I carry his vampire."

"That's not possible," she insisted. "During the transformation, the curse's poison invades the soul. If the person survives the change the magic in their blood creates the vampire. Demons can't be transferred."

His lips turned up in a cruel smile. "Would you be willing to stake your life on that popular belief?" His voice deepened and scratched over her skin as he said, "I would be happy to collect my winnings."

Eva shook her head, ignoring his taunt. "Tell me how this happened."

"He forced his blood on me beneath a full moon. My transformation was immediate." Hadrian paused as the memory crept forward. "My change was violent and my desire to kill the beast that had ruined my life was overwhelming. I held him down and drank deep. He was unable to stop me, already weak from the Death Curse. I drained him. I felt his immortality fail beneath my fangs." Gods, it had been a powerful, drugging sensation that rocked him to the core and poisoned his soul. Evil had strengthened his cells as the ancient's blood filled his body.

Eva held back her shock, masking her expression with a frown. She had never heard of anything like this.

He has said that he isn't like other vampires, she reminded herself.

Her blood turned cold and slowed her heart.

Hadrian could flash from place to place, dematerialize and appear at will, a gift only Dimitri, the last remaining original vampire possessed. And Hadrian's eyes did not turn the customary black of a fledgling. His gaze glowed red as fresh spilled blood when his vampire emerged.

Had Imbrasus's eyes been red?

"Until Titus's death I had been able to control the beast. My mind was strong, which was one of Imbrasus's reasons for changing me. When I watched Titus fall, the barrier between the demon and myself collapsed. The fiend attacked my psyche, extracting its revenge and punishing me for its confinement. Since, I have relived every evil act Imbrasus ever committed." His hands came to cover his ears as if he could muffle the voices. "I hear the screams and the pleas for mercy. I see the pale faces of countless corpses. I taste the blood and the death of every victim. It has attached its memories to mine. Twisting and blending everything together until I can no longer distinguish the memories from reality."

She felt ill. She had heard stories of Imbrasus, legends of his cruelty. He tortured, maimed, raped and slaughtered for the fun of it all. Imbrasus had hunted shifters to near extinction, driving the survivors to flee their homes, abandoning Europe to the vampires. To this day, none had returned.

Her hand came to her throat. She couldn't breathe as realization choked her, cutting off her airway. The vampire had caused Hadrian's madness. It was destroying him from the inside out. It had torn him apart as he mourned his brother, seizing upon his weakness. The vampire imprisoned Hadrian for centuries, torturing him. This was the reason he believed they could not be together. He feared the demon.

"I have the devil in my bones, Eva." His hands fell to his chest. "I cannot control it."

"You are no monster. You may carry one inside you, but you, Hadrian Lucretius, are no monster. Titus's death was an accident. You did not shove him with the purpose of sending him over the edge. He slipped. And I won't, nor will anyone else, hold his passing against you. Hadrian, you had every right to fight back. As for the vampire, you have it on a short leash."

Hadrian blinked. "Last night, in my bed, I could have killed you. When I saw your blood it was all I could do to keep from attacking you. The demon wanted to taste your pleasure rich blood and feel your pulse fade beneath my lips."

"You left"

"I could have—"

"You are no beast. You are gentle, kind, and selfless. There were numerous times when you could have taken my blood or claimed my life, but every time you pulled away, showing restraint. Even when you took my blood, you stopped before taking too much."

"I do not want to bring pain to anyone."

She reached out, her fingers brushing the line of his jaw.

His heart was as still as his lungs. Hadrian closed his eyes unable to stomach her tender display. Why was she touching him? Why was she trying to console him?

"The demon does not have hold of you." Her hands slipped to his shoulders. "Hadrian, look at me."

He slowly lifted his eyelids. Her gaze was so lovely, so pure. He was tempted to look away, those amber orbs could see straight into his soul.

"You need to remember who you are," she said, her voice low, the words soft. "Remember the man you are. Put down the shame and release your guilt." Her fingers lightly skimmed to his shoulders and massaged the tension from his muscles. "You need to forgive yourself and allow yourself to heal. Only then will you be able to begin again, and it is time you started living."

Hadrian had not felt the tears slip from his eyes and roll down his face, but Eva swept them away with her thumbs. He had been told words like these before, but they had never hit him like this.

"Stop living in the past." She leaned forward and kissed the corner of his eye. "Be here with me."

Eva took his hands. Hadrian rose to his feet with her. She pressed him back and he fell onto the throne. A sensual smile graced her lips as she untied her robe. The silk slipped to the floor, revealing her short light blue nightgown.

His brain went into overdrive, desperately trying to process what was happening. She still wanted to be with him. She was not repulsed by his confessions or frightened.

Eva sank to her knees. He reached for her shoulders.

"No," she said as she ran her hands up his thighs.

She was beginning to shiver. Hadrian commanded the balcony doors to close, blocking out the rush of cold wind and locking out the storm.

Her fingers slipped the button of his slacks free. The zipper came next. She parted his torn shirt, pushing it aside, revealing his abdomen.

Hadrian's hands fell and he gripped the arms of the chair. Air hissed between his clenched teeth as she pressed her lips to his ribs. Moving lower, her tongue swirled over his muscles and delved into his navel.

He kicked free of his shoes while she pushed his pants down and off. His erection free, it strained for her touch. She came closer. His groan cut through the silence as she slowly ran her tongue over her lips.

"I have been wanting to taste you," she whispered, her breath caressing his aroused flesh.

Eva took him in her hand, unable to close her fingers around his girth. He was hot and hard, iron wrapped in silk. She stroked him. Her movements agonizingly slow as she learned the feel of him. Dipping her head down, she tasted him, her tongue gliding from the base of his shaft to the swollen tip as she cupped his sac and massaged the heavy weights. She traced the head of his penis with her tongue and lapped at the bead of moisture that had formed. She peeked up at him from beneath her long, dark lashes. Hadrian thought he would faint dead away from the pleasure. Eva pressed a loving kiss to the broad tip before drawing his length into her mouth, taking him deep.

Hadrian's back arched, his nails cut into the wooden arms of the chair. He nearly came right then. She suckled, up and down. Bringing her hands up, she used them both to pump him into her mouth. Her tongue teased and tortured. His muscles strained, his breathing uneven. She worked him until he teetered on the edge of oblivion.

He could take no more. Reaching down, he circled his arms around her waist. Eva pouted as he drew her to her feet. He could not wait. He needed her. He needed to bury himself inside her searing core. He needed to feel her ripple around him as she came. He needed to release deep within her. Gods, he had never wanted anything more in his life. All his energy focused on her, his world revolved around her.

Hadrian was not gentle as he tore at her nightgown, the delicate fabric drifted to the cool marble floor in pieces. Leaning forward, he pushed her thighs apart, his fangs biting through the thin material of her panties. The scent of her arousal hit him like a freight train.

He hooked a hand beneath her knee and raised her right leg to set her small foot on the lion's head. He licked up her center, finding her hot and wet. She was ready for him. He shuddered. Gods, she was divine. Her taste and response were sweet perfection. He laved at her, his tongue thrust inside then circled her clitoris and he repeated the rhythm until she came, her beautiful body trembling from the force of her pleasure.

He dragged her forward. She fell, her thighs parting to straddle his lap. His mouth claimed hers, matching the vicious intensity of the storm that battled outside. The kiss was ferocious, devouring, branding. Supporting her back, he arched her back over his forearm, thrusting her breasts upward to meet his ravenous mouth.

Eva cradled his head as he worshipped her. He suckled, wild and frenzied, his lips pulled at her nipples. With his other hand he gripped her hip and pressed her down. Her sex glided over his raging erection, silk over steel.

His fingers traced down her hip to her find her core. He caressed, teased and sank two long fingers into her. Eva cried out. The combination of his mouth on her breast and skilled fingers was exquisite. She rocked against his hand, desperate for release.

Hadrian lifted his head and watched with burning eyes as she writhed in pleasure. Her breath caught as lightning split the sky and thunder shook the windows. Eva's head fell back, her body arching as ecstasy crashed into her. Needing to feel her, Hadrian thrust upward, impaling her, filling her.

He gripped her nape, pulling her forward, forcing her to meet his gaze. Her eyes glowed, the amber light shown brightly in the dark room.

"Ride me," he commanded.

Panting and weak from her orgasm, Eva hesitantly rocked her hips. Her eyes grew wide, the sensation curling her toes.

"That's it, little one," he groaned, leaning back.

He dropped his hands and once again gripped the chair. He gave her complete control. His vampire roared. It wanted her blood. It demanded he sink his fangs into her throat. With a shove, he forced it back and focused on Eva.

Her rhythm became wild, her body moving frantically. Her hips twisted up and slammed back down. Hadrian gritted his teeth as she took him, claimed him. Their eyes remained fixed on each other. There were no barriers between them, no restraints. Pure, honest passion sizzled around them, connecting them, binding them.

Hadrian felt the warmth of life spread through him. His heart slammed in his chest, his breaths were quick, and both matched Eva's. He could feel his soul strengthening. She had accepted him. She was his redemption.

Hadrian's hand entangled in her silken hair and he captured her lips. His tongue swept inside, tasting her. He swallowed her bliss filled sighs, savoring the heat of her breath in his lungs.

Her nails bit into his shoulders, drawing blood. He threw his head back, howling his pleasure. Gods, she robbed him of his sanity. His hands gripped her hips, pinning her. He seized control. Eva thrashed atop him, her thighs gripping him, her nails scratching down his chest as he buried himself deeper and deeper within her. His thrusts were hard and fast, unrelenting and demanding.

"More," she growled.

Hadrian complied. Her breasts quivered from each powerful thrust. Her body grew taut, her inner muscles tightened around his shaft as he embedded himself to the hilt. The tension in her body built and built, becoming unbearable.

Mark him, her instincts whispered. *Claim him.*

Eva shoved Hadrian back, pinning his shoulders against the throne. Her teeth sharpened and her tiny claws dug into his flesh, holding him in place. Their bodies slapped together as he plunged his thick, hard length into her, his thrust rough.

Her body began to tingle as the pressure mounting within her coiled, tightening and tightening. Eva licked her lips and surrendered to her Drive.

Hadrian roared as her teeth sank into his neck. Her tongue lapped at his blood. Eva's orgasm was violent, her entire body convulsed, her inner muscles clamped around him, milking him, demanding his essence. He joined her. Stars exploded before his eyes, blurring his vision. The force of his climax ripped him apart.

Eva released his throat. Her claws retracted, and she sagged against him. Her strength gone, her body hummed with pleasure. His chest rose and fell beneath her cheek. His heart hammered, the sound drowning out the bellowing storm.

Closing her eyes, she savored the moment. Hadrian wrapped his arms around her, squeezing her tightly. Tilting her head, she peeked up at him. His eyes sparkled like black diamonds and burned with hunger as he watched her slowly lick the last of his spicy, cinnamon blood from her lips.

He bared his fangs and she moaned as his cock hardened within her.

Chapter Twenty-Eight

Hadrian turned the worn envelope over in his hands before removing the letter it contained. He knew what he would find, having read the missive a thousand times over in the last three months. It wasn't until tonight that he realized what Dimitri had meant.

My dear friend,

I have asked Falcon to come speak with you. He knows the facts of my return for I gave him a letter containing the details. The truth is, I was never dead, and Fate has aligned in such a way that it is now time for me to reclaim my throne.

We all possess dark, painful secrets and, if we are not careful, they will devour us whole. Please, Hadrian, I beg of you, do not allow your demons to take you from us. You must remember who you are, remember the man you are. Come back to us and shake free of your shame, your guilt, and your self-loathing. The voices you hear are only your thoughts. Free yourself from the past. What is done cannot be undone.

I too struggle and suffer like you, and unlike anyone else, I know the truth. I know what happened that night all those years ago. I know how your brother died. Fate can be cruel, but they have plans for you. I have only been shown a glimpse of your future and believe me; your life is not over yet. The second act is just beginning.

— Dimitri Arsov

Hadrian had always believed that people made their own destiny. Now, he was not so certain. Dimitri had seen Hadrian's future and knew of his past. His oldest friend knew his secrets and accepted him, as did Eva. He had even suggested that Hadrian request a ward from the Silveria pack, knowing that Eva would be the female sent to him.

"The second act," Hadrian whispered to the darkness; his words bouncing off the cold, stone walls of the mausoleum.

This was the second act. Here and now, but he had to relinquish his guilt, free himself of his shame, and silence the demon. But he did not know where to begin. How could someone free themselves of hate and despair? He had confessed his sins and shared the worst of his secrets with Eva. His heart felt lighter, but shadows still clung to his soul.

Hadrian folded the letter and tucked it back in the envelope. His gaze lifted to Titus's tomb.

"My brother," he said coming forward. He laid his hands atop the stone. "I have spent the last three and a half centuries mourning you and blaming myself for your death. The guilt and madness have stolen my life."

He exhaled, clearing his lungs of air and stilling his heart.

"Gods, I wish you were here, I wish we could have a real conversation. I cannot remember the last time we actually spoke like brothers. I miss the way we were." Hadrian turned and leaned back against the sarcophagus. "I do not know when or why we began to drift apart. I was aware of your jealously of Falcon, maybe that is what pushed you away. And I never liked how much time you spent with Moreau and his men." He shook his head. "The reasons do not matter. Though I suspect you knew I went to South American not purely to study the shifter packs, but to escape you. In those last days before my departure, I could barely bring myself to look at you. Gods, Titus, I know everything you did. I knew you rode with Moreau under the cover of darkness. You swept through villages, killing and capturing more slaves for Moreau's twisted plans."

Hadrian's hands began to shake. Sorrow spread like a web through his chest, constricting around his heart. "I did not want to believe…I did not want to see the changes in you because…fuck." He dropped to the floor, his legs spread out before him, his head rested against the stone. "I was beginning to hate you. I hated you for surrendering to the evil that coursed in our veins, the evil planted in us by Imbrasus. I had to leave, but I stayed away too long.

"I do not know what kind of understanding you had with Moreau and his Second or the true reason you refused to fight beside me during the rebellion.

"When the war ended and I emerged victorious, I did not banish you as I did the other Black Knights that supported Moreau. I welcomed you with love and peace, embracing you as my brother. Foolishly I believed we could regain what we once shared. I had hoped with Moreau gone we could…but you withdrew even more, completely shutting me out." Unshed tears blurred his vision. "I cannot say I was oblivious of the failed assassination attempts, but I had never suspected you…No." He blinked, the tears slipping from the corners of his eyes. "No, that isn't true. I did not want to suspect you. I did not want to think my own brother would want me dead."

He wiped at his face with the back of his hand.

"I want you to know…I forgive you and I pray to our Roman pantheon that you can forgive me…it was an accident." Hadrian choked on the last word. Never had he allowed himself to view Titus's death as an accident, but that is what happened. "I have relived that moment countless times always wishing it had ended differently."

Hadrian pushed to his feet. His chest felt heavy as if it was filled with lead and his eyes burned.

"I have mourned you every second of every day and…I have to stop. I have let you go. I need to release the guilt that grips my soul and the hate that fills my heart. I need to start living." He wiped at his face again, clearing away the dampness. "I need to allow myself to heal for our Clan and, more importantly, for my mate.

"So, this is goodbye, my brother. I will allow you to lie in peace and silence, as is your due. After tonight, I will never again think about our last moments together and I will bury the demon. Never again will the vampire rule me."

Hadrian brushed aside the dust that covered his brother's name. "I will not return to this crypt." He leaned down to look upon with brother's name, tears falling from his chin to speckle the gray stone. "Rest well, Titus."

Chapter Twenty-Nine

"Well, crap," Eva sighed as she added the leather bound book to the pile of rejects.

She had been combing through the library, searching for any useful information about the Shaw and found nothing. Most of the books were written in one ancient language or another such as Greek, Latin, and Rune. Or, they were focused on spells, incantations, and healing techniques. Eva had attempted to use the magic, but nothing ever happened.

She grabbed another book, flipped it open and cursed again. It would take her weeks if not months to translate all the books, that is, if she could. Some of the texts looked very old.

Exhaling a frustrated sigh, Eva slammed the book closed. This entire situation was insane and there seemed to be no answers to the questions that circled in her mind.

Why had her mother not told her she was Shaw? Had she really gone to Brazil for school or had she been banished from her tribe? Did her mother decide to move to Florida after she learned she was pregnant? Was her mother's friend Shaw, and was her uncle really even her uncle?

Leaning back in her chair, she rubbed her brow. She did not know what to think or where to begin searching for the answers. Hadrian could tell her what was in the books, but he did not know the "why" and the "how" of her family's secret.

Saying her world had been turned upside down was an understatement. Her world had been ripped to shreds leaving her heart battered, her soul bruised, and her mind reeling. Nothing that had happened in the past few days made any sense. Not even Hadrian.

Her body warmed just from the thought of him.

The guarded vampire king had shared with her words she knew he had never before dared to speak. He had revealed himself to her, laying his sins at her feet, showing her the scars that abraded his soul. Had he meant for his confessions to drive her away? Well, it had not worked.

He was no murderer. He was no demon. He was Hadrian. He was dark, mysterious, sexy, hard and gentle. To her, he was a wounded angel in need of healing and, god, she wanted to be the one to heal him. Would he allow her to help him? Or would he just ship her off to Florida without so much as a second glance?

No, she would not leave. Not yet. She would stay until the party as previously planned. Every time she thought of leaving pain tightened her chest and her stomach knotted. Her instincts cried in protest and her inner animal violently roared.

A growl rumbled through the library. She slapped a hand over her mouth. God, would she ever get used to making that sound?

Her nerve endings began to tingle. Hadrian was near; she could sense him. Eva whipped around and nearly fell from her chair. The vampire king was entering the library. He was dressed in casual jeans, a black shirt that sported white letters that read, "I bite" and his boots were tipped with snow. Her body instantly responded and she cursed. God, why did he have such an effect on her?

As he came closer she noticed there was something…different about him.

"Having trouble?" he asked, taking note of the books that were scattered across the long table.

"Um, yeah. I used the library database and collected every book that mentions the Shaw. What I didn't realize is that most are written in ancient languages."

"What knowledge do you seek?"

Eva smiled. "You just sounded like some old sage."

"I struggle with modern phrasing from time to time," he said with a shrug. "Could I help you?"

"I don't know. I'm sure you can tell me what each book is about and give me some background on the Shaw, but you are as much in the dark as I am when it comes to my parents."

He nodded in agreement. "Are you certain you want to know why your mother never told you of her family or to understand why your father took you?"

"What do you mean? Of course I want to know."

Hadrian came to the table. Indecision streaked his face as he took up a book. He his slid fingers along the spine, it was a simple gesture but Eva found it erotic. She suppressed a moan as she remembered those long, graceful, deadly fingers caressing her skin, pinching her nipples and teasing her core.

"When the divide in my mind fell, the demon showed me many things I wish I never knew. Information once learned can never be forgotten." His voice was chilling. "If answers are what you want, then I may be able to help."

Her gaze snapped to his. "Really? How?"

"The priestess who has been guiding us through your transition, she may know."

"Oh, my god. Do you think you could ask her to talk to me?"

"If I speak with her again, I will ask her to visit you."

Eva jumped to her feet and threw her arms around his neck. Her body slammed into his with such force she made him drop the book.

"Thank you." She pressed a kiss to his cheek. When she moved to pull away, his arms circled her, holding her to him.

They stood like this for a long, tender moment.

"How are you feeling?" he asked, leaning back to peer down at her face.

Eva could not stop the blush that rose to her cheeks. Hadrian had shoved her over the edge of pleasure with his hands, his mouth, and his thrusts until the sun began to rise. After she had ridden him, he changed their position. He had pressed her back into the throne, hooking her legs over the arms, opening her wide for him. They came hard and fast. Then he had taken her up and turned her around. He placed her knees on the velvet cushion and entered her from behind, his thrusts powerful and deep.

Finally, he had taken her against the mirrors. He pinned her with his massive body. His strokes were slow, his kisses gentle, his hands lightly caressing her breasts, her back, her hips. Her legs wrapped around his waist. He had pressed his brow to hers and whispered soft words in Latin. Eva had wished she could understand them, but she knew they were loving and beautiful.

His gaze had flickered to his reflection as she had kissed his neck. She watched him from beneath her lashes. It was as if he was seeing himself for the first time. He mumbled gruff words before capturing her lips. The force of his release swept her into oblivion. They clung to each other, their bodies sated, their hearts pounding the same frantic rhythm. She did not know how long he held her there. She did not remember falling asleep in his arms, but she had awoken in her bed.

"I was a little sore this morning, but I have no complaints," she admitted.

He smiled and she traced his lips with her finger. He was so handsome when he smiled and she hoped after last night he would share his smile with her more often.

"Have you decided when you will leave?"

"Well, I've been thinking. You know, I never went to a single high school dance. They just didn't seem like my kind of thing, but I had so much fun dressing up yesterday. So, I'm going to stay until after the party. Besides, it is probably a good idea I stay until my estrus runs its course."

She felt his muscles relax before he released her and took a step back.

"You may stay for however long you wish." He folded his arms over his chest and his gaze became intense. "I want you to know, I will help you through your need anyway I can. If you decide to take the Levo I will sit with you until your cycle passes. And if you don't want to take the drug…I'm here for you."

Eva blinked. Even though they had become lovers, she had not expected him to offer her the use of his body.

Be honest, it is more like abuse, she told herself. Shifter females in heat were violent and extremely dangerous. They were known to kill their partners. When it came time to breed, the women were restrained and drugged to the point of unconsciousness, only then would her mate service her.

"Thank you, but you don't have to—"

"I want to."

Eva smiled. "Twenty-four hours of sex, do you really think you are up for the challenge?" she teased.

In a flash of movement Hadrian had her on the table, books toppled to the floor. He pressed her back to the wood, his hips separating her legs, his hands planted on either side of her head, supporting his upper body.

Eva's breath hitched on a gasp as he stared down at her, his eyes alight with the promise of passion.

"I will see your twenty-four and raise you forty-eight."

A lightning bolt of sizzling desire shot through her.

"Throw in a few meals and shower breaks and you have yourself a deal."

"Shall we seal it with a kiss?"

Eva gripped his shoulders and pulled him down. Hadrian's lips were gentle, yet forceful. She growled low as he deepened the kiss, sweeping his tongue into her mouth.

When he finally drew back, her lips were swollen and the scent of her luscious desire sprinkled the air. Gods, he could take her here, now, on the table. He craved nothing more than to hear her cries of pleasure and feel her orgasm around him. Her need matched his own. She was so responsive, pure and wild. Fate could not have given him a better female.

Hadrian groaned when her tiny tongue swept over her upper lip.

"Gods, you are tempting."

"You started it." She ran her hands down his chest. "Should we finish it?"

Hadrian whispered a curse and straightened. "I would love to, sweet, but you need to conserve your energy. Tomorrow is the third day of your transition."

Eva sighed and came to her feet. "Yeah, I know. When the bell tolls twelve I will turn into a raging sex fiend." She frowned. "Why does everything happen at midnight or during a full moon? What is so special about those times?"

He smiled again. "It is one of nature's greatest mysteries." Sobering he added, "Unfortunately, I will have to restrain you whether or not you decide to take the drug."

Eva rolled her eyes. "Yeah, I know that too. So, are you going to give me a guided tour of the dungeon before shackling me to a wall?"

Hadrian laughed. The rich sound invaded her soul and melted her heart, for the first time she saw true joy spark in his cold eyes and she knew what had changed in him. Pain no longer lurked in the depths of his gaze. Power and danger still clung to him, but the beast was buried and concealed behind a thin veil of control. He was being...himself, completely unguarded.

Mine, her soul cried so loudly that Eva barely resisted the need to scream the word.

He began to speak, but Eva did not process a word. Awe numbed her as an overwhelmingly strong yet tender emotion spread through her chest and weakened her knees. She fell back against the table.

Hadrian reached for her. She must have mumbled that she was fine because he withdrew and cocked his head to the side, studying her for signs of illness.

Eva began to tremble as her brain finally understood what her body, her instincts, her heart and soul had already known. Hadrian was her mate and...she loved him. The realization was like a one-two punch. Her shifter had recognized him as her male the instant they met in the dark hall. It had been Drive that compelled her to enter the labyrinth. Over and over again, her instinct had led her to him. She swayed. None of their encounters had been accidents, and the passion they shared... *Oh, god.*

Hadrian brushed his knuckles along her cheek. The contact startled her from her thoughts.

"You are pale. Do you have a headache?"

Eva swallowed hard, her throat suddenly dry. "I just...um...I'm fine." She rubbed her eyes and willed herself to focus. "What were you saying?"

Hadrian's eyes narrowed. He looked her over once more before giving a shrug. "I said I would not mind showing you the dungeon. However, I think you would find my bedchamber more comfortable than a cold cell. Although, if that is what you prefer, I will indulge your fantasy."

Eva shook her head. She should have been paying more attention and not been swept up by her shocking and life changing epiphany.

"What?"

"I had chains built into the wall behind my bed."

That statement caught her attention. "Wow." She laughed, unable to hold back her excitement. "You are finally living up to your naughty reputation."

His gaze dropped to his shoes. God, if he started blushing she was going to lose it.

Desperately needing a change in subject, Eva asked, "So, what kind of torture contraptions do you have down there? I bet it will be like walking through a museum."

"It has been closed off since the beginning of the seventeenth century. I suspect it will be like taking a step back in time." He paused, his brows knitting together in contemplation. "Perhaps I will convert one of the floors into an indoor go kart track. There is already a training facility located on the lower level, but it will need to be updated."

"Wait, how many underground levels are there?"

"Three. The first was used by the knights and is where the armory is located. The second is mainly storage. The dungeon currently occupies the third level."

"This place is even more massive than I originally thought."

"It housed my entire clan for centuries and some day it will again."

A soft knock interrupted their conversation. Hadrian turned toward the entrance.

Mr. Banik bowed. "Forgive me, Your Majesty, but Sir Falcon Kenwrec is holding on line one."

"Thank you," Hadrian said.

The butler bowed again and promptly retreated.

Hadrian turned back to her. "You should eat, relax, and sleep if you can. You will need every bit of your strength."

"I highly doubt I will be able to do any of those things. I can feel my nerves sneaking up on me."

He hesitantly reached out to her, brushing her fingers with his. He stared down at their hands then said, "Come to my room when you're ready."

Chapter Thirty

Pouring his fifth shot of Silver Moon, Hadrian slammed the glass down as he swallowed. The liquor slipped down his throat and he welcomed the burn.

Another haunting growl carried through the wall. With a curse, Hadrian snatched the decanter. Not bothering with the glass, he took a long swig.

Gods, Eva had waited too long to come to him. He had not wanted to pressure her or make her feel any more uncomfortable than she already was. The female had waited until midnight to come to his room. She had collapsed outside his door. Sweat beaded her brow and she shivered with a fever.

He had been as gentle as he could when he stripped her and secured her. The chains were long, allowing her to roll from one side of the massive bed to the other.

Now, he waited. He wished there was something he could do for her, but a female had to suffer for an hour before her body would be receptive to the drug. If he gave it to her now, it would have no effect and could possibly make her feel even worse.

He had hoped the liquor would drown Eva's calls, but there was to be no escape for him. Her desperate pleas, her demanding roars, and seductive growls rang in his ears as the intoxicating scent of her arousal thickened the air.

He was cracking. He could feel his control slipping inch by precious inch with every passing second. Everything within him demanded he go to her, that he help her, that he give her what she needed—him.

He knew the scene he would find if he went to his room. Eva would be writhing on his bed, her breasts thrusting upward… Hadrian raised the crystal decanter to his lips with shaking hands and took another drink. Shifting in his seat, he maneuvered his throbbing shaft, gaining little relief. The damn thing pulsed as if it had a heartbeat of its own.

"Fuck," he exhaled on a shudder, scrubbing his face with his hands.

Pain. Eva was in pain and allowing her to suffer needlessly was cruel. He could give her pleasure and with it temporary release. Then she would be able to make her decision, him or the Levo.

He would help her. He could be selfless, he could ignore his raging lust and he could fight his instincts for her. He could do anything for Eva.

Hadrian released his death grip on the decanter and stood. Determined to maintain his resolve even if it drove him mad, he materialized in his room. Candles flickered while the fire in the hearth blazed, bathing the bed with a soft, golden glow.

Hadrian stood, unable to move, unable to think, his gaze transfixed on the erotic scene before him. Eva's body twisted and undulated, her back arching, her hips gyrating, the rattle and scrape of the chains kissed his ears. Her legs restlessly rubbed together as she tossed about on his bed.

Her eyes fell upon him and Hadrian's lungs turned to stone. Glowing amber gazed at him. Wild. Her eyes burned with lethal passion, they silently beckoned him to come closer.

"I–I'm so hot," she panted.

Her trembling voice snapped him from his trance. He heard her cry out as he vanished.

Hadrian appeared in the kitchen. With shaking hands, he filled a bowl with ice and grabbed a pitcher of water. Taking in a deep breath, he let it out slowly through his nose.

Control. He could do this. He could keep the demon buried. He heard its demands and could feel its sexual hunger and bloodlust, but its voice was distant and the sensations weak.

He took form beside the bed. Eva would have gasped if she weren't panting so hard. Hadrian set the bowl and pitcher on the bedside table then quickly retrieved a crystal tumbler from the set on his desk.

"Where did…don't leave."

He kept his back to her as he poured some water into a crystal tumbler. "Your first hour is almost completed," he said, trying to sound calm.

"Y–Yay for me."

Hadrian closed his eyes, prayed for strength, and turned towards the bed. Her beautiful, smooth mocha skin was flushed. Her dusty rose nipples were hard; her stomach was flat and taut as she writhed, her hips rocking wildly as her legs twisted in the black silk sheets.

Leaning down, he cupped the back of her head. Eva raised trembling fingers to the glass as he pressed it to her lips. She took a few sips before another surge of hot sensations swept through her. Her muscles constricted, her arms fell to her sides as her head thrashed back and forth. Moans slipped past her lips as the tension continued to grow within her core.

Sweat dampened her brow. Hadrian smoothed the dark strands of her hair from her face. He could feel the heat radiating from her body and winced as his fingers brushed her cheek. Eva immediately turned her face towards him and rubbed her chin against the scar on his wrist. Her rapid breaths caressed his flesh.

"Feels good," she whispered. Her body twisted towards him, seeking his cool touch.

Hadrian backed away. Eva screeched in protest. Lunging for him, her claws slashed at his shirt. With a venomous curse, she fell back, wrapping her arms around her waist. She groaned and threw her arms out letting them fall to her sides again. Her skin was too sensitive to touch.

"Oh, god, H–Hadrian. I'm b–burning." Her body bowed, her legs falling open.

Hadrian spun around, squeezing his eyes shut.

Dear lord, she was ready and drenched with need. Tiny rivulets of pearly white ran down the insides of her thighs. His jaw clenched as her scent slammed into him like a slug to the chest, knocking the unnecessary air from his lungs, leaving him breathless.

His body shook as his hands fisted. He wanted to tear his clothes off, cover her body, and thrust so hard and so deep she would come instantly.

Hadrian bit the inside of his cheek, drawing blood, praying the pain would distract him.

"Fire," she helplessly sighed.

"I know, little one," he rasped.

"I d–didn't think it w–would be like this. So bad."

"Shh, Eva, it will be all right." He ran his hands over his head, the stubble of his hair pricking his fingers.

"P–please. Help me." Another longing, sorrowful growl ripped from her throat. "Pain. M–make it go away."

Her words a tormented whisper, seared his soul. The demon roared, not for its own pleasure, but for hers. Hadrian frowned, his hand rubbing his chest as an odd sensation gripped his heart.

"Yes," he hissed past his elongated fangs.

Hadrian sat on the edge of the mattress.

"Oh, yes," she sighed when he brushed her knee with his hand. "Your touch feels...so good."

His fingers slowly traced up her inner thigh. Her hands shot out. She was desperately seeking more contact, but he sat just outside her reach. Her claws swiped at the air.

"More," she groaned, bucking her hips, trying to force his hand closer to her core and the burning, tension that built there.

"Eva," Hadrian warned, his voice strained as he pulled away. "My control."

"No," she snapped. "I want y–you to snap. I need your cock—"

"Enough!" he roared.

He clamped one hand over her mouth, silencing her words as he drove two fingers deep into her heat.

Her climax was immediate. Relief swept through her and her body relaxed. Her breathing remained harsh, her heart did not slow, and the haze of passion still clouded her eyes, but her mind was calm. She did not know how long this reprieve would last.

Hadrian's eyes were closed, his jaw clenched so tightly, she could hear his teeth grinding. His entire body was still. He sat like a beautiful Roman statue beside her. She pressed a thankful kiss to the palm of his hand that remained over her mouth, while she savored the feel of his fingers still buried inside her.

"Thank you," she gratefully sighed.

Hadrian slowly withdrew from her. His gaze dropped to the floor.

"Is the first hour over?"

He did not speak, but nodded in response.

It is here, she thought. *Decision time.*

Eva sat up, the chain's shackles heavy about her wrists. Hadrian had secured her just before her need arose. She had been glad they allowed her movement even though she was restricted to the bed. She brought her knees up to her chest and leaned against the cool wood of the headboard, which concealed the chains home in the wall. She briefly wondered if he had ever been confined on the bed or if they were just for the women.

"It will come again. Each wave more painful and intense than the last."

She nodded. She knew how it worked.

"The Levo will allow you to remain coherent but sluggish. You will be weak, but I cannot release you from the chains."

"I know. We can't have me running around and terrorizing the villagers. Although, I don't think the men would mind too much since I would be naked. Do you think they would notice my glowing eyes and jaguar like teeth and claws?"

His lips twitched with a smile.

"Well," she raised her hands and shook her wrists, "I'm not going anywhere." She licked her dry lips and before she could ask, he handed her the glass of water. She could feel the tension rising in her body again. It started at her center then spread through out her system.

He became tense, sensing the change in her. He shifted on the bed and Eva's eyes fell to his lap. Her eyes widened, she could see the line of his hard shaft straining against his jeans. She ran her tongue over her lip.

She quickly gulped down the water, then wiped her mouth with the back of her hand.

Their fingers brushed as he took the empty glass. It was a light caress but it sent massive waves of need crashing over her.

"You don't have to choose me. You can take the Levo and we can just relax," he offered, his hands clenched into fists at his sides.

That warm, loving feeling crept up on her again. He was not pushing her to choose him. He was willing to just sit with her, hang out and talk. Well, she didn't know how much talking she would be able to do since the drug could affect her speech.

"Kick it or have a repeat of last night?" she said. Her words were shaky as she struggled against the desire that was quickly rising within her. The fever had returned. Her breasts felt heavy and she rubbed her thighs together attempting to ease the throbbing building at her core.

"What do you want?" he bit out. "Tell me so I can help you."

She tried to speak but she could not get the words past her lips. Her throat had become suddenly dry and rough. She swallowed and the action hurt. A blast of energy shot through her and vibrated the room as her need claimed her again. Her vision blurred as the world around her began to spin. She doubled over, falling onto the mattress. She wrapped her arms around her middle and blinked hard, desperately trying to focus on Hadrian. His face was set in harsh lines, his black eyes a strange mixture of lust, sympathy, and determination.

He reached for the vile of the Levo and filled the syringe.

Turning to her, he whispered gently, "Breathe, Eva."

"Not...that." She reached for his arm, but the chains weighed her down.

"I cannot tolerate your suffering," he said, raising the needle.

She shook her head, her tangled hair thrashing about. "You."

"Eva, I want to…service you. Gods, I want nothing more. But this is better; it will be easier on you."

He would deny her? The thought made her see red. No. She would have him. She would *take* him. Her muscles coiled and she lunged for him, her claws tearing at his shirt, laying open his chest. The wounds vanished as quickly as they had appeared.

Hadrian did not flinch. He did not retreat. "Lay back."

She hissed, baring her teeth as she collapsed back on the bed. "You," she whimpered. "You."

He forced himself to his feet and set the syringe back on the table. In a flash of movement, he was undressed. Eva's eyes widened, her hands reaching for him.

"Yes," she panted as her body arched.

Hadrian lowered himself on the bed. Slow. He would need to take things slow. Conserve their energy. This was only the second hour, they had twenty-two more to go and with each passing minute her need would grow until she was mad and completely wild—out of control.

"Eva," Hadrian rasped, drawing the tip of his finger over her slick folds. "I want to feel you come beneath my lips."

His deep, rough whisper sent chills racing down her spine to curl her toes. Damn the vampire and his erotically hypnotic voice. She loved it.

She tried to sit up. She tried to reach for him again. Yes, she wanted to feel his mouth on her but she needed his long, hard length inside her. Pumping, driving into her. She craved to feel him release within her.

His sensual lips curled into a smile as he circled her clitoris. "Will you let me?"

"You," was all she could manage to gasp.

The simple word gave the vampire all the permission he required.

Hadrian caught her waist, dragging her to him. He hooked her knees over his shoulders. Flashing her a devilish smile that stole her heart, he bent his head and scrapped his fangs along the inside of her thighs. Eva shuddered as he masterfully, nipped, slowly kissed and suckled his way up to her center.

Fervent pleas fell from her lips. Now was not the time for teasing.

He drew his tongue over her folds. She violently jerked beneath him. The chains rattled and scraped as her body twisted. He held her hips, pinning her to the bed. Her legs tightened over his shoulders as he claimed her with his mouth. Eva's claws tore at the sheets as her body splintered into a million pieces.

His dark laugh vibrated the bed as he drove her over the edge again.

Eva was gasping for air when he finally released her. She watched him with hooded eyes. His mouth glistened with her passion and she nearly came again when he licked her lips.

Her body sated for the moment, her mind calm for a few precious seconds.

"I made the right decision," she panted.

Heat scorched her again. Flames danced over her flesh, the reprieves were growing shorter and shorter.

Hadrian dipped his hand into the bowl of ice and Eva's frantic breaths caught in anticipation. His touch already felt blissfully cool against her fevered skin but the ice...Her body strained towards him, demanding contact.

Hadrian traced her lips with the ice. She shivered and moaned. Her tongue flicked out and she captured the square and his finger. She suckled both until the ice melted. Eva nipped at him as he drew back.

He smiled and returned his hand to the bowl, removing a larger piece. He drew it down the line of her throat and followed it with his mouth. He circled the ice over her taunt nipples. Hadrian paused over her breasts, his breath teasing her, blowing over the hardened peaks before suckling them in turn.

Hadrian continued to draw the square lower. He dipped it into her navel where it melted. He lapped at the tiny pool of water and flicked his tongue over her hipbones.

Her eyes closed. She was drifting away, wrapped up in the refreshing pleasure.

A cry lodged in her throat, her eyelids flew open as he pressed a square against the ultra sensitive place between her thighs. He rubbed the ice over her clitoris, wringing another world shattering orgasm from her. As her body convulsed, he traced her folds with the tips of his cold fingers.

"Oh, god," she moaned, her body already on the verge and ready for another wave of soul searing pleasure.

Hadrian climbed up her body. His shoulders rolled with power as he settled over her. The hard tip of his cock teased at her entrance. Her hips bucked.

"Not yet," he grated.

Eva held her breath as he snatched another piece of ice. Reaching between their bodies, he drew the cube over her slit.

"So good," she sighed, pressing her hips up, craving the cold contact.

He slipped the ice inside her and Eva came apart. Hadrian did not wait for her orgasm to pass. He straightened and thrust into her, burying himself in her tight, velvet sheath.

Eva rippled around him, her muscles clenched, released, and clenched again. Her hips rocked to meet his, urging him to go faster, harder.

He was lost in pure sensation. She was erotic perfection. Her nipples scraped his chest with every thrust, her claws curled into his shoulders. He heard the demon roar, felt the vibrations in his head. Blood. It wanted her pleasure spiked blood. And so did he.

Eva craned her neck, twisting her head to the side. Her pulse enticingly danced beneath her smooth skin.

Was she offering?

"Bite," she growled.

"No."

He had managed to keep the demon silent all day, but taking her vein would be too dangerous. He could snap. He could lose control. With Eva being restrained, she would not be able to defend herself if he attacked.

"Not...mortal...anymore," she said, emphasizing her words by drawing her claws down his chest.

Hadrian stared down at her. She wanted him to bite her. She wanted him to claim her, to completely dominate her. He would give her exactly what she wanted and the demon could go to hell.

Instinct taking control, Hadrian snatched her wrists and pinned her hands to the mattress as he reared back.

"Yes. Bite," she sighed, pressing her cheek into the pillows.

His fangs sank into the swell of her breast as his hips slammed against hers. Eva's blood filled his mouth and he closed his eyes with a worshipful groan. He had never known such a taste. He had thought her blood addictive before, but now...he was a goner. Her essence slipped down his throat, warm, creamy vanilla, spiced with ecstasy.

Heaven.

He forced his fangs deeper. Eva clutched at his head, holding her to him. He fed voraciously. Her blood flowed through him, burning yet soothing. As he took her into his body, he claimed hers, pounding into her until he felt the blissful tension ripple through her core. Her claws ripped at his back, tearing flesh and drawing blood as she tightened around him, gripping him with soft, scorching fire.

Hadrian released her breast. His back bowed. His head snapped back. With a roar he exploded within her in a great wave, filling her until seed dampened her thighs.

He ran his tongue over the pinpricks, closing the wound, and then rolled to his back, taking her with him. Hadrian tucked her against his side. Eva's chest rose and fell in a steady rhythm. She closed her eyes and savored the quiet stillness that surrounded her. This moment was perfect and she wished it could last forever, but the madness would soon begin again.

Eva pressed her cheek against his chest and traced the lines of his muscled chest and defined abs. He was lean, his shoulders wide, and his body powerful. He was built like a true warrior and he had the heart and determination to match. Hadrian, her male, her lover, was beautiful and true.

I love him, she thought as she began to trace the curve of his bottom lip.

He playfully nipped at her fingertip before rising.

"We are going to have fun, my little half-breed," he said with a smile. Ignoring Eva's protests, he stood and crossed over to his closet. She struggled against the chains, the sound of metal grating over stone rumbled through the room.

"I am not leaving, sweet. Relax," he cooed.

When he returned to the room, Eva was kneeling at the edge of the bed, the restraints pulled taunt. She watched him with glowing eyes as he came closer. He carried two wooden boxes, one weathered and the other new.

"Earlier you expressed an interest in my 'naughty reputation'. Would you like me to show you how I earned it?"

Eva's heart stuttered. "Yes."

He set the boxes on the bed. He opened the tattered box first. The hinges creaked as the top fell back. Her eyes widened. Whips, chains, glass tubes of various sizes and lengths clicked together at the bottom, and silk bands she assumed were used as blindfolds, were piled high.

"Kinky," she whispered.

He closed the box and let it fall to the floor. "I know I should have asked before I purchased these." He ran his hand over the smooth surface of the second box. "Honestly, I do not know what I was thinking. This was a bad idea—"

"Open it," Eva rasped, wiping at her brow. Her temperature was rising.

His cock instantly hardened as he sensed her need preparing to launch another attack.

Hadrian removed the lid revealing handcuffs, feather teasers, body jewelry, a whip with flayed ends and a glass handle, and an assortment of other toys filled the box.

Eva swayed as a wave of lust swept over her.

"We do not have to use them. I thought they might help."

"Fuzzy hand cuffs?" she said with a strangled laugh as her muscles tensed and she shook her wrists, rattling her chains.

He rubbed his nape and cursed.

Eva smiled. Air hissed past her teeth as tremors took hold of her. "I'm interested."

Hadrian's shoulders slumped in relief. "Nothing drastic. We will go slowly," he vowed.

She lifted a shaking hand and pointed to the item that had spiked her interest the most.

He removed the short whip. "This?" he asked. When she nodded, he set the box on the floor.

"Water? P–please."

Hadrian went to the side table and poured her another glass of water. Eva drank what she managed not to spill.

Leaning back against the scattered pillows, Eva managed to say, "Ice."

Hadrian nodded. She was relieved her male understood the tract of her thoughts. He buried the glass handle in the ice and she shuddered in anticipation.

Chapter Thirty-One

"Yes. Hadrian. Yes!"

Eva's back arched so hard it hurt. Her hips pushed back against his. Her arms gave out as her climax slammed into her. Her chest hit the mattress as his name fell from her lips. She gripped the sheets, her claws shredding the already ruined satin.

Hadrian wrapped an arm around her waist, supporting her lower body. He flexed his hips and thrust in deep. He could feel his own release building clear down to his toes. His entire body clenched. His heart pounding so hard he could feel his blood rush through his veins. White-hot lightning streaked down his spine, the bolt exploding in his head. His pure, primal roar vibrated the bed and shook the room as he came, spending into her hot depths.

He slid his arms underneath her, his fingers curling over her shoulders. He lifted her torso and flattened her back against his chest, hugging her to him. He buried his face in her wildly tangled hair, inhaling deeply. Eva reached back and wrapped her arms around his head, pulling him closer.

The delicate melody of the clock rang signaling the end. The sexual tension that had filled the air suddenly vanished and her body went limp. Her arms slipped from him to dangle at her sides, her legs collapsed. He gently lowered them both to the bed, tucking her against him.

Her fever had broken and the flames that had devoured her began to fade. The tension slowly eased from her body. She was so exhausted she could barely breathe. Every muscle ached and her wrists hurt from fighting the chains. Her lips were dry and cracked, her throat raw from her growls and screams of pleasure.

Hadrian kissed her shoulder blades and the back of her neck as he whispered soothing words. The storm within her had passed. What remained was perfect peace. He drew her closer and Eva buried her face in the mass of torn sheets before she could blurt out, I love you.

God, what would he say? Would he balk? Would he try to rationalize her emotions, claiming they weren't real?

"How are you feeling?" he asked, his breath brushing her ear.

Eva had to swallow a few times before she could respond. "Tired." Her voice was like gravel. "You?"

Hadrian dropped his head. He felt...there were no words to describe the euphoric harmony that had settled over him. He had never experienced such ecstasy and he wanted to stay just like this. He held her tightly, their bodies joined, they fit perfectly. He wanted to stay there in the sanctuary of her body forever.

"Blessed."

Eva's head snapped back and she twisted around to face him. His obsidian eyes were warm, bright and...no. Her mind had to be playing tricks on her. Eva moved closer, their noses almost touching. *It was there.* It had not been a flicker of lighting or her imagination.

Hadrian blinked as if he just realized what he had revealed. The emotion vanished, replaced by his mask of control.

"Thank you," he said then placed a light kiss on her lips.

Eva opened her mouth, but she could not find the words.

Hadrian rolled from the bed. Tiny red lines extended from his shoulders to his hips and ran down his arms. There were puncture marks lining his neck with a few scattered about his chest. He turned and headed for the desk. The same marks crisscrossed his back in a frenzied pattern. She had lost control towards the end, scratching and biting—blood rushed to her face—she had even hit him. Repeatedly. But the vampire seemed...fine. His movements were fluid, his muscles rolled with ease as he walked back.

He returned with the key to the shackles. His hands were gentle and he was careful not to touch her tender flesh. He held her hands, his gaze lingering on the circular scar on the inside of her wrist. He traced it with his thumb. Electricity sprinted up both their arms, a sharp shock. Eva gasped and Hadrian dropped her hand and flinched.

He abruptly turned and stalked to his closet.

She lifted her head. Her vision wavered, the room spun and she collapsed back with a curse.

Hadrian emerged wearing loose gray sweats, set low on his hips. His chest remained bare. The evidence of her mauling was gone. His skin was smooth, unblemished, as if nothing had happened.

He did not come back to the bed. Instead he entered the bathroom and the sound of running water filled the silence that hung in the room. Hadrian stepped from the bathroom and came to the bed. He was careful as he took her up in his arms.

She released a grateful sigh as he settled her in the tub. The warm water and heady scent of relaxation aromatherapy was heaven.

Her stomach rumbled. Loudly.

A smile tugged at Hadrian's lips.

"Yeah, I'm hungry."

"I will bring you something to eat. Relax."

Hadrian vanished and Eva sank further into the water, the bubbles floating about her chin. She let out a soft sigh. The soreness was easing from her muscles and she was grateful that her transition had improved her healing process.

Dipping under the water, she wet her hair. Wiping the foam from her eyes, she quickly washed and reached overhead for a towel. She wanted to be out and ready when he returned. She was *starving*.

Eva stepped from the tub and dried. Her legs were a bit unsteady, but she managed to make it to the closet. She snatched one of his plain black shirts and slipped it over her head.

Returning to the room, she eyed the bed. It was mutilated. The sheets were shredded. The comforter reduced to strips and the pillows lay in disarray, cut open, their feathers spilling out. The thick chains hung over the headboard and their "toy box" remained open at the foot of the bed.

Hadrian appeared beside her, a tray piled high with an assortment of sandwiches, sliced fruit, and warm rolls slathered in butter.

"You can sit at the desk," he said.

"I hope you don't mind, I borrowed a shirt."

He looked her over, heat sparked in his eyes. "Not at all."

Eva followed him, picking grapes from the tray. She could not stand the hollow feeling in her stomach; it reminded her of living with the pack.

I'm never going back, she told herself as she sat in Hadrian's massive chair.

Eva knew she should have placed the napkin in her lap. She knew she should have held back, but manners be damned. And Hadrian wasn't watching her. He was busy trying to put the bed to rights. He gathered the sheets, the ruined comforter, and dead pillows. At least the mattress had survived. He rolled the chains and tucked them behind the bed then collected the goodies they had used.

She shoved one sandwich after another into her mouth as he worked. He took the box to the bathroom and she assumed he was cleaning all that they had used. Next, he went to the closet and retrieved a new set of sheets and pillows.

"Sorry for destroying your stuff," Eva said as he passed her. "I'll help." She stood.

"No, you need to eat."

"What about you? Shouldn't you feed?"

"I took in some blood while I was in the kitchen."

"Oh." She resumed her seat and took up a piece of an apple. "Well, if you need a snack."

He paused and turned to her, his eyes darkening with hunger. "You are offering?"

She nodded. "I didn't think I would, but I really—and I mean *really*—like you biting me."

His fangs elongated and Eva shivered. "As do I."

When he finished with the bed, he took a quick soap and rinse shower and joined her.

Eva offered him a strawberry. He took her hand and brought the fruit to his lips. His tongue swirled around her finger, scooping the strawberry into his mouth.

"Sexy," she breathed, her eyes fixated on his lips.

He drew her up and they walked to bed. Eva slipped under the fresh sheets and leaned back against the plush pillows.

"Thank you for everything. You've been so helpful and understanding." She pushed her damp hair over her shoulder. "And I'm sorry for attacking you and being...so rough at the end."

"Eva, don't apologize."

"I don't want to hurt you."

He shrugged. "I heal. Besides, I knew what I was getting myself into from the start."

She covered her yawn.

He sat on the edge of the mattress beside her. "Lay back," he urged. "You should sleep."

She was not ready for sleep. Well, her body was, but if she did not want this moment of peace between them to end.

"Hadrian, will you tell me about yourself?"

Chapter Thirty-Two

He visibly tensed. "You wish to know my past?"

"I want to know how you became the man you are," she said.

There was a long silence.

Good job, she chided herself. Hadrian was not the sharing type, but she had hoped he would open up to her. He had confessed his darkest secrets and fears to her the other night. Was she pushing him? He obviously was not ready to reveal more.

"You don't have to say anything. I just thought...well, it's cool."

His brow wrinkled, his eyes fell to his hands, which were fists in his lap. "I want to share myself with you. I just..." He let out a heavy sigh. "I do not know how or where to begin."

Eva came up to her knees and crawled over to his side. She sat beside him, allowing his silence to fill the room. Her gentle hand rested on his forearm.

"I had a good life," he finally said. "Sometimes it is difficult to remember back to when I was mortal. It was so long ago." He paused as if he were searching for words. "My father was a member of the Roman Senate. Always looking to improve his status, he had selected a beautiful woman who came from a wealthy and well-connected family to be his wife. There was little love between my parents. As I recall, they only had two things in common: political aspirations and their children."

He stopped again and placed a hand over hers. He still did not look at her.

"Titus and I were inseparable. I had brains and brawn and he had charm and charisma. But while I was content to live the life our father had planned for us, Titus rebelled. He joined the military and I followed. Even though we were identical twins, I was stronger, more robust, and a much better fighter. Titus had a startling ability to anger people and I always defended him."

"You joined to protect him?"

"I was promoted quickly for my ability to read the enemy and, well, destroy them. I learned early how to compartmentalize life. War was ugly and I did not allow the death I witnessed and created to disrupt my life."

Eva nodded. That was how he had been able to deal with the demon before his brother's death.

"Emperor Claudius sent four legions to invade Britain in 43 A.D. Titus and I were amongst the soldiers. We were only to be there for two years, but we never returned home." His voice grew strained. "Imbrasus and Uro, the Father of the Voidukas, were warring and Imbrasus was grossly outnumbered. He would use his human slaves as scouts. They watched the legions and reported back to him the names of those that would make good recruits for his army. Imbrasus would then stalk his prey under the cover of night, assessing their strengths and weaknesses."

Her eyes rounded. Imbrasus had used the Roman conquest as a screening session and Hadrian had caught his interest.

"During the campaign, I married a Briton." His eyes closed and his throat went dry. "Her name was Cordelia. My marriage infuriated Titus and my father, who had selected a wife for me back home. Finally, my brother and father had something in common."

"I get your dad being mad, but why would Titus be upset?"

"He viewed my wedding Cordelia as the end of us. We would no longer be inseparable."

Titus had been jealous of Cordelia, just as he had been jealous of Falcon. He had not wanted to share his twin.

"Titus and I were on Imbrasus's list of candidates and he took advantage of our division. He knew how protective I was of my brother, so he approached Titus first."

Rage began to vibrate from him. Eva squeezed his arm. He lifted his head; his eyes were swirling pools of crimson.

"Titus had been wounded in battle and was in his tent when Imbrasus came to him. The vampire offered him immortality, power, riches, women—everything. Titus only wanted me."

"Which Imbrasus knew and he wanted you too."

The temperature in the room dropped as malice thickened the air. "When the fighting was complete, I went to Titus's tent to check on him. I found Imbrasus bent over my brother's lifeless body. He smiled

221

at me, revealing his fangs. Wrapping his arms around Titus, they disappeared."

His muscles had tightened as if he was preparing to strike a foe. He had not noticed the shift in his body until Eva began to stroke his back. Her fingers kneaded and massaged. Comfort and compassion, the emotions warmed him, easing the pain of reliving the memories.

"I had heard stories of the demon that stalked the camps, collecting the dead. It was rumored that he changed them, made them into monsters that preyed on the blood of humans. Naturally, I had thought it nonsense until that night." He took in a breath and slowly let it out through his nose. He could feel the demon stirring in his mind. If only he had the dagger. He did not enjoy cutting himself, but the simple torture kept his mind sharp, focused. "For two weeks, I hunted Imbrasus. I abandoned my unit and followed his trail of destruction and death. Each attack I came upon was more brutal and more gruesome than the last. He was taunting me."

Her hands paused as another wave of anger pulsed through him. Hadrian pressed into her touch.

"Please, continue," he said on a whisper.

She moved her hands in circles over his shoulder blades. "It sounds like he was drawing you to him, setting you up."

"He was. After seeing the devastation he wrought, I knew there was little chance I would survive. I did not care. I would die trying to avenge my brother. Or, well, I thought I would be avenging Titus's death." He cleared his throat. "It was the night of the full moon. I had finally found Imbrasus. He and his fledglings were living in a cave by the seaside. I called for him to come down to the beach…I challenged him. The bastard laughed when I drew my sword."

It was a long time before he continued. "Water slapped at our legs, the sand clotted with blood, and salt stung my eyes and burned in my fresh wounds as we battled. I fought with all my strength, giving everything I had. He pinned me to the ground, my arm broken, my kneecap shattered. He loomed over me, silhouetted by the bright glow of the moon. My vision was blurred with pain, seawater, and blood, but I saw his fangs lengthen. He pressed his lips to my ear and whispered, 'you will be a fine soldier, the strongest in my army. You will be proud to be a Validus.'

"His teeth ripped at my jugular. I struggled beneath his hold fighting him for every last heartbeat. He pressed his clawed hand over my heart, the talons scoring my flesh. I could hear the others above. They laughed and placed bets on whether I would survive the transition or not. As I took my last breath, preparing to be delivered to the underworld, I heard Titus's voice.

"Imbrasus slit his wrist and forced my lips apart. The instant his blood touch my tongue, the change began. My body seized and convulsed. The only thought in my mind was to kill. I sank my teeth into his wrist, locking my jaw. With every swallow I grew stronger. I pulled him down and wrapped him up, securing my arms and legs around him. He thrashed, but grew weaker by the second. I battled through agonizing pain as my body morphed, my organs shifting, my muscles tearing."

"Compartmentalizing the pain," she said in awe. *God, his mind is strong.*

He nodded. "I felt his cool skin turn to ice as his immortality slipped away. Ignoring the terrible burning sensation in my chest, I twisted his head free of his body. There was no blood. I lay on the sand, the water lapping at my feet. Vile emotions pumped through me as his demon invaded my soul.

"My senses were heightened. I heard the others coming down from the cave. Shock and murderous rage laced their rumbling voices as they stalked toward me. I do not know how I managed to get to my feet or match them blow for blow. A red haze clouded my vision…I killed them all. Falling to my knees, all my strength gone, I prayed for death. I begged the gods to end my life. That is when Titus came to me. The sun had begun to rise. He hefted me over his shoulder and carried me up to the now vacant cave.

"I had wanted him to leave me there, but he claimed the sun would turn me to ash if I remained on the beach. We settled in the safety of the shadows and watched the bright rays destroy the demon corpses. Their ashes scattered on the wind. I could not believe my eyes or the words that Titus spoke. He explained what we had become, bloodthirsty fiends from hell that could no longer walk in the sun. I knew then that I could never go back to Cordelia and that we could never return to our family in Rome. It would be too dangerous. Our lives were over and we had to begin again in the realm of darkness."

"How did you account for Imbrasus's and his follower's deaths?"

He shrugged. "Titus had explained to me about the Red Order. The hunters were thick in Britain and the Isles. It is rumored that they began as Celtic and Druid priests. When more of Imbrasus's fledglings arrived the next day, we told them the cave had been attacked. No one besides Titus and I ever knew the truth about my deeds. If the others had learned, I surely would have been sentenced to death."

Hadrian sensed Eva's sorrow. He turned and drew her against his side. He tilted her chin up. "I do not regret going after Titus or killing Imbrasus. In a strange way, I'm glad I ripped his demon from his soul." He took her hands, his fingers closing around her wrist. "I never would have known Falcon or you."

He slowly turned her hand over, revealing the scar. As he traced the circles with the pad of his thumb, the anger eased from his body, allowing peace to settle within him. The demon silenced.

Gods, how was he going to let her go? She had awakened him, brought him back to life. She was the salvation he had sought.

"Hadrian, do you know what that scar means? I woke up with it after my transition."

Should he confess that she was his mate and his queen? That she was his to hold for all eternity? He would have to tell her that even though she had transitioned, she was not like the average shifter. She would not age slowly like her relatives. Eva would never die. She was bound to him.

"Hadrian?"

He closed his eyes. Gods, he could not deny her soft voice. He had already bared his soul, shared his shame, and his secrets, why not keep going? Fear of what she would say, or of how she would react was not going to rule him.

He laid his hand over hers, his palm turned upward. Her tiny gasp kissed his ears and he opened his eyes.

"I do."

"It's the same," she said in awe, her eyes wide. "What is it?"

"It is the mating brand of my people."

Chapter Thirty-Three

Eva stared at him, her amber gaze glittering pools of confusion. Hadrian silently waited for her to process the information. He could have phrased the answer differently. Maybe he should have been less direct.

She shook her head. Her thoughts tangled, her mind struggling to comprehend the meaning of his words.

Her gaze dropped to his wrist. The marking was identical to hers. Two perfect circles.

Finally finding her voice, she asked, "What does this mean?"

Hadrian released a relieved sigh. Curiosity was a good sign. "You are my mate, my intended queen."

"Wait. I think I've heard something about this. Didn't Dimitri Arsov just marry his mate?"

"Yes, last month."

"So, this is a common thing?"

"Not exactly. We are the third couple."

Eva began to twirl her hair nervously. "Okay…can you explain this to me from the beginning?"

Hadrian silently debated where to begin. Should he tell her the priestess had tricked him into performing the binding ceremony or that he only bound her to him so she would survive the transition?

"Everything, Hadrian. Don't leave anything out," she insisted, sensing his hesitation.

"There has only been one successful performance of the bonding ritual, Dorian and Victoria of the Mylonas Clan. Until them, the idea of a vampire monarch finding their intended mate was nothing but a legend, a fanciful story that kept the Rulers of Darkness hopeful."

"Hopeful of what?"

"The only way one can survive the Death Curse is by finding their mate."

"None were successful until King Dorian?"

He nodded. "A mate is only created when the rightful king, or in some cases queen, ascends the throne. It is believed that these monarchs will bring peace and some vampire scholars think the curse that binds us to our demons will be broken. But I don't believe we will ever be freed of our demons."

Eva pushed her hands through her still damp hair. "You are one of the rightful kings."

His gaze returned to his lap. "So it seems."

"How did this happen?" She tugged at her lower lip with her teeth. "Is it because you gave me your blood?"

Hadrian stood and crossed over to the hearth and the dying fire. Suddenly the flames jumped and a wave of heat rolled through the room.

"I did not tell you this before, but there have been others like you. The Shaw priestess told me I would need to bind your life to mine in order for you to...survive. None of the others lived through the change."

Eva swallowed hard. That bit of information was hard to process. If it had not been for Hadrian, her transition would have been a death sentence.

"Did you know I was your mate?"

"Not until the night of your transformation. There is very little known of how the binding spell works." He scoffed. "The priestess had suggested the solution. I should have asked her more questions, but I was not thinking clearly."

"Are you saying she knew, but didn't tell you?"

He nodded. His back was to her, his gaze focused on the flames. "I could not let you die. Not when I had the power to save you."

She fell back on the mattress. If she had ever thought her life was complicated before, she had been wrong. But this was good, right? He was her male and she was his mate. At least Fate had made them a match. God, she could not even imagine how it would be if he were her male but he did not want her.

He hasn't said he wants you, she reminded herself. *He has made a nice plan for your life without him.*

She rolled to her side, propping her head up on her hand. She studied him. He stood, his arms crossed over his chest, shadows covered his arms and back like tattoos. Again she had the absurd urge to just say those three little words, but he seemed to be fighting the truth. Fighting the potential they had for a real relationship, love, and happiness.

"What does all this mean, Hadrian?"

"Our lives are bound, united as one. As long as I live, you live. Eva," he turned to her, "you will live forever."

Her jaw dropped. "As in, for all eternity?"

"You will remain as you are now."

"Forever twenty-six."

He nodded.

"God, this has to be a dream. All of this…it is just too much. I don't know how I can possibly process all of this crap. I'm a witch-shifter half-breed and the mate of a vampire. Oh, yeah, and he is a king preparing to reclaim his throne. Drama to ensue."

Hadrian was beside her in a flash of movement. "Eva, I do not want you to feel as if you are trapped. You can leave. You can go live your life."

Eva felt her brows knit together. Did he want her to stay, but refused to offer believing she wanted her freedom? For so long she had craved nothing but freedom. She had longed to break away from the pack, to live her life how she wanted.

"What of the bond?"

"It will not hold you back."

He could not be more wrong. Her own Drive was holding her here. Every time she thought of leaving she felt ill, her heart and soul rebelled. Her shifter side would not allow her to go willingly. Hadrian was her male. She was his mate. They belonged together. But he would deny them so that she could be free.

Eva took a deep breath. She had to tell him about her Drive. Maybe then he would stop trying to push her away. Hadrian had granted her freedom the moment he decided to send Falcon to the Silveria Pack. Over the last month and half she had lived free of fear and starvation. He had given her everything and reminded her that kindness did exist. And that love was not just something in a fairy tale.

She would tell him she loved him. She would tell him that she did not want to leave. No matter what, she would stay by his side.

A sliver of doubt crept into her thoughts. What if his clan did not approve of her? What if they scorned her like the pack had?

Hadrian must have sensed her worry. He cupped her face.

"Eva, I—"

His body suddenly tensed. He came to his feet. The sound of footsteps pricked her ears. Someone was moving down the hall. A booming knock rattled the heavy wooden door.

"Hadrian," Falcon called, his tone urgent. "I need to speak with you."

Hadrian opened the door with a thought. Falcon stepped in and froze, his eyes instantly falling on Eva.

She clutched the sheet to her chest and waved.

The knight's face flushed.

"I will not be long," Hadrian said pushing a sputtering Falcon into the hall. He closed the door behind them. "What are you doing here? You were not to return for another two days."

Hadrian's sharp tone snapped Falcon from his surprise. "Well, you weren't answering the phone," he answered. "I called nearly thirty times and every time your new butler informed me you were not taking calls."

"I told the vampire not to disturb me unless he wanted to face the sun. He was doing his job."

"I started calling yesterday. What could have kept you..." Falcon's words died as realization crept up on him.

Hadrian cursed and started down the hall to his private drawing room. The knight followed, stammering his apologies.

"Now that you have your answer," Hadrian rounded on him, "explain why you are here."

Falcon straightened and gathered his thoughts. "Two reasons. The first, I have confirmed that Jefferson will challenge you."

Hadrian nodded. "We have been expecting this. I will need a list of all his supporters."

"It is being compiled as we speak."

"Does he have military backing?"

"Some. The majority remains loyal to you."

"Not me," Hadrian said. "They are loyal to you." He shook his head when Falcon began to protest. "This information could have waited. What is the second issue?"

Falcon unzipped the pocket of his jacket and removed a deep purple envelope. Hadrian's eyes narrowed as he snatched the letter from the knight's hand. He ripped it open, his eyes scanning the parchment.

"Who gave you this?" he demanded.

"A Black Knight belonging to the Voidukas Clan delivered the missive directly to me."

"This is an official Shaw summons," Hadrian grated. "All the chieftains are to attend a meeting tomorrow in Tallinn, Estonia."

"Does it state the purpose?"

"Peace talks."

Falcon's brow furrowed. "For what?"

"The Mylonas and Red Order war."

Hadrian read the formal document again and groaned. This confirmed his earlier suspicions. The Shaw priestess was crazy. What could she have planned?

"Do you think it could be a trap?"

"It is possible, but unlikely. However, we will prepare as if it were." He placed the paper back in the envelope. "Call the airport. Have them ready the jet. Collect what you need, we leave within the hour."

"What of Eva?"

"She will join us," Hadrian answered.

Falcon frowned. "We will only be gone one, two days tops."

"I will not leave her unprotected."

"She is safe here and even if someone comes, they won't hurt her. She is no longer your ward since the treaty has been declared null and void, but she is still under the clan's protection."

Hadrian cursed. He formed a fist and thrust his arm out. His wrist turned upward displaying the mating brand.

Falcon swayed as if Hadrian had struck him. Good lord, he had been right. Eva was Hadrian's intended.

"We are saved," he murmured.

Hadrian remained silent, his eyes downcast.

"You are the rightful king of the Validus. The nobles—"

"I do not want them to know of this."

"Don't be ridiculous," Falcon said. "This will make your transition smooth and absolve any doubt the Clan may have."

Hadrian shook his head. "I will not yield."

"For the love of god." Falcon squeezed the bridge of his nose. "Why? This is absolutely perfect."

"Eva may..." Hadrian took a breath and forced the words out, "She is leaving."

"I don't understand. The girl has been after you since the start. It may be too early to talk about love, but any idiot can see that she has feelings for you."

"I told her to go."

Falcon crashed back into a chair, stunned. "Please, explain."

"She craves freedom above all things and...I want to give it to her."

A heavy sigh pushed out of Falcon's lungs. "She is already free."

"She deserves happiness."

Falcon's eyes turned sharp as the true reason was revealed. "As do you. Shit, Hadrian. Fate has dumped happiness on your doorstep in the form of a petite, gorgeous, extremely well endowed woman. And you are just going to toss her aside."

"I will not force her to stay." Hadrian held up a hand. "Conversation, over. Prepare to leave."

He dematerialized before Falcon could speak.

Chapter Thirty-Four

"What the hell is this?" Samuel erupted, stepping into the largest conference room of the swanky hotel. Thick, black tapestries covered the floor to ceiling windows. The sparkling gold and crystal chandelier provided plenty of light.

Silvie smiled. "Welcome to Estonia, the shared territory of the Voidukas and Shaw. Please, gentlemen, take your seats, we've much to discuss."

"The summons said nothing about vampires. I will not sit at the same table, nor breathe the same air as those fiends," Samuel seethed, jabbing a shaking finger toward the vampire royalty.

"This is trickery, priestess," Oliver added.

She shrugged, her shoulders rolling beneath the scarlet red, velvet robe. "The Shaman wanted you here. This is the reason he requested you all attend unarmed."

"Where is he? He should be at this meeting," Lewis pointed out.

Silvie sighed. *Here we go. Kick the plan into action, she told herself.*

Her uncle had given her specific instructions. Her words would set off a series of events and there would be no going back for anyone in the room once she opened her mouth.

Do it, Silvie. She heard her uncle's voice invade her mind. You must.

Have I ever disappointed you before? Bobby was my idea, if you recall. I planted him to separate Denise and Kerstyn. It worked perfectly. I drove Kerstyn right into Dimitri's arms. I also successfully convinced Hadrian to bind Eva to him. Without my help, those two would still be fighting their attraction and now they are well on their way to wedded bliss, she countered.

231

Handle this with care, my girl, he cautioned before fading away.

I always do, she thought with an inward grimace.

"The Shaman will not be joining us. He has been ill of late. I will be presiding over this meeting," Silvie announced.

Samuel's eyes narrowed. *The seed of discord has been planted*, she thought.

"We will not tolerate this. We are leaving," Oliver declared.

The doors slammed shut as the strong sense of magic spread through out the conference room.

"No one will be leaving until I lift the spell," Silvie replied sweetly. "So, have a seat. You must be exhausted from your flight."

The Red Order Council slowly moved towards the table. They sat, their gazes locked on the vampire monarchs.

"Wonderful, let's get started. The Shaw have called this meeting, summoning all the vampire Chieftains and their Seconds along with the five members of the Red Order Council with the purpose of discussing peace."

Samuel and Oliver balked while Carter, Richard, and Lewis leaned forward, interested.

Good boys.

She glanced at the line of vampires. They remained poised and as stoic as ever. Just as expected. They betrayed nothing, all true warriors. Well, Kerstyn was an exception. The newly changed vampire had been named Dimitri's Second. He had named his wife as his heir. King Dorian had Raphael at his side while King Hadrian and Falcon sat together. Queen Sonya and Gwendolyn's expressions were fierce, the women perhaps the most deadly pair.

"The war between the Mylonas and the Red Order has gone on for far too long. The Shaw would like to see it end in a mutually beneficial way."

"Long before your time, priestess, I had tried to end this senseless war," Dorian interjected.

"Yes, King Dorian, I am aware."

"You expect us to call a ceasefire?" Samuel snapped. "You are wasting your breath, priestess."

"Since the invention of bagged blood, the Clans have not been feeding directly from humans," she continued, ignoring Samuel's outburst. "Slavery was abolished long ago and bleeders are no longer necessary."

"But they are still kept," Lewis said.

"Only if they are willing," Silvie countered.

"Those humans have been brainwashed," Samuel argued.

"No mind control or hazing has been used on the humans in question, I can assure you," Dimitri spoke, his voice smooth and even.

"Slavery does still exist. The Outcastes capture humans and keep them in cells, using them as juice boxes until they dry up," Samuel said.

"Before this war, the Red Order hunted the Outcasts, keeping the society under control," Silvie interjected. "But no longer do the scum of vampire society fear you."

Dorian turned to Silvie. "We know the Red Order will never stop killing our kind. However, the four of us would be content if this war ended and we returned to the old ways. We control and police our people. We will see to it that no unwilling humans are used and that those who share themselves freely are not abused. If a vampire disregards the law, they will be banished and the Red Order can deal with them as they see fit."

"That was once the arrangement," Hadrian said, his deep voice drawing all eyes to him.

"And can be again," Carter added.

"No. Our mission is to destroy all vampire kind, beginning with the Mylonas Clan."

Dorian's sea blue eyes narrowed as his gaze fell on the white haired man, Samuel. "That will never happen."

"Nor the ceasefire," Samuel countered.

"Peace can be achieved," Carter insisted. "The Shaw and the Voidukas are a perfect example. They have happily coexisted for centuries."

Silvie held up her hand. "Think twice before you insult my tribe," she said, her gaze fixed on Samuel.

He bit down on his tongue and swallowed his retort.

"The Red Order was founded with the purpose to hunt and kill vampires," Oliver said.

"Has anyone here suggested you stop doing your job?" Sonya asked. "We are not fools. We know there will never be love between our two species, but there can be a mutual understanding."

"A contract can be drawn, laws put into place which will be enforced by both sides," Dimitri offered. "We can come to some sort of an agreement."

"I don't believe we can," Oliver said.

"Let's hear this out," Lewis suggested. "I would like to know what would be in this contract."

"I will never sign a treaty with these leeches," Oliver replied.

The vampires all rolled their eyes at Oliver's derogatory term. It was an overused label.

"Be warned, Councilman," Dimitri said, his tone deathly calm. "If this war persists, the Volkov Clan will join with the Mylonas."

Carter swallowed hard as Richard and Lewis paled. The Red Order was struggling to fight one clan. Two would lead to absolute destruction. God, there was little stopping the Validus from joining as well. Hadrian needed some time to organize his clan, but once they were unified...fear struck like a blow to the chest as all three realized the gravity of the situation.

Death will fall to all. Carter heard the priestess's words as if she were speaking them now.

"You will not see the Red Order tremble," Samuel spat. "You all can band against us, but we will prevail. Not even the traitorous Shaw can save you."

Samuel's blood was heating to dangerous heights. He sensed Oliver's agitation beside him and hated Carter's enthusiasm for a peace pact. Had the young councilman contacted the Shaw? Had he gone behind their backs and arranged this meeting? Then there was Richard, who supported Carter's efforts for peace and the undecided Lewis. This conference had done nothing but show the enemy that the Red Order council was divided. The internal strife translated into weakness.

His eyes shifted to the priestess.

The Shaman would have only sent her for one reason. He was dying, perhaps preparing for reincarnation. The always strong and proud Shaw would soon find themselves weakened by the lack of a leader.

Perhaps the Reds had been going about this war the wrong way. The Shaw supported the vampires, backing them with healing potions, spells, and when necessary, soldiers. Without the Shaw...Samuel disguised his evil smile with a cough. Yes, the Red Order had been fighting a losing war, but not anymore.

"Your hopes for a ceasefire and possible treaty are futile, priestess. I will never sign a pact with these bloodthirsty, murderous demons. They belong in hell."

Carter and Richard sputtered as they argued, but Samuel was finished. Being the oldest council member, he held the most power and, unfortunately for everyone involved, the council had to come to a consensus or no agreements could be made. As they stood, the Red Order was divided and without a ceasefire bringing peace, there would be death.

Dorian's gaze flickered between soulless black and warm blue. His fangs sharpened as he hissed, "I promise you, Samuel. One day soon you will lament your stubbornness."

"I highly doubt it."

Dorian's lips slowly turned up with a smile. "War has been my sole occupation for nearly four thousand years. You cannot possibly win. Not only do we have superior strength, but time is on our side."

"Your population suffers," Sonya stated. "Your numbers fall every day and unlike you, our reproduction is not restricted by biology."

This conversation was not going as Carter had hoped, but it was progressing perfectly for Silvie. She just needed one more retort from the pig-headed Samuel and she could call an end to this meeting.

"Every full moon, we could welcome hundreds if not thousands of our kind into this world," Dorian added.

"You would damn more innocents to hell to win this war?"

All the monarchs knew Dorian was not serious. He loathed the thought of creating more vampires. Then again, he would do anything to ensure victory, which is what had always made him dangerous.

"Embrace a truce and you will never have to learn the answer to your question," Dorian said.

"When you all walk into the glowing rays of the sun, you will have your truce," Samuel spat.

Silvie clapped her hands, drawing everyone's attention. "Enough." She rose to her feet. "I have heard all I need." The doors of the large corporate conference room swung wide. "Councilmen, your rooms will be comped. Airline tickets await you at the front desk of the hotel lobby. I suggest you gather your things and depart immediately. Though the sun rides high in the sky, there are some vampires present that can tolerate its rays." She smiled. "I wouldn't want anything untoward to befall you."

Samuel shot to his feet, his fists shaking at his sides. "This is not over, priestess."

Her pupils dilated and constricted as a vision flickered through her mind. After a long, strained moment of silence, her eyes returned to normal. Her smiled grew brighter. "Yes. I know."

Samuel mumbled heated curses as he stormed from the room, Oliver close behind. Richard and Lewis filed out into the hotel hall. Carter paused just outside the meeting room. He opened his mouth to speak, but quickly snapped it shut and left.

"What the hell were you thinking? Why did you call this ridiculous meeting," Sonya demanded once she was certain the enemy was out of hearing range.

"To talk peace. Where have you been, Sonya?" Silvie teased.

The queen mumbled a curse and slumped back in her chair. She tossed her long golden hair over her shoulder. The silken strands hit Falcon's shoulder. She turned to apologize. The knight gave her a stiff nod.

"Your Majesty," he said, his voice controlled.

She blushed as she sensed everyone watching them.

"Sir Kenwrec," she replied.

Falcon stood and straightened and buttoned his suit jacket. Turning to his king, he said, "If you no longer have need of me, I would like to check on Miss Maldonado."

Hadrian gave a nod of approval. Sonya watched, pained longing glistening in her eyes as the Black Knight left the room.

Gwendolyn leaned over, placing her hand on her queen's forearm. Sonya shook her head and said, "Don't say anything."

Sonya pushed away from the table and excused herself from the room, careful to remain in the shadows and away from the sunlight.

Silvie sighed. She hated seeing her friend in pain. It was no secret that Sonya and Falcon liked each other. Unfortunately, ancient vampire law forbade a union such as theirs.

Something I will have to fix, Silvie thought.

"That poor couple," Kerstyn sighed.

All murmured in agreement.

Dimitri took his wife's hand. "You did well, Kerstyn. Being a new vampire, it is difficult to resist. I am proud of you."

Turning toward him, she smiled. "It was much harder than I thought. I could hear their hearts pounding and their blood…that was really difficult."

"You displayed great restraint," Dorian praised. "I was ready to launch across the table and rip their throats out."

"Now, Vlakhos, that would not be kind of you," Silvie tsked.

"You know those morons will never accept peace," Raphael added.

Silvie's shoulders shook with a hard laugh. "I know everything." Her dark giggles died. "Now, there is someone I must meet. I will see you all at Hadrian's coronation this weekend." Her words echoed through the room as she faded.

Chapter Thirty-Five

Eva paced. The hotel was lovely. Certainly the finest she had ever seen.

They had arrived late last night and after tucking her in the room, Hadrian had gone to meet with the other Clan Chieftains. The Shaw were playing mediator, calling for a peace meeting between the vampire rulers and the Red Order. The idea was great in theory, but could it ever be implemented?

Hadrian had not come back last night and she had not seen him this morning.

He must be staying in a different room, she thought.

Falcon had swung by before the meeting and gave her a credit card. Hadrian had suggested that she "take in the sights" before they flew back tonight. She had been excited to explore the new city and took advantage of the short time she had. It was refreshing to mingle with the public. She had wandered through the city, ducked into shops, had some coffee, and after ignoring them for as long as she could, Eva asked her two Shaw bodyguards where she should go. They escorted her to SadaMarket, which had everything from fashion and necessities, to baked goods and fishing gear. Fortunately, there was no language barrier. Her mother had taught her Estonian since it was her first language. She had also instructed her in Russian and Portuguese.

Now, she anxiously prowled from one wall to the other, thankful the suite was spacious. She let out a frustrated growl, her steps quickening.

She needed to talk to Hadrian. They needed to finish their conversation that Falcon and the summons had interrupted. She had a feeling Hadrian had been about to say...what? God, she wished she knew.

She had been unable to sleep. Her mind kept replaying that last moment. His expression had been serious, his harsh black eyes were warm, his gaze gentle. The way he said her name…it sounded as if he could not live without her.

"That is because he doesn't want to."

Eva slapped a hand over her mouth to hold back her yelp of shock as a woman took form just inside the door. Her red robe swayed as she crossed the room.

"Hi, I'm Silvie."

Eva could only blink. The woman exuded power and strength. The scent of her magic was overwhelming and Eva struggled to breathe. Her vision spun as she felt herself sway. Then in a rush, the room cleared.

"Sorry. My power can make some uncomfortable, especially those that aren't used to the sensation." Silvie waited for Eva's equilibrium to return before she continued. "You wished to speak with me?"

"What? Oh, you must be the priestess Hadrian told me about."

Silvie smiled warmly. "I hope I can help you with your questions. I must warn you, I can't see the past. I only know what the Shaman has chosen to share with me."

"Oh, god," Eva sighed, falling onto the edge of the bed. "These last few days have just been…unreal."

"I know what you mean. Things still need to sink in."

"What was it that you said when you came in?"

"I was just responding to your thoughts. When I first materialize in a room, I can hear, well, everything. Don't worry. I've closed the door to your mind. I will only know what you decide to share with me."

"I've never met anyone who could read minds," Eva said breathlessly.

"It's not a whole lot of fun."

"I can imagine. I'm constantly wondering what King Hadrian is thinking, but…I probably don't want to know."

Silvie came to sit beside Eva. "I think you would be pleasantly surprised."

Eva shook her head. She hoped the witch was right. "Did he ask you to speak with me?"

"No, I beat him to it."

"Well, I had some questions about my mom."

"I'm sorry, but many of your questions can only be answered with speculation. I have yet to develop the ability to speak with the dead." *I'm right on track for that, just another two months of training,* she added to herself.

"I wasn't expecting much. I just want to know a few things about her."

"And your father?"

Eva shrugged, sweeping her hair forward. It draped over her shoulder and fell to her lap. "Can I assume you know about my life and my situation?"

"Yes." *I know more than you could ever comprehend.*

Eva closed her eyes and willed herself to relax. She was too on edge, her thoughts a mess of questions about her mother, Hadrian, and her own future. She needed to organize the chaos. Mentally, she ranked her questions.

"So," she began, squaring her shoulders, "do you know the true reason my mother left her family? She had told me it was so that she could go to school."

"Isabella was in line to become a priestess, but she did not want to fall into the fold. We," Silvie waved a hand at her cloak, "sacrifice much so that we may dedicate ourselves to our craft. She simply wanted a different life. She was not banished or anything like that."

That was a relief. Eva had imagined that her mother was an outcast from her tribe. Alone to make her way in the world, like her.

"Was the story she told me of how she met my father true?"

"Yes, they met at a party."

And had drunk, unprotected sex, Eva finished.

"She knew little about shifters and your father was probably too wasted to care about her being a witch. You know shifter law, any relations with anyone other than shifters are forbidden. So, are you going to ask me the hard questions?"

Eva brought her hands up to rub her temples. Did she dare ask the two questions that burned her tongue? Hadrian had a good point. Information once learned cannot be unlearned. Well, she was not faint of heart. She could handle anything and these past few days were evidence of that.

"Why did she never tell me she was a witch?"

"I was waiting for you to ask that." Silvie reached into one of the pockets that were hidden within her robe. "Your mom sent this letter to her brother."

Eva reached for the paper with trembling hands. "My uncle?"

"Yes, he gave this to me for you."

"Oh, my god."

"When you are ready, he would like to see you. He may be able to explain more of why your mother did what she did." Silvie paused, searching for the right words. "After Hadrian's coronation celebration, you should ask him to send for your uncle."

"Or I could just go to him. I'm planning on leaving the Validus Clan after the party."

"Are you?" Silvie asked, her eyes narrowing.

Eva looked up and met the witch's eyes. "I think it would be a good idea."

"Really?"

"Yes," Eva said with a frown.

"How does Hadrian feel about you leaving?"

"He wants me to go."

"Honestly, do you believe that?" Silvie asked.

"He said—"

"Men say a lot of stupid things that they don't mean. Besides, I didn't ask you what he said. I asked what you believe. What does your instinct tell you?"

He wants me to stay. Eva was dying to say the words, but she could not force them past her lips.

"I know your doubts and fears. I can't tell you what to do or what will happen depending on your decision. But, wouldn't it be easier for Hadrian to reclaim his throne after all these years with his mate by his side? After all, you are proof that he is the rightful king of the Validus."

Silvie stood and stretched her arms over head. Her body ached from lack of rest. She had given Eva too much information. She should have phrased her words more carefully, but damn, she was tired and did not care about being cryptic and mysterious. She needed to unwind. Her lips curled into a smile as she thought of the perfect place to relax.

She glanced to Eva. Hadrian's mate stared at the carpet, nervously tugging on her lower lip with her teeth as her fingers frantically made little braids in her hair.

"I'll leave you so that you may consider my words. My last bit of advice is, don't overthink this. That is what Hadrian will do. Allow your emotions and instincts to guide you. They are never wrong."

240

Chapter Thirty-Six

Silvie took form in a suite that overlooked the Las Vegas strip. It was 4 a.m. here and the street below bustled with life. She took in a breath and relaxed, the scent of sandalwood settling in her lungs.

She had been here numerous times, which probably classified her as a stalker. Then again, Gannon was never home when she visited so it wasn't as if she were spying on him. She had to admit the thought had crossed her mind. The vampire was yummy and completely off limits.

Rule number one: a priestess is to remain chaste.

She fell back on the black leather sofa. The room was simply decorated. Rustic wood furnishings, a colorful hand woven rug covered the dark hardwood floors. There were no pictures on the walls, only a large mirror that hung over the fireplace and an enormous flat screen that loomed in front of her. The place could use a woman's touch.

She shrugged out of her heavy robe, tossed it beside her and leaned back. It felt wonderful to be rid of the stifling garment. She stretched, enjoying the freedom of movement, confined only by her jeans and tank top.

Closing her eyes, she pressed her head back into the leather cushion and welcomed the silence.

Home had become chaotic. Everyone had a million questions for her all about what their future holds. She was not a damn fortuneteller. She was a seer, a high priestess and the heir to the Shaman, although most of her tribe was not privy to that last item on her responsibility list. They assumed the Shaman would elect reincarnation again, as he had for the last thirteen thousand years.

Damn, everyone was in for the shock of the century. Her uncle, the Shaman, was retiring. He would finally move on to the next place and he had selected her to be his heir. Upon his death all of his knowledge, power, and memories, would be passed to her. Their magic would combine and, well, she did not know much after that. She had asked him what was to become of her and, like always, he shared little.

He had said he had been waiting for her, accumulating strength and building his magic knowing that one day he would gift it to her. She was destined to be the most powerful witch the world had ever seen.

Oh, yay, that is exactly what I want.

Silvie groaned. She wanted nothing to do with his plans, but Fate had already cast her for the role, and she was in way too deep to get out now.

She needed a break. She needed to unwind and release her stress. She needed to just be…herself. Silvie. A normal twenty-four year old who liked to shop, dance, and lay out in the sun with a tiny umbrella in her drink.

This suite had become her sanctuary. She had cast a spell to whisk her away to the place she would find peace and it had brought her to Gannon's home.

She had only met him once, but the man certainly left an impression. The instant their eyes had met, he tripped over a line of chairs, disrupting Dimitri and Kerstyn's wedding. They had talked that night, enjoyed a few drinks and danced to a song or two.

Okay, seven. It had been seven songs.

And at the end of the night, they went their separate ways. She had not seen him for almost two months even though she came here at least once a week. Silvie knew she should stop, that it was not right to roam around a stranger's home. But, for some unexplainable reason, this was the one place she could go without her uncle summoning her. It could be time for her training or lessons, but if she was here he left her alone.

Silvie heard a gun cock. Her eyelids flipped open. She had not sensed Gannon's presence, but he had picked up on hers.

He rounded the corner, pistol drawn.

Silvie scrambled to her feet. Her heart plummeted to the floor.

"Holy shit," he exclaimed, dropping his hand.

"I–I'm sorry." *Busted.* Fire spread through her cheeks and she wished she were anywhere but here. "I'll go."

"No. Wait," Gannon called as she began to fade. He dropped the clip from the gun and set the pieces on the side table. He could not get the weapon out of his hand fast enough.

Silvie released a heavy sigh and took form once more. She sat on the couch, head in her hands, her hair spilled forward, hiding her face. She was too embarrassed to look at him.

"I'm sorry."

"Yeah, you said that," Gannon said. He removed his thick, black, leather jacket and draped it over the back of a recliner.

Silvie peeked up at him and stifled a moan. The vampire was even more devastatingly sexy than she remembered. His black hair framed a strong jawline. His hazel eyes appeared to be more green than brown at the moment. And all that muscle, god, she could swoon. His shirt hugged his torso and showed off every hard line.

"You here on business?" he asked.

Silvie considered lying about her reason for coming. She had seen enough of Gannon's and his boss, Gabriel's, future to play out that scenario.

"I needed to get away," she admitted.

"And you came here," he added, his brow furrowed with confusion.

"I did a spell and it brought me here."

"Did you know this was my place?" he asked, suddenly worried she could have arrived at any random person's house.

"I saw you leaving." *The first night I came here*, she thought.

He nodded and removed his gun hostler, setting it on the seat of the recliner.

"So, why are you here?"

Silvie brushed her hair over her shoulder and finally met his gaze. Gannon's steps faltered as he came to the couch. God, she was stunning. Her pale skin was flawless and her dark eyes sparkled like diamonds. Her red lips were thin but perfectly kissable.

"I was searching for a safe place to escape to and, well, here I am."

His heart kicked into gear, heat spreading through his chest. He told himself her appearance was most likely an accident, but a man could wish.

"Drama?"

"Yeah, I suppose you heard of the peace meeting the Shaman called."

She held her breath as he lowered down onto the couch. Could he have managed to sit any further away?

"We caught some mumbles about that. How'd it go?"

"As well as to be expected," Silvie sighed. She grabbed her cloak and placed it in her lap. *Maybe he will move closer now*, she thought. Then frowned. *No. He needed to stay exactly where he was.* "I should not have come here."

"I'm glad you did." Gannon bit his tongue. The woman had finished saying she had come here to escape drama. He did not need to add to it. But damn, he couldn't think of anything other than kissing those luscious red lips.

She smiled and he nearly launched himself across the sofa.

"Well, I've been here too long and you need to pack."

Gannon's brow wrinkled. Pack? Why did he need to pack? Where was he going?

"Oh, shit," he exclaimed, then slapped a hand over his mouth. "Sorry."

Silvie waved her hand dismissively. "Like I care."

"How did you know that Gabriel and I are leaving?"

She tapped her temple. "I'm a seer, remember? The two of you are heading out to Colorado to check up on that woman in the photo."

Gannon rubbed his palms over his knees. Gabriel had found the picture of a beautiful young woman hanging in the empty cell of a slave warehouse. She had been the next victim on the vampire's list. Having been a bleeder and slave during his mortal life, Gabriel had become obsessed with finding and protecting the woman.

"I'm going to get out of here. It was nice seeing you and thanks for letting me chill at your place, even though you didn't know I was here," she said, crimson creeping into her cheeks.

"You can come by any time. I don't mind." The words came out in a rush.

"Thanks."

Silvie stood and shook out her cloak. Gannon moved to help her slip the heavy garment back on. Their fingers brushed, a light caress that made his skin tingle and her eyes flicker.

Her breath seized in her lungs as images of the future hit her like a bullet to the brain. The scene was clear, the colors, sounds, tastes and textures bombarded her senses. Silvie saw herself here, in Gannon's home. She was lying before the fireplace. Flames jumped and excitedly devoured something…red? Gannon was beside her, his fingers stroking her face, her neck, her breasts, and then lower. Their clothes lay scattered about the room, completely forgotten. His mouth came down on hers as he shifted, settling himself between her legs.

The vision released her and Silvie stumbled back, falling to the couch once more. Her heart slammed in her chest, her lungs burned for oxygen.

Oh, god. Oh, god. Oh, god, she chanted, rocking back and forth, clutching her robe to her chest.

"No. That can't happen. It can't."

"Are you okay?" Gannon asked, falling to his knees before her. She continued to stare at the floor, her eyes unfocused as she swayed. "Silvie," he said as gently as he could. She did not respond. He called to her again, but still, nothing.

Gannon brushed her hair away from her face. The contact slapped her out of her shock. She flinched and scrambled away from him.

Her eyes were wide and wild. She slowly backed away from him. She looked terrified. What had she seen? What could have caused this reaction?

"Silvie, are you—"

She was gone before he finished.

Chapter Thirty-Seven

Another growl, a matching snarl, the sound of kissing metal grew louder as Eva rushed down the stairs. Covering her ears with her hands, she used her shoulder to shove open the door to the gym.

Hadrian's head whipped around. His black eyes were wild as they narrowed on her. She choked on a scream as Falcon swung his blade. The king's gaze never wavered, he did not blink, nor did he wince when the razor sharp edge of Falcon's sword sliced a perfect line from the corner of his eye to the tip of his chin. Blood welled and ran down his cheek to drip from his jaw. The tiny crimson droplets landed on his smooth bare chest.

"Oh–my–god," Eva gasped. She pulled free the towel she had hastily fastened over her bikini and rushed forward.

Hadrian stood rooted to the stone floor, unable to tear his eyes from Eva or to find his voice.

If they were alone, he would lay her down on the mats and take great pleasure in untying the straps of her top, freeing her ample breasts. He would trail kisses down her flat belly. Using his teeth he would drag the bikini bottom from her hips and down her shapely legs, leaving her beautiful golden skin bare to him.

He stifled a groan, cleared his throat, and thanked every Roman god he had once worshipped that he was wearing loose workout shorts.

"Please," he said, his voice rougher than he wanted. "This is nothing. No need to worry."

Her steps slowed, but she continued to come towards him. Hadrian nonchalantly wiped his face with the palm of his hand, smearing the blood and revealing perfectly flawless pale skin.

"No need to worry," he repeated, "Thank you for your concern."

Falcon sheathed his weapon. "My king, I apologize."

Hadrian shook his head. "No harm done. It was my fault, I lost focus."

Eva inwardly groaned. She had caused his distraction by barging through the door.

"I'm sorry about interrupting your sparing match. Here," she held her towel out to Hadrian, "you can wipe off the blood."

He gave her a grateful nod and took her offering. He rubbed the cloth across his chest, his muscles flexing.

"Well, carry on," she said.

Turning on her heel, she slipped out the door and sprinted back up the stairs to the pool. It was a miracle she did not stub her bare toes in her hasty retreat.

Eva cursed and grabbed the second towel she had brought down with her, intending to use it for her hair. She stomped back over to the hot tub and sank into the water, resuming her seat, using the new towel as a pillow.

"That wasn't embarrassing at all," she sighed.

What had she been thinking? She was practically naked and had charged down to investigate what sounded like a fight. She should have known better than to barge into a vampire-sparing match. She could have easily become a target, or worse, a victim. And what if it had not been Hadrian and Falcon? The castle was beginning to fill with their Clan members. Everyone was anxiously awaiting the coronation ceremony, which was tomorrow night.

Tomorrow would be her last night at Palatio Nocte and her last night with Hadrian.

It had been three days since their return from Estonia. For three days they had barely spoken, only spying glimpses of each other in the great hall and library. She had hoped Hadrian would come to her room at night. He never did. Maybe he was worried about what his Clan thought. How would the nobles react if they learned their king had been sleeping with a witch-shifter half-breed?

Eva shook her head. She could not imagine Hadrian caring about what the nobles had to say.

Last night, she had gone to his room. She had waited for him, but he never came. She awoke late this afternoon, curled in his bed. Irritated beyond belief, she had stormed to her room, changed, and literally beat the sand out of a punching bag. To relax, she decided to take a dip in the hot tub and here she was.

She had not been surprised to find Hadrian and Falcon together. Ever since they had returned, the two of them spent every moment together. She knew they had been preparing for the coronation and training for the fight Hadrian would have with some guy named Jefferson. Eva reluctantly admitted she was jealous of their bromance.

She smiled to herself as she poked at a cluster of floating bubbles. Bromance was one of her new favorite slang words. She had recently picked it up, knowing she would be out in the "normal" world soon she had doubled her efforts to modernize.

Her smile faded as her thoughts turned serious. She still had yet to decide where she was going to go. With Silvie's help, she had gotten in contact with her uncle. He had offered for her to come live with him. He had a small apartment in Tallinn that they could share. She had been surprised to learn that he had not married in the past nine years. He was such a nice, genuine man. When they had spoken, she could hear the loneliness and hope in his voice.

Her other option was returning to Florida. Her uncle had agreed to move with her. He was a well-known martial arts instructor and he could easily open another studio. She would work for him and go back to school. If she studied hard, she was confident she could make it into medical school and finally become a pediatrician. She did have all the time in the world. Literally. Thanks to Hadrian, she would live forever. Eva knew she would need a really good job and to learn how to invest successfully if she were going to live comfortably throughout eternity.

She slipped further beneath the water, submerging her shoulders.

The honest truth was, she did not want to leave.

"Damn it."

"Damn what?"

Eva shivered despite the hot water. His voice was unmistakable and she cursed her body for instantly responding.

"I was just thinking out loud," she said. "Didn't anyone ever teach you that it isn't polite to eavesdrop?"

Hadrian smiled as he came to stand beside the in-ground hot tub. Eva craned her neck back. The vampire towered over her normally. He was good foot and some inches taller than her. But from here, he looked like a giant—A very sexy giant, who wore nothing but shorts and running shoes.

"Sorry for busting in on you guys like that."

"I'm glad you did." He slipped his shoes and socks off.

Oh, no. Was he planning on getting in the water?

"Why?" she asked.

"You distracted me."

Eva held her breath as he stepped in. He was so close.

"Isn't th–that a bad thing?" she stammered.

He shrugged. "You have the power to distract me."

His velvet voice turned her heart over. She silently cursed.

"Noted," she said. "I'll be sure to stand in the back when you face your challenger."

Hadrian reclined back, his arms spanning over the tiled edged of the tub. He looked like a Roman god enjoying his bath and Eva found it impossible to look away.

"I'm sorry, we have not had much time together—"

"It's fine, I understand. You are a popular guy and I know you have a lot to do."

"I would like us to talk."

"We are talking now."

He gave a stiff nod. "Falcon told me the priestess gave you a letter from your mother."

Eva sighed, the air easing out of her lungs as her muscles relaxed. She had not noticed the tension that had tightened her shoulders.

"It was a letter my mom had written to my uncle."

"Your uncle, the man you lived with in Rio de Janeiro?"

"Yeah, she wanted advice." Eva idly pushed the bubbles around, forming shapes and designs. "She had asked him if she should tell me I was part witch. She did not want me to feel...like a freak. Being a human-shifter half-breed was already rare. A witch-shifter combination was unheard of."

When Eva had read the words she could feel her mother's terror. Everyday her mom had watched her, wondering and worrying if her daughter would experience the change. If so, would she survive? It was a miracle the two of them had even lived through the birth. If it had not been for Jenna, a skilled healer and witch, they would have died.

Eva was amazed by how she had not noticed the stress her mother was under. Growing up, she had been completely oblivious.

"You have been speaking with your uncle."

It was not a question, but a statement and Eva nodded. Before leaving Estonia she had asked Silvie to help her get in contact with her uncle. She still had yet to see him, but hearing his voice over the phone was wonderful.

"He has been able to answer a lot of my questions. My mother never wanted me to worry about the change, especially since she did not know if it was even a possibility." Eva's hands began to tremble. "You must know there was no way my father was unaware of my mom being a witch."

"Yes. It was one of the most troubling pieces of your story."

"Well, he didn't know about me until we moved back to Brazil. The informants he keeps in Rio told him about the Shaw witches that were in the city. He came, recognized my mother and realized I was his daughter."

Hadrian nodded. The story sounded plausible. Shifters could sense their own kind and, if Arsenio had gotten close enough to Eva, he would have felt their blood bond.

"My uncle doesn't know why the alpha came for me. Maybe he was afraid of him taking me to the Shaw."

"It is forbidden for shifters to mate with others outside their pack. Generally, exceptions are made in regards to humans since their offspring, if conceived, have a very low chance of living."

"What would've happened if they had found out?"

He shrugged. "He could have been stripped of his title and banished. If banished, he would not survive long. He has many enemies."

Eva shifted, bringing her legs up onto the seat. The tops of her knees stuck out of the water. "My uncle had wanted to go after me."

Hadrian's gaze grew sharp. "Why didn't he?"

"He would've needed the permission of the Shaman to engage in a dispute with the shifters."

"He was denied."

Eva slowly nodded. God, her life would have been so different if she had remained with her uncle. They would have moved back to the Shaw compound in Estonia and lived quiet, peaceful lives.

But I would have never met Hadrian, she thought.

Despite their roller coaster of a relationship, if it could even be called a relationship, she would not have traded it for "normal." She loved him even though she knew it was foolish. Yes, she sensed he had some feelings for her, but he still wanted her to leave. Did he still think he was protecting her?

She sighed and wrapped her hands around her knees. She did not know his motives and she probably never would. Silvie had made a good argument, stating that it would be better for Hadrian if she stayed. Presenting Eva as his mate would make for a smoother transition back into his Clan. But the fact remained that he had not asked her stay and was instead practically shoving her out the door.

Silvie's words circled through her head again. *Don't over think this. That is what Hadrian will do. Allow your emotions and instincts to guide you. They are never wrong.* Well, she was doing a terrible job at not overthinking this. And how could she possibly follow her emotions and instincts when they were as messy as a kitchen junk drawer.

"Eva?"

She shook her head, clearing her thoughts and turned her gaze to him. "What?"

"Are you going to go live with your uncle?"

"I think so."

His arms dropped into the water. The muscles of his arms and chest flexed. Was he clenching his hands?

"That's good. You should be with family. You belong with them."

"And not with you," she finished his thought.

Why did his words make her feel as if a knife had just been plunged into her heart?

Mine, her instincts whispered. *No, not mine. He will never be mine. He won't allow himself to be mine.*

She felt her tears rising. She had to leave. She could not cry in front of him.

Eva pushed herself to her feet and snatched the towel. She was about to step out, but his fingers circled her wrists. She did not turn to him. She could not look at him. Not now.

"I've got a date with a book," she said, proud her voice did not tremble. "And Falcon will probably need you soon."

"Falcon is nursing a few injuries and…I asked him to give us some time."

"Well, I hope he is okay and I know your time is valuable so I won't keep you."

She tried to pull free, but he would not let her go. Eva sighed.

"What is it Hadrian?"

Chapter Thirty-Eight

Don't leave. Not now. Not ever.

The words were on the tip of his tongue. He just had to open his mouth and they would tumble out. But he could not do it. She was going to leave and be with her family, the Shaw.

Gods, how was he to pretend losing her was not killing him? Had he truly thought he could watch her leave and not fall apart?

He had thought avoiding her would make this situation easier to accept, but it had only made it worse. He thought of her with every passing minute, unable to focus on his work. His coronation was tomorrow night. He would face Jefferson and he would return to his Clan as their king. But his queen would not be at his side. She would be in the crowd waiting for the party to end and for Falcon to escort her to the airport.

How could he concentrate on his fight with Jefferson knowing he only had a few precious hours left with Eva? He would be distracted, leaving himself open and vulnerable to defeat.

"Let go, Hadrian."

She still had not looked at him. He did not have to see her face to know she was on the verge of tears. He could hear the sadness in her voice.

He reached up, took the towel from her and tossed it on the chairs. She mumbled a protest as he drew her to him. He did not ask her to sit or try to pull her down. He simply wrapped his arms around her thighs and laid his head between her hips.

Eva gasped, her body tensed, but the stiffness faded. Her arms circled his head. She held her to him.

Hadrian closed his eyes, silently savoring the feel of her. His heart was breaking with every beat. He could not let her go, he could not release her. She was his mate. She was his Eva.

"Hadrian, I think—"

Her words ended on a moan when he pressed his lips to her navel.

"Oh, Eva," he sighed, nuzzling against the triangle of her bikini.

Eva knew she should push him away, but her arms remained locked around his head.

"Will you let me taste you? I need to taste you."

Every sane thought escaped her. God, she needed him. Needed this, just one last time.

Her throat was dry, her chest ached, and tears blurred her vision as she whispered a shuddering, "Yes."

Hadrian's hands fell to her hips. He drew the dainty bottoms of her bikini down her legs. She stepped out of them and he tossed them over his shoulder. They landed in the water with a soft splash.

The hard sound of locks sliding into place echoed throughout the room. She smiled. He thought of everything, and right now, they did not need an audience.

He stood. Water and bubbles ran down his chest. Gripping her hips, he lifted her and set her on the edge. His hands slipped to her thighs, spreading her wide for him. He drew a finger over her center, finding her creamy and ready for him.

Hadrian pressed a palm to her chest, guiding her to her back before kneeling down. Eva hooked her legs over his wide shoulders and, closing her eyes, she surrendered herself to him.

He teased her hipbones with his teeth before drawing his mouth lower. His breath brushed over her sensitive flesh. She heard him take in a deep breath. He growled low and she shuddered. God, she was close to coming already. It had been three days and her body was starved for him.

He drew his tongue over her cleft. She moaned and Hadrian smiled against her.

"I love the way you taste," he whispered. "Warm vanilla...I will never forget."

His tongue drove inside her and her back arched. Eva's claws dug into his shoulders and he went wild. He lapped at her, his tongue driving into her, his lips suckling at her clitoris.

Under his attack, she writhed. Fire raced through her veins, the heat building and building, burning, consuming. Her hips rocked against his mouth. Her frenzied need matching his. She cried out as everything fell away.

Hadrian swallowed her orgasm and growled. He rose above her. Eva gazed up at him, her brilliant eyes glowing with hunger. She sat up, her hands going for his shorts. She shoved them down as she slipped back into the hot tub. Her hands gripped his buttocks, her tiny talons pressing against his flesh. She pulled his hips forward and took his hard arousal into her mouth.

He caught her hair in his fists, crushing the silken curls. Her mouth was tight and hot around him. She swirled her tongue up and down his shaft, her lips slipping over the sensitive tip. Gritting his teeth, he flexed his hips. Eva took him in further, sucking, drawing on him hard and urgent. White-hot lightning shot down his spine. Gods, he was on the verge of coming.

Hadrian pulled from her grasp and drew her up. Eva only had time for one inarticulate cry before his mouth claimed hers. His lips were hard, his tongue plunging, the kiss hungry, maddening.

Her hands massaged his shoulders and his arms. Then her claws ran down his chest. His growl was rough, masculine and primitive. She loved it.

His fingers untied her halter-top, freeing her breasts. The material fell to the bubbles. He trailed his lips down the side of her neck. His teeth nipped at her shoulder as he cupped her, his thumbs teasing her nipples.

Eva moaned, shuddering as he pulled her back down into the water. She straddled his hips, his hardness brushing at her core. With one thrust, he could be buried deep within her, but he remained still. His lips caressed her breasts while his tongue toyed with her nipples in turn.

She clutched his head to her, wishing this would never end. This moment. Here. Now. It had to last forever.

Her breath caught as he turned her around, settling her over his thighs. He slammed her down. She cried out, the water splashing about them, the bubbles kissing her breasts. She leaned forward, gripping his knees. He reached forward, his palm sliding over her hip, his fingers finding her clitoris. His other hand tunneled through her hair.

Hadrian thrust into her, taking her hard and slow. She stretched out before him, her back long, flawless, and elegant. He bent down, pressed his lips to the curve of her neck. He nipped at her nape, drawing his fangs over her spine as his fingers worked at her. She shivered and sighed.

As he took her, he marveled at how absolutely beautiful she was. She was so small, delicate, and yet strong. Her passion matched his own, wild and hungry. She moved with him, her body urging him to go faster.

Her body arched, her head falling back against his chest. He released her hair to cup her jaw. Turning her head to the side, he kissed her, deep. Their breath became one as their tongues tangled, their teeth hitting. Desperate. Demanding.

Hadrian kissed her with all he had, offering her his heart, his soul. Him. Eva had drawn him from the darkness. She had healed him with her light and passion. She was in his heart. She was in his soul.

Gods, he loved her. He felt whole. He felt complete. The emptiness, loneliness, and madness that had claimed him for centuries had been shoved aside by the woman in his arms. And, gods, he wanted to keep her. Needed to keep her.

Her muscles tightened around him as her breath caught. Her breasts thrust upward as her back bowed. As his name fell from her lips, he sank his fangs into the curve of her neck. A roar of complete satisfaction rumbled in his throat as her blood filled his mouth. He pinned her hips and pounded into her.

Eva whimpered as he thrust through her orgasm. Her mind drifted through a haze of pleasure as the terrible, powerfully electrifying sensation began to build again. His lips pulled at her, drawing her essence into him. He grew even harder, longer inside her. Closing her eyes, she was swept away by the storm of their passion.

Her soft muscles rippled around him as her smooth, vanilla blood slipped down his throat. He could taste her orgasm as it built within her. The turbulent pleasure slammed into him and he came with her. His head snapped back, a roar tearing from his chest as he flooded her with seed.

Eva collapsed back against him, her breaths coming in a rush and her heart pounding uncontrollably. She squeezed her eyes shut, desperately fighting back the tears that threatened to fall. This was a painfully perfect moment. His arms wrapped around her, pulling her tightly to him. He was still stiff within her. His breaths rasped against her neck. She felt him sweep his tongue over her sore flesh, closing the wound.

She swallowed hard, wishing the bite would not heal. God, she wanted to keep his mark. She wanted to wear it forever. But there was no forever for them, no matter how many times she prayed and no matter how hard she wished. Nothing was going to change.

Eva climbed off his lap and stood. Her legs were weak, but she had to leave. She had to get away.

He tried to pull her back, but she jumped out of his reach. She did not bother looking for her bikini. She stepped from the warmth of the water and quickly crossed over to her discarded towel.

"Eva."

She did not have to turn to know he was standing right behind her.

"May I come to you tonight?"

God yes. Please, yes!

She shook her head. "No. I don't think that would be a good idea. Let's just...leave it like this."

Chapter Thirty-Nine

Eva had to get away. She had to get out of this castle and just be…far, far away from Hadrian. She could not do this. She could not stay until after the party. She knew she would be unable to say goodbye. She had to leave. Now.

After a quick shower, she dressed and shoved as much as she could into a lightweight duffle bag. She could always send for her things later. She had to be quick, she had to act, or she knew she would chicken out.

She pulled the door of Falcon's Land Rover open and let out a relieved sigh when she found the keys resting on the driver's seat. Tossing her bag in the back, she slipped in. Adjusting the seat and mirrors, she prayed that driving was like riding bike—you never forget how to do it. She pressed the garage door button on the visor and took a deep breath as the steel door rolled back.

"At least there isn't a storm tonight," she said, turning the ignition. She put the car in gear, took a deep breath, and pushed on the gas.

Good, no one is out in front, she thought as she rounded the circular driveway. The last thing she needed was someone running to tattle on her. She was only borrowing Falcon's car, she fully intended on giving it back.

She relaxed back in the plush seat once she reached the road. It should be smooth going from here. The road had just been plowed in anticipation of the new arrivals. She suspected she would pass a line of cars on their way to the castle.

She turned the radio on hoping some music might help with the butterflies that were fluttering in her stomach.

"Wow, Falcon," she said with a light laugh. "I never thought you were into Frank Sinatra. Metal, hardcore rap, sure, but not this."

She sang along with the songs, surprised by how many she actually knew. Her mom had a thing for Ol' Blue Eyes and the crooners. But the music and the pleasant memories that accompanied it did nothing to quell her nerves. They seemed to be getting worse.

Her chest felt tight and her palms began to sweat. Her heart rate elevated and her throat constricted.

What the hell?

Her stomach clenched, her muscles tightened, and her breathing labored. With every passing mile it got worse. The dull aches of her body turned to sharp pains.

She frowned as the sensation to turn around and go back took root within her. The compulsion grew stronger and stronger. Her instincts screamed, her animal spirit roared.

"I'm not going back," she chanted, her voice a whisper.

Leaning forward, she tightened her grip on the steering wheel and gave the Land Rover a little more gas.

She was leaving her male and her Drive was not going to stop her. The pain would eventually pass. She hoped.

*   *   *   *

Hadrian sat at his desk. He did not bother with a glass. He just took another swig of Silver Moon straight from the decanter.

He was twitchy, on edge. He felt like running. Not because of the beast or the evil memories, though he could feel the demon prowling within him. No, this time he felt like running because of Eva. He needed to escape the unwanted emotions she triggered.

Hadrian brought the bottle to his lips again and drank deep. Wiping his mouth with the back of his hand, he slumped in the chair. The burn of the liquor was not helping.

Hadrian placed the decanter on the desk and pushed to his feet. He knew he should dress and go down to the great hall. A black suit awaited him in the closet, but when he had materialized in his room an hour ago, he could not bring himself to put it on. Instead, he selected a pair of gray loose sweats and a plain white t-shirt.

There was a welcoming party going on downstairs. Guests such as Sonya, Gwendolyn, Dimitri, Dorian, and their queens awaited him. The remaining nobles of the Validus had arrived as well, but he did not care. Falcon had already come to talk to him, but Hadrian had not heard a word the knight said. Eva consumed his thoughts.

He ran his hands over his face. He had not sought her out for sex. Truly, he had wanted to talk. He wanted to know what her plan was. The coronation ceremony was tomorrow night and she had yet to announce where she was going to go when it was over. He was glad she had decided to live with her uncle instead of moving back to the States alone.

Honestly, he did not want her to leave at all, but he would not be selfish with her. He would not ask her to stay. Eva finally had her freedom. Remaining here meant accepting her rightful place at his side. Why would she elect to endure an eternity of confinement? She would be sequestered in the castle surrounded by mountains just as she had been isolated in a hut deep in the jungle. She would be trading one prison for another.

He had to let her go. He had to let her live her own life, find her own way, and maybe she would return to him.

Hadrian scoffed and snatched the bottle back. He would not sell himself on that idea. He would not allow himself to hope for her return. Hope only led to disappointments.

He took another long drink then crossed over to the bed. Sliding the decanter onto the side table, he fell face first into the pillows. Taking in a deep breath, he filled his lungs with the calming aroma of vanilla. Hadrian groaned. His cock grew hard, responding to Eva's luscious scent. He had not allowed the servants to change his sheets. For the last three days his dreams had been plagued by nightmares of the past, of the night they had shared his bed.

Gods, that night he had been ready to tell her of his feelings. He had been on the verge of confessing when Falcon had interrupted, pounding on the door, ruining the moment.

Eva possessed his heart, his soul, his mind, and his body. He had belonged to her since the moment they met. He had tried to fight it. He had managed to think of one logical explanation after another to avoid admitting what his soul already knew.

She was his mate, his queen, his lover, and his friend. She was his everything. He had shared his darkest sins with her and she had not turned from him. Eva had accepted him and all his flaws. When she looked at him, it was as if she could see directly into his soul. Never once did she allow the intensity of the demon to frighten her or dominate her. The beast liked that. It liked her.

Hadrian rolled to his back, clutching the pillow to his chest.

Why was it so difficult to say three simple words?

She had said them, here, in his bed. She had whispered the little words. Although, he doubted she realized they had fallen from her lips.

Did she mean it, he wondered.

Eva had been in the throes of passion, consumed by her need and pleasure. People often said things they did not mean while overwhelmed by emotion.

What if she had purposefully whispered the words?

He had not responded. He had continued on as if she had said nothing. Gods, had she expected him to reply?

Hadrian was up and out the door in a blink. He needed to talk to her. He needed to know if she loved him. If so, freedom be damned, he would not let her go. He would keep her locked in his room or chained to his bed for all eternity if that is what he had to do.

Focusing his energy, he materialized in the hall outside her room. Falcon was coming towards him with an all too serious frown on his face.

"Not now, knight," he snapped, brushing past him.

"My king, she is not there."

Hadrian stopped. "Where is she?"

"Eva left."

His blood turned glacial as he faced the knight. "What?"

"I went to my room to grab the plans on the new gun I'm designing. Sire Dimitri wants to look them over. I found this." He pulled a piece of paper from the inside pocket of his suit jacket. "She must have slipped it under my door."

Hadrian snatched the note, quickly scanning the contents.

Falcon laughed, "Can you believe she stole my car?"

Chapter Forty

Eva slammed on the breaks, sending the Land Rover into a slide. Turning the wheel, she directed the vehicle into a snow bank. The seat belt constricted, snapping her back against the seat. She blinked, rubbed her eyes, and blinked again. Damn, she was dizzy and it was not because of the accident. Her shifter instincts were demanding that she turn around and go back to her male.

What the hell just happened?

She fumbled with the belt clasp, her fingers trembling. Adrenaline hammered through her veins. With a click the buckle sprang free. She shoved open the door and slipped out. Wrapping her arms about herself, she walked around to the front of the car.

"Oh, thank God," she sighed. *No damage.*

She swayed and stumbled. She pressed a hand over her heart as she leaned against the side of the car. Her chest compressed, her lungs seized, her heart clenched as if a vise was squeezing it. Pain shot through her system, her fingers and toes stung with prickling tingles.

She doubled over. Eva gasped. The frosted air burned her lungs. She wiped at her eyes again and lurched for the car door. If her body was going to torture her, she may as suffer where it was warm.

Her fingers slipped around the handle and…suddenly the pain was gone.

Eva felt the blood leave her face. There was only one solution to the pain. Its absence meant that her male had to be nearby.

"No," she whispered, drawing her gaze back to the road.

Hadrian's red eyes glowed like embers, hot and bright. His shoulders rolled as he stalked toward her with predatory grace.

Eva swallowed the hard lump of fear that rose in her throat. She jumped and stumbled back when the door slammed shut. The locks sliding into place told her she was not going to escape him. Eva braced herself as he came to stand before her, blocking the car. He looked furious. Shadows cut across his face, his fangs were long and sharp, and his red eyes sparkled with malice and madness.

"You were not to leave until tomorrow." His words were hard, his voice eerily deep.

She squared her shoulders. She would not be intimidated by the demon. "I changed my mind. Now, move and unlock the car."

"Why?"

"So I can go."

His eyes narrowed. "Why did you leave, Eva?"

Eva shook her head and let out a long, exasperated sigh. "I could not stand to be there anymore. I had to get out."

"You could have gone for a walk," he said with an underlying growl. "You did not have to steal Falcon's car."

"I didn't steal anything. I'm borrowing it," she argued. Crossing her arms over her chest, she asked, "Why are you here, Hadrian? Why did you come after me? I'm leaving, just like you wanted."

He balked, his eyes flicking between red and black. "Like I wanted?"

"Yes."

She tried to step around him, but he blocked her with his body. Eva growled, the feral sound drawing an answering growl from him.

"Unlock the doors," she hissed between clenched teeth.

"You think I want you to leave?"

Eva threw her hands in the air. "That is what you want, isn't it? Ever since we discovered the secret hidden in my blood, making me no longer your ward or responsibility, you have been shoving me towards the exit."

Hadrian took a step toward her, his fingers reaching for her. Eva backed away. She could not allow him to touch her. She would lose her nerve if he did.

"Stay away from me," she snapped.

The red faded from his eyes and they returned to their natural black. Pain and longing flashed in his gaze as his hand fell to his side. "Eva. I…" His voice wavered. He cleared his throat and let the words tumble out, "I don't want you to leave."

Eva stared at him as if he had struck her. Her eyes were wide, her lips parted as she sucked in deep breaths. Anger and confusion danced like flames in her eyes as her hands curled into shaking fists.

"Do you get off on playing mind games?" she spat. "I mean, really? You're my first true lover, but I can say with perfect confidence that I am not into that crap."

Hadrian ignored her anger and realization buzzed in his head. Eva was leaving because she believed he wanted her to go.

"I am not playing a game, I assure you."

Eva rubbed her brow. "Hadrian, I'm going. I can't take this anymore. It was…fun, but I have to go." She brushed passed him and tugged on the door handle. "Damn it!"

She whirled on him, her claws extending, her teeth sharpening. Wild anger flowed through her. Her jaguar spirit wanted out and it wanted Hadrian. It wanted to lash out, to attack him, but it also wanted her to *take him*. To claim him here, in the snow, untamed and savage.

Sensing her conflicting desires, Hadrian came closer. His movements were slow, fluid. He did not want to trigger her instincts. She was feral. Her beautiful lips pulled back over her teeth, her eyes shimmered in the moonlight, and a low snarl vibrated her throat. A warning? A plea?

He did not touch her, but he advanced, backing her against the car. Cornering her. Trapping her. A dark part of him wanted her to attack. The demon? It wanted to feel her claws bite into his flesh; her teeth tear at his neck or his shoulder as she rode him hard.

Something within him snapped. He lunged forward, his palms hitting the glass, his hands framing her head. His body hummed, his heart pounded out of control until it matched the frantic rhythm of hers. He bent his head down to her neck and drew in a deep breath. Gods, she was divine.

Eva told herself to calm down, to breathe, but she was too far-gone to relax. Hadrian loomed over her, his body crowding her, trapping her. Yet, he did not touch her. Her anger twisted with lust. She needed him to touch her.

Struggling to maintain her sanity, she hissed, "Why did you come out here?"

He released a shuddering sigh, "I want you."

Her harsh laugh rubbed over him like silk. "You can't be serious."

Hadrian pressed closer, his lower body sinking into hers. Eva gasped when his erection pushed against her stomach. She wanted to shove him away. She wanted to pull him closer.

"I am very serious."

"Sex. You hunted me down for sex?" she seethed, her anger and need rising together as one.

"No," he whispered, his lips moving against her ear.

Her hands wrapped around his wrists. She clung to him as if anchoring herself. Her nails cut into him, drawing blood.

"I hunted you because I want you." He kissed the sensitive flesh blow her ear.

She moaned. She was on fire. She wanted him to stop, but she needed him to continue. God, she wished she were stronger. That she could break free of the emotional hold he had on her. Eva knew that if Hadrian wanted sex, she would give it to him. Her sanity would not be able to save her.

"Please, Hadrian," she sighed, unable to tell if her own words were a plea for freedom or a request for him to continue.

Hadrian cupped her face. Their eyes met and held. His heart stilled as he slowly exhaled all the air from his lungs. She was beautiful. So strong, so brave, so warm and caring, everything he wanted. Everything he needed.

He swallowed hard. "I need you."

His words hitched as she wet her lips. Her claws retracted from his wrists. He could sense the tension slowly fade from her body.

He came closer, their bodies melding together. His hands slipped into her hair to cradle her head. He titled her face up, maintaining eye contact. Her tiny exhales brushed his chin. Her lips were tantalizingly close and parted. She blinked up at him. Waiting. She was waiting for him to say the words that burned his soul.

"I love you, Eva." The words fell from his lips in a desperate rush. "I do not want you to leave. Please…tell me what I can do to…make you stay. I will do anything."

Her silence was like a dagger to his heart. He closed his eyes as he felt the tears of hopelessness rising. Gods, he had bared his soul and lain his heart at her feet. He needed to hear her say…something. Anything.

Hadrian flinched when her smooth soft hands caressed his face. He did not dare open his eyes, terrified of what he would find in her eyes. Was she looking at him with sorrow or pity? He prayed for anything but pity. He told himself he could survive her rejection. He was no stranger to guilt, loneliness, or despair.

"Hadrian."

He could not stop the tears from slipping. The sensation was unnerving. He never cried. Not even when he was mortal. Tears were for the weak and they achieved nothing. They could not bring loved ones back or absolve anguish.

"Gods, Eva. I cannot lose you," he rasped. "Please, tell me what I can—"

"Just ask me, Hadrian."

His eyes opened. She was crying too. Her amber eyes shimmered with tears. They streaked her cheeks.

"Will you stay?"

She nodded. "Oh, god, Hadrian. I didn't want to leave. I love you."

Eva rose up on her toes and their lips met. The kiss was soft, sweet, tender and tasted of their tears.

The world shifted around them and Eva felt the heat of a fire.

"What about Falcon's car," she asked as his lips trailed down her throat.

"We will retrieve it later," he said between kisses.

Eva circled her arms around his waist, pulling him close. His muscles shifted, tensed, and released beneath her hands. She could feel the power of his body.

He pulled at their clothing, tearing and destroying the fabric. His shirt drifted to the floor in shreds, his sweats dropped as he kicked his shoes free.

Hadrian went to his knees before her. His fingers made quick work of her laced boots. He stripped her jeans and panties away. Eva let out a thrilled gasp when he sliced open the front of her sweater with his claws. He shoved the ruined fleece from her shoulders as he bit through the front clasp of her bra.

Intense. Frantic. Their passion was rising to dangerous heights. Their need was spiraling out of control. His hands and his lips were all over her body, not leaving even a fraction of an inch untouched.

He came to his feet. Wild sexual hunger darkened his black eyes. His fangs glinted in the firelight. Eva could barely breathe. Shadows clung to his muscles, accentuating every hard line of his chest, abs, arms, and thighs. His body was amazing. His face was hard yet gentle, and serious with need. He was her Roman warrior, her vampire king, and her fallen angle. Hadrian was her male.

He loved her. The emotion blazed in his eyes. She had seen it in his eyes once before but she had not allowed herself to believe Hadrian could have feelings for her.

"I love you," she gasped against his lips as he kissed her again.

His tongue delved deep into her mouth, his lips claiming, dominating, hungry. Gripping her hips, he drew her up his body. Eva locked her legs around his waist. He carried her to his bed and followed her down to the mattress, blanketing her with his body.

"Oh, Eva. Say you will give yourself to me. Now. And forever."

He cupped her breasts, feeding one to his mouth then the other. His tongue swirled around her nipples and suckled on the tight beads.

"Yes, Hadrian. Forever," she gasped. "Yours. I'm yours."

He came back to her mouth. "I never thought you would be mine."

"I never thought you would let me," she admitted, tears stinging her eyes again.

His hands slid down her body, tracing the gentle swell of her breasts, her tapered waist, and the flare of her hips. He pressed against her, his hardness gliding over her slick heat. Eva moaned. The tip of him teased her clitoris. He rocked his hips against her, driving his shaft over her until she was crazed with need.

"Now, Hadrian," she rasped. "Please. Now."

He lifted his upper body, bracing his hands on either side of her head. His hips surged forward.

She cried out from his fierce invasion. He withdrew and thrust in deep. Tossing her head back, Eva called out his name, tension coiling through her body. Her toes curled as he took up a demanding rhythm, pumping in and out of her, base to tip, again and again.

Her eyes closed as she let herself go, allowing him to penetrate her heart and brand her soul.

Hadrian thrust, gritting his teeth. He was hardly able to bear the tightness of her searing heat clenching him. So addicting. Hadrian surrendered, losing himself in her. Forever. He would lose himself in her forever. He buried himself to the hilt, taking her and giving himself. Sharing himself. Opening his heart for her. Only her. Eva. His woman. His mate. Dropping his head into the fragrant curve of her neck, he pressed kisses to her shoulder.

Eva clutched at his powerful arms, holding onto him as he drove her over the edge, sending her careening into the abyss of blissful madness.

Urgency built and built until, with a primitive roar, his release shot through him. He came over and over again, flowing into her, filling her. Unable to stop, he continued thrusting, his muscles twitching with pleasure as the haze of ecstasy consumed his mind.

Eva felt the contractions of his climax deep within her; the rough sensations carried her into another orgasm. Her body clamped down on him, squeezing him like a vise, taking all he had to give.

Finally, his arms gave out and he collapsed to the mattress. He wrapped an arm around her and pulled her to his side. Eva settled her head over his chest. His heart thundered and matched the storm that swept through her. She curled into him, not able to get close enough.

God, this must be a dream. Or was it heaven?

She could not believe she was here with Hadrian. The happiness was overwhelming and she felt another round of tears coming.

His hands stroked her back. "This is what I wanted. You. In my arms and in my bed." He pressed a kiss to the crown of her head. "Gods, I just need to hold you."

"You fooled me," she replied, her voice rough from her cries of pleasure. "Why did you insist I leave if you didn't want me to go?"

"I thought you would not want to stay. You are finally free of the pack and...I know how much freedom means to you. I thought staying here and being my mate..." He shook his head. "That this would be a prison for you. I don't want you feeling as if you are forced to stay here."

She pushed herself up, placing her hand above his now still heart. "Well, as far as prisons go, the castle isn't bad. Although, I still haven't seen the dungeon."

He frowned and Eva sighed. He was not referring to the castle. He had thought a relationship with him would be a prison.

"Hadrian, how could you think I wouldn't want to be with you? How many times do I have to tell you? I–want–you. Everything within me wants you. Hadrian, you're my male." She shook her head. "You really have a thick skull."

"Your male?" Pride and happiness spread through his chest like a firestorm. Her animal spirit recognized and accepted him as her male, her mate.

"I had a difficult time believing someone like you would want to be with a monster like me."

"I don't ever want to hear you refer to yourself as a monster or a beast or a demon ever again. You are none of those things. Understand?"

He laughed. "Yes, little one. I understand." Hadrian tilted her chin up and gazed into her eyes. His humor was gone, replaced by heart-stopping love. "You are the only thing I like about me, the only good thing this curse has brought me." He kissed her lightly. "If it weren't for Imbrasus, I would not be here with you now."

God, she was going to cry again. "You are...thankful for what he did?"

"I know now that everything I endured, I endured for you. For us, for this very moment."

Chapter Forty-One

Hadrian stepped from his enormous closet. Eva gasped. He was…beautiful. He wore a thigh length white, sashed robe. It crossed his bare chest, creating a V shape that extended to his navel. His pants were also white and made of a soft, light material, permitting easy movement. His shoes were pure white as well. He had a sword fastened around his waist, the sheath made of gold, the hilt depicting fighting lions with ruby eyes.

The white was a striking contrast to his black hair, which was shaved close to his head, and deep obsidian eyes.

He crossed to her with all the grace of a deadly predator. Reaching out, he took her hands and kissed her knuckles.

"You are so beautiful."

She scratched her nails down his exposed chest. Hadrian groaned, passion heating his eyes. Gods, he wished he had time to take her again.

"I like this," she purred. "You are so sexy."

Hadrian snatched her to him. A sigh escaped her as their bodies met.

Eva teasingly swept her tongue over his lips before she took his mouth in a slow drugging kiss. She drew her hand down his chest again and he growled.

"Seductress," he whispered, pulling away. "You tempt me to distraction. We've guests, a celebration, and a challenger awaiting us below."

Eva nervously smoothed her dress. Anxiety settled like rocks in her stomach. She did not know what to expect. She knew Hadrian was a fierce warrior and she had faith in him. He would win the challenge, but she didn't know if she could watch the fight. Instinct told her it would be brutal and bloody.

A knock sounded at the door.

"Enter," Hadrian commanded.

Falcon opened the door. The knight was dressed from head to toe in black. Eva thought it was a little strange that the vampires wore different, very specific colors for formal functions and battle. Royals wore white, nobles wore gray, while knights and soldiers wore black.

"Eva, you look lovely," he greeted.

She twirled. She felt like a little girl playing dress up. She definitely looked like a princess. The full skirts of her ball grown were white silk. The strapless corset bodice was deep crimson with a lace over lay. Hadrian had made another amazing selection.

"You clean up well, Falcon."

He bowed. "Thank you, my lady." He turned and motioned for someone to enter.

The newcomer was also draped in black. He bowed first to Hadrian then to her. Eva stumbled as she attempted a curtsy.

Hadrian cleared his throat and made the introductions, "Eva, this is Sir Vincent Cassano. He is the head of the guard and he will escort you down stairs."

"I thought I was going with you."

"No, little one. I don't want the nobles to know you are my mate until after I have faced Jefferson. So, Falcon will accompany me." He kissed her frown away. "Please, go with Cassano. He will see you safely below and show you to the other monarchs. They will welcome you and I want you to remain by their side."

He knew if she remained with Dimitri, Dorian, and Sonya, she would be safe. The comfort would allow him the ability to face Jefferson undistracted.

She kissed him again, but her lips were not gentle. They were hard and desperate. She kissed him as if it were the first time and the last, with all the passion and love that burned within her.

"I love you," she whispered against his mouth.

"I love you, Eva. This will all be over soon."

Eva uncomfortably shifted on her feet, wringing her hands. This was it. The moment had finally arrived. She had tried to ignore her nerves all day. But she had been unable to eat and last night, despite vigorous rounds of love making, she had not been able to sleep.

Everything is going to be fine, she told herself. *Hadrian will fight. He will win and take his vows as king.* She inwardly groaned as she thought of him introducing her to the Clan. Would they be glad their returning king had found his mate? Would they scorn her for her breeding? Hadrian did not care about her parentage, but his nobles may. What would they do if his Clan rejected her?

God, please, let them approve of me.

Sensing her weariness and apprehension, Hadrian drew her close. She pressed her face against his chest, her breath made his skin tingle.

"I wish I could be as calm as you."

"Eva, I have fought countless battles and faced foes much more dangerous than Jefferson."

She nodded. Her mother's voice whispered through her mind. "Please, be careful and fight smart," Eva said, reciting the words her mother had always told her before she entered a fighting match.

"I will."

Eva reluctantly pulled away. With one last glance to Hadrian, she turned and took Vincent's arm. He led her from Hadrian's chambers and down to the great hall. The expansive room was void of furniture and filled to the max with people.

As if directed, everyone turned towards the main staircase. Hundreds of eyes focused on her. Her heart pounded so hard and loud she could have sworn it echoed through the hall. Whispered voices quickly turned into a dull roar as she descended the steps. The vampire mob parted as they crossed the floor to the raging hearth. A small group of seven stood, talking amongst themselves, not taking any notice of the collective awe that followed her through the room.

Vincent gave a respectful bow to all within the clique. Eva's hands trembled as she swooped her skirts back to curtsy low, just how Hadrian had instructed her. One of these men was Dimitri Arsov, the last original vampire.

A towering Viking broke away from the group. His shoulder length blond hair was tied back at his nape and his ice blue eyes were sharp. There was a collective gasp when he bent, took her hands and drew her up.

"Hello, Miss Maldonado. It is an honor to meet you."

Eva could only smile in response. She feared her voice would crack if she spoke and she did not want everyone knowing how nervous she was. She was focusing on her breathing, trying to keep it slow and even. A sea of vampires surrounded her, they could sense fear and she *would not* appear weak. She was Hadrian's mate and she would make him proud.

"Please, come join us."

The intimidating vampire pulled her forward. He turned his back on the crowd and conversations resumed throughout the hall, shattering the thick uncomfortable silence. Eva released a sigh of relief when the spotlight eased from her.

270

"I apologize. Where are my manners?" The vampire said with a light laugh. He circled an arm around a young woman with strawberry blonde hair. "I am Dimitri Arsov, ruler of the Volkov Clan and this is my queen, Kerstyn."

"Nice to meet you," she said with a wave, her smile widening, revealing tiny fangs.

"And this is King Dorian Vlakhos of the Mylonas Clan along with his queen, Victoria."

Eva blinked. The couple was…gorgeous. His white suit clung to his massive shoulders and her dress showed every curve of her figure.

Victoria stepped forward and greeted her with a hug. "We are very happy to make your acquaintance."

Dorian took her hand and placed a polite kiss on her knuckles, then he turned to a woman Eva had already met.

"You are stunning," Silvie beamed as she passed the breathtaking couple. She wrapped an arm around Eva's shoulders. "I will make the last introductions." She spun them around to face a pair of women. "This tall, blonde, bombshell who looks like she stepped right off the runway is Sonya, Queen of the Voidukas, also known as the warrior queen. And the pretty lady next to her is Gwendolyn, Sonya's Second."

Eva hoped she would be able to remember all the names. "I'm really pleased to meet you all," she said, thankful her voice was steady.

They all smiled and Eva shifted nervously. Did they know she was Hadrian's mate? They did not seem to find it odd that she wore white, while others in the crowd still whispered about who she was and what her relationship could be to the monarchs. She could hear the rumors of her and Hadrian spreading around the room.

Trumpets sounded, calling everyone's attention to the stairs. A painful, heavy silence fell over the congregation.

Hadrian and Falcon stood at the top, both with hard expressions. Their jaws were set, their eyes sharp. They looked ready for battle.

She took in a deep breath. She laced her fingers together in front of her and released a long exhale. Chills raced up and down her spine as the same sense of danger and malice she had felt her first night here at Palatio Nocte settled over the room. The demon was here.

Here we go, Eva thought.

Chapter Forty-Two

Hadrian welcomed the oppressive silence. Lifting the shield on his power, he loosened his hold on the demon. It roared with life, eager for violence, starved to face and destroy their enemy.

He descended the stairs, his hand lightly resting on the hilt of his sword. His Clan members parted, creating a path to the hearth. As he passed, his people bowed their heads. Some cringed away from him, while others seemed relieved by his presence and his return.

As he gazed around the room he saw that Dimitri stood before the flames, his clear blue eyes void of emotion, a sea of cold ice. The ancient was dangerously controlled. Dorian stood to the left. His hands were clasped behind his back, his face expressionless, betraying nothing of his thoughts. Sonya stood to the side, her calculating gaze cutting into him, her hand clutching a book.

Hadrian could feel Eva's stare and hear her pounding heart. He spared her a quick glance. Her shoulders were thrust back, her chin high. She looked regal and serene, though he could sense her inner turmoil. She was so beautiful and so brave.

He forced himself to look away, not wanting to draw more attention to her. Everyone knew she was the ward given to the Clan, but they also knew she was no longer attached to the shifter pack and the treaty had been broken. They would question her presence and, once the challenge was finished, they would receive their answer.

Hadrian and Falcon stopped before Dimitri. Both punched their right fists against their chests over, their hearts and fell to one knee, bowing their heads low.

"Rise, warriors," Dimitri commanded, his regal tone shattering the spell of hushed awe that captivated the room. Shifting his gaze from Hadrian and Falcon, he addressed the Validus Clan. "Welcome all. We have gathered on this night to celebrate the return of your king, Hadrian Lucretius."

Sonya stepped forward. Extending her hands, she bowed her head and offered the thick black leather bound book to Dimitri. He silently thanked her with a nod.

Dimitri held the book above his head, presenting it to the crowd before tucking it against his chest.

"Vampiric Law states that if a Clan Chieftain chooses to desert the throne, they may return at any time," Dorian stated.

"However, they either must challenge their successor for the right to rule or their heir can peacefully return the crown." Dimitri's gaze fell upon the Black Knight before him. "Sir Falcon Kenwrec."

"Yes, Sire."

"As the legal heir to the Validus Clan, you may either accept the challenge Hadrian Lucretius presents or peacefully return the throne to your predecessor."

Falcon cleared his throat and projected his voice. "Sire, I respectfully select the latter. I will support the return of my king for Hadrian Lucretius is the rightful ruler of the Validus."

Dimitri, Dorian, and Sonya all nodded in agreement. "Your decision has been recognized and is incontestable. Thank you, warrior."

Falcon bowed before retreating to join the line of Black Knights that had formed a barrier between the royals and the masses. Clan nobles swarmed forward, pressing against the knights, their eyes riveted on their dark king. All knew what was to come next.

"Hadrian Lucretius, are you prepared to reclaim the throne and leadership of the Validus?"

"Yes, Sire."

"Then, keeping with Vampiric Law, you must recite the vows, binding yourself to the Clan. However, since you renounced your throne and are now seeking to regain your title as king, you have opened yourself to challengers." Dimitri lifted his gaze to the crowd again. "As is dictated, the king will accept and face those who oppose his dominion. Anyone belonging to the noble house of Validus who desires to challenge the king for the throne may step forward."

A tall, lean man with long, light brown hair broke free of the sea of gray pressing along the stern line of knights. He wore a gray suit befitting his station and a sword was secured to his waist by a black belt.

"I would like to challenge the king," he announced.

"Come closer, Lord Jefferson," Dimitri commanded. "Please, state the reason for your objection."

"Sire, I believe Hadrian Lucretius is dangerous and unfit to rule. He renounced the throne for that very reason, recognizing the threat he posed to the Clan. His madness had driven him into exile, where he spent nearly three hundred and fifty years away from vampire society. I am glad to see his condition has improved, but I would like to present myself as a worthy alternative for the throne."

"Do you know and understand the risks that are involved with offering a challenge?" Dimitri asked. "If you should lose, Lucretius will have the right to claim your life or banish you from Clan territory. However, if you should win, you will then have to immediately confront Sir Kenwrec, since he is legally the next in line for the throne. The consequences of that challenge are the same."

"Yes, Sire, I understand and I accept the terms."

Murmurs rumbled the rafters, shocked gasps and whispers of doubt danced in the air. Dimitri held up his hand, demanding silence once more.

Dimitri nodded. "This will be a standard duel, swords only. The two of you have come prepared," he said, noting the blades hanging from their belts. "If you happen to lose your weapon, you may use your fists. There will be no biting, no tricks, and" his eyes flickered to Hadrian, "no powers."

"Understood," Hadrian and Jefferson said in unison.

"Good. Now set."

Falcon commanded one knight to see to Jefferson then rushed over to his king. He removed Hadrian's sword belt then his white robe. The other vampire took Jefferson's sword, suit jacket and button up shirt.

The knight's held the empty sheaths and discarded clothing as the challengers turned to face one another. The metal of their swords gleamed in the light of the angry fire burning in the hearth.

The Black Knights forced the audience back, providing a secure circle for the combatants. Dorian retreated to stand beside his wife and Kerstyn, while Dimitri remained, front and center. He would be the referee and judge.

The challengers settled into their stance, swords raised, their eyes locked. Tension cracked like lightning through the air and Hadrian felt the demon shudder within him in excitement. He prayed for strength. He needed the beast's power, but he could not lose control.

Hadrian took in a deep breath. Vanilla instantly invaded his senses. He could feel Eva behind him, but he had to shut her out, he had to focus on this battle. He stopped his heart, his breath, effectively shutting everything out. His body was calm and still as death.

Dimitri's voice rang out, "Begin."

Jefferson released a savage battle cry and attacked. Hadrian met his blow. The sounds of clashing and scraping metal echoed through the castle. Jefferson spun, furiously swinging his weapon through the air. Hadrian skillfully blocked, countered and struck. His blade sliced at Jefferson's bare chest. Blood sprinkled the floor.

The wounded vampire roared in pained outrage. His eyes filled with the darkness of evil, his claws extended. Hissing, he flashed his fangs.

Hadrian's demon responded with a snarl, his lips peeled back revealing his own, lethal canines. His gaze burned red, but his expression remained controlled. There was no hint of fear, no sign of anger, no emotion at all. He fought with expertise, his motions smooth and elegant. His fiery gaze was calculating, studying his enemy, and learning every weakness.

Eva wanted to look away, but she had to watch. Hadrian was...beautiful. Deadly. Her shifter growled in approval. Her male was strong, powerful. Alpha. Jefferson had yet to land one blow, but blood flowed from a gash in his ribs, ran down his brow, and smeared across his chest.

Hadrian was a blur of motion, intensifying his attack. He parried and blocked Jefferson's swing then followed it with a right hook. He kicked his enemy's sword free. The weapon slid across the floor, stopping at Dimitri's feet. Hadrian's lips turned up with a taunting smile. He tossed his sword aside and Falcon caught the blade on reflex.

Jefferson's claws grew even longer, his eyes flashing with rage. Hadrian's fists clenched and released, his nails turning into lethal talons. Jefferson charged and Hadrian launched forward. They met and clashed like lightning, the sound of trading blows like thunder. Claws slashed and diced as fists cracked bone. Blood made the floor slick. In a flurry of movement, Hadrian caught Jefferson's throat. He slammed the vampire down, the force cracking the stone beneath him. Jefferson cut at his arm; his claw's prying at Hadrian's wrist.

Hadrian curled his fingers, sinking his talons deep into Jefferson's throat. He could feel his opponent's jugular frantically pumping against his fingertips. With a simple tug, he could tear Jefferson's head from his body. Blood would spout from the corpse like a glorious fountain and rain down upon him. The demon roared with satisfaction and demanded death. It wanted to bring death.

Hadrian dragged in one breath after another, clamoring for control. The beast within him struggled for freedom. Slowly, he peeled his hand from Jefferson's throat, one finger at a time.

He forced himself to his feet, as he trembled with the urge to murder. He willed his chest to expand. The warm rush of vanilla nearly knocked him over. Eva. She was to his left. Gods, he wanted to go to her. He craved to feel her soothing touch and hear her calming voice. But this was not finished.

Hadrian turned his crimson gaze to Dimitri. The pureblood glared back at him, knowing he stared at a fellow original demon. Hadrian blinked, until the red faded and his eyes returned to cool black.

"As victor, you have every right to claim your opponent's life," Dimitri said, his tone emotionless and flat.

Hadrian shook his head. "No. Jefferson had every right to challenge me."

"Very well." Dimitri waved a group of knights forward. "He will survive, but he needs to be tended to."

They took up the gurgling Jefferson and carried him from the hall.

"Are there any more challengers? Come forward now or not at all," Dimitri commanded.

Silence.

"Then I declare the floor closed. Will the victor step forward?"

Hadrian shrugged back into his robe, but Falcon kept the sword. He went to stand just before Dimitri.

"If it does not offend, Sire, I would like to address the Clan before reciting my vows," he said.

Dimitri gave a respectful nod. "As you wish."

Eva took a hesitant step forward. Hadrian held out his blood stained hand, beckoning her to come to him.

The crowd began to whisper, the sound rising and rising until Eva took his hand. She smiled up at him and he squeezed her hand. In that moment, he knew he could never have done this without her. He never would have been able to break free of his guilt, his demon, or his madness.

"Validus, I have been gone for far too long." he began, his gaze scanning the sea of vampires that stretched out before him. "After the death of my brother, Titus, I was no longer stable enough to lead you. I renounced my throne in the hopes of sparing the Clan another crazed, tyrannical king. Madness controlled my mind and ruled my life for centuries, leaving me broken."

He brought Eva a little closer. He could feel the comforting heat of her body.

"But Fate has saved me and has shown her grace down upon our Clan." He lifted their entwined hands, displaying their mating

276

brands. "I present to you my mate and the future queen of the Validus, Eva Maldonado."

Gasps of shock, words of joy, and relieved sighs reverberated through the room. Slowly a roar built, it rose until the stone floor rumbled from the force. Eva was struck speechless. They were cheering, clapping, howling, and whistling in approval.

Chapter Forty-Three

After the coronation, Hadrian returned in a pure white suit and the celebration moved to the ballroom. The Hall of Mirrors was overflowing. The sounds of merriment ricocheted off the glass. The orchestra had not stopped playing since the king and his mate entered. Champagne popped and fizzled as glasses clinked. The Clan rejoiced. Their king had returned, he was mated, and their people would know peace. After so many years of war and oppression, they had finally broken free of the cycle.

The rejoicing carried on throughout the night. Songs of happiness were sung so loudly the chandelier swayed. Nobles welcomed Hadrian back and congratulated him while they introduced themselves to Eva and offered her their best wishes. She could not believe the reception she had received and Hadrian was convinced it would be at least a week until her shock faded.

It was an hour before dawn when the party began to die. Hadrian took the first opportunity to slip away with his woman.

"Hadrian Lucretius, I demand you take me to your room," Eva said as he tugged her down the dark hall.

He laughed, the sound bouncing off the walls and echoing through the narrow corridor. "So eager."

"With you," she ran her nails over his wrist and up the inside of his arm, "I'm always eager."

"Do not forget you said that. I will be enacting our deal tomorrow. Seventy-two hours, my sweet."

"I can't wait."

They stopped and the sconce overhead flamed to life. Eva blinked, her eyes adjusting to the light. She was still not completely used to her sensitive sight.

Hadrian spun her around and forced her back against the wall. A surprised gasp escaped her lungs as he pressed his body into her, his hands braced against the wood paneling above her head.

"Oh, god," she sighed, her voice laced with love and lust.

"This is where it all began," he said. "I stalked you down this hall. Powerless against your lure."

Eva closed her eyes as one of his hands fell away from the wall to encircle her wrist. His thumb brushed over their brand and her pulse jumped.

"Your scent called to me."

She shivered as he bent his head down to her throat. His cool breath tickled and teased.

"Do you remember?"

"Yes," she gasped. His hand moved up her arm to cup her nape. Delicious tension flooded her and gathered at her core. "I remember it perfectly."

Hadrian placed a light kiss to her pulse. "Warm vanilla. You taste so sweet, my Eva."

She opened her eyes and found him gazing down at her.

"I had borne centuries of loneliness, of emptiness. My world was consumed by the darkness of madness. I was hollow." His other hand came down on her shoulder, pinning her to the wall. "Then you arrived and everything changed. You are the light that chased away the shadows that clung to my soul."

Eva cupped his face as tears slipped down her own cheeks.

"You freed me of my pain," he whispered. "I can look in the mirror and not see my guilt, or Titus, or the demon. I see me. For the first time in centuries, I can see myself. You made me remember who I am. I only wish I had not taken so long to realize you are mine."

She smiled and more tears slipped from her eyes. "Oh, Hadrian, I love you." She pressed a gently, trembling kiss to his lips. "And we have all of eternity to be together."

He gripped her hips. Eva wrapped her legs around his waist as he slid her up along the wall. He held her with one hand as the other tossed up her skirts. Her breath caught as she felt cool air caress her core.

Hadrian groaned, finding her wet.

The world spun as he teleported them to his room. The sound of a zipper kissed her ears and she bit her lower lip in anticipation as he pressed her down to the bed.

"Hadrian, I love you. Ever since we met here in this hall, I loved you. I wish I had realized it sooner."

He captured her lips in a gentle, soul-binding, mind-numbing kiss as he entered her with a painfully slow thrust.

"Eva, you are my savior," he whispered against her mouth as he claimed her.

*   *   *   *

Sonya hooked her duffle bag over her shoulder and started down the stairs to the main hall. She had done quite the costume change, from an elegant ball gown, shining jewels, and strappy heels, to slim dark jeans, leather trench coat, red leather corset, and knee-high, laced boots.

She paused on the last step, her eyes closing. God, she could not believe she was going through with this. Her hand slid over her hips, her fingers checking the buckles of her gun holster. It was secure. The weapon was loaded and she had plenty of spare clips. Her father's hunting dagger was strapped between her shoulders blades. A small dagger was concealed just under the lining of her corset, the hilt forming a Y shape over her breasts. She shifted on her feet, feeling the cool slide of metal against the side of her lower leg and ankles. It was odd, she could not remember the last time she had been strapped for battle.

"Are you leaving?"

Sonya's eyes flew open and she stumbled from the step. Falcon reached out, but snapped his arms back to his sides before making contact. Sonya held back her sigh of disappointment. She remembered with perfect clarity, what his arms felt like. His hands. His mouth. Had it really only been two months since their encounter at Dimitri and Kerstyn's wedding? Two months since they almost…

"Yes," she said, desperately needing to focus on anything other than *that* night. "There is some place I need to be."

Falcon clenched his jaw to keep it from dropping. Her light blonde hair was pulled back and tightly secured in a bun. Her yellow-gold eyes glowed with resolve and her soft pink lips were set in a hard line. And she was dressed for battle. She looked every bit the warrior queen of legend and, damn, she was sexy.

She stepped around him and crossed the great hall. All the guests had moved to the Hall of Mirrors once the challenge had been finished and Hadrian had taken his vows as king. Her steps echoed, bouncing off the high, arched ceiling.

Falcon went after her. "Is Gwen not going with you?"

"Her presence is unnecessary," Sonya replied. "She will remain here. No need for her to miss the celebration."

"Are you coming back?" he asked as they entered the foyer.

Sonya paused and slowly turned to him. Her shoulders were squared, her heart-shaped face titled up, as she took his hand. She met his gaze for a brief moment before pulling away.

What the hell is going on, he wondered.

Cold, angry wind rushed in when the front door opened. Her driver greeted them with a low bow before taking her bag. Snow covered the silver Jaguar XJL, the windshield wipers thrashed, fighting to scrape the ice from the glass.

A strange foreboding sense coiled around Falcon's heart as he gazed down at the car. Something was not right.

"Goodnight, Falcon," Sonya said.

She stepped out into the furious blizzard. Falcon followed her down the steps.

"Wait." He snatched her wrists, spun her around, and pulled her back. Their bodies hit. Heat enveloped them despite the frigid air. They stood for a long moment, their eyes locked, each searching for the right words.

Something inside him demanded he not let her go. Danger awaited her.

"Sonya, I—"

She cupped his face and placed a light, butterfly like kiss upon his lips. She drew away. Stepping back, she gripped the top of the car door, her knuckles turning white.

"You are coming back." Not a question, but a stern statement.

Sonya smiled, but no warmth touched her eyes. "Try to enjoy yourself tonight. This is a wonderful celebration." She slid into the car. The chauffer closed the door and quickly rounded the hood.

Falcon's hand shot out. He could not let her go. Something bad was going to happen, he could feel it.

"Falcon," Dimitri's voice rang out from the top steps of the entrance. "Dorian and I are going to have some drinks and I think Hadrian will be joining us…some time." He gave a light laugh. "Come inside. The celebration is not over yet."

Epilogue/Preview

"Your Majesty, we will be entering the Voidukas territory of Poland shortly," the driver called.

Sonya shook her head and banished her fantasies of Falcon. Now was not the time to be thinking about him. She had to focus.

She released her seatbelt. Leaning forward, she scanned the road and spotted movement up ahead.

Hunters.

Sitting back, she thought of her conversation with Silvie. The priestess had hauled her off to a corner and shoved a flute of champagne into her hand, insisting that their conversation needed to appear casual.

"They will be waiting for you at the boarder," Silvie had whispered. "You could escape since they did not bring enough, but I need you to allow yourself to be captured."

"Are you mad?"

Silvie shushed her. "Keep it down. We can't have anyone overhearing this. Everyone needs to think we are having a normal conversation, hence the champagne."

The priestess glanced about. When she was confident no one of importance was in earshot, she continued, "You won't be held captive for long, I swear."

"Explain to me why the Red Order is planning on attacking me."

Silvie sighed and shook her head. "I wish I could. Believe me, I really do. But I am already altering the Shaman's plan by warning you and sending you out a day early. Your entire entourage is to be caught unaware."

"You expect me to surrender to those—"

"I said nothing about surrendering. I just need you to be kidnapped." Silvie gave a careless wave of her hand. "You may kill as many as you like."

I intend to, Sonya thought as she drew her gun free and cocked it.

"Giles," she said. The driver met her gaze in the rearview mirror. "Do you remember the plan?"

"Yes, Your Highness, and I see the spikes in the road now."

"Good."

Sonya let out a slow exhale, clearing all the air from her lungs, causing her heart to seize mid-beat. Her fangs punched down into her mouth as the whites of her eyes were consumed by black.

The tires blew and she kicked the door open. Tucking her head, she rolled from the car. She saw Giles bail seconds before the car wrapped around a tree. He glanced her way and she nodded. She knew he did not want to leave her to fight on her own, but he knew the plan. Silvie had given them specific instructions. Giles turned and ran. Sprinting to the waiting car they had arranged to be left a little further up the road. He would call for back up.

Sonya slowly straightened as the witches jumped out onto the road, their weapons drawn. She bared her fangs. A joyful murderous smile curled her lips.

She raised her gun, leveling it on the hunters. "Come and get it, bitches."

Gunfire splintered the peaceful silence of the night.

*   *   *   *

Falcon leaned back in his seat. The sound of softly scraping metal hissed through the council chamber as the shutters slid down, covering the windows. Dawn was approaching and Sonya had yet to return to the castle.

The celebration had ended about an hour ago and by now all the Clan members had retired to their rooms, preparing for the day. Most vampires found it difficult to function while the sun ruled the sky. Only a handful of elders could resist the call of slumber and three of them were with him now.

"I would like to say, Hadrian, that your coming out party was a success," Dorian said, holding up a shot glass full of Silver Moon.

Hadrian raised his own drink. They both tossed the liquor back and slammed their empty glasses on the table.

"I am so very glad you have returned to us," Dimitri said, clapping Hadrian on the back. "Did you find the words in my letter helpful?"

Hadrian smiled. Dimitri had written nearly exactly what Eva had said.

"Yes, but only after I heard similar words from my mate."

283

A rhythmic, hurried, pounding carried down the hall. All four men frowned as they turned to face the entrance. Someone was running at a frantic speed and was headed their way.

The door flew open with such force it slammed against the wall. Gwendolyn rushed in, her hair swung about her face as she skid to a stop.

"Our Black Knights just received a distress call," she said, her voice and body trembling with rage. "Sonya's car was ambushed by Red Order Hunters and she has been taken."

The men jumped to their feet, their chairs sliding along the floor hitting the wall and one or two toppled over.

"How long ago?" Dorian snapped.

"Maybe ten minutes. Her driver is the one who reported the attack."

"Was she attacked on Validus land?" Hadrian demanded.

"No, she was heading to our compound in Poland. They had just crossed the border," she answered.

"Fuck," Dorian growled. "They timed this perfectly. We can organize a team to head out at sunset, but they will be long gone by then, their trail cold."

"If you would like to join me, I can teleport us to the border and see if we can find anything," Dimitri offered. "They may not have counted on Dorian and I being able to walk in the sun."

"The Voidukas's knights have already assembled, but we need computers and phones to begin our tracking of the hunters," Gwendolyn said.

"Yes, of course. Falcon can provide all you require," Hadrian said. He turned to face the knight and cursed.

Gwendolyn gasped, Dorian groaned, and Dimitri did his best to hold back his smile.

The secret door hidden along the wood paneling of the room lay open, revealing a dark passage way.

Falcon was gone.

Turn the page to read a preview from Caressed by Shadows, the next installment within the Rulers of Darkness series.

Caressed by Shadows

Rain ran in rivulets down his face, the droplets caught on his lashes like tiny crystals, a delicate contrast to the harsh gun metal gray of his eyes.

Falcon observed the group of Red Order Hunters that gathered in the alley below. Shadows clung to him, concealing him with their darkness. His prey's laughter sailed on the wind, their merriment grating his nerves. Falcon's hand tightened about the grip of his dagger, his knuckles turning white.

Poor bastards, they were peacefully oblivious to the specter of death that stalked them.

The hunters had taken from him, stolen what he loved most in this world. Sonya Rebane, the queen of the Voidukas Clan.

Three weeks. Sonya had endured imprisonment for three weeks, and if she had one bruise or a single scratch to mare her smooth skin, he would roast every last Red Order hunter.

His fangs burned as his vision darkened, his gray eyes turning black as the pits of hell.

Tonight, he would save her. Tonight, he would have Sonya in his arms.

The gentle hum of a car's engine drifting on the air disrupted his thoughts.

Glancing up at the night sky, Falcon judged it to be about eleven-thirty. It was time for the changing of the guard. He watched as the hunters piled out of the old black van. They fell in line behind their commander, a tall, slender, balding man. He would open the secret door and go down into the dark pit where the cells were located, where Sonya was being held.

The commander was the only hunter permitted to check on the prisoners. Once finished, he would return to the group, close the wall, and take the van back to the Red soldiers' headquarters.

Falcon moved to the edge of the roof. Tension coiled through his body. Crouching down, he balanced on the balls of his feet. Lightning cut across the sky, the flash causing the chrome of his holstered twin 1911's to sparkle in the darkness.

The witches turned to face the wall. Their commander reached out and pressed a single faded brick. The stone moved revealing a soft glowing blue screen. Falcon's breath froze in his lungs as he watched the commander flatten his hand on the screen.

Just a few more seconds, he thought. Anticipation knotted his gut.

The sound of scraping bricks kissed his ears as the wall shifted. The bricks drew back revealing the secret entrance and a set of stairs covered in shadows. His nostrils flared and his lungs expanded as he sucked in a deep breath. The unmistakable, unforgettable scent of fresh lilacs mingled with the putrid smell of human waste and dirt. Sonya was down there. His fangs burst from their sheaths, long and sharp. His black eyes burned with rage. Sonya. They had *his* Sonya and he was going take her back. Falcon gracefully jumped from the roof, landing silently on the concrete below. He pulled and cocked one gun, tightened his grip on his dagger, and stalked toward his enemies.

About the Author

Amanda J. Greene creates paranormal romance for ravenous readers. She lives in Southern California, where she enjoys escaping the rewarding but hectic world of writing by spending time in the sun and sand with her husband and their two dogs.

Amanda is also an associate reviewer on The Book Nympho Blog.

46942570R00173

Made in the USA
San Bernardino, CA
19 March 2017